Ave Maria

Charles D'Amico

AVE MARIA

Cover & Interior Design: Blue Handle Publishing, LLC

ISBN: 978-1-7347727-2-2

AVE MARIA

To everyone that has helped me along this journey, I thank you. From the criticism, closed doors and a blind eye turned to the praise and acceptance of what I'm doing. I thank everyone for their role in this process.

Here's to hitting 1 Million words before my 40th birthday.

Sis, thank you for continuing to be my literary inspiration. Thank you to my wife for all the support and belief in this crazy dream.

To all the fans and supporters, thank you.

Thank You, Bryan, Mike, and Joe. Without your early support, none of this would have happened.

1

Even without Sheila, I'm always going to have at least one other female in my life, that's my daughter.

"I still can't believe today marks six months since that day in Mexico City, to think I'm still second-guessing everything that happened. I know everyone back at the bureau said it was the right move, but I still wish I would have gone a different route."

"Neil, you need to stop worrying about this. The case is over, and there is nothing left to worry about. Sometimes the hardest thing to do after being involved in such a case is to let go. You need to let go if not you're going kill yourself fighting these demons."

"I know, but it is a lot easier said than done, you of all people know that. What we want and what we get are usually two different things."

"That's true, but that involves things that are out of your immediate control. This is all on you, Neil, no one else, just you. You have to let go or your ulcer will turn into something worse."

"How did you know I had an ulcer? I didn't tell you about it; hell, I didn't tell anyone about it. But I do understand what you're trying to tell me. I have to admit, ever since I started training hard again,

4

my ulcer has felt better. Hitting that punching bag and running seem to be very therapeutic."

"That's the spirit. You don't need to forget the stress. You need to work through it, just as you are. As for noticing your ulcer, that was an easy one. You've been sucking down those antacids like they're going out of style. That and you haven't touched your coffee since you've been here. And we all know that you love your coffee."

"That is probably the worst part of all of this stress, the lack of coffee drinking I can do. It really is hell without my coffee. I've even resorted to eating coffee beans in place of the coffee itself. It seems to sit better in my stomach."

"You genuinely have a problem, Neil, eating coffee beans whole? I mean seriously, you've lost it. But I digress. How's the home life been with your daughter and Sheila?"

"They're doing well, as good as can be. It's hard trying to be a family with an ex-wife and a daughter. Don't get me wrong, I love both of them dearly. It's just hard."

"I can only imagine, since Sheila and you still have a lot of love for each other, it can get very complicated at times. At least I imagine it can."

"'Complicated' is a nice way of putting it. I'm still a little upset with the way things ended up with Maria. I thought after the case with me limited to consulting for the FBI, it would be okay for us, but it didn't help the situation any."

"Oh, yes, Agent Garcia and you, I almost forgot about that. That did end pretty badly, didn't it? Are you guys at least on talking terms now?"

"We try, but it just ends up being small talk, pointless conversations. I can understand Maria's point of view, but she knew my relationship with Sheila going into our relationship. To demand that I stop seeing my ex-wife was ridiculous. Sheila and I stopped all physical contact on account of my relationship with Maria, but that wasn't enough for her; it just got worse the longer we dated."

"It's understandable, though; eventually it came down to Maria not wanting to share you with another woman. You've got to understand that, at least?"

"I do, trust me, I do. But even without Sheila, I'm always going to have at least one other female in my life, that's my daughter. If someone can't understand that you don't get all of me, all of the time, then I can't help them."

Sometimes I wonder why I even bother coming here and talking to him, but I have no one else to talk to, at least no one that understands me like he does. I just wish my life wasn't so complicated. I thought ending the Cappelano case would simplify my life, but it hasn't changed since that day. Hell, the only thing that has changed is Cappelano and the chase. Maria and I aren't talking anymore, and now I'm simply consulting for the FBI, which is nice because I can concentrate on my own business, CB INC.

"We're almost out of time, Neil. Is there anything else you would like to cover this week before you have to go?"

"There really isn't anything I can think of. If I think of something I know where to find you, that's for sure. It's not like you're going anywhere."

"Very funny. It's been six months since I've been stuck in this hellhole thanks to you, and you're still cracking jokes. Glad to see one of us can smile about my situation."

"I didn't force you to go on a killing spree, now did I. Not to mention killing an FBI agent. Are you fucking nuts?"

"We've been over this, Neil, not now. These meetings are to talk about you and your problems, not mine. Have a good week, but for now I need to get going."

"I'll talk to you later, Franklin."

"You know I hate that name. Just call me what you've always called me: Cappelano."

"Are sure you don't want me to call you 'Veritas'?"

"NO!"

Cappelano got tired of me ragging on him about his ass being in prison for life thanks to me. Hey, I did the easy part, tracking him down; he was the one that had the hard job of going crazy and killing everyone. As for the past six months, life has been just as crazy as it was when I was chasing him down. I talked to him about how Maria and I tried to have a real relationship. Still, it only lasted about four months; it ended about two weeks ago when we had a huge fight about my relationship with Sheila. I understand her side, but she has to see it from my point of view as well. That was something she just didn't want to do.

After that night in Mexico, the guys and I sneaked Cappelano back into the States and brought him to Detroit so he could be tried in the state this all started in. The DA and the FBI worked out a deal to keep him at a Michigan prison instead of shipping him to a federal penitentiary somewhere else. Cappelano said he would plead guilty to all counts, twenty-seven in all, for first-degree murder. As long as he could stay in Michigan; he said he wanted to be close to me. It's that mentor obsession I was talking about a couple of months ago; I think he has a little man-crush on me.

Joking aside, Cappelano and I have been meeting once a week and talking. It has done me a lot of good to talk to him; he really helps to put things in perspective. It's hard for a lot of people to understand why I would want to talk to a man that I chased for so long, not to mention who killed so many people, but it's simple: he understands me. I don't know why he does; he just does, and that's good enough for now. Plus he comes in handy when I need to talk to someone about a killer that I might be tracking down; nothing quite like talking to a psychopath when you're trying to track one down. Like the old saying, to catch a fox, you need to think like one.

"Hey Neil, how was the visit today? I still don't understand how you can talk to that guy; he's crazy."

"Some say the craziest people are too sane for anyone to notice."

"What the fuck is that supposed to mean? All I know is he doesn't say a word to anyone, not even other inmates. He only talks to you. Like I said, he's crazy."

"He might be, but he's helped me catch a couple of killers already, not to mention it's kind of fun to give him a little shit about being behind bars. I mean, after all those years he taunted me, now I get to taunt back. So what if I'm enjoying it a bit."

"Whatever you say, Neil. I need to do my rounds. Have a good day, and drive safely."

"Thank Officer Daniels. Be safe, and keep an eye on Cappelano; he's starting to warm up to you, trust me."

"I could care less, this is just a paycheck to me, and these inmates are just numbers in a system. That's the only way to look at this job; otherwise I'd go crazy working here."

"You do what you have to, to get through the day. See ya, Daniels."

"See ya, Neil."

The drive home seems to get shorter and shorter every time I leave Cappelano's office. He'd rather me call it that than what it is, a federal penitentiary. I guess it's all semantics when it comes down to it, I'm just going to visit an old mentor who just happens to be a serial killer that I recently put behind bars, but hey, you can't always pick your friends.

The last couple of months have been pretty good to me, especially since I collared Cappelano. I did a small lecture circuit at colleges and a few conferences sharing my expertise when tracking down a serial killer over a long time. It was fun, I met a lot of very interesting people, made a few new friends, and oh yeah, I made a lot of money. I spoke at a three-day conference in Florida and made seventy-five K for the weekend, which was nice; I paid off my mortgage with that one.

With a couple others, I finally finished remodeling the inside of my house. The bedroom is finally completed as well as the basement. Now when you walk into my bedroom, you see a massive walk-in closet, king-size bed, customized oak dresser, matching nightstand, and a temperature-controlled dog bed for the girls to sleep in. I know I spoil my dogs, probably a little too much, but they keep my sanity in check.

As for the basement, I finally have it just the way I like it; I didn't go the route of a big entertainment area like most. Instead, I turned half of the basement into an office. Complete with a custom oak desk and shelving units that you would expect to find in a political figure's office. I also made sure the whole house was wirelessly hooked up to my laptop.

The other half of the basement is where I keep my sanity, a workout area. Not your average weight setup; instead, I built myself a dojo—a fancy word for a training room—with wood flooring, mirrored walls, heavy bag, speed bag, and anything else I could fit in there. It looks like someone filmed a martial arts movie in that room. I made sure the walls have extra insulation for those late nights when I turn up my music to concert decibel levels.

Most of my friends were surprised when I turned down a full-time job with the bureau, especially with the promotion they offered me. We worked out a compromise that allowed me full access to the bureau as well as the free time and freedom I enjoy. We settled on a consulting job, allowing me to keep my foot in the door, but it mainly keeps me from driving the bureau up the wall.

As for the other part of my work life, I've been keeping busy with CB INC. When it became public that the main reason I was able to catch Cappelano was due to the work of some of my investigators, the jobs just started pouring in. High-profile cases, which translate to a lot of money for everyone at the warehouse.

It's almost midnight as I make my way downstairs to the dojo. I cranked up the radio and started to do my routine on the heavy bag. About twenty minutes into my workout, I started to hear a faint noise that had been drowned out by the music. It sounded like my cell phone. What is Ken doing calling me this late?

"Ken, what's up? How are you doing tonight? Are you still at the office?"

"Yeah, I am, and good thing too. You've got an urgent message."

"Urgent message? From whom?"

"It's your old high school. Orchard Lake St. Mary's. The headmaster asked for you personally and said it was urgent and to be as discreet as possible."

"Do you know what's going on? Why is my high school trying to track me down at midnight?"

"He wouldn't say anything else; he just said to meet him at the main building, in his office. Do you need anyone to go with you? I can swing by and pick you up. You're right on my way."

"I'd say yeah, but you said he wants me to be discreet. I'll call you when I get there and let you know what's up. For now I need to get changed and get out of here."

"No problem. Just let me know if you need anything. I hope everything is okay. Drive safely."

"Thanks, Ken, I'll talk to you later."

2

*Actually, I would like to see your commanding officer. Tell him
Agent Baggio of the FBI is here and would like to look around.*

I wonder why the headmaster of my high school is calling me in the
middle of the night. No matter the reason; it can't be good. I hope he
doesn't expect me to turn in my final paper from high school; it's not
my fault the dog ate it. When I was a senior in high school, my
literature teacher was James Glowacki. We called him Glow for
short; no idea why. Glow taught for another seven or so years before
he was promoted to the headmaster, and what a fantastic job he's done
since then. Glow was not only a teacher turned headmaster, but he
was also an alumnus of St. Mary's—he bled eaglet red and white, and
does to this day. Glow and I had an interesting relationship. I was a
very talented student but also extremely lazy. My senior year, I
missed some forty or so days of school. The sad part was that I was
there for the majority of them; I just didn't go to class, too busy
hanging out in the headmaster's office or with the monsignor of the
school. I was the school's son, for lack of a better phrase. Most of my
friends were faculty; that's just the way it was growing up for me. St.

Mary's was my second home; I wouldn't be where I am today without those four years.

I finally gave that old Jeep to the warehouse for the guys to use on stakeouts. I'm driving a new Cadillac Crossfire, which is a sweet car, let me tell you. Reluctant at first to try it out, Ken coaxed me into test driving one; needless to say, I fell head over heels for this car. I also bought a used Jeep Wrangler to use when I take the girls out. It wasn't anything special, and it's actually pretty old. It's a 1981 Jeep; currently I'm remodeling it. I always need to have a project outside of work to keep me sane. Since the house is pretty much done, fixing up a car seemed like a fun task. The system in my car is turned all the way up, and I can feel the bass on my skin—I love that feeling. First thing I did when I bought the car was to bring it to the warehouse and let our mechanics modify the hell out of it. It doesn't have missiles or machine guns like James Bond, but hey, it still rocks.

Driving up M-59 to I-75 and then a short trip to Square Lake Road, for those of you not from Detroit. If it weren't midnight, I'd be stuck in construction and traffic the whole way there. It's about a twenty-mile drive from my house to Orchard Lake. Some people think we should change our state bird to a construction sign. I for one agree; it's pretty bad here. From what I understand, some manufacturers have been given permission to overfill trucks, which causes our roads to break down quickly. The crazy thing about all the construction is that each road still sucks; you would think that the roads wouldn't be so bad, but alas, that is not the case. And yes, I said "alas"! I made my way through the subdivisions, taking an old shortcut along the lakes that I remember from high school. I know it's been years, but I still come out for the school fund-raisers and try to make it to a couple of sports events every year. Making my way on the campus, I'm reminded how spoiled I was in high school. It truly is a beautiful place to go to high school in more ways than one.

The main office was directly in front of me. Parking in the street I ran up to the main building, where I saw Glow in his office. Not much has changed in this old building. Orchard Lake St. Mary's used to be the Michigan Military Academy. It was opened more than a hundred years ago; I think it was 1899, if my memory serves me right. There's a lot of history between these walls; it felt like home the instant I stepped inside.

"Sorry to have to call you so late, Neil. Thanks for coming on such short notice."

"You know I'd do anything for the school. What's going on? I noticed as I pulled in that there were a couple of Oakland sheriff police cars down by the dorms, as well as an ambulance."

"One of our students was found in his room hung, and they believe it to be a suicide. It was a horrible scene; the RA found him. The student's name was Andrew. He was a student from Poland and his mother worked here to help pay his tuition."

"I'm just going out on a limb here, but you don't think this is a suicide, do you? That's what I'm doing here, isn't it? Also, why you said, 'they believe.'"

"You always were good at reading people, Neil. That's why I called you here. Andrew wouldn't have committed suicide; he wasn't depressed, and it just wasn't in his nature to do so. It was too clean, too perfect for a suicide if in fact it was a suicide."

"I still don't know what I can do. Do you want me to call in a few favors, get the locals to look at it closer?"

"No, I need you to do this for me, for us, for your school. I don't trust anyone with this situation, but you. Your stubbornness is the only thing that will get to the truth. Plus I think this is bigger than just a local problem, but I can't talk about this much more. Let's go over to the scene; I'll show you what I mean."

"No problem. My car is right outside, I'll drive us over there. Let's go."

We drove slowly over to the dorms. It's a short drive, probably could have walked, but Glow didn't look like he was in good spirits. It was best that we drove there. St. Mary's campus is shared with a small college and seminary, which makes for a decent-size high school campus. With graduating classes capped at approximately 120, it makes for a very tight niche of young men. I almost forgot: St. Mary's is an all-boys school, and we don't even have a sister school. Going to high school here was like being in one large fraternity, which is probably why I never felt the need to join a frat in college. I already belonged to a fraternity, the St. Mary's Prep alumni fraternity. Making our way around the bend, I could see students standing outside, talking to the police; they had looks of confusion on their faces. There weren't many students in the dorm, since graduation was last week, which meant most of the students had gone home for the summer. The few that were still on campus are mainly exchange students or those staying around for the summer sports camps that the school puts on. If this was a murder and not a suicide, that limits the number of witnesses for us to interview. Making it a problem for us, as well as making it easier for someone to come in and murder a student without anyone really knowing what happened.

"Just pull over and park right here. We'll walk from here."

"No problem. So tell me a little bit about the student. How old was he?"

"He just graduated last week, and yesterday he found out that he was given a full ride to Oakland University, which isn't too far from here, as you know. It's not the biggest school in the country, but it was still an amazing feat for him. He has only been in the country since eighth grade. He struggled with the language barrier for a couple years and it wasn't until the summer of his junior year that he really blossomed."

"That's why you don't think it was a suicide; he had gotten a lot of good news lately, so there really wasn't a need for him to feel down?"

"That and I've known Andrew for four years, and the two of us had a strong bond, similar to the one you and I had when you were at school here. He told me everything, even down to when he lost his virginity. That's why I think this isn't a suicide. If he were down, I would have known about it."

"You mentioned losing his virginity. Did he have a girlfriend? Was he seeing anyone?"

You may ask why he knows that. When someone is an exchange student, they go to anyone they feel they can confide in; there is no judgment. There is no rhyme or reason why they communicate with someone in particular.

"He's been seeing the same girl since that very same summer. Her name is Christine, and she really did wonders for him. And no, she isn't capable of doing this; she cared about him too much."

"Just as I was about to respond to Glow's remarks, I was interrupted by an Oakland County sheriff, who wasn't in too good a mood. You would think, the fact that I'm walking with the headmaster, I might get a free pass, but they didn't care. Now the only question is, do I show them my license or my FBI credentials?

"Sorry, guys, I can't let you in there. We've got a crime scene to protect. Yes, even you, Headmaster. I'm sorry, I'm just doing what I was told to do."

"That's okay, officer, I'm sure you're just doing your job, but I really need to get to the dorms. I would like to console my students."

"I'm sorry, but I can't let you do that. By the way, who is this with you? I'm going to need some form of identification."

"Actually, I would like to see your commanding officer. Tell him Agent Baggio of the FBI is here and would like to look around."

I really wasn't planning on pulling out my ID tonight, but it comes in handy. Having that trump card for many occasions doesn't hurt. I have been able to walk the line of bureau and investigator for a few years now, and it has served me well.

"Let me see your ID. I'm going to have to call this in before I can let you go by. But the headmaster will have to stay here. Sorry, those are the rules."

"In the meantime, while we're waiting, please call your CO so I can talk with him."

"All right, suit yourself, but he's not going to be happy that the feds are here."

"Just shut up and do what you're told."

"Neil, calm down; it's not worth it. We'll get there in due time."

We stood there for fifteen or so minutes waiting for this idiot's supervisor to show up. Don't get me wrong—the local police do a great job around here, especially in Oakland County, but this is just ridiculous. There is always some idiot that ruins it for everyone out there, no matter where you work.

"Hi, my name is Hank Rollie. I'm the lead investigator here, and I understand that you're with the FBI?"

"That's correct. The name's Neil Baggio. I work—"

"Officer, give this man his credentials back, this is Agent Baggio, the man that caught the infamous 'Veritas' killer."

"Sorry, sir. What would you like me to do about the headmaster?"

"He can come through and be with his students. We've gotten all of their statements anyway; he can't do any harm to the investigation. Just make sure to stay out here with your students and the other officers. Got it?"

"Very well. As for you, Neil, see what you can get from the investigator and the crime scene. I'll be over there talking to my students."

"You got it, Glow; I'll let you know what I find. Officer Rollie, you lead, I'll follow. Let's get going."

"Right this way, Agent Baggio."

It's amazing that after all these years the dorms are still the same, always old and rustic. Don't get me wrong, they're not dirty, just old. As for Officer Hank Rollie, he's a putz—an unimaginative bureaucrat. Although he's a nice guy he's a putz nevertheless. From what little I've gotten out of him walking from the parking lot up the stairs, I'm not too impressed.

"Here we are. Room three-ten. You know the drill: don't touch anything without a glove on, and here's a pair for you in case you get nosy."

"So what makes you believe this is a cut-and-dried suicide case? I'm just wondering what you guys have pulled together so far."

"There are the usual suspects that we came across. A suicide note written in his handwriting—"

"Before you go any further, how can you be certain that the handwriting is a match? You haven't analyzed the handwriting yet."

It looks as if they had taken him down for processing, the rope set to the side of the body, not surprising with the timeline. It wasn't instantly that Glow thought to call me. As things unraveled, he realized something didn't look right, and that's when he contacted me. The scene was staged well—or cleaned up is more like it—not common. If you're going to end yourself, you're probably not going to take the time to tidy your room.

"It's our guess at the time being that the handwriting was his; it matched his classwork. We are going to have it sent to the lab for testing first thing in the morning."

"I'm going to need a copy of that suicide note. After your lab processes it, fax me a copy to my office, would you? Here's my card with my fax number on it."

"Can do. We'll work with you in any way we can on this case. May I ask why the feds are involved already? It's not as if this kid was anyone special. He was just an exchange student."

"'Anyone special'! What the fuck is that supposed to mean? I'm just going to chalk that phrase up to a brain fart and not rip into you." I guess I already did.

"I'm sorry I didn't mean it that way. It's just that it's odd that the FBI is involved in a simple case like this. Can I ask why?"

"No, you may not. I wish I could tell you, but that's not for either of us to know right now. All I know is I got called out here tonight, and I intend on doing my job."

I don't need to tell this guy that the headmaster called me out, it's not like I'm lying, I'm just telling half truths, which are better than lies because they're true. So you can cover your ass no matter what people have to say when they catch you in a half truth or a lie. The next hour was a waste of time. I now understand what Glow was saying, the scene was too clean, it looked like a professional job. When someone commits suicide, it is rarely planned out and executed perfectly. When someone commits suicide, they are not in the right frame of mind, and they are definitely not worrying about cleanliness or anything else like that. It's been my experience when dealing with a suicide crime scene; it's usually a mess, from the turmoil of the last couple of seconds. A lot of people struggle with their own decision after they make it to commit suicide.

The walk from the dorm room down to the parking lot seemed to take forever, and it wasn't because of the scene I had just looked at. I kept having flashbacks of that semester I spent in the dorms here at St. Mary's. There was a lot of maturing during those months; I changed quite a bit, and I'll never forget that semester. The smell hasn't changed over the years; it still smells like a locker room, probably because teenage boys live here, but just like the advertisement says, they leave St. Mary's as men.

"How about you, Neil, what do you think? Do you see what I mean? It's just—"

"Stop right there, Glow. Let's talk in private. Do you have somewhere we can hide out for a couple of hours and talk, and I mean about everything?"

"I know just the place. If we go back to my office, someone will track us down. We won't get any privacy. Let me finish up here, and we'll head out."

"All right. I'm going to talk to some of the officers who were first to arrive at the scene."

"Say fifteen minutes or so? Is that long enough for you?"

"That will be fine."

All I can think of right now is that room, and how clean it was. It just doesn't fit. Glow was right: something is definitely going on here. But what would the police be trying to cover up? And why would they be covering it up? It doesn't make sense. Also, where are his parents? Where is his mother? Glow mentioned her, but I wonder where she is in all of this. I'll make sure and ask Glow.

"All right, Neil, are you ready? Any luck talking to the other officers?"

"I keep getting the same story regurgitated over and over. Apparently they don't feel like thinking for themselves tonight; they keep referring me back to the lead detective, and he was just a waste of time. By the way, where are we heading?"

"Now do you see why I called you? As for where we are going, we'll make our way over to the church; we should be able to get some privacy there. The few people that might be lingering around don't speak much English, so we should be able to talk about anything there."

"Speaking of the church, how's the seminary going? Are you still having the Polish seminarians assist the priests at Mass from time to time? God, that drove us nuts as students; you could barely understand a word they said."

"It was hard for the teachers too. And no, they don't do that anymore, they have separate, smaller Masses that they allow the seminarians to participate in."

"It's amazing, even with the few new buildings, this place still looks the same. It brings back a lot of good memories. Except for those winters. Walking around campus when it was freezing got old really fast."

Entering the church, I was overcome with old memories; the smell, just being in there gave me this amazing sense of calmness. The church isn't very big, but then again, it isn't small either. As you approach the church from the front, you are greeted by a hanging iron statue of Mother Mary. Probably a good ten to twelve feet in height, it really is a sight to see. I remember growing up, I was always wondering if that thing would ever fall off, but they keep her in great shape. Once you made it under the feet of Mary and through the doors, you'd find yourself in a small entranceway that is the width of the church but only about twenty feet long. During school Masses, this area would be full of backpacks and coats from all the students, since you weren't allowed to bring in your backpacks to church—just one less distraction, I guess. I still can't believe I'm back at my old high school; it really is an amazing thing how sometimes life comes full circle. Orchard Lake St. Mary's did wonders for me and my life; now it's my turn to give back.

"What is it you wanted to talk about, Neil? Now that we're private, we can talk about anything you would like."

"Let's start off with this Andrew kid. Is there anything you left out? I keep feeling like there is something more, I just can't figure it out."

"There really is nothing more than I can say. My hands are tied with this matter. As for yours, that's a different story. You can do all the digging you would like, but I would be as swift as you can be."

"What do you mean, your hands are tied? Does this have to do with the archdiocese? Are they telling you to be quiet about information, about things that could help me out?"

"There are very influential people leading those handling this case. That is why I called you; you're the only person I could think of. I really have said too much already; we probably shouldn't be seen leaving the church together. I'll hang around and do some praying for Andrew's family as well as you."

"I'm so lost right now. Why me? I'm sure there are other people you could have called to help you out. What makes me so special in this case?"

"Let's just say your ability to ignore authority as well as your unwillingness to believe that an organization should be running a church. Makes you the only person I can trust."

"So you're saying that my belief in God but lack of trust in the Roman Catholic Church are what make you believe I'm the guy for the job? I guess I've always had trouble believing in organized religion, it just didn't make sense, but that's neither here nor there."

"I'd have you call me, but I'm afraid there will be too many people listening in on our conversations."

"I've got that covered. I'll send out one of my guys with his son, and we'll have them look at St. Mary's. While out there visiting him can you slip a cell phone that you can use to contact me, and I contact you? Also, where is this kid's mother? I thought you said you knew both of them."

"Okay. But you can't tell too many people what's going on. I'm already putting my neck out there enough by calling you tonight. As for Ms. Malinowski, I have no idea, I'd ask the cops, maybe follow up tomorrow."

"Does she live on campus or nearby?"

"She lives in Keego Harbor, up the street. She lived on campus for a few years but decided to move off campus last year when Andrew got older to give him some privacy."

"I understand. And don't worry, my guys are extremely discreet; only those I can trust will be involved. I'll be in touch."

"Thank you, Neil. One last thing before you go."

"What's that, Glow?"

"You've only got a week or so to do your digging. As I said, some very influential people don't want the truth being brought to the light. Every day you take means that much more information is being taken care of. I'm not sure why, but it's just my gut feeling."

"I hear you loud and clear. And don't worry about anything; this O

As we parted ways in the dark, I couldn't help but wonder what was going on. My mind was racing a mile a minute, trying to figure out what is up with this kid Andrew. Why does the archdiocese— well, the Church, in general—want to cover this up and make it look like a suicide? It's not as if they would have had the kid killed—I mean, I don't agree with a lot of the churches' views or policies, but I don't think they have it in them to murder someone. Or do they? For that matter, is this a suicide and they are covering up something else?

AVE MARIA

There are just so many unanswered questions right now; I have no idea where to start. Hopefully, in the morning, things will be a little more in focus.

3

My dad got pissed at me; that's putting it nicely.

I could barely keep my eyes open as I made my way to the expressway for the trip home. No matter how loud I turned up the music in the car, I couldn't seem to snap out of a trance, constantly phasing out. To think of it, I'm only a mile away from Maria's place. I should give her a call and see if I can crash on her couch, just to be safe. Hopefully she's awake; then again, she always was a night owl.

"Neil! Are you okay? It's almost three a.m."

"Actually, I'm right down the street from you; I was out in Orchard Lake for the past couple of hours. I'm having trouble keeping my eyes open. Would it be okay if I just crashed at your place for a bit to be safe? I just don't feel like pressing my luck right now. If you don't want me to, I'll understand."

"No . . . no . . . it's okay. I'll leave the front door unlocked; just let yourself in. I'll throw a blanket on the couch for you."

"Thanks, Maria. I'll see you in a few."

"I'll probably be in bed already, so I guess I'll see you in the morning."

Five or so minutes later, I pulled into Maria's driveway and made my way into the house. This has to be one of the most awkward situations I've ever been in, walking into my ex-girlfriend's house only two weeks after we broke up. I don't have much of a choice, though; it just wouldn't be smart to try and make the drive as tired as I am. It didn't take me long to fall asleep on her couch, the floor looked just as inviting. It was more a matter of crashing anywhere other than in my car behind the wheel. "Restlessly" would be the best word to describe how I slept; I couldn't help but think about the nights I spent sleeping upstairs curled up with Maria. When I sleep, I can sometimes work through a lot of my deepest, darkest problems. It has always been a problem of mine, to consciously think through a problem while sleeping. I would be the first person to tell someone that it isn't possible to consciously think while sleeping, but since I'm the one doing it, I'll believe it's possible.

The smell of freshly brewed coffee filled the first floor, working its way to my nose, waking me up ever so gently. There really isn't anything quite like waking up to the smell of coffee brewing in the pot, it sends such a promising message as I start the day; with a good cup of coffee will come a good day. Before I get a chance to move, I realize there has been a visitor sleeping on my chest for some time now. I woke to see Nancy asleep on my chest, purring ever so quietly in tune with my breathing. I know Nancy isn't your average cat's name. At the time, Maria and I were still dating, and I knew she hated coming home to an empty house. With her job, a dog would be too much work. A fish just is not enough company. So I picked Maria up a seven-month-old domestic short-hair kitten. I named her Nancy after Frank Sinatra's daughter. She's all black with the darkest green eyes I've ever seen. Jade would have fit her a little better, but I liked Nancy.

"I see you had company last night. Don't the two of you look too cute?"

"I didn't know she was sleeping with me until I woke up. I wonder how long she's been down here."

"She spent most of the night with you. I came down to check on you at about four a.m. and found her curled up on your chest."

"Thanks again, Maria, for letting me crash here. While I've got you here, can I apologize for the way things ended a couple of weeks ago?"

"There's nothing to apologize for, Neil. We've got a lot to work through. Especially if we are going to have a chance for anything, even a friendship. And right now I need a friend more than anything."

"Wait a minute. Are you okay? You look like you're going to cry. Come here and sit down. What's wrong?"

"The reason I haven't called you lately—"

Maria broke out in tears; I had no idea what to do. So I just leaned in, put my arms around her, and let her cry it out; I knew she would tell me when she was ready. After a good fifteen minutes of tears and curling up on the couch, Maria finally filled me in.

AVE MARIA

"It's my dad. He's dying, and there's nothing they can do about it."

"Oh, my God! What's wrong with him? When? How?"

"About two days after our big fight, I got a call from the hospital. It was my mom crying and telling me to meet her out there. When I got there, I found my dad hooked up to a bunch of machines, fading into and out of consciousness."

"I . . . I don't know what to say. Is there anything I can do?"

"Can you just be there for me? No one makes me feel safe like you do. I just need to feel safe right now."

"How long did they say your father has?"

"That's the thing. He had a massive heart attack, but no one saw it coming. When they went in for surgery, they noticed tumors all over the place. If the heart attack wasn't bad enough, he has cancer, from the looks of it; he's had it for years without knowing about it. They said he only had a couple weeks left in him, the latest is that they don't think he's going to make it through the night."

"Oh, Maria! I'm so sorry for you and your family. I know how close you and your father are; this must be extremely hard on you right now. I'll tell you what: we'll just lay here on the couch until you're ready to get up."

"Thanks, Neil. That would be great."

I spent the next two hours lying on the couch asleep with Maria, just holding her close. And I would be lying if I hadn't been thinking about the relationship I have with my father. About a year ago, my family and I got into a big disagreement. My father decided to give my younger sister control of his butcher shop. It wasn't the fact that I didn't get the butcher shop, I could care less about that, but there's a lot more to the story.

We'll start with high school, since that is where important stuff started to take shape. As I mentioned, I went to high school at Orchard Lake St. Mary's. I didn't grow up rich or affluent in the Orchard Lake area, like most of the students there; I grew up in East Detroit in a small brick home. Don't get me wrong, I loved every minute of my childhood growing up in the city. My parents never let us know that we weren't rich. What we didn't have in monetary rewards we made up for in family; we were too busy to know we were poor. Our family had a friend at Orchard Lake St. Mary's, a very close friend of my mother and who taught morals and ethics there. She also drove me to school every morning. My father was an Italian butcher shop owner who ran the business with help from his old friend and father to my best friend. Father Roberts, or as I knew him growing up, Vincent Joseph Roberts. My mother was an Italian stay-at-home mom. Which, in an Italian family, is more than a full-time job; she made her family her job, and she did an amazing job at it.

As for my sister Katrina, or "Kat" as we call her, she was a wild child. She was never happy with where we lived or what we did as a family. I know some of it was just going through a phase, but as she got older and I ended up at the FBI, her problems became my problems all of a sudden. I was bailing her out of trouble at least once every six months for something. The first time I was asked to take care of one of her problems, she was dating some loser who asked her to hold his stash of drugs at her apartment. He was a local drug dealer and didn't want the product at his house where the cops could get him on possession, so he put it at her house. The problems kept getting bigger and worse every time. The last time was about a year ago, and her new addiction was gambling. At least it wasn't drugs or alcohol; she had been and is still sober for almost two years now. I'm so proud of her for that, back to why I'm mad at my dad. She got in trouble with some bad people when she lost a poker tournament that cost her more than twenty K. She had most of the money but was short on the last five K, and when she asked me for the money, I told her that I wasn't helping her anymore. She got herself into this; she could get herself out of it.

She couldn't get out of trouble any legal way, so she called an old friend and started to steal cars for him to raise the money. Needless to say, she got caught, and this time our parents came to me and asked me to take care of it. I told them I wasn't going to make it go away, as I had been doing for the past couple of years. This time she had to learn a lesson. I told them I would get a lawyer for her and pay the retainer, but that was it. I was washing my hands of the situation; I wasn't going to put my job on the line anymore for my sister's mistakes. My dad got pissed at me; that's putting it nicely. It was also nearing a time in his life that he was looking to retire, and he wanted to leave the family business to someone in the family. So he decided to give it to Kat instead of me, thinking I would be mad. I was mad, but not because I didn't get it. I was mad because he was putting it in the hands of someone who has never cared about anything given to her since the day she was born. I knew the family business was going to be run into the ground by my sister.

Luckily for me, I'm not a betting man. Kat has done a great job with the butcher shop and has cleaned up her life to an amazing point. She has finally gotten the message; I think some of it was the ninety days she had to do in jail for the grand theft auto charge, as well as the parole she will be on for the next year. Although I think it was the right move. My father hasn't forgiven me for my decision, and I haven't forgiven him for being pissed at me, and not letting Kat learn a lesson for a change. Everything went right back into the family business, which means we all worked there. I worked there during school, putting myself through college during the week. I worked at the butcher shop with Dad, on the weekends working at local bars. I received my undergraduate degree from the University of Detroit–Mercy, in psychology and criminology in three short years, and received a master's degree in clinical psychology from Wayne State University. I started working for the FBI shortly after that, in 1996, and then I left in 2001 after a parting of the ways with the bureau was forced because I didn't catch Cappelano. Luckily for me, Cappelano was nuts. He came out of hiding four years later, and the bureau called for me one last time. But that is neither here nor there. What matters now is taking care of Maria and figuring out what happened to this kid at St. Mary's last night. Maybe, just maybe, I'll give my dad a call someday to try and work things out before it's too late.

"Thanks, Neil, for being with me for these past couple of hours. It really means a lot."

"No problem, kid; you know there will always be a place for you with me."

"I like it when you call me 'kid' for some reason. But I really need to get going; I want to be at the hospital before noon, to let my mom go home and get some rest."

"I completely understand. I have a lot of work to get done today, but you always know my cell phone is on. Just give me a call if you need anything."

"Thanks for everything, Neil. Maybe we moved too fast, maybe we just bit off more than we could chew. Either way, I'm glad you're still around. You're a great friend to have in my corner. Thanks again for everything. Have a safe drive home."

"Give your dad a hug from me, would you? I'll make sure and light a few candles at church today or tomorrow, and I'll say a little prayer for him. Do you guys still go to St. Pat's Church downtown?"

"Yeah. That would mean a lot. Thanks again for everything."

"One last thing: any way you can look into this kid and his mother for me? Just run their names through the basic checks such as immigration. And something seems funny about their names."

"Yeah, I can do that. Just email me the info and we'll get on it."

"Thanks again, Maria."

4

*Barely in the door, I was ambushed by two female Dobermans
whose tails were about to fly off.*

There really is nothing quite like driving in the middle of rush hour in
Detroit. Whenever I would take trips out of town to Ohio or Indiana,
I would always get the same response from people when I tell them
I'm from Detroit. "You guys drive like assholes up there. I mean,
you guys are really nuts up there." It's always some variation of that
or about the crime level in the city, which is getting a lot better; we're
no longer in the top five for violent crimes. It's almost nine a.m. and
I'm making my way back home to put the girls out, shower, shave,
and change before the long day ahead of me. With my brain going a
mile a minute trying to figure out what to make of Andrew and the
scene I saw last night at St. Mary's Prep. Already with my conspiracy
theories about the Catholic Church, I couldn't help but let my
imagination run wild, especially after my conversation with Glow.

The way the conversation was left by Glow, telling me that I was
his only choice because I had faith in religion but no faith in the

Church; it was too much for me to handle right now. On top of that, I find out Maria's father is dying; it was just a month ago that I was helping him refinish his basement; he seemed fine. I need to get home and take a shower, which always helps me to think. I should probably call Ken and get him and the boys together for a meeting this afternoon. Ken or Kenneth Chamberlain is my partner and friend at the private investigation company that we now call BCI. It used to be called CB INC, and we tried to shorten it to CBI, but we kept getting alls for some medical offices. So we went with BCI, which stands for Baggio and Chamberlain Inc, although most people think the "I" stands for Investigation. We made it a corporation for tax and liability purposes as well as business purposes.

BCI does more than just private investigative services. We specialize in high-profile security for athletes and celebrities, as well as setting up security systems for corporations, small businesses, and anything in between. Thanks to one of our tech guys, we have a new computer division that has grown from one man to a team of six that can do computer surveillance as well as extensive background checks. We've come a long way in a very short time, and catching Cappelano had a lot to do with that. Thanks to the short-lived celebrity that I had gained, our company has gone from local boys to national attention in six short months. Although media attention has pretty much died off, I am still recognized for my work among my peers, which is the most important thing to me. Fame will come and go, but respect among your peers lasts a lifetime.

"Hey Neil, what's going on? Isn't it a little early for my little celebrity?"

"Yes, it is too early. If I'm a celebrity, then that means Armageddon must be right around the corner."

"Nice. I have to admit you are funny when you're cranky. So what's the call for this early? I highly doubt you just wanted to chat."

"I'll get to the point. I need you to have the tech department to hack into St. Mary's records ASAP. And get me as much information as they can on a student that committed suicide last night. All I have is a name: Andrew Malinowski. But part of me feels like it's fake."

"This should be easy," Ken said sarcastically.

"Wait a second. He just graduated in the top tier of his class and was supposed to go to Oakland University this upcoming fall. He was born in Poland, and that's about all I know about the kid. That's where you guys come in."

"I'll put them to the task right away, partner. Oh, I have a message for you."

"Let me guess it's that editor from the publishing house?"

"Yup. She's just calling again to see if you've thought about her proposal."

"I mean, hasn't she gotten the hint? I never return her calls. Don't get me wrong: writing a book would be cool, but I don't have time for it right now, and I don't want any more attention publicly than we're already getting."

"Look at you, Mr. Celebrity. You think if you write a book, you'll become even more famous. Don't you?"

"You know what I mean. I just don't need any more attention, no matter how much . . . or how little. I'm enjoying the family right now. Sheila and I are thinking of taking Carol Lynn to Florida for a vacation, I'm thinking something more like the Bahamas."

"Now, that sounds like a plan. I'll let you go, Neil; I need to get ahold of our tech department and get those guys over here. You know how hard it is to get these guys in here before noon. They are definitely night owls."

"Thanks again, Ken."

"Thank you for catching Cappelano. Hell, we have to turn down jobs now; it's crazy. Be safe driving home. I'll call you when I get something."

"Sounds good, but before I forget, why don't you buy lunch for everyone down at the warehouse today, maybe subs or something like that, as a thank you for all the hard work."

"The boys would love it. I'll let them know you send your best. The guys really miss you around here. Talk to you later, Neil."

It really is nice having a team of almost forty people at my disposal to get things done; even though I prefer to do things myself, it's a trust issue. We have specialists in almost everything now, and we are always looking to expand our workforce with the right people. I know that sounds like a now-hiring advertisement, but what can I say? I love my job and the people that work with me. I hate saying that people work for me because it makes me feel like an authority figure, since I have trouble with authority figures myself. They work with Ken and me at the company we founded, but not for us. There's a difference.

Before I can even shut the door to the car in my driveway, I could hear the girls going nuts in the house. I don't know what I'd do without those two: Jackie and Danielle, aptly named after my favorite nightcap, Jack Daniels. Barely in the door, I was ambushed by two female Dobermans whose tails were about to fly off. It really is the next best thing to being greeted by a happy wife and kids. I'm close, I have a happy ex-wife and a daughter that I love very much. They live nearby, about three blocks away in my old house. The only thing I regret about the divorce is giving up that kitchen; I wish I could have brought it with me. That's neither here nor there What is important is that I still love Sheila, my ex-wife, and our daughter Carol Lynn. They are the true ladies in my life; just don't tell Jackie or Danielle I said that. If they heard me say that, I might get something worse than a horse head left in my bed come the morning.

Before I made it to the shower, I went into the kitchen to get a pot of coffee started because a morning without coffee is definitely sacrilegious. I need caffeine in the morning and lots of it, and since I don't drink pop or any carbonated drinks anymore, that only leaves me with coffee, that sweet nectar of life. I love the feeling of hot water running down the back of my neck and back while sipping on a cup of coffee and jamming out to Frank Sinatra. If I failed to mention it earlier, I'll fill you in now, I am a huge Frank Sinatra fan. There really isn't anything quite like Frank on vinyl. Well, okay, I can think of a few things that might be a little better, but not by much.

AVE MARIA

It's almost ten in the morning on Monday, and I still haven't the faintest idea of what to think about what happened last night. As a matter of fact, the only thing I'm sure of right now is that the ladies are driving me nuts because they have to go out. I don't know if they have to or need to, but I'm sure they want to. Probably to go wrestle around and get dirty, especially since they just finished getting groomed the other day. Almost all dog owners know that if you get your dog groomed, they will spend the next couple days doing anything and everything to get dirty, just like little kids. It looks like my phone is ringing; either that or my pants are just vibrating.

"Baggio's cell phone, this is his secretary. May I direct your call to him?"

"Aren't you in a good mood this morning? I saw the news this morning, and I saw your car in the background of the news coverage. Is everything all right out at St. Mary's?"

"I really don't know, Sheila. They say it was a textbook suicide, and that's what scares me. There is no such thing, even you know that much. From years being around me."

"Aren't they going to at least look into it a little further? Or is that why you were there?"

"You always were good at figuring things out. That is why I was called out there, by my old headmaster."

"Thanks. I learned from the best."

"Glow doesn't think it's a suicide, and he couldn't really say much to me last night. He said I have to do this as quietly and quickly as possible. I felt like I was in an espionage movie from the fifties."

"I promise I won't tell anyone about our conversations, Alpha One."

"Very cute. You know I was thinking of taking you out to lunch today while Carol Lynn's at school. Are you up for it?"

"I can be ready in fifteen minutes."

"I knew there was a reason I loved you."

"Aw, you said you loved me. I love you too, even if you can be difficult most of the time. I'm just kidding."

"You know you and Carol Lynn will always have a place in my heart. You guys mean the world to me."

"Speaking of that, I really am sorry for the way things turned out with Maria and you; I could tell you really liked her. Maybe it will work out."

"I don't think so. She wants something I can't give her."

"What's that, if you don't mind me asking?"

"All of my heart, without you and Carol Lynn involved. Although it's dysfunctional as hell, it makes me happy, so I guess I'll just keep trying until we get too old and we end up together."

"Sometimes I ask myself why we keep playing this game. But we were just so miserable being married, I'm scared to try it again, scared to ruin what happiness we have, especially with Carol Lynn so young."

"I know, cutes. Go get ready; I'll be by in a few minutes."

"See ya, hot stuff!"

Sheila and I have a peculiar relationship. However, the older I get, the more I realize we are far from the only people in the world with the same relationship. Sheila and I were married in 1996 after a short period of dating—a little less than two years, to be exact. Our marriage was rocky, lasting five years, which is impressive if you ask either of us. We really hated living together. Carol Lynn was two when we filed for divorce, but it was odd because it seemed like the moment we filed those papers, we could put up with each other. I remember the moment, to be exact. I was moving my stuff into a small apartment, preparing for the worst, I had little furniture, and even fewer items in the kitchen. Sheila came over my second night there, with a few boxes of stuff from the house that I could use: towels, dishes, etc. We stayed up all night, reminiscing about the times when we dated. It was weird, just sitting there talking, no fighting, no snide remarks, just enjoying each other for who we are. It's been the same ever since that day. That's why we are both scared to try again, at least try in the formal sense. We still have a very healthy sexual relationship, better than when we dated. Not to mention a complete 180 from when we were married. Sheila and I couldn't be married, not from a lack of love. It is just a matter of two people whose personalities clash in close quarters; if you put them in the same room together for too long, they snap at each other.

"Thanks for lunch, Neil, and the talk; it was just what the doctor ordered. Now I've got to get home and be there when our little spitfire comes   home   from   school."

"It was no problem at all, cutes; glad I could oblige. It helped to bounce some of my far-fetched notions off someone else. I'm just at a loss right now about everything. Give Carol Lynn a hug from her dad, would you?"

"No problem, I'll talk to you later, might even let you come over for a little late-night wrestling."

"We'll see where I'm at with everything."

"Don't be turning me down before I even get a chance to offer. You know I hate that."

"It's better than letting you down after you get all riled up."

"Very true, but you need to get out of here and get to work on this mess at St. Mary's."

"I'll talk to you later, Sheila."

I probably should have pointed out to Sheila that we have been tailed from her house and all through lunch. Judging by the car model and the men in it, it isn't a government tail. It looks like someone hired a PI to tail me. This is quite ironic, since I'm a PI. It looks like it's time to call Ken and have fun at the expense of the two guys trailing me.

5

What do you have in mind? It better be worthwhile. Otherwise
I'm going to your boss, for lack of a better word.

"Ken, it's Neil. I've got a little bit of a problem."

"You mean the guys tailing you? Yeah, I already know about it."

"What? Why didn't you call me? Did you figure out who Andrew really is?"

"Almost. We have a name, and a lot of empty holes, which means there is something up with this kid. As for your tail, we were trying to figure that out too."

"And? Do we have an answer to the latter question?"

"Well, I can tell you who it isn't. It isn't any of the PI companies, at least none of the ones out here."

"You don't think it's someone working for the Church, do you?"

"Well, it isn't a government tail, I'm sure even you figured that one out. It just doesn't add up. I have no idea who it could be."

"There's always one way to find out."

"What are you going to do?"

"I'll call in a favor and have them pulled over by a cop buddy of mine so I can find out for myself."

"It's decisions like that that make you the 'B' in BCI. Good luck. Let me know how everything goes, I'll have our guys keep an eye on you like I've had them all morning. They are working on their tailing skills."

"I forgot about that; good timing, I guess. I'll call you when I get something."

"I'll have the guys email your account the little information we've pulled up on our suicide kid, Andrew. I'll keep you posted on everything."

As soon as Ken and I got off the phone I started to dial an old friend of mine, Brian Potter. It's probably a good thing we just had lunch last week. The two of us went to college together and worked together as bouncers at a couple of different places. He was a tall, lanky kid back then, but he was always good at his job, and that's all that matters.

We reconnected about a year ago; he was having an issue with his bar when some guys were trying to run drugs through there, and he was having trouble getting the cops to stop them. It's not that they didn't want to—the police, that is—they were just spread thinly. Ken and our crew put in some work and helped the cops get the intel they needed to stop the local ring. Since then, Brian and I have been hanging out, looking out for each other when we can.

"Brian, this is Neil. Can you do me a huge favor?"

"What's up, bro? Anything I can do, you know I'll do it."

"You said you've got some cop buddies who work for Macomb County. Can you do me a favor?"

"Yeah, what's up? One of them is actually working right now. Where are you at?"

"I've got a car tailing me, and I don't know who it is."

"Just give me the info and I'll call him right now."

"Just give me one minute and I'll get everything for you."

I had to end the call with Brian so that he could call his cop friend for me. While I was waiting to see if Brian could get ahold of the officers, I pulled into a gas station to allow them to catch up to me and pull the car over. I guess it is somewhat ironic that I'm being tailed by a private investigator right now. Eventually even those of us in the business are going to be tailed. We probably have a higher chance of being followed because we are always sticking our noses in business that isn't ours. It looks like Brian is calling me back already; I hope it's good news.

"Hey Neil, they said you should see them any second now. Do you see them anywhere?"

"Yeah, they just pulled up. Would it be okay if I go over there and talk to the guys?"

"I told them who you are, and they said just approach them and identify yourself. And it will be no problem at all."

"Thanks again, man. I owe you one big. Just let me know."

"I'll save that one for a rainy day. Talk to you later, Neil."

"Thanks again, Brian. Now let's go see who these guys are that have been trailing me all day."

Feeling like one of those scenes in old Western movies at high noon, I made my way across the street to identify myself with the officers. They were surprised that I was an FBI agent, since Brian had just informed them that I was a PI who was a partner in BCI, a company that has made quite a name for itself lately. I guess I should have just told them that I was Neil Baggio and not Agent Baggio, but then again, it's a lot more fun to say Agent Baggio than Neil Baggio.

"Hey guys, so what do we have here? Do we have identities for these two fine gentlemen yet?"

"As a matter of fact, we do, Agent Baggio."

"Don't call me Agent Baggio; just call me Neil. As a matter of fact, for helping me out with this, here's my card. If you guys are ever looking for some extra work, just give me a call; I'm sure I can find something for you guys to do."

"Thanks, Neil. As for your two friends here who were keeping an eye on you. The driver's name is Father McMahon, and the man in the passenger seat is Father Strickland. They appear to be Catholic priests for the Archdiocese of Detroit. They aren't saying much, and they are trying to act like they don't know what we're talking about."

"That's okay. I've had a couple of guys trailing me all day as a training exercise, and they were the ones that noticed these two guys first. Let me have a chat with them if you don't mind."

"Go right ahead, Neil. We'll be in the cruiser if you need anything. Just wave us over."

"Thanks again for everything."

Two priests. Glow wasn't kidding. This is interesting shit. I've got to talk to these guys and see what's going on. I can't believe I've had two Catholic priests tailing me all day in a beat-up old Reliant.

Good to see I'm paying attention. If I had known they were priests, I would have stopped off at a strip club and gone out the back and had a friend pick me up just so they had to sit in front of a strip club all day. That would have been fun.

"Good afternoon, Father."

"Good afternoon, son. How are you doing today?"

"I should ask you. You've been following me all afternoon. Would you care to enlighten me as to why? And don't say that you haven't been. I have had trainees tailing me all day, and they noticed you earlier, so I know you have been."

"We are not at liberty to say, Mr. Baggio. It is not our place to say anything."

"All right, then how about you point me in the direction of someone that can fill me in on why you are tailing me."

"We really aren't allowed to say anything. I'm sorry, but that is just the way it is."

"All right, I'll just go to the cardinal with pictures of two priests tailing me for several hours and I'll ask him myself. Thanks, guys, for everything."

"Wait a minute, you don't have to go and do that. I'm sure we can work something out."

"What do you have in mind? It had better be worthwhile. Otherwise I'm going to your boss, for lack of a better word."

"We can't talk about this here, not now. Do you have a card, so we can call you later?"

"Here you go, you've got until midnight to call me, or I make my move without you. Got it?"

"We hear you loud and clear. I'll call you before midnight tonight."

"Be safe today and tell your superiors to stay off my tail. Next time I'll have you guys thrown in jail. Trust me, I have the power and connections to do it."

"We've already seen enough; we won't be bothering you anymore."

"Sorry, Fathers, but I just don't take kindly to being followed. Have a good night."

That was definitely not what I expected, two priests. One of them is in his late forties and the other in his early fifties; not very sprightly, if you ask me. I have seen an awful lot in my days as a private investigator and as an FBI agent, but I never thought I would see the day come where I would be tailed by two priests. With each new day, I can see the Catholic Church for what it is. A big organization or corporation, and trust me, the Church is a corporation, especially with all the money the Church raises every year. Just like any other corporation, you have a lot of shifty people at the top, making decisions. The only difference is that when the Church makes a decision, they can say it's in the name of God, which takes the blame off themselves if it doesn't work. I'm not saying everyone in the Church is corrupt, I'm just saying a lot of the important people in the Church are.

A good example happened not too long ago right here in Detroit. We have had a lot of the archdiocese's schools closing down because the Church said they didn't have the money to keep them open. And then someone did some digging around, and we just found out our cardinal gave a large sum of money to another archdiocese for a monument or some crap. The amount he gave away could have kept ten schools open for at least five more years. That money would have allowed more than a few people to keep their jobs, not to mention keep the students where they need to be. Instead he shipped the money out, closed schools, cut more jobs, and told our kids to go find somewhere else to go to school.

I understand decisions get made on paper that have real-world implications. Still, we as a society need to be better. I also know I wasn't in that room. for all I know they realized that money would have kept schools open for only a year or less. But be upfront—hiding it never looks good.

Ken is never going to believe me when I tell him who was tailing me this whole time. I can't wait to see his face. I'd call him, but it would be better to see his reaction in person. I guess I'll be making an appearance at the warehouse today. The warehouse is the center of BCI's operation. It's down on Eight Mile on the right side of the tracks. If you've never been to Detroit, that means it's on the side of Eight Mile that the cops will show up to if you call. It's sad, I know, but true. The drive downtown is as expected, seeing as it's nearly six o'clock. Meaning that it's rush hour and everyone is trying to get home or to their local pub to take the edge off of working all day. I'm flying down the expressway in my new crossfire, taking full advantage of my federal government official license plates. Isn't it ironic that I hate everything about the FBI unless it gives me an advantage when and where needed? I guess my situation with the bureau works out for both sides.

They get a top-notch serial homicide detective on the payroll, and for very little money, I might add. I, on the other hand, get to use my FBI clearance when needed. Also, not being on call is glorious. Technically I'm not getting paid by the bureau. All I'm getting is a tax-exempt status for myself and that of my business. That, along with my clearance and a few perks. I do get my expenses covered, but no real salary. As I got off I-94 and made my way down Eight Mile, I pulled out my security card so I could gain access to the warehouse. Ken and I love our tech toys, especially when it comes to the security of our building. With the area, we have set up shop, and with all of the equipment we have stored there, we need all the security we can get.

The security cards follow the same algorithm that our security entrances follow. Every hour on the hour, our security codes change throughout the whole building, and determined on your job and level at the company, your access to certain areas changes. Accesses to the car bay or the tech lab are all determined by job code. It's quite an amazing system that costs quite an amazing penny, but as I said, Ken and I love our toys. As for security cameras, we have them stashed all over the property. The majority of them are hidden, and when it gets slow around the warehouse, some of the guys try to find out where they are; thirteen cameras have yet to be found.

If anyone can find all of the cameras before the end of the year, they'll get a ten-thousand-dollar bonus. I made my way into the VIP area as it's called now because Ken and I are the only two who have access to it. It's a small bay that we park in that is just below our offices, making it especially nice in the winter and for a quick exit. As I pulled in, Ken was surprised to see me at the warehouse. If he thinks he's surprised now, wait until he hears who was following me.

"What are you doing here, Neil? I thought you weren't coming today."

"I just had to grab a few things from the office that I needed to work on. Before I forget, what was Andrew's real name?"

"Pardon me if I slaughter the pronunciation of his name: Andrzej Malinowski."

"Have you sent out some of the guys yet to gather information on our mystery boy's past, friends, or family?"

"I've already put the tech guys to work on tracking him down through the INS. I needed to talk to you about possibly bankrolling a couple of guys making a run out to Poland. It might be the only way we can get any truth from this situation."

"Run the numbers and see how much we are probably talking about. I'll decide in the morning. Wait a minute: do we even have a guy that speaks Polish around here?"

"We don't have anyone that speaks fluent Polish, but we do have a guy whose cousin is fluent in Polish, German, French, and English.

And apparently this cousin can also speak a decent amount of three or four other East European languages."

"Do we know anything about this cousin? I'm guessing you've already done a background check on this person, since you're bringing it to my attention."

"She checks out fine, in more ways than one."

"Whose cousin is it that we are talking about? It's not Snyder's, is it? I like the guy. I just don't trust him with my money."

Snyder is what we call a grunt or a pup around here. He is eager, ready to work his tail off, but he makes dumb decision after dumb decision. He once fell asleep for twenty minutes into a stakeout because he was up the night before playing Madden.

"No, it's not Snyder's cousin. It's Christian Dombrowski's cousin. She's twenty-three and one hell of a find, that's for sure. She could make it easy for everyone over there. You know guys love giving information to women."

"Twenty-three? That's a little young for such an important case; I'll need to meet her first. If she's anything like Christian, then I might think about it, but we'll have to see."

"I figured that you might want to meet her first before the decision is made, so I set up lunch for the four of us at Miles tomorrow at noon. Will that work for you?"

"Yeah, that should be fine as long as I don't get another middle-of-the-night emergency call from anyone."

"Before I forget, did you figure out who was tailing you?"

"I almost shit myself when I walked up to the car and saw these two guys sitting there. I would never have guessed it in a million years, and I'm usually good at figuring out things like that."

"This must be a great story; I'm going to have to sit down for this one. You always beat around the bush when you've got something quality to tell me. Wait a second and let me get comfortable in my chair. Okay, shoot."

"There I am walking up to the police officer that stopped them for me when he informed me of whom they were and who they work for. I almost died laughing when he told me, and when I finally saw the two guys, it took everything in me not to laugh right in front of them. Although they did do a good job, at least for a little while."

"Who was it? Was it someone we know, someone we fired? Wait, who did they work for?"

"They work for the man upstairs. The Big Cheese."

"What? I'm not following you. Who do they work for?"

"It was two priests that were following me all morning. I shit you not."

"Holy shit. You've got to be kidding me. The Catholic Church already has a tail out on you? It hasn't even been twenty-four hours since this whole thing started. This kid must be special for one thing or another."

"That's what we need to figure out, and we need to figure it out right away. If the Church has already got a tail out on me, they obviously have someone keeping a close eye on the whole investigation."

"I need to figure a few things out; I'm going to need to hit the bag. You know that it always helps to clear my mind. If anyone calls, just take a message unless it's about this case. One last thing, what's Christian's cousin's name?"

"Nicolette Milewski. I'll have one of the guys prepare a bio for you right away; you can take it home with you if you want."

"Thanks, Ken, for always being there when I need you. You really are a good friend."

"Neil Baggio is getting all emotional and soft on me; this must be really hard for you. You never get like this; you've been a prick since the day I met you."

"Thanks, Ken, I can always count on you to remind me that I can come off a little brash."

"A little brash would be nice, you can be downright mean, but we love you for it, bro. Go hit the bag, I'll put some Frank Sinatra on for you and I'll hold your calls."

6

Regardless of how the meeting goes tomorrow, at least I'll have some good food in me for the day.

There really isn't anything quite like the moment of clarity I get when it's just me, my wraps, and a heavy bag. Another example is the sensation a friend of mine describes when he gets to the baseball field early enough before a game to lay on the freshly cut grass and take in that smell. I can definitely relate to the freshly cut grass, but for me it was getting to the football field early in high school. We had the softest grass. I know it sounds weird, but I used to get there at about seven in the morning, especially when it was warm outside, and I'd curl up in the sun and take a nap for about an hour. I have so many great memories of high school, and to think I sometimes hated going to school there, now I'm glad I went there. I wouldn't be who I am today without that experience. I could only imagine sitting across from the eighteen-year-old me; I think I would strangle him. I mean, look at me now; now imagine me as an eighteen-year-old, a know-it-all, not a good mix.

There has got to be some connection between Andrew and the Catholic Church, something big. Otherwise the Church wouldn't be tailing me like this. Just because a student commits suicide at a Catholic high school doesn't mean you need to tail a private investigator. Especially an alumnus of the school unless you have something to hide. You don't want anyone to know what it is. The problem is, did Andrew have information on the Church, or was the Church doing something for Andrew? Either way, this isn't looking good for the Church; this has got cover-up written all over it. The crime scene was enough to convince me there was something wrong, but after being tailed by those two priests, I'm certain this isn't a suicide. This was a murder, and it's being covered up by the Catholic Church.

I'm not about to say that the Church killed this poor kid, but they are definitely hiding something about his death, and they are making sure no one looks into it. If you ask me, that's just as bad as if not worse than killing someone. To be letting a killer go because you're afraid of something negative coming out about you is just wrong. Church or no Church, it is wrong to let a child's life to be taken and then brushed under the carpet like that. I can feel the anger building inside me. I know this case is going to test a lot of my convictions as well as my patience, and I'll have to try and be on my best behavior. But what could an eighteen-year-old Polish student know or be connected with that would have the Church so worried that they would send a couple of guys to tail me? I feel like I'm in a bad movie right now, and there's no end in sight. With the way things are lining up, I should have a week to maybe ten days to wrap up this case. Needless to say, I have to get to work, and it's probably going to take some finesse and a lot of bullying to get the information I need. I'll leave the finesse up to the other people; I'll stick to what I do best, and that's intimidating people both physically and mentally. There's nothing like a good mind game to get someone's juices flowing in the right direction, and by right, I mean in the direction I need them to be headed.

I've spent a good hour down in the gym trying to clear my head and to grasp the situation at hand. Each repetition of a basic combination releases frustration and clears my head. Jab, cross, step back, hook, and uppercut. I repeat this over and over, switching when I dodge. Focusing on my footwork, increasing my snap as I turn over my hands, feeling the stress drip away with each punch.

As I take a deep breath, I focus on tracking down the mother and trying to talk to her about her son and her husband, like who the fuck is he? Not to mention, I need to figure out where her husband/Andrew's father is; this could all be linked back to him. First things first: I need to figure out who Andrew's mother is and where I can find her, but something tells me finding her won't be as easy as opening up a phone book and calling her.

"Hey Neil, how was the workout? Did you get anything worked out?"

"A few things, but we'll see. I think I just need a good night's sleep. Do we have the tech guys working around the clock trading off, as usual, to track down any info they can on Andrew?"

"You know it. Those tech guys live for this crap; they are all about nonstop work. Do you have something specific in mind?"

"See if they can track down the mother. I have a feeling she can help me out, but I also have a feeling that the Church is going to have her hidden pretty well. It's not going to be easy to track her down."

"That's true. If they already have a tail on you, there's a good chance they've already hidden her away somewhere that no one will find her."

"My guess is that she's right under our noses; it's just that we have to find out where. As of right now, we don't even have a name for her, just her son."

"It shouldn't be too hard to track down the mother's information. If she came over with her son, we should be able to get almost anything from the INS."

"If she was brought over under the Catholic Church's wings, it will be a little harder than you think. The Church still has some pull. People will always fear God; it's just a natural state of being."

"That's true. With that fear of God pretty much instilled in most of us at birth in one way or another. It gives the Church great power to control situations that they might normally not be able to control."

"Now you're getting it, Ken. But it's getting late, and I need to get out of here. Just call me if the tech guys come up with anything."

"Don't forget the file I had the guys put together on Christian's cousin Nicolette. You should go through it before tomorrow's lunch at Miles Place."

"You got it. At least you picked a good restaurant. So regardless of how the meeting goes tomorrow, at least I'll have some good food in me for the day."

"Nice, Neil. Way to always look on the positive side. You crack me up, you know that?"

"Glad I could oblige you tonight. But I really do need to get out of here. I'll talk to you tomorrow at lunch."

"Try not to be too late for once and get home; you need the rest."

Over the years, Ken and I have really built a strong bond both in business and in friendship. He has become my go-to guy for almost anything. He's been a friend when I needed him to be and a partner when need be. He knows how to balance our friendship with our business relationship quite well. It's gotten to the point that he has things done before I even tell him I want them done; he just knows what I'm going to ask for. I know I can be a little demanding at times, but it's just because I like to do the best I can at everything I do. On the drive home, I couldn't help but think that the only chance I have of getting anywhere with this case is by tracking down Andrew's mother. She is the key to set my path. Without her I'm just guessing at anything and everything along the way. I've got an idea that just might work, but this is going to take a lot of man-hours and a lot of money. I slammed on the breaks and did a U-turn and made my way back to the office. First things first: I need to call Ken.

"Ken, it's Neil. Get on the wire and have everyone who's not working a high-profile case meet us at the warehouse ASAP. I need to address everyone."

"What's this about, Neil? Do you have an idea for finding out what happened to this kid?"

"Just get everyone there; I'll be there in a few minutes. Tell everyone this is important and to get here ASAP."

"You got it, boss man, see you in a few minutes. I'll round up the troops. Anything else I can do for you?"

"Just get everyone there fast and meet me in the conference room."

"Done. See you in a few."

I know this case is all about time, and the more time that passes means the harder it will be to get anything done and find anything. With every minute passing part of this kid's life is being erased from not only the record books but also from people's lives. People forget a quiet kid such as Andrew. This is a race again, and I'm going to need all the hands I can get on this case. There is just no way to fund this without a backer; I'm going to need to ask for volunteer help and lots of it. I looked down at the speedometer and realized I was doing well over a hundred miles an hour. That's not a good thing, but I just couldn't get my foot to lighten up off of the gas pedal, not until I pulled into the warehouse. I was taking turns at forty plus miles an hour flying through downtown as if I were driving in an Indy car race. As the bass from my stereo filled me with energy, I could feel the engine roar through the floor and up my legs. Making me even more dangerous behind the wheel, but luckily for me, I'm about to turn into the parking lot.

To my surprise, I noticed car after car similarly piling into the employee lot as I did. Cars were flying in off the street at high speeds. As if they were trying their hardest to get to the warehouse as quickly as possible for this meeting. It gave me a sense of loyalty that I have always gotten from the employees, and it's moments like this one that make me proud to be a partner in BCI.

"All right, Neil, we have almost everyone here, we're just waiting on a few more bodies to come piling in. Is there anything I can get you?"

"I need you to get the projector set up with all of the crime scene photos of Andrew's case. That's what this is all about; I will need to ask   for   help   on   this   case."

"You've got it. I'll get everything up and running. Do you have that disc I gave you just before you left?"

"It's right here. Thanks again for everything, Ken."

"You really need to stop saying that, Neil, I know you're thankful, we all do."

I had a few moments to collect myself and think about how I was going to present everything. Without the help of everyone here, I would have no chance of getting the truth out of this case. I'm going to need multiple tails around the clock on a lot of people. This is going to be a major operation; it's going to take every bit of manpower we can spare, every last drop.

"Neil, we're ready. I did a head count; we have everyone, and I mean everyone, here. There isn't anyone that isn't accounted for."

"Are you serious? What about—"

"Don't worry about a thing. Everyone's here because you asked them to be. Now let's get this show going."

"All right. Can you hand me the employee list so I can work some things out?"

"Here you go. That's everyone."

I can't believe everyone is here, I mean literally, everyone that works for BCI is here right now. It took only thirty minutes to round up more than forty employees, and it's nearly eleven at night. Ken and I must be doing something right if we can get this kind of a turnout on such short notice. But enough of that; I need to get this meeting going.

"All right, everyone. Some of you know why we're here, and some of you don't. So let's get right to it. As some of you know, a student at my prep school alma mater committed suicide the other night; the only problem was it wasn't a suicide. Anyone who was at the crime scene would know that it was just too clean. Ken, can you put up the photos for me on the projector?"

"All right. Here you go, Neil."

"As you guys can see, it was a pretty clean scene for a suicide. Especially a suicide that was done by hanging. Ninety-nine percent of the time, when you get to a scene where someone hung themself to commit suicide, there will be signs of a struggle at the end to try and free themself. Kick stuff over, etc., as the last chance of guilt or remorse for what they had just done. I know this is graphic stuff, but the reason I brought you all here is that there is a huge cover-up in process with this kid. We need to find out why, but I can't do it

64

without everyone's help; I mean everyone. We only have a week to ten days to figure this puzzle out, and it's going to be many long days and long hours, but it's the only chance to figure out the case. Oh yeah, one other thing, the people that are trying to cover everything up, they are the Catholic Church. I wish I could tell you why, but that's the truth. I've been tailed since the other night by the Church, and it's only going to get worse; we need to figure out what is going on. This is going to be volunteer only. I'll cover expenses, but hourly is out the window; we're going to be at the max as it is. I understand if you can't and won't take it personally, this is me asking for help, not demanding it."

"Come on, guys, Neil is asking us for help, and we all know if it weren't for him, none of us would be here. What do you say? Let's show those assholes who they are messing with. Nothing like taking on the whole Church; this could get ugly, especially for us who are Catholics. Still, we need to set our beliefs aside and figure out what is going on with this kid."

"Thanks, Ken, for that. So what do you say, guys? You can ask anything now, but this is it, I'm just going to ask once."

"All I have to ask is why we are talking about it; let's get this shit going right now."

It was right then that I heard a loud roar go through everyone. People started chanting "Let's go!" "Let's take it to them!" Andrew deserves to have the truth be brought to light. It was a very moving moment, a moment I will remember forever. Now all we need to do is come up with a plan of action. Talking about a huge faction like this is one thing, but organizing it is another. Luckily for me, I have Ken with me. The next couple of hours were spent making teams and getting them set up with missions and goals to achieve.

The next twenty-four hours are going to be crucial. We need to pull together as much information as possible that we can on this kid and his family. Fortunately, I know I have a team of more than forty to help me accomplish this goal. We have teams of tech guys hacking into files left and right trying to track down financial movement to a third party to maybe pay for a hit. We have teams that are going out to track down and tail key people in the archdiocese in hopes that we might be able to catch someone with Andrews's mother. The only problem is, as of right now, we don't know what she looks like.

"Ken, we are going to need people all over the place tailing and investigating. I would start with what their papers mentioned for when they got to the States. Also, find out who was their sponsor, and go from there."

"I've already got TJ and his team digging in their past they've been doing that all day. I've got him red-flagging key people, to investigate, interview, and track down. We're also looking for anyone that might have come in contact with them in the past six months."

"Thanks, Ken, I need to get to Glow for some follow-up. We'll follow up more later, have TJ email me regularly, you know his usual drill."

"We got you, Neil, go do your crazy shit, we'll take care of the rest."

AVE MARIA

I need to make a phone call to Glow, and I need to do it fast, but it needs to be a secure line. I'll have to send out a couple with a child tomorrow to drop off a cell phone to Glow for me to keep in contact with him. That way no one will think twice about a closed-door meeting with the headmaster and a future student.

So much to do and so little time to accomplish it. This is going to be one hell of a ride, regardless of the outcome. One thing is for sure, I don't like to lose, and neither do any of my employees, so this could get really ugly. I might need to light a couple of candles for prayer just in case I tick off the wrong people. But who am I kidding? I know I'm going to piss off a ton of people, but as long as the truth comes out in the end, that's all that matters.

7

*I came over to get a piece of ass, and all I get is an ass with a
cup of coffee.*

In college I ticked off plenty of professors, I almost got thrown out of
school on more than a few occasions, and we all know my track record
with the FBI by now. The one thing that I can say about myself is
that I consistently drive people of great authority crazy. In college
and high school I was the kid that could goof off, skip class and still
graduate with an A- average. I've always been someone who learns
how to work the system in my favor. I think it's that ability that made
Glow call me for this case; plus the fact that I'm tops in the field of
investigative work in both the private and governmental sectors.

Many believe me to be cocky, but I don't agree with that statement
at all. Particularly after my divorce, I learned to make sure and do
things right the first time around. Do I regret my divorce with Sheila?
No, and I'll tell you why; I don't regret anything I've ever done. I
only regret not learning from my failures the first time around. It's
when I start to repeat the same failures that I start to regret things. As

AVE MARIA

for this case, I only hope that I can use all the knowledge and manpower at my disposal to figure this thing out.

It's almost three in the morning when I pulled into the driveway, and to my surprise, Sheila's car was parked there. I wonder what she's doing here, and I wonder if our daughter is with her or at her grandmother's. I guess I'm about to find out in a few minutes what's going on. Not to mention Sheila has been seeing a nice guy for about six weeks now; this means they are probably not seeing each other anymore. I made my way into the house, trying to be quiet just in case our daughter was here. Sheila had fallen asleep. I noticed inside the door that only Sheila's shoes were kicked off and there weren't any small children's shoes that would give me a reason to believe Carol Lynn was here. As I finished taking off my coat and putting it in the front closet, I noticed there were candles lit and leading up the stairs. Sheila must be in one of her moods tonight; normally I would be all for her proposal. The only problem is that I don't think she's here for the right reasons. I might as well throw on a pot of coffee instead of running up the stairs with a bottle of wine.

"Hey, cutie, it took you long enough to come home. Didn't you see the candles lit? You had to know I was here. Why didn't you come upstairs? As you can see, I'm wearing your favorite outfit."

"Yeah, I can see you're not wearing anything at all. I take it that it didn't work out with you and Clint? Do you want to talk about it?"

"I'm not talking about that tonight. Tonight I want you in your room and naked. There will be time to talk later."

"I can't believe I'm about to say this but why don't you go to the room, grab a pair of my sweats and come back down. Let's talk about this. It's just not right, you know that."

"Is Neil Baggio turning down sex from a naked lady standing in his house? I don't believe it! Did you just come from some other girl's house? You did, didn't you? Or is that I'm not pretty enough for you anymore? Am I getting too old—"

"Calm down. It's none of those things. To answer your questions you are still gorgeous, you're not too old, No, I did not come from another girl's house, and I take it Clint left you for a younger girl?"

"You can be a real ass sometimes. I came over to get a piece of ass, and all I get is an ass with a cup of coffee. I'm going to grab some of your sweats and I'll take my coffee with—"

"One cream and no sugar. I know, babe, I haven't forgotten. Just go throw something on. I'll be on the couch."

"Thanks, Neil. I'll be down in a minute."

The next couple hours, Sheila and I spent talking about her and Clint. More than anything, though, we talked about getting older and why it seems to get harder with each passing year to find that special someone. We talked about the possibility of getting back together and giving it another shot. Still, we are both afraid of the fighting and what it could do to Carol Lynn. We figured it is just better to keep things the way they are. Carol Lynn is comfortable with her parents' situation, and we are more concerned about her growing up healthy than we are of our love life. For now we will just make it work and hopefully not hurt anyone else along the way because of our situation.

"If you want, you are more than welcome to crash here tonight. I'm guessing our little one is staying with your mother tonight?"

"Yeah, I called her when Clint and I got into a big fight; I didn't want Carol Lynn to see me in that kind of shape. I called her and told her I would pick her up from school tomorrow, and she seemed okay with everything."

"I've got to get some sleep before tomorrow. So how about the two of us make our way down the hall and crash. We can talk about everything else in the morning."

"Sounds good. Thanks again for everything, I can always count on you to think of me first. You really are a good guy; I don't care what everyone says about you behind your back."

"Shut up and get your cute little butt under those covers. And keep those cold feet of yours off my legs; if you need socks, I've got plenty."

"Now that I'm in and all comfy, where are you going to sleep tonight?"

"Very funny. Move over." Sheila looked at me with that evil look.

"You know they like me more than you, Neil. Watch—I'll call them over on the bed. Come here, girls, curl up with Mommy. Daddy is going to sleep on the couch."

"You really are an ass sometimes."

"I guess that makes two asses and two bitches in one big bed. Come on in and warm up Mommy."

"I can't believe you actually thought you weren't hot enough for any man. You put twenty-year-olds to shame; for crying out loud, you still have six-pack abs. Now move over. I need some covers. And sorry, Jackie and Danielle, but I need you off the bed."

"Aw, you just kicked off the bed warmers. That wasn't nice of you. Just for that, I'm going to put my cold feet all over you." Fuck, her feet are cold.

"Holy shit, they're like ice. I swear that's not healthy. No one's feet should be that cold. If it's warming up you want, then it's warming up you'll get."

"Just shut up and kiss me; my little feet warm you."

I have to admit I am kind of a softie when it comes to situations like the one last night. When the mood wasn't right, I couldn't just ignore what was going on and hop into bed with Sheila. We've known each other for way too long, I can't just do that to her—or to anyone, for that matter. We still ended up messing around last night. But now it was for the right reasons. That makes the morning a lot easier for both of us, I'm not about to cheapen something so special, not after everything the two of us have been through. As I said, I try not to repeat failures in my life, and rushing into sex is definitely one failure I have had.

"Thanks for last night, Neil. You really know how to make a girl feel special, you know that?" Sheila is special.

"No problem, you looked like you could use a good massage. Plus, you know me; I like to do things like that."

"I know, but it was nice that you turned me down when I threw myself at you because I was vulnerable. Because of the way you handled it I don't feel bad for last night, I'm just in a good mood because Momma got a massage and some good loving."

"You are so cute the morning after we mess around. You have a glow about you; it's really cute." Almost like when we were dating the first time.

"Oh, shut up! You know I'm still shy about that kind of stuff. It's only with you that I feel free when it comes to sex and stuff like that. But we both need to get a shower in. So who's first, you or me?"

"You can go first. I need to make a few phone calls. Just don't use all the hot water."

"You know I'm going to. So, you might as well just come on in and join me. Just give me a ten-minute head start so I can shave without you bumping into me."

"All right, you've got ten minutes, Sheila."

Sometimes I wonder what life would be like if we all lived under one roof. By all of us, I mean Sheila, Carol Lynn, and myself. I just miss waking up to her smile, although there wasn't a lot of smiling going on when we lived together, and that's when the reality check hits me in the gut and reminds me why we got divorced. Our situation is so unorthodox, but it works, and I guess that's something to be happy about. Right now I need to call Ken and check in.

8

Walking out of the police station I dropped my shoulder into one of the officers trying to ignore me.

"Good morning, Ken. How are you doing? Has anything popped up yet?"

"So far we have tails all over the city. We've got a tail on the cardinal, and we did a little background check on his staff and are tailing six others as we speak. Hopefully we can find out where our kid's mom is hiding, or shall I say being hidden?"

After the meeting last night, Ken and I went back and forth with text and emails about where to send the team. Who to tail, who to interview, and how to attack this problem. We were working against a clock. This was about trying to chase a rabbit running away with a few clues about this kid, and it didn't make sense. There didn't seem to be any real reason why the Church was interested in him.

"That's more like it. I have a feeling she's the only connection we are going to have to piece everything together. Are we still on for lunch at Miles this afternoon?"

"As far as I know, the four of us are still meeting up; you, Christian, his cousin Nicolette, and myself at noon. Don't be late, but then again, I've never known you to be late for a meal."

"Aren't you the funny one this morning? Don't worry, I'll be there at noon and not a minute later. Hell, I might get there early and hang out with Miles and wife. I'll see you there at noon. Have everyone check in with both of us via email and text. I have a few more calls to make before I make my way out to Miles's place."

"No problem. I'll send out the word ASAP. I'll see you for lunch."

It's amazing what can be accomplished when you have a team of many behind you and working with you in pursuit of a similar goal. It's a good thing too because it's going to take everyone working around the clock to get anything accomplished. I don't even want to know how much it's going to cost me to send two people over to Poland to try and find a needle in a haystack. My guess is somewhere around ten thousand or so to pay for the room, board, and payoffs for information. I guess in the scheme of things, what is ten thousand dollars when we're talking about the truth? There is no price on a life, especially when the truth is being hidden on how he died.

Sheila and I can be a great couple when we're not a couple, if that makes any sense at all. We just don't get along when we have pressure on the relationship, as we did when we were married; both of us need an out. It really is dysfunctional, but the important thing is that our daughter knows we both love her very much. And that we are both happier for the decision to be divorced. For a young girl, she has a very grown-up grasp on the idea of love, and she understands she is loved equally by both her mother and her father.

"Hey cutie, how's Ken doing these days? I haven't talked to him in months." Sheila was checking in.

"He's doing good, and so are his two boys. I can't believe they are both in high school already. Our kids are growing up so fast. Before we know it, Carol Lynn will be in high school."

"I know exactly what you mean, time really does fly. It seems like yesterday that Carol Lynn fell asleep in her crib. Where did all the time go?"

"I don't know, but it's gone too fast. But for now, I really need to get going and make some phone calls before I get ready for lunch today with Ken and a couple of BCI employees. We're thinking of sending a couple of investigators over to Poland to see what information they can dig up."

"Well, I will be out of your hair in a few minutes. I just need to find my pants, and I'll be on my way."

"I saw them in the kitchen on the table. I have no idea how they got there, but that's the last place I saw them."

"Sure enough, that's where they are. Thanks, Neil. Are you staring at my butt?"

"It's kind of hard not to. You are walking around the house in a T-shirt and your cute boy-cut underwear. You know how I love it when you wear those; your butt looks so great in them." I can get really flirty with Sheila when we hook up.

"Sometimes I wonder how any other girl can see anything in you when you say things like that. Then again, I've kept you around for a long time."

"Nice. You're always good for an ego boost. It's not my fault you still look just as good as you did the day we met years ago."

"Thanks, babe, you know I try. I'm always working out and watching what I eat. It's a pain, but I can't be stuck with you for the rest of my life. I need a real man."

"Ouch, that's twice. You really are on fire this morning, Sheila."

"I know, I always get witty after good lovin', you know that."

"True, you always do get a little hyper the morning after we mess around. But seriously, Sheila, I need to get going; every minute I spend off this case is another minute that information is getting swept under the rug. It makes my job that much harder."

"Don't worry. I've got my pants and I'm getting out of your hair. Good luck with the case. If you need anything, don't hesitate to call."

"Can you check in on the girls at some point today? I should be gone from lunch until eight or nine o'clock tonight. They will just need dinner and to be put out."

"Yeah, I can do that for you. I'll bring over Carol Lynn. You know how much she loves the girls."

"Thanks again for everything. Thanks for always worrying about me, it means a lot."

"I still love you, babe, no matter how crazy you drive me sometimes, and you know I'll always love you."

"Me too, cutie, me too. I have to get going so I'm not late to lunch with Ken."

It took me a bit to get ready, go through all my routines, yes, a few cups of coffee to get going, but I did. By the time I got to Ken, met him at the restaurant, he had some files out, waiting for me. It seems we had checked off more than we had gained, doors kept closing, with no windows in sight. More and more, I started thinking they were protecting this kid from something, not just hiding him, hiding the truth, something doesn't add up.

The meeting with Ken at Miles Place was needed, more for me than for him and the team. Nicolette and Christian would do great. I just needed to meet her, look both of them in the eye, give them the speech, and feel them out. I know it's a bit old school, and you have to trust your team, but this is overseas, it's not like I can check up on them easily. The meeting went better than I thought it would. Hopefully we can get these two out of here tonight. It's going to be hard, but if anyone can pull it off it's going to be Ken. He has so many friends in the military, especially as a worst-case scenario we can always see a military transport. Although I try not to call in too many favors when it comes to the military because I know a lot of people can get in trouble when we do call in these types of favors. But we might not have any other choice.

"Hey Ken, I'm heading out of here, I'm going to swing by the police station to see what if anything they might have found since the other night."

"Can't you just call?"

"I could, but the way this case is going, I'm trusting my eyes, not my ears."

"I feel you. Call me if you need anything."

Just like that, I headed over toward the other side of town to the police department to see what gives. I feel like a phone call might be more efficient, but I want to be there when they tell me what I fear the most. Some bullshit that the case doesn't exist, there was a call, but no official case was ever opened, or some shit. The drive took about forty minutes, which gave me time to relax my mind, clear my thoughts, and listen to some music. There's nothing quite like cruising down the freeway and at a cool thirty to forty miles an hour. Oh yeah, that's right. I live in metro Detroit, and the highway is closed from four lanes to one.

Once there, I noticed the parking lot was pretty empty, which isn't too surprising for the middle of the day, but I hope I can get somewhere with this case. Though if I get nothing, that might be something, as long as I can find out why there is nothing.

"How's it going, sir? Can I help you?"

"Yes, I was here to follow up on a case from the other night at St. Mary's. There was a student that was found hung on campus. Do you know who the active case is assigned to?"

"I can call up there and find out for you. Give me a moment."

Judging by the way the phone call is going, they have no idea what I'm talking about up there. This is what I wanted to be here for, I wanted to read people's body language, see if they were lying to me, or if they were in the dark as well. You can get only so much from a call.

"I'm sorry, but they are confused about what case you are talking about, but they said you can go up there."

"Thanks, I'll head that way."

Walking up to the second floor, I noticed two of the officers from that night, but neither would make eye contact with me. They were almost trying too hard to ensure I didn't notice them or make eye contact. Walking down the hallway, I noticed some photos of prominent people of the community with their arms around the police chief and some of the softball leagues, etc. I couldn't help but notice one person that stood out and showed up in many of the pictures, Cardinal Kelley.

"Hey, I'm Officer Daniels. I was on the phone with the officer downstairs. He said you had questions about a case involving a kid found hung on campus over at St. Mary's the other day?"

"Yes, he said you guys didn't know what I was talking about."

"What I can say is that there is no case here involving anything like that. We're all on the same boat with this one. Sorry we couldn't help you."

"Thanks for your time, Officer Daniels."

That was the most professional courtesy he could give me under the circumstances. He was telling me he couldn't say shit, but to keep barking up that tree. If he didn't want to help me, he would have told me to beat it over the phone. But he wanted me to see his reaction as he told me. This doesn't make me any less pissed, but I do appreciate the support.

Walking out of the police station, I dropped my shoulder into one of the officers trying to ignore me, knowing they wouldn't say anything. He wanted to, oh he wanted to, but he knew he would have to address the big ass issue in the room. I guess I'll just call Ken, pissed off as I walk to the car and tell him the great news.

"Ken, are you fucking kidding me? They claim there's no such case. But one officer was nice enough to allude to the fact that they're all covering it up."

"So you're telling me, according to the police station, that there is nothing there. No case file, nothing? It doesn't exist?"

"Jesus, you are kidding me!"

"There were also plenty of pictures of the cardinal in the building too. I'm sure that played a role."

"This is getting out of control, man. If this was a killer, I'd get it, but part of me wants to either give up or just grab a gun and threaten some old dudes in a church."

"I know! Ken, I don't know who is this powerful, and why they keep doing this, but it's starting to concern me. What the FUCK did we get ourselves into?"

"Anything involving the Church is always scary. They have something big to protect and will often go to extreme lengths to protect it."

"What do you mean, kill a kid?"

"No, I mean faith, they protect faith, and if Andrew was involved in something, then they are going to find a way to cover their tracks."

"Hey Ken, I need to let you go. I need to visit a very influential member of the Catholic Church."

"Where are you headed to? Cardinal Kelley's office?"

"Nope. We are still having him tailed, right?"

"Yeah, around the clock. What do you have in mind?"

"I thought I might surprise him while he's out and about today. Don't worry about it; I'll take care of everything."

"I don't like the sound of that. That usually means you're about to do something that most people would deem idiotic or insane."

"Like I said, Don't worry about it; I'll take care of everything. But just in case, be ready to do some major spin control if anything goes wrong."

"I knew it. Just don't get your ass arrested. We don't have the time to deal with that shit right now."

"Drastic times call for drastic measures. Time to get a little creative and stir things up a bit."

"Just be careful, Neil, and remember who we are dealing with. This is a global organization that can really fuck with us if they truly want to. Let's try and stay out of trouble today, okay?"

"Fine. I'll do my best to keep things from getting out of hand, but I can't promise you anything. It all depends on the reaction I get from Cardinal Kelley."

9

If I tell you, will you give me the antidote?

According to the guys who have been keeping an eye on him, Cardinal Kelley should be getting ready to leave a church in downtown Detroit. It's called St. Patrick's, and it's down by the Fox Theater. From there, they believe he will be making his way to his residence; little does the cardinal know that I have something else in store for him. All I need to do is call up an old friend who's already helped me once this week. Let's try him again, good old Brian Potter. He loves this kind of stuff; we're going to put on a good show for the cardinal so I can get some more information out of him. Before I go any farther, I realize that my earlier statement sounds like I'm going to assault a cardinal of the church. Don't worry; I'm just going to play a little trick on him. I know I've been negative about the Church lately, but I also know that the whole Church isn't corrupt, it's just the bad apples ruining it for everyone else. And that's enough preaching for one day. Back to calling Brian.

"Hey, Brian, it's Neil. I need you to do me a huge favor. Do you still have that beat-up old Thunderbird out back?"

"Yeah, the one I let my guys use if they don't have a ride to work. Yeah, it's here. Why do you need a car?"

"Sort of, I need you to get in it and meet me out by St. Patrick's Church; we're going to cause a big accident and scene down there so I can get to the cardinal."

"Wait a minute, what's going on? And why are you trying to talk to the cardinal like this? Why don't you just make an appointment to talk to him?"

"Never mind, I'll fill you in later. Call your friends at Detroit PD. I'll call my guys. Have them all meet up in the Fox Theater parking lot in twenty minutes, got it? I'll fill everyone in on what's going down when we get there."

"Yeah, no problem. How many officers do I need to get down there?"

"I should be able to get two squad cars' worth, so I would say about the same for you. We're going to box in the cardinal and corner him at the church. Long story; I'll fill you in later. You game?"

"You know it. I live for this shit, and you know that. I got you covered. See you down there."

Off the phone with Brian and immediately I called the guys tailing the cardinal and filled them in. They are actually tailing him in my old Jeep; I can't believe I'm about to crash up my old car just to talk to this pompous ass. I've never met him, but he's a cardinal, so I'm guessing he's a pompous ass. I hope this works, because if it doesn't, then I'm going to get a lot of people in trouble and piss off a very influential man in the Detroit area. Again, I have to catch myself because I keep taking my emotions from this case out on the Catholic Church. I need to keep myself in check before I do something stupid; I have a feeling that in about an hour that stupid thing will have just happened.

I called a couple of guys that pick up extra work from BCI to supplement their income as police officers, and they said they would gladly help me create a scene. This is going to be great; I can't wait, I feel like a kid just before Christmas. Instead of opening presents, I'm going to cause a big ass accident in front of the church and corner our friend Cardinal Kelley. I know it's a little crazy and probably way over the top, but as I said to Ken, desperate times call for desperate measures. I figure if I can get under the cardinal's skin, he might do something stupid and try to move Andrews's mom to a new location. Making it that much easier to try to find out where she is, as long as we're tailing the right people. I might as well call Ken and fill him in on what is going down so that he can try to get something ready for damage control. I've got only a few minutes because I'm not very far from the parking garage where everyone's meeting up. From the looks of things, it looks like almost everyone is there already. I see a couple of police cruisers and Brian's old beater of a car; his car is going to be finished after this, and I can't stop grinning.

"All right, Neil, fill us in on what the hell is going down."

"I'll make this short. We need to block off the parking lot and street access to St. Pat's Church so that I can corner the cardinal and question him. It's the only way I'll be able to get to him. I know it's over the top, but hey, go big or go home."

"That's true. So what's the plan? Why do you need so many officers here?"

"I need them to be here in the area to close off the street before the cardinal can get in his car and get out of here. The plan is to have you, Brian, crash your car into the Jeep on the street. But we need to make a huge scene and confuse the shit out of everyone so that we can delay the whole situation. That's where you guys come in. I need two of the squad cars blocking off the street. The other two were trying to figure out what is going on at the scene. I need you to constantly fight with each other and delay long enough that I can get to the cardinal inside the church. Do you guys have it? It's going to be a lot of acting off the cuff, just shooting from the hip and hoping for the best."

"Sounds like a plan. I think we can do a good job for you, Neil. It's the least we can do. You've always been there for us, it's our turn to return the favor. When do you want us to get started?"

"Give me ten minutes. I'm going to leave my car here and walk over to the church and sit in the back pew while the cardinal is still in there. I'll send you a text when I get a confirmation that he is still there. We don't want to do this if he's not in there, you know?"

"Brian, you and my guys head down the street, so when I call you, you can pull out down the street and get right into it. As for the officers, I need one of you to block off Cardinal Kelley's car right away, and then the other two can block off the road, so we'll have him boxed all over."

"Sounds good, Neil. You really are a crazy son of a bitch, but we love you for it. We'll be waiting for your call."

As I made my way into the church and sat in the pew, my phone started to vibrate. It was Ken sending me a text about the travel plans for Christian and Nicolette. Looks like he'll be able to get them on a plane at nine o'clock tonight. Not bad, Ken. But for right now, I need to concentrate on the situation at hand. Looks like Cardinal Kelley is still here and he's going to hear confessions today. Oh, perfect—this is going to go down beautifully. I'll call the guys and make my way into the confessional; he'll never know it's coming.

"Brian, he's here, and I'm about to get him in the confessional. Give me three minutes, then go."

"Got it. Good luck, Neil; we'll try to do you proud out here."

"Thanks again for everything, Brian, I owe you guys one. Tell everyone else. Three minutes are all I need."

"See you outside when this is all done."

I made my way to the confessional and noticed that it was empty. It looked as though the cardinal was saying a rosary while waiting for the next person to come to confession, probably because he feels guilty for covering up a young man's murder like this. I know I have no proof, but I need to psych myself up for this if I'm going to go through with it.

"Forgive me, Cardinal, for I have sinned. It has been four months since my last confession."

"That is okay. God is just happy you are here now. What lies on your heavy heart?"

"I   covered   up   a—"

Right then, I heard the huge crash outside followed shortly after by sirens. I noticed that the cardinal paused for a second but waited for me to continue.

"It's okay. Continue; we are in God's house on God's time. Right now we need not worry about anything else."

"Thank you, Cardinal. As I was beginning to say, I covered up the murder of a young man and made it look like a suicide. For this and all the sins of my past life I am heartily sorry."

Right at that moment I could hear the cardinal's breathing pattern change. He started breathing slower and deeper, trying to keep his heart rate down. He wasn't sure if I was confessing to him about the murder that just happened or if I was confessing about something completely different.

"I am not here to judge, only to offer absolution from God; I cannot help you with the laws of this land."

"I understand, Cardinal. It's just that I feel really guilty and I don't know what to do. Do you think I should turn myself in?"

"I cannot tell you what to do, I can only offer you prayer in hopes that the Holy Spirit will help to guide you. May I ask you when this occurred?

Rule number one when you're a priest hearing a confession, you don't ask about the specifics of the deed. It is your job to offer absolution without details if he is convinced that the penitent is truly sorry for his sins. It is not to inquire more about the person's sins. In this case he is fishing for information; things are starting to move in the right direction. I think it's time to make my move. I opened my curtain and noticed that the church had emptied from the accident outside; you have to love our society. We love a good crash and violent scenes. This gave me ample opportunity to press him. I told him I needed water and that I would be back in one minute. Instead I grabbed a chair and wedged him into his booth so that he couldn't get out. Then I returned to my side of the confessional and started to have a little fun at his expense.

"Cardinal, we both know why I'm here. I'm here about Andrew, I am here because you are covering up a murder. You're trying to make the whole thing disappear by calling in favors and making it look like a suicide. The only problem is I know it wasn't a suicide and you know too, that's why your breathing has changed since I brought up a similar story to yours."

"I don't know what you're talking about, and I am not going to sit here while you accuse me of great falsehoods."

"You're not going anywhere, Cardinal Kelley; I've boxed you in, and there is no one here to let you out. Everyone is outside watching a little show I'm putting on. I'll ask you one last time: why is the Catholic Church covering up a murder? I know it is not common practice in the Church. At least I pray it isn't."

"I don't know what you're talking about. Why do you think the Church would do such a thing?"

It was at that moment that I blew a little bit of baby powder through the vent we were talking through. He is going to flip; this should speed things up a bit.

"What is that? Is that anthrax?"

"No, Cardinal, but you wish it were. It's something our friends in the lab have worked up. You've got about twenty minutes to get an antidote into you or you'll die before the end of the day."

"You are crazy. You'll never get away with this."

"Maybe not, but that doesn't help your situation now, does it? I ask you again: why is the Church covering up this murder?"

"If I tell you, will you give me the antidote?"

"I've got it right here. Just answer the question."

"All right. I can't tell you much because it goes above me, but what I do know is that the Church didn't kill Andrew. They were supposed to protect him, and they didn't, so they made it look like a suicide. That's all I know, I swear."

"Thanks, Cardinal Kelley, for your time. I'll be on my way now."

"But what about the antidote? You can't leave me here to die."

"You're not going to die. That was just baby powder. You might smell good and feel soft, but you're not going to die. Sorry."

"You'll never get away with this."

"Sorry, Cardinal, but I just did."

I made my way outside to one hell of a scene; the guys did me proud. Brian took it a little too seriously and just destroyed his car; luckily he didn't hurt himself. From the looks of things he was okay, but his car was smashed. I don't know how, but the Jeep ended up on its side on the sidewalk. The two guys in the car were outside walking around and looked all right. They had fun with this whole thing, that's for sure. I'll have to have them fill me in later; I need to get out of here before anyone notices me. I sent a text to Brian saying thank you and to call me later with the details and that I would pay for any medical attention needed as well as replace his car. At least now I have a little more to go on than I did a few minutes ago.

It felt like a scene from a movie in many ways in that I got away free as a bird from the whole situation. There was chaos everywhere, people just standing around watching the show that Brian and the others were putting on with such ease and fun. You could see them smiling a bit while the whole thing was going on. As I walked past everyone, I was given a silent nod of approval that was returned in a way that let us all know everything worked to plan. I can't wait to get these guys out to the bar tonight to talk about this, this is pretty funny shit. I climbed into the crossfire and took in a deep breath before I turned on the ignition. The whole situation was starting to catch up with me; it usually takes me a minute or two after something big like this goes down to catch up, at least from a physiological standpoint. Ken isn't going to believe any of this, and that's why I'm going to let everyone else tell the story, then maybe he'll at least believe half of it. I pulled out of the parking garage and made my way past the street where all the commotion was. It was then that my cell started to ring.

"Hey Neil, it's Brian. The guys and I just wanted to tell you that you're buying the beers tonight. Say my place around nineish. Hell, it will probably take us that long to get out of here and clean this mess up. We went a little overboard, but it was all in good fun. So did you get anything that could help you from the cardinal?"

"I got something; it was helpful, I guess. It's just not a ton of information, but it will help point us in the right direction. I've got to make a few calls before it gets too late. I'll see you tonight at your place. Thanks again, Brian, for everything."

"No problem. We all had a blast pulling this off."

Brian is an old buddy of mine that I used to work with in college. We used to work at this club that was strapped for money. We'll just leave it at that for now. The owner overextended himself by building the place from the ground up, without any help from investors or partners. Brian and I were managers together there. I focused on the security in the building and scheduling, and Brian took care of parties and more of the inventory aspect. We worked together for a little less than a year, but we've been friends ever since. He has since gone into business for himself, opening up a small club in Detroit. I say small because he didn't want to overextend himself, as our old boss had. He figures he'll start small and work his way up to a bigger club when he gets the first one established.

Don't get me wrong, it's not a hole in the wall by any means. It is a very high-class place; it's got more of a martini bar feeling to it with a small dance floor. He ended up naming the place "Shootr's," which if you knew Brian fit him and his bar perfectly. It looks like I'll be spending a little bit of money tonight at Shootr's. I guess it was worth it for the information I got tonight from our good friend Cardinal Kelley. At least I have somewhat of a direction to focus the search on. Before I had no idea what was going on. I still don't know much, but now I know this Andrew kid was important enough for the Church to offer him and his mother protection. This means, at least, my guess is that his father or maybe a sibling has something brewing over in Poland.

I guess I'll find out more when Christian and his cousin get over to Poland; at least that's the hope. Christian has excellent instincts when it comes to tracking down information, and I liked his cousin's demeanor. She really knew how to carry herself. Plus she's Polish, and she speaks the language, which will help to speed up the process tremendously. I need to get back to the warehouse, to fill in Christian and Nicolette on their trip.

10

To be honest with you, his last name, Malinowski, is very common in Poland, so it might be hard to track down his family or anything about him.

As I made my way into a parking spot, Ken noticed me and apparently decided that the situation at hand couldn't wait for me to make my way upstairs. He didn't have the greatest look on his face, either; my guess is he heard what happened over at St. Pat's Church. To be honest, he probably knows more about the details than I do. I was too busy getting information out of our friend Cardinal Kelley to pay attention to what was actually going on outside.

"Holy shit, Neil! Where the hell did you come up with this one? It's not like you had a lot of planning ahead of time to pull this off. Did anyone spot you?"

"The only people that spotted me were the same ones that were helping pull it off. Don't worry, everything is going to be fine. Are Christian and Nicolette here?"

"Yeah, they're downstairs. As for you, did you at least get any useful information?"

"Yes I did, and it was worth the whole production. It seems that our friends at the Catholic Church were entrusted with protecting Andrew and his mother. Our friend Cardinal Kelley didn't know why, but he did say the Church was covering up the truth behind what happened."

"It's not a ton of information, but it's a start. It gives us a chance to find something. What do you think they were trying to protect Andrew and his mother from?"

"My guess is it has to do with a sibling or a father or both. If my current events are right, I think there is some form of political change going on in Poland. Where there is political change in a country like Poland, you can be sure the Church has something invested in the government, whether it be for the new or the old. But usually it's old; the Church isn't always known for being modern."

"Not to mention the Church is not a big fan of change. Well, let's get downstairs and get everyone up to date. I'll send a mass text/email out to everyone, and I'll meet you downstairs in five minutes."

"See you down there."

I couldn't help but wonder what type of luck we might have in the next twenty-four hours now that I have gotten Cardinal Kelley all riled up; more than anything, I think I got the Church riled up. If they think that someone is on to them, they might do something stupid; for instance, they might and try to move Andrew's mother from wherever they have her stashed away. At least that is my hope. I need them to mess up if I have any chance of catching a break in a case like this. It's hard when you are going into a case blindly. Imagine you walked out of a supermarket with anything and everything imaginable you would need to cook. Then someone asked you to make a dish for them that you had never heard of and without a recipe. That's what it feels like to be involved in this case right now. Except that our friend Cardinal Kelley just gave me the first ingredient; now I can look for things that would most likely be used with that first ingredient.

"Hey Neil, how is everything going? We are all packed and ready to go. We've been going over the information on Andrew and St. Mary's, trying to see where we might want to start when we get to Poland."

"Not bad, Nicolette. I guess you were right, Christian—she definitely has a knack for this kind of stuff. I got a little headway on our case; it seems that the Church was entrusted with protecting Andrew."

"But if they were supposed to be protecting him, why cover up the fact that he was murdered? That doesn't make sense."

"Actually it does, Christian. If you look at it from a standpoint that they were trying to protect something that Andrew stood for, not necessarily the person himself, but an ideal he was attached to."

"So, what do you think should be our first step when we get over to Poland? Do you have any ideas, or should we just start with trying to find out everything we can about his family?"

"Do you have any ideas on the situation at hand, Nicolette? I mean, you are the one that grew up in that culture, and it's just a guess, but I would think you are more familiar with what is going on in Poland from a current events standpoint."

"Yes and no. To be honest with you, his last name, Malinowski, is very common in Poland, so it might be hard to track down his family or anything about him. Not as common as, say, Smith is here in the States, but it is similar to Johnson or Jackson."

"We definitely need to find out where this kid came from and what his family background is. And there is no way that we are going to get any of that information here in Detroit; the Church has pretty much made this kid nonexistent."

"We will definitely do our best to get information to you as fast and as accurately as possible. I know that Nicolette and I are not going over there thinking we are going to sightsee, we know we are going to have to work our asses off."

"That's good to know, since we are talking about days; we have to get the information on this kid. I can't stress this enough. With every passing day, we are losing information. The Church is a world organization, and they are working around the clock to make sure this kid becomes a shadow forgotten."

I spent the next twenty or so minutes going over strategy and means that they might have to use to get information, and both were well aware of the situation. Nicolette understands that she might have to bat her emerald green eyes at a couple of guys to get the job done where needed. Christian knows he is probably going to have to rough up more than one person to get what we need. I hate to sound like a gang of thugs trying to force information out of people. When you are dealing with the Church, you are dealing with an organization that has had social control over billions of people for centuries. It's not going to be easy to get information from people who are being intimidated by an organization that strong.

I just hope this doesn't turn into something more than what it already is. From the looks of it, things are probably going to get really ugly, fast. This is going to become worse than anything I've had to deal with. I know I'm ready for it because I've had a chip on my shoulder about the Church my whole life. I just feel that a lot of these people helping me are going to dwindle off. It's just too much to ask people to put their faith aside from their job, but I know that is what it's going to come down to. I know everyone truly wants to help me find out what happened to this poor kid. But a person can only question their faith and beliefs so much before it starts to take its toll on them.

I am working against so many different variables in this case, and I wonder if I even have a chance to figure everything out before it's too late. I'm forty strong with my team right now, and before tomorrow ends, that number will fall to half of that. I'm fighting an organization that has been around for two thousand years. Not to mention, I'm working against the clock. Add all of that up and you don't have a very high probability of success. Then again, I always did defy the odds a bit. Hey, I put Franklin Cappelano behind bars when no one thought it was possible. Needless to say, I've never been someone to play the safe bet, I've always been somewhat of a long-shot type of a person. So why quit now?

"Hey Neil, sorry it took me so long. I was on the phone with a couple of Detroit Police lieutenants. I was getting an earful and reminding me that we are going to be making a substantial contribution to any and all Detroit PD-related fund-raisers this year for the stunt you just pulled today." Ken was getting cranky.

"In other words, nothing is going to change from what we usually do from year to year."

"Basically, but I didn't need to hear it from three different people yelling at me through the phone. By the way, when did I become BCI's PR guy? I don't ever remember seeing that one in the contract when I signed on to work with you."

"We could always hire a PR firm to help out, but that would be a waste, if you ask me. You have been doing a great job with everything you really have."

"Quit patronizing me, Neil! Oh yeah, by the way, I've got our two fly birds on a connecting flight through New York to Poland; they have to be at the airport in about an hour. I'll have one of our lower-level guys give them a lift out to the airport. Is there anything else you want to talk to them about?"

"Not really anything else I can think of. Except for one thing: did we make sure that their cell phones are internationally ready so we can still communicate with them while they are overseas?"

"Christian is already set up with the same plan that we put all of our guys on. All we need to do is call the provider and let them know that he is going to be over in Europe for a couple weeks, and they will take care of the rest. As for Nicolette, I really don't know. I'll ask her, and if she isn't sure, I'll just give her one of our backup cell phones."

"Sounds like a plan. As for me, I need to get out of here and talk with Glow. Did you get that cell phone to him today like I asked you?"

"Yeah, we had that all taken care of this morning; everything went as planned. I sent out Johnson and his wife with their son, who's in eighth grade, so it just looked like any other official visit. They dropped him the cell phone in his office when no one was around. Glow wrote them a note that said he would call you on it later tonight when he had a chance to step away from everyone and everything."

"Thanks again for everything, Ken. I know I'm always saying that, but I truly do appreciate everything you do for this company. Without you we wouldn't be nearly as organized as we are. You really are the backbone of BCI."

"Thanks, Neil, it's nice to know the big guy doesn't forget who takes care of everything for him."

"I could never forget what you do, Ken. Without you I don't think anything would get done. You're the true backbone of this place, not me."

"But without you, we wouldn't have the business we do have. So I   guess   we   need   each   other?"

"I guess so. We're stuck with each other, but I'm happy with our situation if you are."

"I have to say that I am; can't complain one bit. Except for the fact that I'm married and you're single. I wish I could enjoy some of the things you get to."

"Oh, shut up, you don't mean that. You love your wife and trust me. There's nothing like coming home to that special someone."

"That's true. I do love her, she drives me crazy, but I love her."

My conversation took a weird turn at the end, but it was good. It was one of those bonding moments that two men will have from time to time. Ken has always been a dear friend, and his drive to succeed has always helped keep this company and me on the right track. He is a man of resilience and direction, and I'm a man of vision and creativity. Together we make one hell of a team that brings a lot to the table; we balance each other out quite well. Ken is the practical one that keeps things balanced, and I'm the one who comes up with all the new ideas. Ken makes those ideas come to reality; without him I'd just be a dreamer stuck working for the FBI somewhere.

He made his way back to his office to make sure everything was taken care of for our long-distance travelers while I gave them a few last-minute pointers on how and what to look for while in Poland. I think the two of them will do just fine; I'm not too worried about them. I'm more worried about what the Church is capable of doing now that I know they have the guts to cover up a murder. As for me, I'm off to Brian's club for an evening of drinking and socializing with everyone involved in today's little spectacle. I know what you're thinking right now, but it's the one thing that's nice being the boss of a big investigation firm, I get to have other people do all the legwork while I figure it all out.

11

Growing up as kids in the same neighborhood and with fathers that were and are still best of friends.

After stopping in and buying a few rounds for the guys, I decided to head home. After struggling to sleep for hours, I decided to get up since it's two in the morning and I can't sleep a wink. I really don't know what to do. I can't get my mind off this case, I might even have to hang out with my boys Frank and Jack. There really isn't anything more relaxing than listening to Frank Sinatra while sipping a Jack Daniels on the rocks. I think I've already made a choice, since the girls have already noticed me moving them out of the way so that I could get to my sweatpants and out to the main room. Where I'll throw on some good music and even better drink. I know that I shouldn't talk about a drink like that, but it's how I feel right now.

My back is starting to tense, and I'm starting to feel the stress catching up with me. I just hope that this case doesn't end up with me getting excommunicated from another world organization. It's bad enough that I've pretty much alienated my own government, at least those involved in the FBI. I don't think I need to throw a whole religion in that group either. I'll try to do this under the radar, but I can't promise myself or Ken anything. Today could have gone a little better, and I guess I could have just talked to Cardinal Kelley at his office, but I didn't want to take the chance of him seeing me and figuring out what exactly is going on. At least this way, he didn't see my face, and I still got the information I needed. Okay, maybe not all the information I needed. But it is a start, plus I startled him a bit so I can expect them to probably do something rash and give me a chance to get a little more info out of them. If I'm lucky, I'll get a chance to find Andrew's mother and figure out what the hell is going on with this kid. It just isn't right that a murder is being covered up, especially something like this.

There really is only one person I know that is up right now and who will be there for me. But the problem is he works for the bad guys, or in this case, he works for the Church, for the Big Guy upstairs. If you haven't caught on yet, I'm talking about my old friend Father Roberts. I've known him for years, and I hate to get him involved in something like this. But he really is the only person I think I can turn to for advice right now. Let's just hope he isn't involved in the situation already.

"Hey, Father Roberts, sorry for calling you so late. But you're the only person I could talk to about what's going on."

"You know you're not sorry for calling me in the middle of the night. To be honest, I don't think we've ever talked on the phone during normal hours. It always seems to be in the middle of the night or first thing in the morning with you. Is everything all right?"

"Not even close. I've happened upon a case that is much bigger than me and those working on it. It's not just a matter of the case but also that of my faith and that of my employees."

"What are you talking about, Neil? You have to give me a little bit more information than that."

I want to tell him everything, I really do, but I don't know, I just don't know. I know I can trust him, but something is telling me to tread carefully with this whole situation. I've known Father Roberts, or as I've known him for years as Anthony Roberts. Growing up as kids in the same neighborhood and with fathers that were and are still best of friends, we had a bond that was decided for us before we were even born. The problem isn't my trust in him but trusting his faith and his beliefs. He joined the priesthood because he felt the Church was his calling. He gave something of himself wholeheartedly, and no friendship or past can break that; at least that's what I think.

"Anthony, you know we go way back, we were basically born together, only weeks apart. And I've always backed you with your choice to join the priesthood. Even when our fathers were opposed to your choice."

"It wasn't a choice I made; it was chosen for me. And where is this going, Neil? Why don't you just come right out and say it? Does this have to do with that student at St. Mary's?"

"I take it your superiors have already come to you for information on me. What did they ask you? What did you tell them?"

"Calm down, Neil. All I told them was that we grew up together and that we are still friends. But I told them I wouldn't help them get information from you."

"Thanks, I guess. But back to what you know about the whole situation."

"I really don't know much outside of what has been in the papers. People tread very softly around me, probably because they know that I know you and that you are investigating Andrew's death. I really can't say much more; there's a good chance we're not the only ones on this call."

"Then how about we talk later—say, somewhere a little more private?"

"I hear you loud and clear. It will take some work, but I will be there if I'm running late. Please wait for me, I'll be there."

"Then I guess this conversation is done for the evening. Be safe, Anthony, I'll talk to you later."

"Night, Neil."

Our usual time and place is in the basement of my father's butcher shop right after school got out. From as young as I can remember all the way through high school, the two of us would always meet there at 3:00 p.m. every day. In high school we used to smoke cigarettes there and even bring girlfriends there to make out. It wasn't much, but it had a couple of couches in it. Our fathers used it as a place to get away from their wives whenever they were in trouble. As I said, it wasn't much, and it still isn't, but it's there, and no one knows about it except the four of us.

The four being myself, Anthony, and our fathers. I should really look into finding a better way to spend my sleepless nights than calling Father Roberts and reminiscing about the old days. Or in tonight's case calling him and bugging him for information in hopes that I might get another lead. There is always working out in my basement, especially now that my workout room is all done. I might just have to throw the MP3 player on shuffle and get a good sweat in on the heavy bag. At least working out will be somewhat productive. Hey, it's a lot better than drinking myself to sleep; better on the waist and when it comes time to get out of bed in the morning.

The girls made their unhappiness evident with me as I made my way out of bed. I barely nudged them when I got up, but that didn't stop them from giving me a little huff. I think Danielle actually growled at me for upsetting the balance in the bed. They crack me up. I have to stumble my way through the room in the dark because I don't want to risk upsetting the girls any more than I already have; sometimes I wonder why I baby my dogs so much. But then I come home after a long day feeling all stressed out, and the two of them greet me at the door and curl up with me at night, and that's when I realize they are much more than just pets to me.

After about fifteen minutes of stumbling around the house, trying to get my things together, I finally made my way to the basement. Just as I grabbed my gloves, I realized I had left my MP3 player in the car. Seeing that it's all the way upstairs, I didn't feel like going all the way back up there. Then going into the garage because I knew if I opened the door to outside, the girls would wake up. They'd also want to go for a walk, and right now I need to beat the crap out of my punching bag. It looks like I'm going to have to throw on one of my CDs and just jam out. As for my neighbors, they stopped calling the cops on me when I decided to buy them all new triple-pane windows for the sides of their houses that shared sides with mine. It's really made a big difference; at least that's what they've told me.

I don't know if I want to go with classic Frank Sinatra tonight or if I'm in the mood for something a little newer, such as Michael Buble. I think I'll go with a little Buble tonight, especially with the sound system I have down here, you feel like you're in concert with him. Music blasting, heavy bag taking a beating with me all covered in sweat, nothing like a workout in the middle of the night. It's probably moments like this that have brought my six-pack back to the party.

12

She's one of those people that makes it look easy, She could wake up out of bed and look like a million dollars, whereas I wake up and look like $1.25.

Why is it when you need sleep, you can seldom get it, but when it's not that important, you seem to get plenty? I don't know if that makes any sense, but it's six in the morning, and my alarm is screaming at me to get out of bed with a little bit of sports talk radio in the background. I think I've reached a point in my life when I can feel the lack of sleep really starting to catch up with me. If the bags under my eyes get any bigger, I'll look like a champion boxer's sparring partner. Looks like Ken and the boys had a long night last night, since I've got three missed calls and seven new text messages. All the calls are from Ken, and the text messages are from a couple of different guys working last night and one from Brian.

Dude, you didn't have to leave us high and dry like that.

Nothing like getting made fun of by drunk buddies for trying to get some sleep. Although I probably would have had more fun staying out and hanging out with them, it's probably best that I came home and struggled to fall asleep. Even though I had three missed calls from Ken, he didn't leave a voice mail. It must not have been something major if he called me three times and didn't leave a message. I really need to get some sleep one of these days. Maybe I'll go on vacation after this is done and just lay out somewhere and do nothing.

As I got up, I decided to reach out to Maria, see how she was doing, but also follow up on a favor I had asked for the other day on Andrew and his mother. I have this suspicion that something isn't adding up with them.

"Hey Maria, how's your day going? I was just calling to see if you had time to check on those names yet."

"We ran them through most of our databases, but we're waiting on a response from overseas. We haven't heard anything from Interpol, Poland immigration, or other European contacts. As far as we can find out, these names were created when they got here some six years ago. But we don't know that for certain; they could have just had bad paperwork too, so many possibilities."

"True, they could have just immigrated illegally and tried to hide out. Thanks, Maria, hope you have a great day. I won't take up your time."

"If we find anything, I'll let you know, Neil. You can just call to say hi, it doesn't have to be for a case."

"That obvious?"

"Yeah, but I appreciate it. Talk to you later."

She's one of those people that makes it look easy. She could wake up out of bed and look like a million dollars, whereas I wake up and look like $1.25. She puts in the work, thinks through things meticulously, but she does it so well, it looks effortless. It's about time I got moving, headed to the warehouse, and got focused with Ken and the team. The drive to the warehouse is a short one, since I can just shoot down Gratiot to Eight Mile and make my way down from there.

It's almost eleven in the morning as I turn on a local AM radio station and listen to callers talk about the Detroit Tigers. I have to admit this year they are doing pretty damn well, especially the young guys they've brought up over the past year or so. Speaking of the Tigers, Ken and I bought season tickets to the games, four seats for every home game, set us back a couple grand, and I think I've been to one game all year. Go figure that's life, but the guys like it when Ken and I don't use the tickets because we'll usually give them out on a first-come, first-served basis. We've also used them to thank the employees for going above and beyond.

Before I could really get into any part of the show, I made my way into the BCI parking lot and then to the private garage that Ken and I share. It's one of the perks for being a founder of the company, and it drives the other guys crazy. They have to park outside all year long regardless of the weather, while Ken and I have a climate-controlled garage to keep our cars in. It really isn't as fancy as it sounds; it's just a garage that's hooked into the same heating and cooling system that the rest of the warehouse is run on. I was hit with a moment of clarity

AVE MARIA

about Andrew and his mother as I exited the car. The biggest reason that the Church would be covering up Andrew's murder and hiding his mother from the rest of the public. Someone he's related to, whether it is a brother, father, or even a cousin; his family has to be involved in something big in Poland. The only thing I can think of is something political or something dealing with the Church. In Poland, as it is in many countries, religion and politics go hand in hand.

"Hey Ken, how are you doing this morning? Anything coming across the wire from any of our employees out in the field since last night?"

"Nothing major to speak of, just the lead that we have about Andrew's mother being moved tonight at about midnight. I've had some of our guys researching likely areas all night, and we've got operatives checking them out one by one as we speak. We've only got half a day to figure out where she is, and you and I both know there isn't going to be a second chance on this one."

"Trust me, Ken, I know the severity of the situation; there isn't any room for fucking up. Why do you think I look like shit? I couldn't get any sleep last night."

"You always look like shit, Neil; I didn't even notice when you walked in."

"Very funny, Ken. hy don't you just shut it? All joking aside, how are we coming on narrowing the field down for tonight?"

"We are making progress, but we won't have enough time to narrow it down enough. It's going to take some luck and good guessing to figure out where she's going to be tonight."

"On the matter at hand, I'm going to go down to see TJ in the tech offices and see where he is right now; hopefully I can speed things up over there. Throwing a little experience into the mix might help a little bit."

"Sounds like a plan; can I ask you one thing before you head down there? Why are you grinning from ear to ear? It's not like you to smile this much during a case. You are almost always in a shitty mood on cases like this. Did you get some last night, or better yet, this morning?"

"Not even close, but I am smiling because of a lady. I hung out with Sheila."

"Your beautiful ex-wife that still puts up with you for some reason. That one?"

"Yup, I know, right," I said with a smile.

Our offices are on a makeshift third floor in the warehouse. This way we can overlook everything that goes on in our building. Plus it gives that power of high feeling to the rest of the employees. We learned it from some business manual, I think they stole the idea from Sun Tzu's *Art of War*, but that's beside the point. The only reason why CEOs put their offices at the top of the building is that it's a social status to be at the top; that's it. I would offer a guess that if you were to poll people in power why they have their offices on the top floor that they wouldn't be able to give you a decent answer. At least not an answer that really made sense.

"Hey TJ, how's it going down here? Are you guys making any progress in the search?"

"Hey Neil, to what do we owe the pleasure of your visit? It's not like you to be hanging around the warehouse, especially the tech wing. As for the search for Andrew's mom, we're making progress, just not enough progress. There are a ton of different locations where they could be hiding her."

"Where did you start your search? Like what was the variable you used to decide where to start?"

"We started with the farthest out and are working our way into the middle, in hopes that we will have a smaller area to work with in the end. If not by the amount of possibilities but a smaller area dealing with the mileage."

"Not bad, not bad at all. I've got an idea: why don't you print me out a list of all the buildings we've got to work with and what they're used for? If I know the Church, they'll be hiding her in an obvious place; it's the best way to do it."

"What do you have in mind? I could use all the help I can get on this."

"Let's start with any place that's affiliated with St. Mary's or any of its charities. The Church is probably going to try to keep as many people involved in this to a minimum. They will most likely keep it within the St. Mary's family or archdiocese. Does that make sense?"

"I've got it, boss. Give me like thirty minutes and I'll get you a list to go through."

"All right. Well, I've got a meeting to get to pretty soon, so I'll just check back in thirty minutes to an hour and see where you're at."

"All right. See you then, boss man."

It's getting to be about noon, and sooner than later I'm going to have to head out to the butcher shop to meet with Father Roberts later this afternoon. I really hope he can help me out on this one, although I can imagine the position I'm putting him in. This isn't like working for a company that is doing something wrong. This is much more. This has to do with a life decision based on faith and religious beliefs, and to ask someone to risk all of that to help you out is asking a lot of them. The sad part is that even if he doesn't help me with information, the Church is probably going to think he did, just because he knows me.

"Hey Ken, how are things coming on your end? TJ is working on something for me so that I can make some cuts on the list, in hopes that we can create a smaller field to work with."

"Just paying some bills. You know, the fun stuff that comes with the job. I'm thinking of taking your suggestion and just getting an accountant to take care of everything now."

"I told you, Ken; especially now that we are making more than enough money and need to save and invest, we should probably pay someone that knows what they are doing. The only question is, do we bring in an outside company, or do we hire someone to do it for our company full-time?"

"I'll tell you what: as soon as everything with this case is done, I'll start looking into it. But for right now, I don't have the time to look into accountants or investing firms."

"I have no problem with that, we just need to make sure to follow the one rule that's kept us in good financial standings this whole time."

"Oh, you mean don't let friends or family give us advice on what to do with our money?"

"That's the rule. My advice is that we just bite the bullet and look into an accounting firm to take care of everything; that way they have nothing to worry about. And if any of our money ends up missing, we'll be covered by an insurance policy."

"You make a very good point, Neil, my partner in crime. I'll have one of the new guys get some information together on companies in the area we can work with so that we can go over everything when we get a chance."

"Sounds good. As for right now, I'm going to bring my car around back and get it cleaned and then head to the butcher shop."

"What are you doing out there? I know you're not going there to chat with your sister."

"I'm meeting with Father Roberts to talk about the case. He thinks he might be able to help us out with it."

"I almost forgot about him. How's he doing? It must be hard for him to be in the middle like this, seeing as you two are old friends and he's been a priest in the Catholic Church for some time now."

"I know, I hate to put him in this situation, but we're running out of options and time. I just wish there were some other way I could get information in this case, but I can't seem to come up with anything."

"I know what you mean, Neil, but I'm sure he wouldn't be helping you if he didn't feel strongly about it. Sometimes we have to draw a line between our faith and the Church as an organization. I don't need to tell you that, though; you know how it goes."

"That's true, I've always held the belief that religious beliefs can be and should be totally separate from religious affiliation. It's similar to politics; you can think Republican without being a registered Republican."

I hate when Ken does this—he always finds a way to get me going on one of my two hot topics. What I mean by that is, if you start talking about religion or politics, I get up on my soapbox and start preaching. He always likes to get a rise out of me and get me going; he gets a kick out of me, making an ass of myself by getting all preachy. Speaking of preachy, I should get going pretty soon and head out to meet Father Roberts. I can't be late. If anything, I need to be early and wait for him, just in case he has to get out early.

"Well, Ken, I need to get going here pretty soon. I'm going to go get my car washed really quickly and while I'm down there I'll swing by the tech lab and see what TJ has come up with."

"Sounds good. Let me know how the meeting with Father Roberts goes. Also, while you're at the butcher shop, do you mind picking me up a couple of T-bone steaks?"

"Every time I swing by there, you ask me to pick you up T-bones. Any reason why?"

"To be honest with you, you're not always out there, and I like a good T-bone, especially one I don't have to pay for. Hell, you're

Italian, and you own a butcher shop. You appreciate a good steak just as much as I do, so who are you trying to kid?"

"Point well taken. I'll make sure and pick you up a couple of steaks while I'm there. Is there anything else I can do for you while I'm out?"

"Nope, just the steaks will be fine. I need to get back to work on these bills, and you need to get out of here soon. How about you give me a call when you get done talking to him, and we'll see what's up."

"All right, Ken. Have fun with the bills while I meet with Father Roberts in the basement of the butcher shop. It's days like today that make me question my career path in life."

"I hear you completely on that one, bro; I'll talk to you later. Try not to get caught, and be safe."

Let's hope we don't get caught; I feel bad enough that I've involved Father Roberts as much as I have. Even though he has offered to help just as much as I have asked, I still feel bad about the whole situation. I don't like to put someone in a position to choose between something as strong-willed as their faith and a friend. I know I'm not someone who is known for his conviction when it comes to religious affiliation. I do understand faith and believing in something greater than oneself as well as faith in one's religion. Many people view me as a person that doesn't believe in religion, or in God, for that matter. The truth is I'm very religious; I just have my problems with the organization as a society that we have built around our religions.

See, I told you, Ken likes to get me up on my soapbox and start preaching my philosophical beliefs; he gets a kick out of it for some reason. I pulled my car around to the wash bay and tipped our maintenance guy twenty dollars and asked him to make it shine inside and out in thirty minutes. He looked at me like I was crazy but said he would give it his best shot. Now it's off to see TJ and see how that list is coming; let's hope I can do some good guesswork so we have a shot at finding Andrew's mother tonight.

"Hey TJ, what's the word? Do you have anything for me to look at yet?"

"I was just getting ready to give you a call; we are almost done. If you give me five more minutes, the computer will be done, generating all the locations for you. I will organize them by years in operation so you'll know how long they've been open. You know, new operations versus older ones; it's the only way I could organize them on such short notice outside of alphabetically."

"Thanks, TJ, you never cease to amaze me. You are definitely a whiz kid. Speaking of kids, how's the family doing?"

"My son's doing great; he just had his fourth birthday last week. It's amazing how fast they grow up, isn't it?"

"You can say that again. It seems like just yesterday when Carol Lynn was born. I still can't believe she's already seven; before I know it, she'll be bringing home deadbeat boyfriends to drive me nuts."

"Although it will be hard for her to get away with anything, seeing as you own the largest private investigating company in the Midwest and you're connected all over the city."

"True, but I wouldn't want her to feel like she was looking over her shoulder twenty-four seven. Okay, maybe just a little bit."

"All right, here it is, boss man, do your best and work through the list."

"I've got a meeting to get to shortly with someone that can help me work through this list. I'll get it back to ASAP. Worst case scenario, I'll just fax it over to you guys to get to work on. I should have it for you by four o'clock at the latest. Is that cool with you? I know it's cutting it close, but I'll pare the list down to something a lot more manageable."

"As I said, you're the boss; just let me know what you want me to do and I'll get it done. What would you like me to do in the meantime?"

"Have everyone take a couple-hour breaks and get some rest and meet back at the office at four. I'm going to need everyone as clear-headed and rested as possible for tonight. It's going to go by extremely fast tonight, and we can't have any mistakes because we're tired."

"Neil, I send the word out to everyone. I'll be waiting for your fax at about four."

"Thanks, TJ, for everything. I really mean it; you've absolutely been an asset to this company. After this case is done, we'll have to sit down and talk to you about a raise or something like a company car. You deserve it."

"Thanks, Neil. Don't worry, we are going to find her, and we'll find out what really happened to this kid."

Making my way back to the car, I couldn't help but think about what TJ said about him knowing that we're going to find out what happened. What if we don't figure this out? What if this is one puzzle, one mystery we can't get to the bottom of? It's not just the failure that would get to me, but also the fact that I would be letting down a fellow eaglet from St. Mary's; that's the part that drives me.

"Here you go, Mr. Baggio, all done, inside and out. I had to have someone help me, but we got it done for you, with time to spare."

"Nice job, kid, real nice job, the car looks great. Thanks for putting in the extra effort; you'll do just fine around here if you keep up that kind of work ethic."

"Thanks, Mr. Baggio, and good luck on the case."

"You know you can call me Neil. Mr. Baggio makes me feel like your dad. We'll just stick with Neil. Cool?"

"All right, Neil. Drive safe."

It looks like it's time to get down to the butcher shop and wait for Father Roberts to meet with me. At times like this my stomach starts to get knotted up. I know you're thinking that I should stop with the coffee too. If you've learned anything from me and big cases, it's that I treat my body like shit when I'm pushing on a case. The coffee beans just aren't enough of a fix for me, not right now. The really scary situations that are life-threatening don't hit you until some time after the event. It's the times leading up to the pressure situations that get to you the worst, not the situations themselves. It's like the anticipation before the big game; for example, when NFL players are interviewed after the Super Bowl, they'll tell you that the game never lives up to the hype and anticipation. The thing that separates the great ones from the rest is the ability to make it through that anticipation without losing focus on the goal at hand.

13

Why do I have a feeling that here is a lot more to the story than what I read in the newspaper?

The drive to the butcher shop seemed to take forever; it was as if I hit every red light along the way. It was probably for the best, since I couldn't seem to focus on driving. I was too busy worrying about how I was going to handle this meeting with Father Roberts. The problem isn't that Father Roberts and I don't talk—we talk about once a week— it's that we haven't seen each other in more than a year and he lives only ten minutes from my house, in parish housing. We've just never found time to meet; it's always late-night phone calls, usually from me to him. The other thing I'm worried about is running into my sister, whom I haven't seen since Easter, and before that, it was Christmas. We're starting to become one of those siblings that only talk during the holidays. If I'm lucky, she won't be working today, and it will be some regular employee that I can just scoot by. But my luck hasn't been that good this week, so I highly doubt it. And judging by the car that's parked in the lot, it looks like my sis is here.

AVE MARIA

If I haven't already talked about the situation involving my sister, I'll give you a quick tour of our history. Basically, my sister has been a screw-up all through the teenage years and beyond, but I love her to death. I'm not saying I don't get in trouble, it's just that she has this amazing ability to do it with a special touch and a little flare, to be exact. The problem isn't that she gets in trouble; it's that I was always getting asked to get her out of trouble. My parents would always ask because I was working for the bureau. Even before I worked for the bureau, I had a lot of connections in our area with judges and police officers. At first, it was just stupid things that young kids do, but eventually she just wouldn't stop. The last time she got in trouble, I refused to get her out of it, and my parents—well, mainly my father— got very upset with me to the point that we haven't really talked much. It's not like I didn't help her at all, I mean fuck, I paid for her lawyer and all her court costs. I just didn't want her to get away with it again; she needed to learn a lesson for once in her life.

Shortly after that, my dad decided to give my sister the butcher shop to run, which made me even more upset at him than he was with me. It didn't bother me that I wasn't getting the butcher shop, I just felt like he was flushing a family business down the drain to prove a point. If anything, he should have let his old-time friend and partner run it, or his son, for that matter; either one of them would have been better choices than my sister. Luckily for him, my sister has done a complete 180 since those days. And the butcher shop is thriving to this day. Which is hard to imagine with all these supermarkets everywhere. That's the abbreviated version of what happened with us, and it still comes between us. We don't talk about it, but ever since then we haven't been the same; we just don't talk like we used to. It's probably because we never really talked about everything after it happened; well, that and because we both take after our father's stubbornness.

"Hey, bro, what are you doing here today? I wasn't expecting you."

"I know; I'm meeting an old friend here. We're going to be meeting downstairs. You remember Father Roberts, don't you?"

"Oh, my God, he's coming today; I haven't seen him in years. Why are you guys meeting in the basement of the butcher shop?"

"It's a long story but it involves that kid that committed suicide at St. Mary's early in the week."

"I remember reading about in the news. I'm sorry to hear about everything. Why do I have a feeling that there is a lot more to the story than what I read in the newspaper?"

"Because you know whenever I'm involved in a story, there's always a lot more to it than what everyone is telling you."

"That's true. Sometimes being your sister has its negatives, other than having to put up with your stubborn and arrogant ass."

"Ouch, that one hurt."

"You know I'm just messing with you, bro. I'll always love you. It's those things that drive me nuts about you that make you so special."

"Thanks, sis, you really know how to make your big bro smile. You know I love you, and it's not just because I have to."

"Nice one, bro. If you want, you can grab something to eat before you run down there. We've got fresh sandwiches in the case, grab one and something to drink, and I'll send Father Roberts down when he comes in."

"I told him to meet me at the back door just in case someone is tailing him, so I'll grab two sandwiches, and I'll see you when we're done. If anyone comes in and looks suspicious, can you text my cell?"

"This is big-time, isn't it, bro? You can count on me. Go take care of what you need to, and I'll keep an eye out up here."

She wasn't kidding. The basement is dingy even though she's cleaned it up pretty well. There's a fresh coat of paint on the walls, some new lighting, some new furniture, and there's even a TV down here. It's tempting to turn the television on while I wait, but I really need to go over this list while I'm waiting; hopefully it won't be too long before he gets here. It truly is amazing the memories that sitting down here bring back, the nights I stayed here when I ticked off my dad. I wanted him to think I ran away, but I'm sure he knew I was here by the food missing by morning. I remember the late nights I would sneak back my old high school girlfriend to the butcher shop basement. I know, how romantic? Hey, we were young and curious; not to mention, the only place we could get any privacy was the butcher shop basement. When you're seventeen and eighteen, the ambience doesn't really matter. It's more a matter of just being private.

Josephine Tortuni, I'll never forget her; we were each other's firsts for a lot of things. Young love with access to a very private little room, not a good combination, but at least we kept it within reason. We grew up together in the same community, went to church and school together, our mothers even played cards together every Thursday night like clockwork. We really did grow up in one of those small Italian communities you read about in books or see in the movies. The only difference was that there wasn't a mob affiliation, at least not in my neighborhood. They tried, don't get me wrong, they tried many times. I remember the conversations I would overhear with my mom and dad about paying protection money. He was very old-school; he was very proud of what he had built from the ground up, and he wasn't about to ruin that by letting some bully come in and muscle him for money.

"Neil . . . Neil . . . you there? Open it up, it's me."

"Oh, fuck, sorry about that, Father. I got lost in some memories."

"This place can do that to you. Let me guess: you were thinking of Jo, weren't you?"

"Yup, good old Josephine, my first love. She was perfect in so many ways; I wonder why we ever broke up."

"If I remember it correctly, she went to Florida for school, and you stayed home."

"Geez! I forgot; I can't believe you remembered it, but I didn't."

"It was a pretty ugly breakup, remember? I was on the phone with the two of you every night. It seemed like for months helping you two get over . . . well, each other."

"That's always the problem with your first love; it's also your first heartbreak. And we can all remember our first heartbreak, definitely not something I would want to live through again."

"Enough nostalgia for one day. I don't have too much time to spend here. I'm almost positive I'm being followed."

"Good point. I've got a list of locations here where we think they might be holding Andrew's mother. I need you to help me go through it and cut it down from a list of more than eighty to about twenty, so we can sit on them tonight and see if we can spot her."

"I'll do you one better: I'll tell you where she is and where they're going to move her. Will those do?"

"Uh, yeah, those will do. How did you get your hands on this information in just a few hours? I just talked to you a little while ago."

"I was lucky enough to be in the cafeteria when a couple of guys were talking about it. They were trying to hide what they were talking about, but they did a bad job of it."

"All right, so where are they stashing her? I know that sounds kind of bad, but I'm really excited, it's finally a break in the case."

"There's only one problem; well, one really big problem."

"You've got to be kidding me. What the hell is wrong now?"

"You can't just grab her; you're going to have to get someone inside to get your info from her. If you just grab her, the Church will make it look like you were covering up the murder. Imagine how easy it will be for them to frame you if you do something like kidnap her."

"But we're not going to kidnap her; they are the ones that kidnapped her. We're just trying to save her and get to the truth about her son."

"Don't forget the Church has been in the politics business longer than most if not all. The Catholic Church has been around for quite some time, and needless to say, they've had quite a bit of practice in turning the public's eye in the right direction. At least the direction they want them looking."

"I hear what you're saying; we should tread very softly. This is going to take a little bit of subtlety and precision—"

"Definitely not two of your strong suits, to say the least."

"Hey, I was getting to that if you would let me finish. So what do you have in mind? Try to get someone on the inside to talk to her and get the information we need? Or try to get it from some other source?"

"That's where you come in; you were always the more creative one when it comes to schemes. Hell, just look at the stunt you pulled the other day in front of St. Pat's Church."

"How did you know that was me? I didn't say anything about that to you."

"It had Neil Baggio written across it; it wasn't that hard for me to figure out you had to be involved. I was certain of it when through the grapevine I heard about Cardinal Kelley's incident in the confessional. Did you really have to lock him in there and scare him like that?"

"Probably not, but it did speed up the process, and he never found out it was me, so what's the problem? It's not like he was hurt in any way, shape, or form; technically, I didn't even touch him. Although amid all the excitement, I feel like I could have gotten more out of him. I guess time will tell."

"You and your technicalities, always trying to find a loophole to keep the guilt out, aren't you?" Aren't all of us? That's human nature.

"You're the priest, you would know better than me. Before we get off track any farther than we already have, where are they keeping her? Every minute wasted is more information lost because it's being covered up, or worse, destroyed."

"You promise me you won't try removing her from wherever she is?"

"I promise I will not move her in any way, shape, or form wherever the Church is keeping her."

"All right, here's the address; I better not hear about any funny business from you and your guys. You know the building quite well."

"Are you serious? They're moving her tonight? You've got to be fucking kidding me."

14

You really like calling me "superstar,"don't you?

The drive from the butcher shop back to the office to talk to Ken has me speeding recklessly. I am just so furious that I have this great intelligence where Andrew's mother is going to be but I can't act on it just yet. I'll have to have some of the guys sit on it tonight and see what comes up. Then we'll have to keep watch around the clock until I can get someone inside. The confidence the Church has in itself is amazing; it's as if they want me to try to grab her back so they can turn the story around on me. As I try to focus on the next move, I'll need to make myself glance down at the speedometer in my car and realize I'm doing nearly 100 miles per hour down I-94.

For those of you not familiar with the Detroit area, that's a good 30 miles per hour over the speed limit, and I don't see the needle move back down; it keeps moving up. Nearing almost 120 miles per hour, I start to remember why I bought this car; it handles beautifully at high speeds.

Cruising down the interstate weaving in and out of traffic effortlessly, as if I were doing a practice run. No jerking, no swaying, just a fluid movement of speed and precision; it really is an amazing feeling to be driving at such speeds with amazing ease due to great mechanical technology. Just as I started to get lost in the traffic, I noticed my exit coming up, and at 100 miles per hour you don't have a lot of time to get over, since you're moving at nearly twice the speed of the rest of the traffic. Amazingly, something so simple as speeding can clear your head. Don't get me wrong, I'm not condoning it and telling people to go out and speed.

As for me, I love to go fast, whether it is driving, flying, riding, or anything else that gets the old adrenaline pumping. It just seems like when I get to that place in my brain where I'm driving so fast, I don't have time to think but instead just react. That's when my brain does some of its best work. It's quite complicated and odd, to say the least, but I seem to think better when I'm distracted. If I can't seem to work out a problem, I either hop in the shower or wrap my hands and hit a bag. As soon as I start hitting the bag, time slows.

The brain truly is an amazing machine, capable of some amazing things. There are a lot of times I really have no idea how I come up with solutions, I just relax, focus on something else, and let my brain do what it knows how to do, and the rest falls into place. A lot of times I think we get too caught up in thinking we have to be aware of our brain working to know it's working. Just because you are consciously aware that you are thinking about something doesn't mean that you are effectively thinking about it. Many times, not thinking about it is the most effective way to sift through something; allowing our subconscious to be utilized is the key.

Pulling in the lot at the warehouse, it looked like there was a small concert going on inside. The lot was packed with cars and people congregating outside, waiting for the show to begin. Everyone besides Father Roberts and me are still under the impression that we are going to have to sit on a ton of different locations just to find Andrew's mother. They don't have the piece of information I have. I still can't believe that they are going to move her there; without Father Robert's info, we would never have found her, at least not in time. I can't wait to give the news to Ken. He's going to be happy, he had a feeling using all the manpower to track her down would spread us too thin on all our other current cases. Speak of the devil, here he is coming down the steps to greet me.

"If it isn't our superstar. Everyone has been waiting for you to show up and give the word. Speaking of which, what is the word?"

"Let's just say we can call off the dogs tonight, we've already got an address where to find her. The only problem is we can't act on it, at least not in the fashion I'd like. We need to handle it with a little more care, so tonight we'll have to brainstorm on the next step to take."

"Where are they going to move her? Don't be holding out on me; you know I hate it when you do that."

"Look for yourself, here's the address; it looks familiar, doesn't it?"

"Is   this—"

"Yup!"

"You've got to be kidding me. This is where they are going to put her up?"

"The worst part is that we've got to find a way to get someone in there to talk to her so we can get the intel we need from her."

"You aren't kidding; this is going to take some major precision and planning. We'll have to get input from anyone and everyone tonight and see what we can come up with."

"I think that's the best bet, that and we need to get you drunk tonight, you always seem to think clearly when you're hungover. I know it sounds crazy, but we both know it's true, so we might as well stick with what works. Since we know where she's going to be, we can have surveillance on her twenty-four/seven until we can figure something out."

"Sounds like a plan; let's get going downstairs and break the news to the rest of the team and hope we can come up with something to do."

"Lead the way. superstar. This is your show, not mine."

"You really like calling me 'superstar,' don't you?"

"I know it gets under your skin; that's why I do it. You know I like to ruffle your feathers a little bit every now and again."

"You mean daily, don't you? I can't say anything, though I do it too; an old man."

"Ooh, low blow; you know I'm sensitive about my age."

"All right, let's get focused before we walk out there and start talking to everyone. I need to use the bathroom really quickly; I'll meet you out there in like five minutes."

"All right, superstar. Would you like me to introduce you?"

"Shut up, Grandpa; I'll be out there in five."

I didn't really have to use the bathroom. I just needed to clear my head really quickly before I go out there and share the news with everyone. There's no reason for me to be nervous. It's not like I'm delivering bad news to anyone, but for some reason, I'm all knots inside. I think it's because I see things falling into place, and I'm starting to get a rough picture of where this whole thing is going to end up. The question is, will BCI be better off if we don't get to the bottom of this case? I'm starting to think that the company could get hurt the longer we stay involved with this case; I might need to pull the company out of this before too long, just to be on the safe side. I definitely need to talk to Ken about this, since he deals with our PR more regularly. To be honest with you, he's usually cleaning up after me from some stunt I pull while working a case. What's one more chink in the armor?

"All right, Neil, are you ready to do this? Almost everyone that works here is in the house tonight. The only ones that couldn't make it are currently working other cases for us."

"Damn, we've really got a full house out there, don't we? I guess I'll have to speak up just a little bit."

"I don't think that will be a problem for your big-ass mouth. You've never been known for your soft-spoken voice."

"True, very true; I am quite the loud-mouthed son of a bitch. I guess the sooner we get this going, the sooner we can get to work on getting me a hangover tomorrow morning."

"That's the plan, isn't it?"

AVE MARIA

As I made my way through the doorway, I was met by thirty or forty pairs of eyes waiting for me to say something. We really don't do this much, so it was kind of hard for anyone to see me unless they were in the front row, so I decided to climb on top of one of our trucks and address everyone.

"As you guys all know, tonight we are supposed to be set up all over Detroit in hopes of finding Andrew's mother, but luckily for us, I've done some digging around, and we've found her. The only problem is we can't make a move to get to her tonight because of her location. And this is the reason we decided to keep everyone here tonight even though we aren't going to need to do a citywide search. Instead, I'm going to need everyone's help in brainstorming about a way to get to her."

As I finished talking for a moment, I could see the wheels in everyone's head starting to turn. Trying to figure out why it's going to be so hard to get to her and why I'm asking everyone for help. Just as I was about to tell them, I heard someone from the crowd.

"Where is she? I mean, why is it going to be so hard for us to get to her? It's not like they can enlist her in the army, although that would be one hell of a way to hide someone."

"Very funny, guys. That would be a nice trick if they could enlist a fiftysomething Polish lady in the army. All joking aside, though, it's going to be just as hard for us to get to her. They have admitted her to a psychiatric facility downtown. Ken is handing out a packet with all the information we've collected so far in this case. Tonight we are going to map out everything we are going to do to get to the bottom of this as well as assign people to work the case. We are not going to use any more man-hours than we already have on this. We will need only six volunteers for the remainder of the case. If you are interested in working the remainder of the case, just sign up outside Ken's office, and tomorrow morning Ken and I will inform everyone of who is doing what. Everyone else will be given new assignments in other cases. We've got a big caseload, and we can use the money, especially with the price of gasoline these days."

The meeting started off pretty well, with everyone giving their support. Almost everyone signed up to help the remainder of the case, so tonight Ken and I will have to go over the list and pick out the guys or girls we are going to want to work the case. It shouldn't be too hard to pick out the group, especially now that we have a general feel of where the case is headed. We are definitely going to need someone that can speak a little Polish or at least be able to understand it. We're going to need our best surveillance people to get into the building and tap into their system so we can try to figure out the best way to get to Ms. Malinowski, Andrew's mom.

"I guess this means it's time to go grab a bite to eat and a drink or six so that we can come up with something to do in the morning. What do you say, Neil?"

"Yeah, I think the meeting went pretty well. I mean the last hour or so went pretty well. I think we got a few ideas on how to get inside and talk to Ms. Malinowski."

"I'm not sure if we are going to be able to get someone on the inside by admitting someone. I think they would catch on too easily.

We might have to go about this the old-fashioned way and bribe someone that's already working there."

"I think we might have a better chance of getting someone on the inside as an employee than a patient, at least from the standpoint of getting information."

"I'll have some of the guys get to work on doing background checks on the employees at the hospital to see who we might have the best chance of manipulating. And we'll have to go through the list and see who a good fit might be to place inside the hospital as an employee."

"Don't we have a guy who's got a psychology degree or something close to it?"

"Actually, yeah, we do. Tony has a degree in psychology, and come to think of it, I think he's working on his masters."

"Let's get to talking to him because if there is someone best fitted for this situation, it would be someone with the knowledge needed to convince those who work there that they belong."

For now I just want to get back to my house, curl up in my big-ass chair, pour a drink, and listen to some good music. I doubt I'll get to do any of that, but a boy has to dream. Thinking about the next steps has my mind reeling. Replaying everything that happened tonight, the way the team came together really made the hair stand up on my neck. Now it's about calming down, focusing on the next move.

15

To give you an idea of how serious I am about my showering and coffee, I have a coffee cup holder in my shower.

It felt good to finally walk in the door of my own place and be greeted by those two smiling faces. I don't know what I'd do without my girls; Jackie and Danielle really are the best companions anyone could ask for. They don't ask for much, just that I look out for them, and in return they give me unconditional love. That is, unless I come home smelling like another dog; then I usually get the cold shoulder for a couple of hours. As I made my way through the house, Jackie was more interested in the closet that held their dog food than wanting to play. As for Danielle, she was in the mood to wrestle, so I obliged her for a few minutes while Jackie waited patiently in the kitchen. Just as Danielle grabbed me by the collar of my shirt, I started to hear my cell phone ring. Judging by the ring tone, it has got to be someone calling from the warehouse; more than likely, Ken checking in on me.

"Hey, old man, how are you doing?"

"'Old man.'" Look who's talking. Don't sit there and act like you aren't hurting today."

"Hey, old man, how's the eye treating you? I was surprised how well you took it; you didn't even fall down. You stayed on your feet, I was impressed; I haven't met too many people that can take a shot like that and stay on their feet."

"Ken, it's not like you toot your own horn like this. You must be feeling good about yourself today, now that you know you are the 'Billy Badass' of the group."

"I guess you could put it that way; I like knowing next time we get in an argument that if it gets to the point where we start throwing punches you will give me a decent fight."

"Very funny. Aren't we chipper today? For someone that should have a huge hangover just like Brian and me, you are acting awfully cheerful this morning."

"That's because I know something you don't know. We've got a way in; we've got a way to get to Ms. Malinowski; well, at least a way to get to her. Apparently one of the doctors has one hell of a gambling problem as well as a problem for self-medicating. Still, we are going to have to handle him very carefully, as to not lead on suspicion."

"That's an understatement. I have a feeling this is going to be a good job for one of our female investigators. As you've said, sometimes things need to be handled with soft hands, not guns blazing."

"Hey, I think you are starting to catch on, at least a little bit. But I'm not going to get my hopes up just yet."

"I was going to say that we are only talking about a decision I'm making, not an action. Let's not get ahead of ourselves. There's still a good chance when I get involved, I'm going to resort to my usual brashness."

"Isn't that the truth. But we both have to admit you do get the job done, and you seem to know when to take a step back, observe for a bit, and let someone else do some work."

"It's just simple mathematics; the more people that shed light on a problem, the better the chance of overcoming it."

"Hey Neil, I hate to cut this conversation short. I just wanted to tell you about the good news and to tell you to get out here soon so we can get started on this. I've got a couple of people getting more information on our doctor as we speak. Everything we can think of in his background is both good and bad."

"Make sure they do the usual credit check and Dumpster diving; I want to know everything about this guy. The more we know, the better chance we have of getting him to cooperate."

"Will do, Neil. How long do you think it will be before you get out here?"

"I should be about an hour. I need to make sure and give the girls a little bit of attention, since I was out all night. But I should be there before too long. How about we set up a meeting with the whole team for five o'clock? I'll pick up some subs and chips for the meeting. If you just want to make sure that we have plenty of stuff to drink."

"I can do that, no problem; I'll make sure that everyone is here at five o'clock. Just make sure and get here yourself, Mr. Punctual!"

"Look at you with all the witty comments; don't worry about me. I'll be there early so we can go over a few things before the meeting. You'll probably see me at about four or four thirty."

"All right, see you then, Neil. Talk to you later."

"Sounds good, Ken; see you in a couple of hours."

See, I told you if I went out last night and got hammered, we would get some good news today. Okay, so maybe that was a little luck, and I doubt the drinking had anything to do with it; let me rephrase: I know the drinking had nothing to do with it. It is just like I said, though; sometimes you just need to turn the brain off for a bit and start anew. Sometimes I think I'm trying to convince myself that it was okay for me to go out last night. To be honest, I do feel kind of guilty for taking the night off the case even though there was really nothing that could be done. Sometimes it is a waiting game whether you like it or not. That's just part of the business. There is a lot of waiting, whether it is because you are on a stakeout or just because you are waiting for other field agents to get information back to you. Think of it as a big puzzle and that all the pieces are spread out around your house. You don't know what you are looking at until you get enough of the puzzle pieces and get a chance to see how they fit together. I know it's a good analogy, isn't it? I wish I could take credit for that one, but I can't. Believe it or not, that one came from my daughter Carol Lynn. I was trying to explain to her what I did for a living, and that's what she explained back to me.

The girls are still looking at me with that look of starvation. As if they haven't eaten in weeks; for anyone that has had a dog, you know the look. I had forgotten that I needed to feed them when Ken called and distracted me. I guess since they are so good, I will feed them; even if they were bratty, I'd feed them. I have to take care of them as they do me. I know I get really sappy when I talk about my two dogs, but hey, they mean a lot to me just as much as my daughter does. Speaking of which, you should see her play with Jackie and Danielle. It really is an amazing sight; they are just so gentle with her, licking her and listening to every command she says. It's like watching three kids play.

Now that the girls are eating and can get out when they want, I can finally make my way into the shower. For those of you not familiar with my ways, I truly have an obsession with showering. That and coffee, which reminds me I haven't had but one cup of coffee today. I need to make sure and take care of that when I get out of the shower. But back to the shower thing, if I don't get a good shower in with a cup of coffee, my day is shot. To give you an idea of how serious I am about my showering and coffee, I have a coffee cup holder in my shower. I'm serious. I put in a cup holder in my shower so I can drink coffee in the morning while showering. I like to take nice, long showers in the morning, usually in the area of twenty minutes. I was taking such long showers and running out of hot water I had to put in one of those new hot water systems. The ones that heat the water through the pipes as it passes through, as opposed to the old-fashioned hot water heaters. That has got to be one of the best things I've ever done to this house.

AVE MARIA

Finally, in the bathroom, I turned on the water with a sigh of relief, knowing I'm just moments away from the feeling. That amazing feeling you get when that warm water runs down your head and neck and down your back. I usually just lean in the shower for a good five to ten minutes while the water runs down my back, slowly releasing all the tension from the previous day. That first step is always my favorite because you get that extreme rush of relaxation; it's almost as good as sex. For an old guy like me who doesn't always know when his next romantic interlude is going to be, you begin to rely on nice, long showers, and contrary to popular belief, I am all about a good, hot shower, not cold. I can't stand a cold shower; to me, it's a crime against nature. I have a theory about people who enjoy cold showers; I think they are the same people who think that jumping out of a plane with an oversized pillowcase is fun. For those of you who are a little slow on the uptake. I'm talking about adrenaline junkies such as skydivers, cliff divers, and those guys who think it's fun to jump off bridges hooked up to oversized rubber bands.

I know I repeat a lot of things, but some of that is old age; if you ask my ex-wife, Sheila, she'll tell you I repeat myself because I run out of things to say and that I enjoy hearing myself talk. I don't know if I agree with her view of my habits, although I can agree with her that I have a problem with silence in a room. I tend to ramble on when a conversation ends; it probably stems from my childhood with my parents. I was always worried whenever it got quiet that someone might be thinking of something else to yell about. When I was in middle school and the early years of high school, my parents went through a rough patch where there was a lot of fighting and screaming, and at times things were getting thrown around the house. I guess that's where I get most of my nervous habits, from growing up in a loud Italian family household.

Back to the important stuff, though, how are we going to get to Andrew's mother? I know Ken said we have a doctor that we can work to our advantage to get close to her, but I just think we shouldn't stop looking for another way to get to her. I've never been happy when you have only one solution to a problem that could be solved in many different ways. This isn't mathematics, where there will only be one finite answer. These are highly complicated problems with just as complicated answers that can be answered in more than one way. Imagine giving directions to someone across town; it could be any town, whether it is big or small. Now think of all the different ways you could get someone from point A to point B; that's what it is like when working a case like this. You know the starting point, and you know where you want to end up, but the problem is deciding the route by which to get there. Now you have a general idea of how I have to look at problems like the one that is in front of me right now with Andrew's death. I know he's dead, I know it wasn't a suicide, but I don't know exactly how to get there.

I made my way across the cool tiles in the bathroom, over to the sink to shave. It was there I was attacked by Jackie and Danielle. They were in a playful mood, probably since I was gone for the night. Without even breaking stride, I went right into shaving, ignoring my girls, which was a major mistake. Any man should know that by my age the only thing worse than ignoring one female is to ignore her and her sister. Jackie and Danielle decided to have a little fun at my expense. Before I knew it, my towel was halfway down the hallway, being tugged back and forth between the two of them like a rag toy. It really was a sight, that's for sure; the two of them really keep me upbeat at all times. It's that unconditional love that just keeps me smiling, simplistic in all its glory.

After I finished shaving, I made my way into the bedroom to get ready for the day, and this feeling of uncertainty just kept overwhelming me. I just felt like there is something wrong about this case, whether it was the murder/suicide itself or the manner of which we were going about finding the truth. I couldn't help but doubt myself and wonder if I was going at this all wrong; maybe I've narrowed my view too much. I think I might have to look at this case from a new perspective. There has to be something I am missing, or maybe it's just something I'm not acknowledging. If there is anyone that can help me work through all of this, it will be Ken. He's always good at helping me shed new light on things. I've got to go to the warehouse.

Before I do anything else, I need to get ahold of Ken. I'll need every bit of information we have on this case for me to go through and start all over from the beginning. The next twenty-four hours are going to be extremely important because I've got to decide which direction to take in this case. Whether it is to find who really killed Andrew or to look at the possibility that Andrew actually may have killed himself. But if he did kill himself, why would he do such a thing? As Headmaster Glowacki had said to me earlier, it just doesn't make sense that a young man with such potential and a positive outlook on life would kill himself. Of all the people we contacted and talked to about Andrew, not one person said he was depressed in any way, shape, or form. As I said, it just doesn't make any sense that someone who has come so far with so little would commit suicide for no evident reason. Before I forget, I should call Ken and have him get everything together for me.

"Hey Neil, what can I do for you?"

"I need you to have a group of guys get together every bit of information available on the case and set up a makeshift office in the gym. I'm going to be working out there for the time being."

"You always did think the best listening to some loud-ass music while hitting a bag. I'll make sure to have everything set up for you within the hour. Is there anything else you need me to get set up for you?"

"Just make sure the makeshift office has a big coffeemaker; you know how I love my coffee. I should be there within an hour or two; I need to make a stop before I get there."

"We could always have one of the guys swing by and keep an eye on the girls for you, or we could just bring them out to the warehouse."

"We'll talk about it later. For right now, I need to get going. I'll see you in a bit, Ken."

After I got off the phone with Ken, I got my things together and took the girls for a walk. They seemed to really enjoy everything, especially a nice puddle they found along the way that seemed to cool them off in an extremely muddy manner. I guess I've spent enough time doing everything but my job; it's time to get to work and head out to the warehouse.

16

Tony is not your average computer geek by any means; he stands at six feet, three inches tall, with a frame equal to only Muhammad Ali.

The drive to the warehouse was the usual. A little traffic mixed with a lot of construction, and this is just the spring; soon it will be summer, and the construction will be in full effect. Who would have thought that it would be easier to get around Detroit in the middle of a blizzard than in the middle of summer? Road construction is what we do best here. I really should have thought twice about buying the crossfire with these roads; I wasn't thinking at all. Then again, I love opening her up on the expressway, and then I couldn't care less about everything. Before I even had time to finish the coffee I had picked up at the gas station I stopped at along the way, I was already at the warehouse. I pulled around back tonight instead of into my usual spot because I was going to have one of the new guys clean and detail my car. I drove the girls over to the park in the crossfire because I was too lazy to move it out of the way for my Jeep. So now I have to get it clean and get all of the dog hair and dirt out of it. Oh well, it's just one of the many perks of owning your own company with a wash and detail bay for all of our vehicles.

"Hey boss man, how are you doing tonight? I'm guessing you need 'the works' done tonight on your baby?"

"You know the deal; there is mud and hair in the back from the girls. I took them to the park today before I came; sorry, but I left you a bit of a mess."

"No problem, boss man, you know I'm always up for a good challenge. I'll have it done for you before the end of the day; is that okay?"

"Yeah, that will be fine. I'm not going to be out of here for quite some time. I have a lot of work to get done tonight; as long as you get it cleaned for me by midnight, everything will be fine."

"That should be no problem with that kind of time. I'll have your car looking brand new. I might even throw in a free oil change for you if I have time."

"Thanks, kid; I knew I liked you for a reason. Here's a twenty for helping out with this; it's not much, but it should buy you a couple of beers later."

"Thanks, boss man, but you know you don't need to do that. You're already paying by the hour to be here; cleaning your car is the least I can do."

"Don't worry about it; just take care of my baby and remember you know I hate it when you call me 'boss man.'"

"Sorry about that, Neil; I forget from time to time. I'm sorry; I'll try to remember from now on."

"It's not that big of a deal. I just don't care for being called 'boss man.' It makes me feel important and old, and I'm just old, not important."

"I'll make sure and have everything taken care of for you. Don't worry about it."

Making the trip from the car bay up to the office reminds me of walking through the hallways in high school. All the half-assed smiles and handshakes saying hi to people you know you are going to talk about behind their back in minutes. I know it's juvenile, but we all know it still goes on. We like to tell our kids that it doesn't go on past high school. We all know it goes on everywhere you get a group of people together who work together in an enclosed environment. But these are all trivial things that keep invading my mind and are keeping me from the important things at hand, but then again, it's probably best, since I'm going to be spending the next couple of hours sitting in a makeshift office in a gym.

I know I'm a little weird. Let me rephrase that: I know I'm extremely messed up, but the important thing is that I get the job done. I know people are going to look at me like I'm crazy since I'll be going through case files. While listening to loud music, hitting a heavy bag, and maybe working the gloves with Ken or one of the other guys. Even TJ has been known to work with me lately. It's been a great way to keep our teams in shape, hand-to-hand-ready, and competitive.

"Hey Neil, it's about time you got out here. I've got everything set up for you on the court. Are you going to need any help on this, or do you want to go it alone?"

"No, I'm going to need some help sifting through everything and someone to bounce ideas off of."

"Well, you can count me in, and if you want, I can call in some of the other guys if you want."

"You know what? Why don't you get at least one other guy that hasn't been working on the case so we can get a fresh perspective on everything."

"Can do. I'll grab Jacob; he hasn't been on the case."

"I need someone who has no knowledge about the case, not someone who's clueless in general. But this guy's a complete idiot; he's great with cars but just clueless otherwise. Do you have anyone else in mind?"

"I have an idea. Why don't we call Maria and see if she wants to help   out?"

"Didn't you just tell me that I should keep my social life a little more simplified and now you're telling me to ask Maria for help? You have one sick sense of humor."

"I know I just felt like throwing it out there. How about we just get Tony from the tech team to come over and help? He's always been good at helping us out with a fresh perspective."

"Yeah, why don't you tell him to meet us down there in a few minutes."

"Sounds good; I'll see you down there in five minutes."

I really like Tony; he's really been influential in the growth and expansion of this office. Tony is the head of our technical support team; they are very much a huge reason why we can get a lot of the information we gain on these cases. Tony is not your average computer geek by any means; he stands at six feet, three inches tall, with a frame equal to only Muhammad Ali. The only way Tony looks any different from Ali is in his skin tone. Tony is more of dark mahogany, which makes him a picturesque statue that commands a room not only with his stature but also with his intelligence. When Tony isn't hammering away on a computer in the tech wing, you can find him in the weight room. He'll be lifting heavier weights than any other employee there. He really is a unique kind of man. Then again, most of us who work here are somewhat different in our own way; we all have something unique to bring to the table, and that is another reason we are so good at what we do.

The walk from the office to the gym is a short distance, but it is not a straight shot by any means. The offices have become somewhat of a maze over the years, with additions and remodeling. Ken and I have an eye for toys, but our interior decorating skills are borderline juvenile. It's quite funny when we have new people come on board, because in the first couple of weeks they are constantly getting lost and having to ask for directions. It's quite the scene, if you ask me. A lot of times the guys will have fun at the expense of the new guys.

We had this new kid in here about a week ago; I think his name was Tanner. The guys had him walking around the office for forty-five minutes, trying to find his way out of the building. It was funny to see from the office; we have a view from above of the whole outlay in the warehouse. It was funny watching this kid run around like a rat in a maze for the longest time, getting frustrated beyond all belief. Finally Ken and I started to feel guilty about the whole situation, so we ended up talking him through his way out of the building over the PA system. Everyone was having a good laugh.

By the time I made it to the gym, Tony and Ken were already there, setting up shop for the long night ahead. I could see that Ken was starting up a fresh pot of coffee for Tony and me; Ken isn't much of a coffee drinker. He used to be, but nowadays he is all about those big-ass energy drinks; he's always got one in his hand. It's worse than my addiction to coffee. At least my habit doesn't keep me up for days at a time, as Ken's does from time to time. Before I can even get a chance to say anything, Ken looks at me and starts to lay down the ground rules for this long night ahead.

"We are not going to leave here until we have at least three different explanations as to why Andrew is dead. And by different, I mean different views than the one we currently are working on. Does everyone understand why we are here?"

"I hear you loud and clear, Ken; that's why I told you to grab Tony. We needed a fresh perspective on the whole case."

"That's what I'm here for; you know I'm always up to put a new twist on things. That's why I brought over my laptop; I've been imputing data and trying to come up with different combinations to the facts we currently have. Think of it as a big mix-and-match program; a lot of the time it's a waste of time, and it doesn't make sense, but a good portion of the time it can help to broaden your thought process."

"You know Ken and I aren't that big in the computer lingo, so you just walk us through it, and together we can make this work. You know me with files. I'll just make a mess of everything, so I figure you and Ken can sift through everything while I write notes on the dry erase board and drive everyone nuts hammering this bag."

"Yeah, you'll drive us nuts, but you think well when you're pounding away on a bag. I guess it is the exact definition of a Catch-Twenty-Two."

"I guess that's true. Most of my habits are pretty annoying; luckily for me, I'm good at my job."

"Speaking of annoying habits, hey Ken, have you ever noticed how Neil likes to crack his knuckles just by making a fist? He'll do that shit over and over again; sometimes, I just want to smack him."

"I know that shit is annoying, or how about the way he bounces his pecs to music when he's drunk? He doesn't even know he's doing it; it's fucking hilarious. At times he's like a little kid with no direction."

"Oh, wait a minute, my favorite is the way he—"

"Hello, guys; I am standing right here, and you two are digging into me like I'm not even here."

"We know you're standing right there; that's what makes it so much fun. Isn't it, Tony?"

"I would have to say it is fun to watch Neil squirm like this, getting all worked up over nothing major."

"'Nothing major.'" You guys are going to town on me and all of my bad habits—"

"See what I mean, Ken? This shit is hilarious. But enough kidding around, we need to get to work."

"Finally one of you guys is speaking something other than crap about me, and it's music to my ears. Let's start with the facts and what we know, and then we'll go from there. Why don't you start us off, Ken? You've got the police photos in front of you."

"Well, we know that there were none of the usual signs of suicide. That it was too clean, as if the body were put there after the fact."

"Let's not get ahead of ourselves right now. We are just talking about the facts. Once we get the facts stated, we will go from there and start to construct a feasible explanation for all of this. But until we get the facts straight, we aren't going to start throwing out ideas."

"I'm sorry about that, Neil; it gets hard sometimes not to get carried away when we get into cases like these; you know that."

"That is true; I have noticed around here that when the two of you get on a case, especially when it is a case with no answer in sight. The two of you go crazy like two kids in a candy store; it's actually quite amazing to watch you both get into it and run with an idea."

"Well, I'm glad that Ken and I can be of some amusement for you, Tony. Is there anything else we can do for you?"

"Oh, give it a rest, Neil; I swear you can be such a baby sometimes. You know that you get so defensive when people razz you a little bit; I'm just messing with you."

"I know; I'm just trying to focus on this case and not joking around. Is that okay with you? I'm sorry if that came out wrong. It's just that this case is driving me nuts. There are so many holes and so little to work with; I can't remember a case that gave us so little to go on." It's like having only five pieces to a twenty-piece puzzle.

"The only time I can think we had even less to go on was that missing persons case we did back in 2002. Where it ended up, the girl wasn't missing, but instead she was back home with her real family. The family that was trying to find her was the one that had kidnapped her years earlier."

"You guys worked that case; I remember reading about it in the paper."

"Well, it was before the company became a company and wasn't just two guys working out of their homes."

"That case did suck; we worked on it for nearly two months without any breaks, and then all of a sudden, the last three or four days of the case exploded, and we got on a roll."

"That's true. I can't remember a case that was as messed up as that one; we were really grasping at straws for a long time. I remember when—"

"Before the two of you get into a flashback of an old case, we might want to focus on the case at hand, since we are, as you said, working with a short hand."

"Good point, Tony. Thanks for getting Ken and me back on point. The facts in the case are as follows: Andrew was found dead in his dorm room by his girlfriend Christine. According to her alibi and the crime scene notes, there is no sign that she would have had any part in his committing suicide. We also know that Andrew drugged himself, and it wasn't with a prescription that he had access to. Not to mention, there was no sign of a break-in down in the nurse's office of the dormitory. And then there is the problem with the Church being overly involved in this case as well as hiding Andrew's mother from not only us but also anyone, for that matter."

"Hey, have you guys had a chance to get back into Andrew's dorm room since the night you were called out there? I have this feeling that something is missing in this case that we might be able to find there. Just an idea I'm throwing out there."

"Tony, that's a great idea. How the hell did I miss that?"

"Well, Neil, it might be because they have had the room locked and sealed off from the public to keep people out of there. And the fact that we probably assumed that the police would have done a thorough job searching the whole room. But you and I both know that if the lead detective on the case had already made up his mind that it was a suicide, he wouldn't have been nearly as thorough as if he thought otherwise."

"Well, I guess the first thing to do on the list is get into that room. I'll have to call Glow to see if I can't get a key for his room or if I can't find another way in, such as the windows. Those windows always did suck at staying locked, and I highly doubt they've replaced the windows of the building."

"Well, then I guess we will have to reconvene this tomorrow after we gain access to that room and see if we can't come up with anything. What do you think, Neil?"

"I think it's time for you and me to gain access to that room, Ken, regardless of how we do it."

"Sounds good to me; I'll have one of the guys get everything we'll need together. As for you, Tony, I'm going to—"

"As for Tony, we are going to need him to set up a wiretap into the phone system at St. Mary's. Something is telling me that Headmaster Glowacki isn't telling me everything. Whether it's because he can't or because he won't, it doesn't matter; I just need to figure out what that is."

"We're also going to see if you can pull up any financial records on the Catholic Church in the Detroit area. There's a good chance the Church is paying off the people involved by giving their respective areas a boost in funds."

"All right, can-do guys, I'll get the team on it right now. Is there anything else you need from me tonight?"

"No, Tony, thanks for everything you've done, but Ken and I will take it from here. I'm sure we'll be getting together tomorrow to talk things over; we'll get ahold of you."

"All right, guys, have a good night, and good luck getting into Andrew's room. If you need anything, don't hesitate to call me."

What we're going to need is a little bit of a miracle to find anything substantial in his room. There's a good chance that we won't find anything and that whoever is behind this cover-up has already been through his room to get anything that would link them to Andrew's death. I should also get in contact with Andrew's girlfriend Christine tomorrow. I haven't had a one-on-one chat with her yet, I've only read her statement and talked to Headmaster Glowacki about the relationship she had with Andrew. Tomorrow is going to tell a lot about the next week or so, although I might just say fuck it and call Glow right now and see if I can't get in there tonight.

17

Here I am a veteran in private investigating and snooping around, and I'm taking orders from a high-school cheerleader.

I had a short talk with Ken before I got in my newly detailed car; I have to admit that kid knows how to detail a car inside and out. I swear it looks better now than it did when I drove it off the lot; I'll have to give him a raise or something tomorrow. We're not talking about something huge, but enough that will show him we appreciate what he is doing around the warehouse; he's always staying around and helping us out. As for the conversation I had with Ken before I got on the road, I told him to track down Andrew's girlfriend and see if he could set up an appointment for us to meet tomorrow night. I just pulled out of the driveway when I decided to go out on a limb and give Glow a text on the phone I had my guys drop off earlier in the week. I know I can be a little too cautious at times, but it's better to be safe than sorry. I know it sounds like something your dad would say to you or has said, but it's the truth. The text I sent him said: I need Andrew's room and I need in there ASAP. Can we do it tonight?

AVE MARIA

While I'm waiting for a response from Headmaster Glow, I decided to take a chance and head in that direction. As I was coming up on I-696, I decided to get on and take a late-night cruise on the highway instead of making my way home. Once I get something in my head, it's hard for me to stop until I finish it. What can I say? Sheila calls it being bullheaded, I call it being focused, and my mom just says I'm as stubborn as my dad. I guess it just depends on your view of the situation. I'll go with Mom on this one; they say Mother always knows best, and in this instance I would have to go with her. Right now, I'm cruising down the highway pretty smoothly, at about ninety miles per hour. I could be going faster, but I'm trying to enjoy the ride and not worry about cops. It is quite easy, since I had the guys at the warehouse install a top-of-the-line radar detector in the car internally, so it's not out and easily seen by cops.

It looks like my exit is coming up; I just passed the sign that says Orchard Lake St. Mary's next exit. I guess that could be a clue that I could be getting close, which isn't good, since I haven't heard from Glow yet. I guess I'll just have to get a little creative and break into the room or something. I'm sure I could bribe the head of the dorms into letting me in unless the doors are still as loose as they were when I went to school there. If that is the case, then I can easily break into the room without anyone noticing; the only hard part will be getting into the dorm itself. If I hang out, I might be able to get in through another student's window on the first floor; all I'd have to do is bribe a student. And the students in the dorms can usually use a couple of extra dollars to line their pockets. As I pulled off the expressway and made my way toward the campus, I decided to stop at a gas station and fill up in case I got into a jam and needed to jet out of there. You never know when you might need a full tank of gas, so to be on the safe side, I pulled into a gas station, not to mention it has been almost three hours since my last cup of coffee, and I was due for another one.

I wasted a good fifteen minutes or so filling up my car and grabbing a cup of java; I even talked to the clerk for a bit just making small talk. All in hopes that the longer I took, the better chance I would have that Glow would tell me he could help me out and let me in tonight. At just about the same time, I was pulling onto the campus. Glow sent me a message saying he would call me in a few minutes to give me a way to get into Andrew's room without him having to come out there. It wasn't what I had hoped for, but it's better than not being able to get in at all. The other thing is that hopefully I will have total privacy so that I can spend a couple of hours in there looking through everything with a fine-tooth comb. However cliché, it is very true to the situation. Going through his room is going to take more than just sifting through his things and looking under the bed. I need to sit there and try and get a feel for what he might have been going through. The one plus I have is that I can relate to living in those exact dorms, and I have an idea of how the guys made it through the long summer days and cold winter nights. There are a lot of hiding places in those old rooms that a lot of people aren't aware of.

As I sat waiting for Headmaster Glow's call, I started driving around the campus, trying to get reacquainted with my old stomping grounds so I would be in the right frame of mind when I entered

Andrew's room. Eventually I settled into a parking spot along the road between the church on the campus and the dormitory. After a good ten or so minutes, I finally got the call I had been waiting for from Glow, and it was about time, too. What can I say? I get impatient when I'm on the verge of hopefully breaking open a case.

"Hey Glow, how are you doing tonight?"

"I'm doing all right, Neil. How is the case coming?"

"We're grinding it out right now, but that is how it usually goes in the beginning. So what do you have for me? How am I going to get into Andrew's room tonight?"

"I've already put the call out; Christine will be out to meet you in a few minutes with a copy of Andrew's keys."

"I thought the students were only allowed one copy. How did she get her hands on a copy of his dorm keys?"

"You remember being a student in the dorms; where there's the will, there's a way. I don't know how; all I know is that she has a copy, so I called her. It wouldn't look good for anyone if I were out there with you. She'll show you how she successfully sneaked in and out of his room on many occasions undetected."

"Works for me. Where am I going to meet her?"

"She said to meet her out across the street at the elementary school. She knows what car you're driving, so she'll probably approach you when you get out there. If anyone asks, though, I had nothing to do with this. Correct?"

"Why do you think I gave you a prepaid cell phone that can't be traced or bugged? I want to keep you clear of this as much as possible in case it gets ugly. You've done great things for this school, and I'm not about to ruin any progress you've made or plan on making."

"Thanks again for everything, Neil; I always knew you'd turn out to be something special. You just had that drive about you; no matter what you got in trouble for you always found a way out of it, and not like most kids, you always knew a way out before you got in trouble."

"Hey, my motto is if you are going to get in trouble, you might as well have an exit strategy."

"It's a good one to have; well, I'll let you get to your job, and I will stay in touch. Good luck and Godspeed, Neil."

"Good night, Glow, and rest assured, I will get to the bottom of this."

I hung up the phone, pulled a quick but quiet U-turn in the street, and headed out toward the elementary school. It was the equivalent of a city block from where I was parked; my guess is that is where Christine left her car when she stayed the night in Andrew's room. I guess I won't have to set up that interview with her tomorrow, since I'll be meeting with her in a few minutes. I really have no idea what this girl looks like, so I hope and pray that she finds me because I'll have no clue what to expect. Just as my mind started to wander off into old high-school memories, I heard this loud knock on the car window that scared the shit out of me. I felt like an idiot because I almost let out a high-pitched scream, but luckily for me, I was too distracted to do that. It was Christine, or at least I hoped it was. She stood a towering five feet tall and weighed maybe a hundred pounds soaking wet. She was your basic high-school cheerleader type, or at least I was guessing that. Once she opened her mouth and started to talk, I realized I was in for a long night with a Valley girl misplaced in Michigan.

"You must be Mr. Baggio; Headmaster Glowacki told me I would find you in this car. Are we having a little bit of a midlife crisis?"

"Aren't we the blunt one tonight? I'm Mr. Baggio, but you can just call me Neil, and no, I'm not having a midlife crisis; I've been stuck in one since my eighteenth birthday."

"Cute, really cute, Mr. Baggio; I mean Neil. Sorry that we had to meet under these conditions."

"I'm sorry, too; it must be hard to do this. I thank you very much for helping me out with this; I know it can't be easy."

"I just want to find the truth out; I just don't think Andrew would have killed himself. It just isn't in his nature; he was always the kind of person who believed the hard times only made you stronger and prepared you to better appreciate the good times."

"It sounds like he was one mature eighteen-year-old—"

"Eighteen? He wasn't eighteen. He was twenty; when he came over from Poland, he started high school over because of the language barrier."

"I didn't even think about it; I just figured he was eighteen or nineteen, like the average high school senior. Age aside, though, was there anything in the past couple of weeks that changed for the worse? Was there anyone that he pissed off or upset? Is there anyone or any reason you think someone might have wanted him dead?"

"Not at all; Andrew was liked by everyone. He carried himself like the most popular kid in school but treated everyone with equal respect no matter if they were the classroom geek or the number one jock. As I said, everyone liked Andrew; none of this makes any sense to me."

"Well, that's why I'm here. I'm going to get to the bottom of this since the police don't seem to want to do anything about it. So how are we going to get into Andrew's room?"

"First, we need to head over there. It will be best if we walk. If we drive, the night patrol will notice a car out of place, and they will probably call the head of the dorms and let them know someone might be in there that shouldn't be."

"His room is on the third floor, though, so how are we going to get in? Won't they notice if we go through the front door? And the stairwell doors can only be opened from within."

"Not necessarily; the stairway on the south side that is closest to Andrew's room has been rigged. Andrew flipped the locking mechanism one night so I could get in by sliding my ID into the lock, and it would just open up as easy as pie. He was one smart kid; he's got hiding places for his things all over his room that only I know about."

"What kind of stuff would he have to hide? If you don't mind me asking."

"Well, he had to hide the condoms; it's not like he could just leave them out. He also hid his cigarettes; he started smoking pretty badly over the past couple of months."

"All right. Well, let's get over there and make our way to his room. You go first, and I'll follow."

It did strike me as a little odd that Christine, just days after her boyfriend was found dead in his room, was walking around in the middle of the night. She was also wearing a miniskirt and tank top, as if she were looking for a date. Then again, she could just be a girl who is constantly worried about her looks, which would make her an eighteen-year-old girl. It was amazing to me that she could run in those flip-flops; then again, I've always been clumsy in flip-flops. I always end up overstepping or dragging my feet, bending the toes, and tripping over my feet.

"All right, here we are. Now all I need is a credit card or ID. Do you have something I can use?"

"Here's my driver's license. Will this work?"

"Looks like it; we've got to be extremely quiet now. No talking until we get into his room. Just stay close to me and keep a lookout for any other students."

I felt like I was in a bad spy movie with me as the older domineering spy, and Christine the young vixen helping me out. Here I am a veteran in private investigating and snooping around, and I'm taking orders from a high-school cheerleader. There are some days on this job when I really need to question my sanity, but when you are investigating a case, you have to take what you can get and roll with it. There really isn't any other way to go about it except to cross my fingers and say a prayer that this works. We made it up the stairway to the third floor, and that's where the fun started. One of the priests that lived on the third floor, at the other end of the dorm, was making his way from our end to the other side. Christine and I kept our backs against the wall and our breathing low as we waited for the priest to make his way around the corner. In this way we could make our move toward the other hallway, where we would find Andrew's room.

"All right, looks like the coast is clear; now's our only chance to go. Follow me and stay close."

"You got it, Christine."

We made it around the corner and down the hall to Andrew's door, where Christine stopped for a second. She seemed to freeze up as she realized this was the very same place her boyfriend was found dead just days earlier. There didn't seem to be anyone around, so I just let her take a moment and collect her thoughts. It was just at about the second deep breath she made when I heard a couple of guys talking down the hall behind their door, and it sounded like one of them was getting ready to leave the room to use the bathroom.

"Christine, we've got to get in the room now. It sounds like someone is about to come out in the hallway and catch us snooping around."

"I can't do it, I just can't. I'm shaking too much. Here, you're going to have to do it. Take the keys; it's this one right here with the marker on it."

"All right, no problem."

But there was a problem as I put the key in the door and started to turn the key. Nothing happened. It wasn't going to unlock; it wouldn't even budge, and now the key was stuck in the lock and not coming out. The voices got louder and louder, and I could see the door down the hallway begin to open. Now you could see the body in the door. It was a young male, probably a junior here for the summer, but he hadn't turned around just yet. Christine still couldn't stop shaking, and I had no clue what to do. I started to panic a little bit inside.

"Move, Neil; the door tends to stick in the humidity with these old locks and new keys. You just need to know how to do it."

It was right then that she snapped out of her funk and got the door open. Just before we were about to get caught, we slipped inside the doorway and quietly closed the door behind us. We were afraid to turn on the light just yet, knowing that someone was going to be in the hallway. So I took off my jacket, rolled it up, and covered the crack at the bottom of the door so we could turn on the light while Christine went over to the window and hung up a makeshift drape that Andrew had made as to give complete privacy from anyone outside of the room. He was a smart kid, that's for sure; he seemed to have his entire basis covered. This would allow Christine and me ample time to go through his room and look for anything that might help me out. It won't take me nearly as long to do it now because I have a guide who can show me through his room, including all his hiding places.

"So, besides the obvious places to look, where would he most likely hide something important to him that he might want to keep from someone else?"

"What are you looking for exactly? If I have an idea of what it might be, I might be able to figure out where he might have hidden it."

"That's the problem. I have no clue what I'm looking for. I just doubt that the police found everything that's in this room. There has to be something missing from the equation."

We spent the next thirty minutes going through the room inch by inch. We started at the door and worked our way across the room; I looked in the obvious places, and Christine looked in all the places she knew Andrew hid things. I have to say I was quite amazed by some of the places he hid things. He chiseled out a brick block from the wall and kept his condoms back there. The kid was definitely a sneaky one; Christine showed me how he had unscrewed the paneling to the wall heater and built a small box to keep his money in. I don't know if he were extremely bored or extremely paranoid; why would a high-school senior feel the need to hide so many things? There is definitely something in this room and about this kid that I can't figure out.

"Didn't it ever strike you as odd that he had all of these hiding places for his things and he didn't even have a roommate to worry about?"

"At first it did, but then he told me about the random searches they had been doing in the dorms because of a few guys getting caught with drugs and alcohol. So, he decided to be on the safe side and find a hiding place for anything and everything. He said when he was a freshman, his roommate used to steal his money and homework assignments all the time; that to me is reason enough to be a little paranoid."

"I guess that would make anyone paranoid. Being in a new country barely knowing anyone and your roommate is stealing anything and everything he can from you. It doesn't seem like we are going to find anything. I guess I could check under the bed. I know there's probably not anything down there, but it's the last place to check. Why don't you look in his chest of drawers next to the bed."

It was right then when I was looking under the bed, and I looked up at Christine, and noticed there was an envelope taped on the bottom of one of the drawers. It didn't look like much, but it's a start. It was addressed to the dorms, which didn't help much, but it was the return address that was interesting.

"Hey Christine, hold up a second; there's something taped to the bottom of that drawer."

"That's odd. I've never seen Andrew put anything there. What is it?"

"It looks like an envelope, and the return address is somewhere in—"

Right then, my phone went off, and for some reason, I forgot to turn it on vibrate. Instead, it was on full blast, and you could hear old Frank cranking out a tune. By the time I grabbed it, Christine was already at the door with the lights off, and I could tell her heart was beating just like mine. These old walls aren't as quiet as they once were; you can hear a mouse fart four rooms down the hall. I know it isn't the prettiest picture to paint, but it is the truth; this old building is as soundproof as a cardboard box. By the time my mind was done wandering off into neverland, I realized that I had Ken on the phone, and Christine was now hiding in the closet.

"Neil . . . Neil . . . are you there? Man, what's going on?"

"Quiet, Ken; I sneaked into Andrew's room with his girlfriend Christine, and my phone wasn't on vibrate. Hold on a second until I know the coast is clear."

"You fucking idiot! Now you're breaking into your alma mater's dormitory. Is there any law you aren't willing to break anymore?"

"Oh, give me a break; I've found something. It's a letter addressed to Andrew, and its return address is from somewhere in . . . I've got to let you go. I'll call you when I can. If you don't hear from me in fifteen minutes, you know the drill. Send out the boys to find me."

"Click."

18

*That's how you get anywhere as an investigator; it's putting
yourself in the right position to get lucky.*

"I think it's okay to come out of the closet, Christine. Just guessing,
but is that where Andrew would have you hide when someone would
knock on the door?"

"Could you tell? The moment I got startled, I ran for the closet. I
guess I'm just used to running there when there's a chance of getting
caught."

"Yeah, you could tell a little bit; it was a bit odd when you went
running for the closet at the drop of a hat. Either way, I think we're
in the clear; we should get out of here while we still have a chance."

"All right, I'll lead the way. As I said before, just stay close and
everything will be fine."

"I guess I don't have much of choice in the matter right, now do
I? All right, you lead the way, Christine, and I'll stay close behind."

"You know, for an old guy, you're pretty cute—"

"Let's focus on the task at hand, and what do you mean by 'old guy'? Never mind that; let's just get back to our cars, and we can talk about things there."

Getting out was a little easier than getting in; there wasn't anyone walking around or even making any noise. It only took us about ten minutes to make our way from the dorms back across the street to the elementary school, where we finally had a chance to look at the letter. It turns out that Andrew had found out who his father was. The problem is there is no name; that part is conveniently missing. The letter does go on to say that the boy isn't his, he needs to stop communicating to him, and if he doesn't stop, he will take matters into his own hands. There is also a bit in there where he tells Andrew to stop threatening him with lawyers.

It wasn't much, but it was something to go on and something to get the ball rolling, hopefully in the right direction. It may seem like a lot, but it's a lot of vague details that really don't get us anywhere. Almost like someone telling you their favorite movie is that one movie with that actor that had that one scene. I mean, they used words, made a sentence, but it was completely useless. As I stated, it's not much, but it's the only thing to go on, and sometimes you luck out on that only thing being the best thing for you to do.

"At least we are finally done with that; thanks again for everything, Christine."

"Oh, it was no problem. If you need anything else, just call me; I want to get to the bottom of this just as much as the next person. The only problem is that I'm only eighteen, and it's not like anyone will take me seriously if I go around asking questions."

"I can understand how it would be hard for me to do my job if I were just a senior in high school. I couldn't have done any of this without you; thanks, Christine. Here's my card if you think of anything at all that might help; just give me a call. Or if you need someone to talk to, I have a good friend that's good at lending a sympathetic ear."

"Thanks; I might have to take you up on that offer. For now I need to get home and get some sleep; it's getting late, and I've got to work in the morning."

"Have a safe drive home, Christine. It's late, so be safe. I'll do my best to get to the bottom of this for you, me, and all of us involved."

Christine and I each pulled out of the parking lot heading in opposite directions but probably thinking the same thing. Why would Andrew tape an envelope under his drawer? Did he just use the envelope to put something in it, or was he saving the envelope itself? It is going to be a pain trying to figure out why the envelope was there, but that's why it is such a good find. It may take me to a dead end, but hopefully it will lead me to find something else I can run with. That's how you get anywhere as an investigator; it's putting yourself in the right position to get lucky. I would be lying if I didn't say that being a good investigator took some luck; think of it like playing poker for a living.

AVE MARIA

I was almost off the expressway and a short distance from home. Which was good because I was getting both tired and anxious to send the information from the letter out to Christian and Nicolette to see what they could do with it. I hope they can come up with something from the address. If they don't get anything from it, then we are pretty much back to square one, and I do not want to break back into Andrew's room for information. With each closing of my eyelids, I became closer and closer to home. You know what it is like after a long day and night of work, and you finally make your way home, and as you get closer, it seems like with each passing blink of the eye, more and more time passes. I swear there are some nights when I'm driving around that I am surprised I made it to my destination in one piece. I could understand if there was alcohol involved, but more times than not, I am sober and dozing off behind the wheel. I guess it is true what Sheila, Ken, and my parents have been telling me for years—I need to get more sleep.

As I pulled into the driveway, I could see the girls asleep in the front window and waiting for me to get home. I know I've said it repeatedly, but I love them to death. I don't know what I would do without them. Jackie and Danielle are the spirits behind my every move, they are the reasons I keep going on. Don't get me wrong: I love my daughter more than life itself, and I would give my life to save hers without thinking twice about it, but my girls keep me going daily. They are the ones that keep me warm at night, they are the ones that greet me at the door, and they are the ones that know how to pick me up when I'm down. Just to see those smiles on their faces when I come home is an uncontrollable joy when I've been gone working; it just warms my soul. Tonight was no different from any other late night. They greeted me with as much enthusiasm as they could muster before they made their way into the bedroom to curl up and sleep. All that was left was for me to curl up with them and pass out; before I could do that, I needed to get this envelope scanned and emailed to Christian and Nicolette.

I made my way into my office downstairs and quickly got to work so I could join Jackie and Danielle in that lovely place called dreamland. I was in major need of a good night's rest curled up with the girls, and tonight was just the night for it. After about ten minutes of working in the office, I stumbled my way back up the stairs, where I was greeted by the girls in my bedroom. I quickly changed out of my clothes, slid into bed, and was off to sleep, or at least that's what I thought. About an hour into sleeping, the case took a turn toward the unforeseen.

"Neil, wake up; wake up, Neil. I know it's in the middle of the night there, but Nicolette and I are at the address that was on the envelope you scanned and sent."

"So what's the big deal? What is so urgent that there is something that will help the case?"

"I really don't know, Neil; we're standing in front of the headquarters of the Archdiocese of Warsaw, Poland. According to the address from the envelope, it means that days before Andrew's death, he was contacted by someone from the archdiocese in Warsaw. What the hell is going on here, Neil?"

"I wish I knew, Christian; I wish I knew. I'm going to need you and Nicolette to do your best, trying to track down who wrote that letter. Try anything and everything possible, from seduction to bribery. If it comes to it breaking and entering, we need to figure out why the Church is so involved in this kid's life and what they are hiding from us."

"That's where we come in. It's our job to get to the bottom of everything; I guess you guys will just have to keep an eye out on the building and see what you can come up with."

"Nicolette and I should be able to figure something out; we'll start with getting ahold of everyone that works in the building, and I mean everyone. We'll even hit up the janitors, since they usually know more than many will believe; you taught me that."

"That's right, start at the bottom and work up the ladder; a lot of times you'll be able to get dirt on the higher-ups from the cleaning help and secretaries. That's how you get to the people you need information on; you need to work with the people that work for the people you are trying to get information from."

"You got it, boss. We'll get to work as soon as I get off the phone with you. Just one question: if I have to bribe, what should I keep the budget at?"

"You should be able to bribe the lower-end employees with simple amounts, such as fifty or a hundred. But you should never make the first offer over twenty dollars, mainly because it's pointless and because I'm not made of money."

AVE MARIA

"Got it, Neil; we'll make sure and only use it as a last resort for information. I'll keep you up to date with any information we get along the way."

"Sounds good; you guys are doing a good job over there. Keep up the good work, and I'll talk to you later."

"All right, go back to sleep, and we'll keep you informed; talk to you later, boss."

Go back to sleep? Like I'm going to be able to go back to sleep after news like that? My mind has just gone into overdrive, and it is not pretty. I'm going to have to throw on a pot of coffee because it's going to be a long-ass night. I've got to figure out a reasonable explanation for all of this. I should probably call Ken as well and tell him of the breakthrough; even though it's late, he would want to know. This is the same old shit with all the cases I seem to get myself into; just once I would like a simple case that wasn't like trying to find a good disco record. There just isn't one. I know it's a low blow to a disco, but it's the truth. As for Ken, I need to grab my cell phone and call him; the only tricky part is going to be sliding out of bed without disrupting the girls' sleeping, since I have one on either side of me right now. With a little patience and trickery, I should be able to get out of this without waking them up.

"Neil, what the hell are you doing calling me at four in the morning? Do you ever go to sleep, or do you just stay awake twenty-four hours a day?"

"Christian and Nicolette called me with some information about the envelope I found in Andrew's room."

"What envelope?"

"Oh yeah, I forgot to inform you of the find. I found an envelope taped to the bottom of his dresser that was postdated about five days before his death. On top of it, the return address was from Warsaw, Poland."

"So what's the big news? Did they find something to finally blow this case open?"

"Not quite. It just complicates things more, but it helps us stay in the right direction. The return address on the envelope is for the headquarters of the Archdiocese of Warsaw, Poland."

"Are you fucking kidding me? That means there is something that was in that letter that we need to get our hands on. Either Andrew hid the letter, or someone from the Church got in there and grabbed it before anyone could read it. There has to be something in that letter worth killing for—or worth dying for, for that matter."

After I got off the phone with Ken, I couldn't help but wonder how Christian and Nicolette will be able to get into the archdiocese office. It's not like they could just walk in and just start poking around without anyone noticing that they are there in an archdiocese, especially in a country such as Poland, which has a very strong religious background. There aren't going to be strangers in the building at any time unless they are a new priest. Last time I checked. Christian wasn't much of the religious type, so that shoots that idea; maybe Nicolette can seduce someone and get information out of them. There really isn't anything else I can do right now except go downstairs and put a good hour or so in on the heavy bag and try and come up with some ideas on where the hell this case is taking us.

The girls seem to have the same idea as I did; that is an early morning workout before I could even make it to the kitchen. The two of them flew out of bed and over to the back door and out into the yard, just rolling around in what looked like a nice mud puddle. Lucky me, it's raining outside; it looks like I'm going to have to lock the girls out so I can clean them off before they come back in. They should be good for at least a good hour out there; they've got their doghouse as well as plenty of mud puddles to splash around in. I need to get downstairs and get to work on that heavy bag while I still have the motivation within me. It just drives me crazy that every time I think I might have come up with a feasible explanation to what is going on in this case, something like this letter pops up and throws me off course.

Imagine that you were a cross-country runner. Just when you think you were on the right path to get to the finish line, someone came up behind you, blindfolded, you spun you around and threw you off the beaten path. That's what it feels like right now; I am at a loss for explanation and for words. For those who know me, it is a rare occasion that I am at a loss for something to say, so you can imagine how frustrating this case is right now. I just don't understand where this case is leading. One of the biggest problems is I don't have a concrete starting point; it would be like getting dropped off in the middle of a large cornfield and someone telling you to find your way out. You don't have a true starting point, so it is extremely hard to figure out where to go.

This case started at Orchard Lake St. Mary's, and it keeps bringing me back there, but to no avail. I keep finding a few small pieces of information, but nothing I can really sink my teeth into and run with. I've gotten to the point that I'm even questioning the whole idea that it was a murder; I'm starting to think it could have been a suicide except he didn't do it there. I am almost certain that whatever happened, whether it is a suicide or a murder, it didn't happen in his room. There are just no signs of struggle for it to have happened there. Even with a suicide almost all (I would say all of the time, but there's always an exception to the rule) the time the person will struggle with themselves at the last minute, regretting the decision, except for when using a gun. Once you pull the trigger, you've pretty much given up hope for changing your mind; there's no going back once that bullet leaves the chamber.

Before I even get started, I decided to go with a change in music tonight; it wasn't a Frank moment. Tonight called for a different sound track, something light on the lyrics and heavy on the track. That's right, it's a BT night. For those of you not familiar with techno music, BT is the only techno/electronic musician I can listen to. He just has a different sound about him that draws you in. When I throw on one of his albums, I just get lost in the music, and it really makes for a good meditation, even when I'm putting some work in on the heavy bag.

AVE MARIA

As the music starts to fade in and take over the room, I begin to put on my wraps and get my hands ready for the next hour of hell I'm going to give this bag. The music continues to get louder and louder with each passing minute, slowly building to an explosion of raw energy. It's at this moment that I start to work the bag with professional precision, leaning in with the jab and following up with a cross and working to a four-punch combination jab, cross, hook, and uppercut. With each blow I'm focusing on the frustration this case has been, and as each fact in the case comes into view, I begin to hit the bag harder and harder. As the sweat starts to drip down my face, I start to cross over from hitting a heavy bag to dealing with all the emotional baggage I've been carrying with me since the last time I worked out on this bag. The fears I carry of failing as a father to Carol Lynn or as a friend to Sheila; I know we've been divorced for years, but I still love and care for her. I can feel my arms starting to fatigue as the CD enters the sixth track, which on a BT CD is about thirty minutes in. I don't want to stop, but I know I need to make a transition from hitting the heavy bag over to the speed bag for a while.

The emotion runs from my thoughts and into my arms; I get lost in the rhythm from the music, allowing the beat of the speed bag bouncing back and forth so effortlessly. My vision starts to blur as sweat drips down into my eyes, causing me to focus that much harder; I'm on a roll right now, and I'm not about to stop just to wipe the sweat from my brow. At just about that moment I felt an odd feeling just below my knee; it felt like something was rubbing me. It was Jackie licking the sweat from my leg; I've never understood why dogs do that, although they say it's for the salt. Besides the fact that Jackie had somehow made her way back into the house, the interesting thing was that Danielle wasn't down here, which meant only one thing: Sheila must have stopped by. I say that because the only time Jackie and Danielle aren't attached at the hip is when Sheila is over. Danielle has always had an attachment to Sheila ever since Danielle was a pup.

"Don't stop on my account, babe; you know how much I love it when you work up a good sweat."

"Glad I could oblige you this early in the morning. What brings you by the house so early?"

"If you want me to leave, I can leave; do you have company? I didn't notice any other car in the driveway, so I figured it was safe to come in."

"You're fine. There's no one here; I was just wondering what had you out and about so early."

"I just wasn't feeling good, and I took a chance that you would be up. Mom's at the house, keeping an eye on Carol Lynn; she ended up staying the night last night. We were up late talking, and she decided to stay the night."

"How's your mom doing these days?"

"She's doing all right; her age is catching up to her. Then again, I guess it should, seeing as she's almost ninety."

"You would never guess it, though she's always out and about doing something, it seems like. You'll have to tell her that her favorite ex-son-in-law says hi."

"Can do, babe. So, how's the case coming? I didn't hear from you the past couple of days, so I figured you are either rolling or you're extremely frustrated."

"The latter of the two; I just can't seem to catch any breaks with this one. I'm worried that I won't be able to figure out this one. I know I can't solve every case I take on."

"Even though you have finished every case so far to date, the only case you didn't finish took you a few extra years. The important thing is that you did finish it, regardless of how long it took you."

"I guess so, but I worry about failure; you know I don't take it very well. Look how I took it when we decided to get a divorce—you almost shot me, I was being so difficult. I just don't like to admit defeat of any kind."

"I remember very vividly; you were a poor sap of a man. That's why I worry about you; sometimes you push too hard. Then again, it is probably that very same reason that makes you so good at your job. What kind of problems are you having? Maybe I can help you; I've always been good at deciphering your thoughts for you."

"All right. Let me turn the music down a little bit and we'll get to work on it. Is it okay if I keep hitting the bag while we talk?"

"As I said when I walked in, I love it when you work up a good sweat."

"As for the case, the reason I'm having so much trouble is there just doesn't seem to be any consistency in what we find."

"It might be the way you are looking at it. Ever think of that?"

"Let me give you the facts in no particular order and we'll see what you come up with. There was an envelope addressed to Andrew from the Archdiocese of Warsaw, Poland, and it was received just days before his death. Andrew's body was found in his dorm room; the only problem is there is no evidence that he died there. In fact, it is nearly impossible that he did die there. And the other piece of the puzzle we have is the fact that the Catholic Church has a vested interest in this case because they are hiding Andrew's mother as well as covering up evidence. Not to mention the fact that they have been tailing me since the night I was out at the crime scene."

"No wonder you are having trouble with this; you really don't have much to go on. It seems like you are trying to figure out the puzzle with very few pieces. Regardless of it's a murder or a suicide, the big question that needs to be answered is why does the Catholic Church have such an interest in this boy and his family? Do they think he was a saint?"

"I highly doubt it; according to his girlfriend, that would not be the case."

"I have an idea. Why don't you focus on the connection between Andrew and the Church and start there? Once you figure that out, you should be able to come up with reasons for his death. I think you need to narrow the picture a little bit before you can broaden your spectrum."

"Thanks, babe; I knew there was a reason we got married and divorced. You know me too well; I can't believe I couldn't figure that out on my own."

AVE MARIA

"Like I said, babe, sometimes you think too hard and try too much. You need to step back and take a fresh view of everything."

"Well, since you're here, how's about I cook you up some breakfast?"

"I've had your cooking, and don't get me wrong, you are good, but you can't cook an egg to save your life. How about you hop in the shower and clean up while I throw together some breakfast?"

"Sounds good, Sheila. Thanks again for everything; you truly are my best friend."

"Quit being such a sap; you know you suck at it. Go shower up, stinky, and I'll get some grub together."

A swift kick in the pants was just what the doctor ordered, or as many know her, Sheila. She has always known how to get me refocused and remotivated. Then again, we've been through it all, from the happy dating period all the way to the not so happy divorce. Now we are the best of friends whose friendship was probably saved because of our divorce. We were just beating each other up as a married couple; some people are meant to be friends, and we are definitely those people. As for the shower, it was great as usual. I could have stayed in there a lot longer, but I decided it would be best if I got out in a decent time since Sheila is cooking breakfast.

"Hey, Sheila, thanks for making breakfast; everything smells great."

"I made everything just like you, like cream and sugar with a little coffee—"

"Ha, ha, very funny. Aren't we the comedienne this morning?"

"I also made your eggs over easy on toast with a side of bacon, just like you like it."

"Not bad, not bad at all. I am very impressed you can still cook a mean breakfast, can't you?"

"Well, our daughter has to eat something in the morning. You know I don't allow her to leave in the morning without a healthy breakfast."

"That's true. We wouldn't want her ending up like her old man, addicted to coffee and any other form of caffeine. We've seen the wonders it's done for my body and being mistaken for a lot older than I really am; that wore off in about my early twenties."

"You are so cute when you get all neurotic about getting old, do you know that? I see why Maria couldn't get over you the first time you guys went out. Then again, she didn't marry you, as did I."

"That was a low blow, and you know it; we had a lot of fun together. Although I have to admit, I think we had more fun before and after the marriage."

"I didn't say I wasn't glad I married you because if we never got married, we wouldn't have had Carol Lynn and gotten divorced, and I'm happy with the way things are now. It works for us, and you can't debate that fact."

"That's true. Things have really turned out pretty good. We still care about each other and have a great daughter and an even better friendship."

"That's the spirit, babe; well, I should be getting back. I have a doctor's appointment at eleven to have some tests done."

"That reminds me—how everything is going with that? Have the doctors pinpointed anything yet?"

"They really aren't sure yet, but they are pretty sure that after these tests we should have a better picture of everything."

"Well, why don't you give me a call later tonight and give me an update on how things are doing. Sound good?

"Can do, babe; take care of yourself, and good luck with everything. I'll give Carol Lynn a big hug for you. You should give her a call later tonight or even stop by if you can."

"I'll try my best to be there. Talk to you later, and good luck on the test today."

Now that Sheila is gone, it is time for me to hit my second wind with Andrew's case and begin to break down the connection between the Church and Andrew. I figure the best way to figure out what the connection is would be to come up with a list of possibilities and then look into each one and see how many I disprove. Sometimes one of the best ways to find the right answer is to find what it isn't and go from there; that way, it narrows the field. It looks like it is the only way I'm going to find any solid ground in this case. I guess it's time to call Ken and Tony and get a meeting together at the office for some brainstorming.

19

As I made my way down Eight Mile toward the gentlemen's club, I noticed the two priests slightly drop off.

I finally made it out of the house and into the car, eventually starting my way out to the warehouse before I even had a chance to call Ken or Tony. The one thing I was positive of was that Ken and Tony were going to be there: Tony pretty much lives there. He even has a futon in his office for those late nights working on a tech job; he's worse than I am when it comes to working too much, if that can be possible. Neither I, Ken, or Tony has a life outside of work; at least not much of one. But that is the reason that we are so good at our jobs; we are overly dedicated. Enough about that, though; I need to call Ken before I get out to the warehouse to make sure everything can be set up.

"Hey Neil, how's it going? Thanks again for the late-night wake-up call."

"No problem, Ken. You know I'm always there to keep you on your toes. Is Tony there by any chance?"

"Yeah, he's around here somewhere. He got here shortly after I did, at about nine this morning. We figured you'd be here already wired out of coffee from being up all night."

"Close. I was up all night wailing on the heavy and speed bags, and then this morning Sheila stopped by and made some coffee."

"Sheila stopped by this morning, huh. That means that you probably have a new clear view of where to take this case. So what are we going to do when you get here?"

"We are going to come up with any and every possible connection between Andrew and the Catholic Church, and then we are going to look into each one. And every time we disprove one, we'll move on to the next until we are left with a very small window of possibilities to focus on."

"Sounds like the only way we are going to have a shot at this case. I'll have Tony get some things together, and we'll get a few teams together that can start researching the ideas we get before the day is out."

"Sounds like a plan; I'm going to stop and pick up some coffee and doughnuts on my way in for everyone. I'll be out there in about twenty minutes. Is there anything I can pick up for you or Tony?"

"If you stop by a gas station, can you pick up a few energy drinks for me. I forgot to pick some up today while I was out getting gas. I think Tony will take his usual French vanilla cappuccino from any gas station you can find. You know he's not much for the fancy French vanilla."

"Yeah, I know what he wants; I'll be out there with the full order, and we'll get to work on everything."

"I'll see you in a little bit, Neil; get here safely and say hi to the priests behind you in the old blue reliant. I sent out a couple of guys to scout your house, and they called in and told me you were being followed by the Church again."

"Well, then I might not be there right away. I think I'm going to have a little fun with them. I'm thinking of dropping my car off at a strip club downtown and sneaking out the back door and having one of the guys pick me up, just to see if we can get the two priests to walk in the club to check and see if I'm in there. We'll have to keep a tail on them so we can get some surveillance of them walking in."

"You know you really have issues, Neil? Then again, it really does sound like a little fun; plus we could use some blackmail photos to use on some of these guys to try and get some information from them. How's about you go to Players on Eight Mile, and I'll have a couple of guys waiting for you out back so you can get out of there without them knowing?"

"Sounds good. How about you have them meet me there in fifteen minutes or so?"

"I can have a car out back, waiting for you."

Shortly after I got off the phone with Ken, I looked in my rearview mirror and noticed the car with the same two priests that had been following me days earlier. I know it's wrong for me to try and find a way to get two priests to walk into a strip club, but hey, it's what keeps me smiling and keeps these guys guessing. I look at the situation as if I'm teaching the Catholic Church the art of surveillance. This way, the Church will be better prepared the next time they are trying to track down information by following someone. Not to mention I'm giving two older priests a legitimate reason to walk in and look around a strip club; I know I care about my fellow man.

As I made my way down Eight Mile toward the gentlemen's club, I noticed the two priests slightly drop off. I had a feeling they knew where I was heading, and they wanted to do their best to stay back and not to get caught. I made my way into the turnaround to pull into the parking lot of the club and found a place to park. At the very same moment, I saw the car that was following me pull into a gas station across the street and sit and wait. Little did they know that I was only going to be in there for about ten minutes to say hi to a few people. Then I'm sneaking out the back and hitching a ride with a couple of my employees. I wonder how long those two guys are going to sit there and wait before they go inside to check and see if I'm in there. I think this situation calls for a square bet; I'll have Ken get something together at the warehouse.

"Hey Ken, I know I just got off the phone with you, but can you have the two guys following the priests stay on them until they go in?"

"Why? What do you have in mind?"

"Get a betting pool together on how long it will take those two priests before they go to the club; it should be some fun. In blocks of fifteen minutes to see how long it takes for them to drive across the street and walk into the gentlemen's club."

"Now you are having twice the fun at the expense of your two shadows. Aren't you nice?"

"Hey, it's not my fault that I get my kicks out of messing with two middle-aged priests that are stuck having to follow me around all day. The least I can do is treat them to a little skin bar, seeing as they are serving the Lord and have taken a vow of abstinence."

"Why do I have a feeling that has nothing to do with it? You just want the guys following the guys following you to take pictures of the two priests walking into a skin bar."

"Never mind the reason; all that matters is that I win the bet. Put me down for three hours before they go in."

"You think they'll wait that long? All right, you're the boss; I'll put you down for three hours. Have fun sneaking out the back, and say hi to Carson 'The Keg' if he's there."

"You got it. I'll make sure and say hi to him for you. See you in a few, Ken."

I got off the phone with Ken and walked into what is definitely a depressing sight. It's bad enough to be in a skin bar, but to be there during lunchtime is even worse. Let's just say you see the best of the best when you walk in. Usually, the dancers are girls who have nothing better to do, or they are new, so it's not much of a show. To be honest, usually, the lunchtime girls are somewhere between a four and a six on a scale from one to ten. I don't make the rules. I just state them and break them occasionally. As for the patrons in the bar, they are even better; you'll find a few guys that have been there all night and morning and have nothing better to do. Or you can find my favorite guy, the one that has fallen in love with a dancer and who eats up everything she says to him. Spending every dollar, he's trying for a chance at what he thinks is a relationship. Before I even look at the girl who is there to take cover, paying cover at lunch for a skin bar is hilarious, but regardless I have to talk to her and tell her what's up.

"Hey honey, it's going to be ten dollars today."

"I'm not here for the dancers; is Carson 'The Keg' here?"

"Yeah, he is. Want me to get him for you?"

No, I just wondered where he was; I just figured I'd drive out here to see if he was working and leave without talking to him. What kind of idiotic question is that? People do that all the time on many different occasions; hell, I do that shit still. It drives me up the wall.

"Yes, if you could get him for me, that would be great. Tell him Baggio wants to see him."

"Can do; just wait right here for a second."

After a few minutes of smiling and waving off the limited selection of dancers, Carson finally came around the corner and greeted me with a big bear hug, lifting me off the floor.

"Hey Baggio, how you doing, bro? I haven't seen you or Ken around here in quite some time. Not since you and Ken were doing some work for one of our dancers who lost her daughter. Which reminds me the owner said if you guys ever come in again, everything is on the house."

"Why would the owner say that? Did he end up marrying Candy?"

"You better believe it; they got really close while her ex-husband kidnapped her daughter, and they fell in love. Now the three of them are living happily ever after and running this place. Candy's actually taken over as a manager here, and she's done a great job. The place is doing better than ever."

"I'll have to tell Ken about that; we're working on a big case, but when we're done, we'll have to come out and kick it for a night."

"Sounds good to me. Hey, if you guys ever have any bodyguard work and you need someone to fill in, you think you can call me? I'm always looking to make some extra cash."

"That's no problem, Carson. Here's my card; give me a call in about a week, and we'll set some stuff up for you. As for right now, I need to slide out the back door to evade a tail. I've got some guys waiting out back to pick me up."

"No problem, I've got you covered. Follow me, and we'll get you out of here undetected. If anyone comes asking for you, I'll say you are in the VIP room dropping coins. Just to make them hang around even longer."

"My man, thanks a lot. Oh, by the way, I'm being followed by two priests you'll know when they eventually work their way in here to look for me."

"I'm not even going to ask why you've got two priests following you. Just take care, and I'll call you next week."

I made my way out the back door and down the alley, where the car was waiting for me. It was two of the guys from the warehouse tooling around in my old Jeep Cherokee. I can't get away from this car, I swear; this thing will be running longer than I will. The good news is, according to my guys that are tailing the two priests, it doesn't look like they've caught on to what's going on, which means I should be tail-free for the rest of the night.

"So guys, how are we doing today? Anything major going on?"

"You mean other than the usual when working for you?"

"Good point; it rarely is a dull moment when you have to work with me. At least you can say you never know what each day of work is going to bring."

"True, very true. Now keep your head down; we are about to pass the gas station where they are staking out your car and what they think is you at a strip club."

Before we could head to the warehouse, I made sure and had the guys drive by a gas station so I could pick up Ken and Tony's beverages. Although I am having plenty of fun at the expense of those two guys following me around, I still needed to get the drinks I promised Ken and Tony before I show up at the office. If I didn't get them their drinks, I know I wouldn't ever hear the end of it. Especially since I've got my coffee in hand, and it wouldn't look good if I showed up with my coffee but not their drinks. In Tony's case, it's a French vanilla cappuccino from any gas station, and Ken will take his usual energy drink. I mean Ken has got his favorites for the most part, but he's more interested in gaining an energy buzz than in how good it tastes.

After a detour to the gas station, we finally made our way back to the warehouse, where it seemed to be empty; there wasn't a soul around. The lot is full, which means there should be at least fifteen or so people around here somewhere; I'll just drop off the drinks at the gym, where Ken has set up the temporary office that we used last night. From the looks of things, though, that is where everyone seems to be. It looks as if Ken is leading some kind of brainstorm.

"All right, guys, can we come up with any more ideas of how these two are connected?"

I could only assume that Ken was leading a brainstorm of how the Church is connected to Andrew in this case. From the looks of the dry erase board, they seem to have a decent amount of ideas listed there; I knew I could count on Tony and Ken to help me stay on top of this case. They know how to work with and around me at the same time. In that way we are continuously working together instead of against each other. It really is an amazing thing to see all these people willing to help on a case for which they know they won't be getting any money or any other form of reward.

"Hey Neil, nice of you to join us; the guys and I were just brainstorming to come up with as many ideas as we can that might connect Andrew and the Catholic Church. Some are off the wall, and others seem unlikely, but the fact is we have a bunch of different ideas to roll with now."

"Sounds good; we'll go over the list in a few minutes. As for now, I've got your energy drinks in the bag here. As for you, Tony, I've got your coffee here in my hand; I already drank my cup."

"Thanks, Neil, for picking that up. I was running out of energy to burn. I was in major need of a French vanilla cappuccino. I'm working on an algorithm that will help us figure out the likelihood of each connection between Andrew and the Church. It will help with the probability the connection is—"

"Stop what you are doing right now; we are going to have to disprove any and all of these ideas with cold, hard facts from investigations and nothing less. I know it is a little old school, but I don't want to jump to any conclusions with this case. We are going to have to look into every possibility we can think of until we come up with more information."

"Are you thinking once we have an idea of the connection between the two parties that we might be able to track down what exactly happened to Andrew?"

"That's exactly what I'm saying, Tony; we should be able to investigate the majority of these in the next day or so in groups. We'll have to go through and group together the ideas by means of how we will investigate them. This way, we will have an idea of where to start looking; before we can find the finish line, we need to figure out where we are starting. That's the problem with this case right now; we don't have a starting point. We have a good idea of where it might be or where we might want it to be, but other than that, we are pretty much at a loss for ideas."

"Let's get to work, then; the sooner we get this list grouped and separated, the sooner we can start investigating it, and the sooner we can find our starting point in this case. Ken told me about the envelope and how it had come from the Archdiocese of Warsaw in Poland."

"I don't get it why the hell is the archdiocese in Poland or at least someone there is involved with Andrew. I really don't understand it—"

"Nobody does; that is why we are coming up with as many connections between them that we can think of. If it did make sense, we wouldn't have any problems, now would we? I'm sorry if that came out kind of shitty; I'm just going crazy with this case, and it's starting to get to me."

"I know it isn't anything personal; we all know that you get worked up because you invest so much into each case you work. It's because you take things so personally that you get the job done so consistently."

"Thanks, Tony, it means a lot that you guys around here understand. But it still doesn't make it right when I start to snap back and get sarcastic."

"Can we please stop this behavior? You two are acting like high-school girls making up after fighting over a guy. Can we get back to this case and focus for a bit?"

"All right, let's get started by separating all connections we came up with into groups. From there, we will send some people out to investigate the connection, and with each failure, we'll get a little closer."

"Okay, guys, let's get down to business and start separating. What's the first connection we've come up with?"

AVE MARIA

"First up is the idea that he is related to someone at the archdiocese in Poland. Whether it may be his father, uncle, or even brother; either way, it would fall under family connection."

We spent the next couple of hours going over every idea everyone had come up with and set up a plan of attack. There wasn't anything we could do more than setting up a plan of attack. We sent Tony off to get the tech team on the project with background information on anyone and everyone at the archdiocesan office in Warsaw. As for Ken and me, we went up to the office, then began assigning some of the other investigators to look into each connection. The one thing that is driving us nuts more than the fact that this case is like trying to find your way through the labyrinth. For those of you not familiar with the labyrinth, I'll give you a quick lesson in Greek mythology. The labyrinth was built and designed by a man named Daedalus, who was commissioned by a king to create a maze that would entrap a monster known as the Minotaur. The Minotaur was believed to be the half child of a bull given to the king by Poseidon, the god of the sea. When the king didn't sacrifice the bull, Poseidon had presented the king's wife, then fell in love with the bull and, in the end, gave birth to the Minotaur. It was after the birth of the Minotaur that the king asked Daedalus to create an inescapable maze that no one could enter or leave.

I know this seems like a bit off course. This case is a lot like the labyrinth in that we fell in love with the idea that took us off course. Now we are lost in the labyrinth that is this case. Every time we find a way to the end, the puzzle changes on us, and we have to start over.

I know it seems like I've smoked too much whacky tobaccy and that I'm getting a little off course, but that's what happens to me when I get a case that takes so many turns like this. When I start to get stuck in a case, I start to compare my situation with historical events. You can thank my high-school mythology teacher for that one. I seem to hang on to some of the oddest things I learned in high school. I guess it's a safety net for me; when I have no direction to go in a case, I resort to a comfortable place, such as historical knowledge. Before my brain could take me on a historical flyby, I felt my phone vibrating in my pocket. Of course, now I have it on vibrate, not last night, when I needed it to be. It is just my luck that I have it on vibrate for no reason whatsoever, but the time I need it to be, I have it on full blast.

"Hey babe, how are you doing today? How is Carol Lynn doing?"

"We're doing great. I was wondering if you might be interested in grabbing some dinner. We could even just order in if you would like."

"That sounds very tempting, very tempting, indeed. What time do you think you want to meet up?"

"Well, it's only a little after one in the afternoon now, so that puts me back in Detroit at about three o'clock. Plus the time it would take me to get ready, so I would say any time after five or six. Will that work for you?"

"I can make it work; we are at a bit of a stalemate anyway with the case right now. Tomorrow should shed some new light on everything; at least that's the hope we all have."

"Well then, shouldn't you be doing any work on the case? I mean, it seems like you're always waiting for information to get back to you."

"That's one of the nice things about running and owning your own investigation company. You can do the hard work, such as sifting through all the information and figuring everything out, and you can leave the rest of the work to the other employees. Plus we are on a short timetable, and I've got more than thirty people working on this case to get as much information as possible and as quickly as possible. I've actually got to meet up with an old friend before we get together for dinner tonight. So how about we say that we meet at my place at seven thirty and we can order in. Sound good?"

"Sounds just great. I'll see you there, and if you are running late, just let me know, and I can come a little later."

"Okay, I'll see you at about seven thirty tonight. I'll call you if anything comes up."

As I got off the phone, I decided I needed to talk to Father Roberts and track down where Cardinal Kelley is. I require some information and some feather rustling. I have a feeling there is something that the cardinal isn't telling me, even though I scared the crap out of him early in the week with the whole anthrax thing in the confessional. Even I impressed myself with that one; I was proud that I came up with that whole scheme on such short notice. I know it's not cool to toot one's own horn, but every once in a while it isn't so bad to give yourself credit for something you did, as long as you don't run around telling everyone you're happy for yourself. I hope Father Roberts has time to talk. I really need to get some guidance on this one, and I'm not talking of spiritual guidance. I'm talking of the kind of guidance only someone that has known me since we were in diapers kind of guidance.

"Hey Neil, how are you doing? I see you haven't completely pissed off the whole Church just yet. How are things going with the case?"

"They could be a lot better, but we might have just stumbled on some key evidence as to what happened with this kid. It seems as though someone from the headquarters of the Archdiocese of Warsaw in Poland wrote a letter to Andrew that he received less than a week before he died. The only problem is the letter is nowhere to be found, just the envelope it came in."

"How do you know it was a letter and not something else? It could have been anything in that envelope."

"I'm just making an educated guess that it wasn't anthrax and that the Church wasn't sending him cash or checks in the mail for a job well done. All I'm left with is the usual suspect that comes in an envelope: a letter."

"All right, smart-ass, you could have just said it was your best guess. You didn't need to be pompous as usual about it. Anyway, what can I do for you on this fine afternoon?"

"I need some guidance, Father; I'm at a cross in the road, and I just need someone to talk to about things. Do you have time now, or would it be best to meet later or tomorrow?"

"I can talk now. It's okay, there isn't anyone around, and I'm talking on the cell you got me, so we are pretty much in the clear of eavesdroppers."

"It's this case—it's driving me mad; I just don't understand how or why the Church was protecting or what seems like hiding Andrew and his mother. On top of it, now I'm at a complete loss because someone made contact with him from the Archdiocese of Warsaw just days before his death. It just doesn't add up, and I can't think of a reason for any of this."

"I think your problem is your faith is still getting in the way a little bit. You—"

"You and I both know that has never been a problem with me. I'm always able to put that aside, sometimes a little too easily."

"Wait a second and hear me out. What I mean by your faith is the fact that you were raised a Catholic that believed priests and cardinals and anyone else that does the Lord's bidding is infallible. And you and I both know that is not true; people who devote their lives to serving the Lord are just as vulnerable to temptation as the next person. I think you need to stop looking at this like it's a matter of faith and imagine if it was just another organization that was contacting him and ask yourself why."

"I get it; you're saying that I might be missing some obvious connections because I am not allowing them in the picture because of my past beliefs and the view of those who serve the Lord that I have created or was created for me."

"You have always been one to be skeptical of those around you, especially those who work in the Church, and it seems to be like this time, of all the times you need to be, you aren't skeptical at all."

"Is there something you know but aren't telling me?"

"No, there isn't, but there is one thing I do know, and that is even those who serve the Lord make mistakes and have regrets for things they have done or continue to do."

"I'm starting to hear you loud and clear, Father; thanks for everything and have a blessed evening."

"You too, Neil, and may your thoughts be clear of any doubt or disbelief of your own abilities."

The phone conversation was just what I needed. It seems like the people I have counted on most in my life are helping more now than ever; without Sheila or Father Roberts, I don't know where I'd be. Wait a minute: I forgot to ask him if he knows where Cardinal Kelley is today, but then again, I don't need to drag him into this. I am sure that we are still tailing him and a few other key people the cardinal has been in contact with. I just need to call Ken and ask him to track him down for me so I can have a little chat with him.

20

I've grown accustomed to doing it this way.

It's about two thirty in the afternoon, and I need to track down Cardinal Kelley to see if I can get any more information out of him about Andrew and this case. The hard thing isn't going to be tracking him down, since we've had a tail on him and his assistant since the incident at St. Patrick's Church a few days ago. The hardest part is going to be getting information out of Cardinal Kelley without letting him know what little information we have. I'm sure I've got an email on my phone somewhere from Lenny, who is one of three guys keeping an eye on Cardinal Kelley. Let's just hope he isn't doing some sort of event tonight; I wouldn't mind getting to him privately at his home.

"Hey Neil, how are you doing? Did you get my message I left you earlier about Cardinal Kelley?"

"Yeah, I got it. I was just calling to see where he was and if you know he's going to be around for a bit because I was thinking of dropping in on him and having a chat with him. Do you think he's going to be available for me today?"

"Judging by his behavior since the run-in he had with you, he's been pretty quiet. He hasn't done anything outside of going to church during the day, and he's usually back to his condo between five and five thirty like clockwork."

"You said he's got a condo, correct?"

"Let's put it this way: if I knew I'd be driving a brand-new Chrysler Three Hundred M and be living in a condo like his, I would have joined the priesthood right out of high school."

"Wow! It's amazing to me that they put them up so well. Where is the condo? Are we talking downriver, or are we talking out on the West Side?"

"To make it simpler on everyone, I'll just send the address to your phone, and you can just plug it into the navigation system. I'll keep you updated if anything changes; it doesn't seem like he's going anywhere today. He's been holed up in his condo since early this morning, and I highly doubt he's going anywhere. He hasn't even had any visitors all day, and from the looks of things, he's there all alone."

"Not bad; it should be pretty easy for me to get in there and talk to him then. Surprisingly, something, in this case, is actually going to be easy for a change."

"Now that you just said that though you probably just jinxed it, especially with our luck we've been having lately."

"That's true, very true indeed. I'll be heading out there shortly; just give me a heads up if someone shows up or he decides to head out."

"You got it, Neil; I'll be here keeping an eye on him for another couple of hours. After six I'm out of here, and Lisa comes on for the night run."

"All right, Lenny, I'll make sure and see you out there shortly."

As I got off the phone, I realized that I had made plans to go see Cappelano at the prison to get his perspective on everything. I'll have to make sure and call the prison and let them know I won't be able to get out there until tomorrow. Although by now, they are used to me standing him up. I've done it so many times over the past couple of months; then again, it's not like he's going to be headed anywhere any time soon. I know it's meant to use him only when I need him and stand him up all the time, but hey, I earned it after it took me four extra years to catch the bastard. Then again, it was nice of him to give me a second chance to catch him. Either way I look at it, he's stuck behind bars for the rest of his life, so I might as well use his crazy ass and the knowledge he's gained from being a former FBI agent/ psycho killer. He has the knowledge of the system and investigating that I have. Plus the habits of a crazy son of a bitch that likes to kill people for shits and giggles.

After tonight, hopefully, the team will be able to unearth some information on the connections we've come up with. The odd thing about it all is that I'm hoping that they disprove about 90 percent of them so that I will have something to work with. I know lately that it seems like I don't do any work at all, especially with researching this case, but I've learned over the years that in cases that hit close to home and that involve you on a more emotional level sometimes it's best to have someone else to do the footwork and then I just have to worry about piecing everything together.

I've grown accustomed to doing it this way, especially recently, because this case has just gotten my mind all clouded and full of doubt in myself and what little faith I have left. The nice thing about having the investigators at my disposal to do the research is that their judgment is not clouded, as is mine. They will be completely objective when investigating this case, and when you are in a case like this, you need to be as objective as possible. Because the amount of information to deal with is very limited, and you can't have one's judgment clouded when investigating a case that has very little or thin facts. I guess the best way to look at it is I'm trying to make sure that my own overthinking doesn't get in the way of the investigation.

As my mind wandered off into a reality in which I question myself and every move I've made in this case, I found myself driving down the road and heading out toward Cardinal Kelley's condo, where I was hoping to find only himself and Lenny, the investigator we've been paying to tail him. I'm only about ten minutes from the condominium complex, which is good because it's already a little after three o'clock. I need to get out there and get this out of the way so I can get back to the house and clean up and get dinner started. I have a decent idea of where this is all going, and I'm not too happy with it.

That is the reason I wanted to see Cappelano today; I needed to bounce some ideas off him and see if he saw this going in the same direction as I did. I just have a feeling that things are going to get really ugly fast. I'm not saying that I plan on finding out that the Church is involved in Andrew's death, but regardless of the reason the Church is involved, this can't end well. This case is a true test of my faith, not only my beliefs in church but also my beliefs in a Higher Being, the overall truth behind a culture of religion. Just because the people that are in charge of my religion of choice piss me off, it doesn't mean I need to lose faith in my religion. Man is fallible, and there is no reason to let that stand between my faith and me. There I go again, getting on my soapbox preaching to the congregation. Before I get too lost in thought, I realize I'm getting close to the cardinal's condo. It looks like Lenny is calling me; this can only mean that someone is at the cardinal's condo, or he's leaving.

"Okay, Lenny, what's going on? Please tell me he isn't going anywhere."

"No, as a matter of fact, it's good and bad news. I think someone just brought Ms. Malinowski to Cardinal Kelley's condo. What the hell is going on, Neil? Why would Cardinal Kelley have Andrew's mother at his condo?"

"I have no idea; whatever you do, don't lose Ms. Malinowski. I'm calling for backup right now; I need you to call your backup and have them meet you up there ASAP, so they can keep a follow on the cardinal in case Ms. Malinowski heads out."

"I got you, Neil, but from the looks of it, I don't think she's going to be leaving soon. It looks like she's packed a bag and that she might be staying there for quite a while."

"Oh, FUCK! Well, still call your backup. I'm going to make a phone call, and I'll meet you out there soon enough. I'm only a few miles from the cardinal's condo."

"I'll be here keeping an eye on everything."

Holy shit, what the hell is going on? I am at a total loss for words right now. Just moments ago I was thinking I needed a plan to get to Andrew's mother inside the psych ward. Now Lenny is telling me that it looks like she is bunking with Cardinal Kelley. I need to call Ken right now before I do something stupid; it is at moments like this when I need a clear view of the situation, and Ken is that perspective for me. I am about to snap because it seems like every time I get a grasp of the situation; it slips through my fingers. I feel like I'm trying to hold one grain of sand; the problem is that I can't see the sand to grasp it, and every time I think I have it, I realize I'm holding nothing. I hope that he answers; I cannot be leaving a message right now.

"Hey Neil, how is everything going? Are you on your way to Cardinal Kelley's?"

"Just listen very carefully right now, Ken. I need you to get in your car and head out here right now. Lenny just told me that it looks as though Ms. Malinowski was just dropped off at the cardinal's condo with a bag packed."

"You mean Andrew's mom is staying the night at Cardinal Kelley's?"

"Let's hope that's the worst of it and that they aren't sending her out of the state or country to somewhere else. The problem with the

Church is that they are a world organization that could send her anywhere, no questions asked."

"I'm on my way, Neil. Just hold tight and don't do anything stupid. But let me rephrase: don't do anything at all. Just stay where you are and wait for me to get there. I shouldn't be any longer than thirty minutes."

The silence at the end of the phone was deafening. Although there was no sound in the phone I could hear all the screams of everyone that had been hurt or killed because of a killer I failed to catch or allowed to stay on the streets one more day. My mind started to consume me with self-doubt and fear; in this business, you can't have this kind of mentality, where you are always questioning yourself. Once that happens, you are finished when it comes to investigating.

So much of this job comes from instinct and blind faith in one's decisions. I've had moments of doubt; however, my ego usually doesn't allow me to hold back but instead push through even harder. I've ended up on the wrong end of the stick because of it several times, but I wouldn't be where I am today without that drive to find the truth regardless of convention. It's been about fifteen minutes since I called Ken, and I'm starting to get extremely anxious, but I need to calm down and fast. This is just another snag in the case; everything will be all right; just take it as it comes and adjust. As I begin to reinforce my image, I start to feel my heart slowing down and my brain coming back to reality. Just then that I heard my cell phone, but it wasn't Ken calling.

"Lenny, son of a bitch, this better not be more bad news."

"Sorry, Neil, it looks like that bag is packed for her to stay somewhere else. Cardinal Kelley is pulling out of his condo with her in the passenger seat. I'm going to tail for a little bit and have my backup pick up in a few so that the cardinal doesn't spot my car."

"Did you get that GPS tracking module in his car like we planned yesterday?"

"Yes, I did. I'll send you the serial number so you can track him yourself from a comfortable distance. I'm sorry that he isn't staying here, but I won't let him out of my sight until Adam gets here to take my place in the tail."

"Good job, Lenny. I'm sorry if my voice is coming off like I'm pissed, but I'm just going crazy with this case. I'll be following behind, far behind tracking with the GPS. Just keep me and Ken updated with anything that goes on."

"No problem; I'll keep you guys up to date with everything. Don't worry, Neil, we'll get to the bottom of this soon enough, that's why we are all helping you. We've never seen you so eaten up with a case before, not like this."

"Thanks, Len, for helping me out; it means a lot. I need to get going and call Ken to let him know there's a change in plans."

As soon as I got off the phone with Lenny, I called Ken to let him know everything that was going on. I can't believe this is the second call in fifteen minutes about this case that is going to change everything completely. Sometimes I wonder how I stand this job; then again, the adrenaline rush is unbelievable right now. Right now

I'm just trying to keep from tearing off my steering wheel. *For the love of God, Ken, answer your phone!*

"This can't be good news. What's going on, Neil? It's bad, isn't it?"

"It looks like they took Andrew's mom somewhere, and judging by her bags being packed, my guess is that they are going to try and get her out of the state if not the country."

"Do we have someone following her right now, or is it just you?"

"I'm following the GPS tracking unit Lenny was able to put on Cardinal Kelley's car last night. I'll send you the serial number so you can track him and meet up with him somewhere along the way. This way, you can hop in the car with me and help me focus on everything, so I don't do anything stupid."

"All right, it doesn't seem like it would be that hard to meet up with you, since chances are that she is going to the airport."

"Sad but true. I'll meet you up on I-Seventy-Five. Just hit call my cell when you're getting close to me and the other tail. It won't take but a moment to switch from your car to mine."

"No problem, Neil. Judging by your location to that of mine and the direction that Cardinal Kelley's car is traveling, I should be able to meet up with you in about ten minutes. I'll meet you up near the I-Six Ninety-Six and I-Seventy-Five interchange."

"Sounds good to me. I'll see you there, Ken. Thanks for helping me keep my head on this one, Ken; I'll meet up with you soon."

21

It's not like the old days at the airport, when you could follow someone for no reason whatsoever.

I did my best to stay half a mile back from Cardinal Kelley and his tail so I wouldn't be spotted. It looks like we are on our way to the airport; I can only guess where the cardinal might be sending her. If it were my choice, I would send her back home to Poland, since there is no more reason for her to be in the United States. At least that's my guess. I have to believe Andrew is part of a big lie or cover-up in the Church. There is no other reason they would be covering up what happened to him that night unless they were hiding him from something or from someone. There is always the chance that he could have been a bastard son of someone such as the pope and they were hiding him. With his death comes blood on their watch, and they don't want anyone to know of his existence. At least that's what it seems to look like to me. I just don't see it playing out any other way. I'd be lying if I didn't have my doubts in my hypothesis, but I'd also

216

be a fool if I believe I couldn't be wrong. Even the truth can be wrong to a certain extent; just because it's true doesn't mean it's completely true.

It looks like Ken is calling me, which is about time, because I noticed his car in my rearview mirror about a mile back. I bet he assumed I would pull over to do the switch right on the expressway. Plus it looks like he has someone else driving his car so he can just hop out of his car and not have to worry about leaving it anywhere. This way he knows that his car will be in good hands and eventually back at the warehouse waiting for him when we get done with all of this.

"So Neil, are you planning on stopping anytime soon so I can hop in your car with you?"

"Don't get all worked up for nothing; there will be plenty of time for that later. I'll pull off the road right now. Just slide behind me and hop in; I'll have the door unlocked. Let's make this quick, so be sure you've got everything you need on you right now before I pull off. Are you ready to do this?"

"Yeah, I've got everything packed in my bag; just pull over, and I'll hop in your car. It's not like we can't make up for any lost time in your car; I'm sure your baby can catch up to the cardinal's car."

"Let's do this."

As I hung up the phone, I slowed down quite abruptly, pulled off the expressway, and leaned over to open the door for Ken. As I leaned back to my seat, I caught a glimpse of Ken running up to the car with a messenger bag over his shoulder. What the hell does he have packed in there? It's not as if we need surveillance cameras for this or anything. Knowing him, he has a little bit of everything in case we get in a jam and need a way out; he's good for things like that. Fake passports, false IDs, extra ammo, anything you can think of. I know it seems a little spy movieish, but it's just how things are in this business. They are definitely not glamorous by any means; you just need to be ready to get down and dirty at any moment.

"Jeez, Ken, did you bring enough stuff with you? We are just following Cardinal Kelley to see where he is taking Andrew's mother, we're not going camping."

"Shut up and drive, Neil. I just brought a few things if this case takes a turn for the worse."

"What did you grab, if you don't mind me asking?"

"I grabbed Lenny's passport from his office; some spending cash; an international cell phone; a GPS tracking device we can try and get on Andrew's mother, so we can keep tabs on her; and a few other things."

"Good idea, Ken. You've got us covered if the worst happens and Cardinal Kelley is sending her overseas somewhere. Have you called Lenny yet to fill him in on everything?"

"Yeah, I called him shortly after you gave me a call and told me what was up. Everything is arranged in case we end up at the Detroit Metro Airport."

"I hope we're wrong about this, but I highly doubt that we are. As you said, judging by the direction he's driving in, the best guess is that they are headed to the airport."

"The plan, if he does take her to the airport, is to have Lenny get a ticket, then hop on the flight with her. That way we can keep an eye on her and where she ends up. If we luck out in that instance and she ends up in Poland, then we'll have three agents over there to keep an eye out for her and see what's going on."

"I guess that is the only chance we have to keep an eye on this thing if this ends up at the airport. At least if they are sending her somewhere, we can only hope that it's Poland."

"Wait a minute: how are we going to know where she's going, and how are we going to be able to get someone on the flight in time?"

"If and when we get to the airport, I'll hang back in with Lenny at the ticket desk, and we'll have yourself and the backup, I don't know who it is right now. Follow Cardinal Kelley and Andrew's mother."

"I believe it's Terrance that's following closest to Cardinal Kelley's car right now; I'll call him and see how it's going. Why don't you call Lenny and give him a heads up on what we are going to do if and when we get to the airport."

"Sounds good. We might as well game-plan now to save a couple of minutes when we get up there."

The two of us grabbed our cell phones and began to call the other people involved in this tail right now. It's not every day you have four people in three different cars following someone. Then again, it's not every day you are involved in a case that involves one of the world's biggest organizations and a dead teenager. I guess there's a first for everything in this business, and today is no exception. Lenny seemed to get the gist of things quite easily; it didn't take much explaining. I actually told him to get a head start and go to the airport so it won't seem odd if he's keeping an eye on Ms. Malinowski because he will already be there. I told him to get a random plane ticket that will get him through the checkpoint. Something local and cheap, so I don't have to pay much for the reimbursement.

It's not like the old days at the airport, when you could follow someone for no reason whatsoever. You could just show up and get through the checkpoints with no questions asked. Now you have to get a ticket before you head through the checkpoint, and it's not as if you can just say give me the cheapest ticket because they will know what to look for. We've pretty much told our guys to go for a certain flight and a certain airline to keep the cost down.

"Is everything squared away with Terrance? I told Lenny to head up to the airport and grab a ticket so he can be waiting on the other side of the checkpoint and keep Cardinal Kelley off track that way."

"There's a little bit of a problem with that. I can't get Lenny his passport to him if he's already over there. We were going to have him follow Andrew's mom where she's headed."

"That's right. In that case, why don't you call Terrance and see if he happens to have his passport on him, and that way, we can just have Terrance do it."

"Especially since it looks like Cardinal Kelley's car just pulled off the expressway onto the airport exit, I think we should call now and get this taken care of."

Luckily, for us, Terrance keeps his passport on him so that he can prove he is who he is with the fake IDs he uses for his job. I know it isn't the best thing to be carrying around multiple forms of ID in today's society with everything on high alert, but it comes with the job and territory. We need to be able to blend into the background and not have anyone be able to put a name with our face—at least one that matches. I understand the times we live in and the reason why. But, son of a bitch, it gets expensive every time some jackass runs off with his secretary and one of my guys has to buy a plane ticket just to make sure they got on the same plane.

"How is everything with Terrance? Are we going to be good to go still?"

"Luckily for us, he carries his passport on him. I should rephrase that to "lucky for you since you told Lenny to drive ahead to the airport."

"At least we are going to have a guy inside already, and we'll have a good tail on Cardinal Kelley and Andrew's mom. Let's hope that Cardinal Kelley just puts her on the plane; that way we might be able to get to her on the plane and not have to worry about where she's going."

"Chances are Cardinal Kelley will escort her all the way unless someone else is flying with her. It's not like the Church to leave anything to chance."

"It looks like we're here, so enough with the speculation. Let's get going and see what's going on."

"Drop me off here. I'll run in and keep an eye on them from a distance. I'll have you meet up with Terrance inside in a bit. We don't need Cardinal Kelley recognizing you; I know you said he didn't get a look at you at St. Pat's Church, but I just want to be safe instead of sorry. We're only going to get one chance at this."

"You and I are thinking along the same line of thinking, Ken. This looks like as good a place as any to drop you off. I'll meet up with Terrance in the parking garage and make our way in a few moments behind you. Just text me when it's clear to come in; I wouldn't want to have Cardinal Kelley catch me and realize what's going on."

"It wouldn't be good having a cardinal telling the local authorities that we need to be detained at an airport. That could get messy, even for you."

As I dropped off Ken, I got on my cell and quickly texted Terrance to park and wait for me to find him. It wasn't too long before Cardinal Kelley was parked and heading toward the concourse of the airport. Judging by the parking lot he chose, overnight, it looks like he will be escorting Ms. Malinowski on the flight. I should have known something was going to happen. We got the jump on Cardinal Kelley and Ms. Malinowski, and now we're going to have to sit back and wait for something to happen again. I know this business is a lot of sitting and waiting, and normally I have no problem doing that, it's just that this case is driving me insane. I can't seem to figure out why this case is getting to me so much; it's not as if I have any connection to Andrew except that he attended St. Mary's. I'm sure there are a lot of people that have attended that school over the years, and something has happened to them. But why is this case getting to me?

I pulled up alongside Terrance's car and took a moment to compose myself before everything was about to go down. For all, I know everything could happen smoothly, and this could end up with us having three investigators in Poland tracking down lead after lead. On the other hand, this could blow up in our face. Cardinal Kelley could be flying with Andrew's mother to Rome. This would be the worst-case scenario because if he gets her to Rome, we have no chance of ever finding out the truth. My biggest fear isn't failure in my own doing but failure in that we may never be given a chance to figure everything out.

"Hey Terrance, thank you for being prepared for something like this, I can't tell you how much this means to Ken and me."

"I've actually packed a bag for this very occasion. Nothing too major, just a few necessities and a few days' clothes, because you never know where a case may take you."

"So you're telling me that not only do you have your passport on you but that you also have a bag packed for such an occasion in your car? That is awesome; remind me after this case to talk to you about a raise and give you more leeway in pursuing cases on your own for the company."

"Thanks, Neil. That means a lot, coming from you. I have to admit I have never met bosses quite like yourself and Ken; the two of you are always helping and allowing us to grow in the company. It really helps to motivate us, at least me."

"We want everyone to feel like they are just as important to this company as myself or Ken. The truth is that without the entire team Ken and I would still be working out of my house on cases."

"It's nice to know, though, that you guys aren't full of yourselves and that you understand you need us just as much as we need you. But enough about that stuff. What are we doing right now?"

"I'm just waiting for Ken to text/call me, letting us know that it is clear to go in and get a ticket on the same flight that Cardinal Kelley and Andrew's mother are going to get on."

"With security nowadays, we could be waiting here for a little bit. Is it all right if I make a phone call to my girlfriend to let her know what's going on so that she doesn't expect me home anytime in the next couple of days?"

"Yeah, that is no problem; you might want to tell her that it will be closer to a week to ten days, just to be a little bit more realistic. That way, if you're back sooner, then it's a surprise. It's always better to come home earlier than later, that's what I always say."

"That probably is best. The only way it would suck is if I came home early and found her in bed with someone else, but then again, that isn't always bad."

"How do you figure that wouldn't be bad?"

"At least this way I'll know sooner than later how well I can trust her."

"That's a little pessimistic, but I see where you're going with it. Make the phone call. Once we get in there, everything is going to speed up a bit, and you won't have time to talk to her."

"No problem, boss; I mean Neil."

For some reason, the more they say it, the more it's growing on me. Maybe I need to just accept it: I am the boss. While Terrance

224

made a phone call to his girlfriend, I decided to email Christian and Nicolette in Poland to give them a heads up and make sure that at least one of them would be available to head over to the airport to head off Cardinal Kelley, if, in fact, that is where they are headed. The thing that is working on our side is that if they are headed to Poland, then the flight will be a long one, and it will allow time for Christian and Nicolette to set things up on their end. It's not as if the flight will be anything less than ten hours. I mean, it takes four hours just to fly across the United States. I would think flying over the ocean and part of Eastern Europe would take a little bit longer than that. Just as I finished putting my phone back in my pocket, I felt my phone vibrate. Chances are that it's Ken letting me know what is going on.

From the looks of it, Ken did more than just tail Cardinal Kelley and Andrew's mother, he was also able to get the complete flight information that the two of them would be flying on. For the moment, I'm happy that he was able to attain that kind of information, but I'm a little worried that it was that simple, seeing that our security at airlines is supposed to be stepped up. No wonder people are worried about flying on planes today. After we get settled in at the airport, I'll find out from Ken how he was able to attain the information so easily. I waited a moment for Terrance to get off the phone with his girlfriend, but it didn't seem like she was going to let him get off the phone anytime soon, so I had to tell him to wrap it up ASAP so we could head in and get his tickets.

"Wow, that was quicker than I thought it would take for them to get through security. Then again, it is a cardinal and an old lady; I highly doubt they are going to check them over too thoroughly."

"Good point. Luckily for us, Ken was able to find out more than just the direction in which they are headed. He was able to get the flight information from the desk attendant. From the looks of things, it looks like you are going to be headed for Poland. You're lucky in that they are flying first class, and I don't want you to take any chances in losing them, so I'm going to be paying for a first-class ticket for you."

"Nice a full paid trip to Poland, including first-class airfare; although don't you think a tall black man like myself is going to stand out a bit in Poland?"

"Don't worry about that; I've got two investigators over there already. This is the second break in the case that we've been able to get."

"Well, I guess we should get the getting and get our asses in there."

"That was more 'gets' than I would normally use in a sentence, but hey—"

"Shut up, Neil; let's go get me a first-class ticket to Poland."

"And here you were worried about your girl cheating. Just wait until you meet one of the investigators I have over there in Poland. She's definitely easy on the eyes."

The two of us made our way from the parking garage to the main concourse to pick up a ticket for Terrance to follow Cardinal Kelley.

This reminds me that I can't believe Cardinal Kelley is flying first class; couldn't he at least fly business class? I mean, first-class costs a lot of money that I don't want to spend. Then again, Terrance is doing us a huge favor by flying over there at the last minute like this. At least I'm going to save some money on buying him clothes, since he has a bag packed for such an occasion. That in and of itself, I guess, deserves a first-class ticket; he was prepared for any situation.

Walking in the concourse, I could tell right away which counter Ken was able to retrieve the intel from. She just had that look on her face that she was easily persuaded. It didn't hurt either that I had all the flight information. So I knew which airline we had to get the ticket from. Three people were working over there, and it still didn't matter, I knew exactly who he was able to persuade. She was a short, stocky girl in her midtwenties; maybe it was the bubbles she was blowing, or maybe it was the extreme amount of makeup she had on; either way, she had a target on her face. She looked like a character on *Saturday Night Live*; it didn't seem to be true. Terrance went up first and got his ticket without any problems while I went over to one of the cheaper airlines and picked up a cheap ticket costing me about seventy dollars so I could meet up with Ken on the other side of the metal detectors to grab a drink and wait to see what happens with Lenny, Terrance, Andrew's mother, and Cardinal Kelley.

Standing in line behind Terrance at the security checkpoint was a little hard to pull off without laughing for some reason, maybe because everything seemed a little too easy. I felt as if I was in grade school all over again and was told to form a line and be quiet. It seems so hard to stay quiet and stand in line for some reason. It might just have been my experience, but I have an idea that I wasn't the only one that had a similar experience in grade school. The crews working the metal detector and X-ray machine were nothing but our nation's finest; I hope you can sense the sarcasm even though you are reading this. They looked like a group of overmedicated ex-cons. It was not a pretty sight; hell, the guy working the X-ray machine had his three front teeth gold plated, I shit you not. If I didn't know any better, I would have thought nothing has changed at all at our airports except for the perception of increased security. Right now I need to track down Ken to talk to him about how he obtained the flight information.

"All right, Neil, I'll text you once we're seated on the plane and everything is lined up, and I'll call you when I land in Poland and meet up with Christian and Nicolette."

"Sounds good to me, Terrance. I'm going to track down Ken so I can ask him how he was able to obtain the flight information. Good luck and have a safe flight to Poland. If you can, use your cell phone to take some photos of Cardinal Kelley and Andrew's mother so we can have something to show the Church later if we need to show them what we know."

"No problem, Neil, I've got it covered. I grabbed a surveillance camera from my car before I left. So I could take photos and videos without looking too obvious with my phone."

"You really have impressed me today, Terrance. Be safe and do what you can to talk to Andrew's mom, on the off chance that Cardinal Kelley gets up and uses the bathroom or falls asleep."

"Well, I better get going because I am running out of time; I should get to the flight so I have enough time. Lenny just texted me and told me that they are about to board first-class cabin passengers soon. I'll be in touch shortly."

"Talk to you later, Terrance."

Shortly after letting Terrance get to his plane, I called Ken to see where he was. He told me he was at a concourse bar near the terminal from which Cardinal Kelley's plane would be leaving. He also informed me that the cardinal had already boarded the plane so that I would not need to worry about him noticing me and realizing what was going on. Amazingly, we were able to pull this off, and even more amazing is that we lucked out and already have two investigators in Poland that have set up camp. Now we'll have three investigators who can rotate and keep a constant eye on Andrew's mother.

"Hey Neil, I took the liberty and ordered you a Jack on the rocks with lemon. I figured after everything that has happened, you could use a drink."

"Thanks, Ken, that is definitely the situation. So where do you think this case is going to take us?

"I really have no idea; it seems like every time we get a good grip on this case and where it might get going, we end up lost and back where we began—in the dark."

"I completely understand what you are saying; this case just won't let up. I know we are trying to uncover something that a very powerful organization is trying to keep quiet. Still, it's not like this is the first time we've had to dig deep to uncover the truth."

"You said it in the beginning when dealing with an organization that deals in faith and religion. You are not only working against them but also those who believe and follow the same belief system."

"I guess now we have a couple of hours to wait and see where this case takes us. I'm going to go home and work out a bit and then go over all the information we have on this case and see what I can come up with. Why don't you give me a call when you hear from Terrance?"

"I can do that for you, no problem, Neil; go and do what you do best. Figure out what's going on when all is lost."

"I'll try my best, and make sure we don't do any more drinking or partying until this case is done. I don't care if it takes me months or years, I'm done waiting around and being reactive. It's time to be more proactive in this case."

"You got it, boss man; I'll give you a call when I hear from Terrance."

Right now I can't help but let my mind run away with every possible solution to this case. Why would the Church be so interested in this case and Andrew? I know it is the million-dollar question that everyone is asking me right now. Don't get me wrong, I like being the go-to guy, but sometimes the stress of it all just wears on me a bit. As I made my way out of the airport concourse, it dawned on me that I just paid nearly two hundred dollars for a Jack on the rocks. In all actuality, there was no reason that I needed to pay for a ticket and follow Terrance through the checkpoint. I guess it was the little control freak inside me; it really was a waste of time and resources to do that. I need to get home and take some frustrations out on my punching bag and then begin systematically going over every bit of information we have in this case.

22

It was almost two in the morning, and I'm running out of time to pack and hang out with Sheila.

The drive home was long and unproductive; I couldn't seem to focus on one thing at a time. I had music blasting in the car, trying to clear my head. In the end, I had to turn everything off and just listen to the simple sounds of the car and the road. The hum of the engine began to melt away my fears as the purr of the road lifted my spirits. It truly is amazing the feeling one can get while behind the wheel of an amazing machine. It was just what I needed to clear my head; I wasn't even upset anymore. While driving, I couldn't help but refer back to something Father Roberts had said to me about giving some of these men of the cloth too much credit; after all, they are human just like you and me. I have to take all plausible reasons behind this connection into account and not allow my prejudgment of the Church to affect my decisions. I think Father Roberts was trying to lead me down that path. What if Andrew was the child of someone from the

Church, whether his mother was a nun or his father a priest? This is something I need to take into consideration.

As I pulled into my driveway, the feeling was bittersweet since the drive had calmed me down to a point where I could focus clearly again. On the other hand, I was looking forward to being chased around the house by my girls Jackie and Danielle. As expected, when I opened the door, the girls came flying in from the bedroom. They tackled me to the ground, attacking me with a barrage of kisses; I couldn't help but laugh and smile at the sight. I know my life has its problems and drama, but at the end of the day I have a daughter I love, a best friend in my ex-wife, and two dogs that greet me smiling every night. I don't think I could enjoy any of the monetary things I've been able to gain over the years if it weren't for the four most important women in my life.

After some time, I finally made my way into the shower with a cup of coffee in hand. As the steaming hot water ran down my neck and back, I began to have flashbacks of this case. It was like watching a slide show of the case and the information we had gained over the past couple of days. Everyone has their talents, and mine seems to be piecing together puzzles; I do a lot of decent things, but there is only one thing I'm genuinely good at. I know there are things that people are better at than I am, and that is why I put so much faith and trust in Ken and TJ. Without them I wouldn't be where I am today. They allow me to do my job to the best of my ability, and I know that; that is why I pay them so much.

I kept reanalyzing the relationship between Andrew and the Church; there had to be something that I was missing. If he wasn't of any great importance to the Church, maybe his mother or father were or are important to them. The mother could be a likely candidate, since they keep moving and hiding her from the public eye, and it seems that they have been doing that for years. My guess is that if she is the key, and she is now allowed to go home because of her son's death, then Andrew was looked upon by the Church as a stain of sorts. There is an exceptionally good chance that Andrew was a child from someone who has power in the Church; whether it be his mother or his father, I am not sure. And perhaps who I know as Ms. Malinowski may not be his real mother. My head is hurting just thinking about everything in this case.

The other thing I am having trouble wrapping my head around is even if he was the son of a priest or nun, why do they have to cover up his murder? It doesn't make sense. Why hide it from the world? It's as if they don't want any record of Andrew ever existing. The scary thing is that they are doing a good job erasing his life. By next week, I would bet there isn't a trace of him ever existing. It's scary to know that, because we live in such a technologically driven society that someone's life could be erased from time with a simple brush of a key. It really makes one realize how important it is to touch people's lives for the better daily, to make sure you will not be forgotten. I know it sounds vain, but doesn't it scare you a little bit that your life could be erased as if it never happened?

AVE MARIA

After a good twenty minutes had passed, I finally made my way from the shower into the kitchen to grab another cup of coffee and to let the girls in. I didn't see the importance of putting on anything else but a comfortable pair of jeans and my favorite Tigers hat. With the girls inside to warm up, I made my way downstairs to my office. I needed to go over everything I had been thinking about in this case. I needed to map out my ideas and disprove them one by one until I am left with a smaller list. This is the only way I know how to break down what seems like an impossible list to consider into something manageable. I think by now it is safe to say any possibility we have thought of that takes the mother or father into account could be true. If it were the son that was important and not the parents, the Church wouldn't be wasting so much time and energy into hiding as well as exporting one Ms. Malinowski. My guess is that Andrew didn't even truly realize his importance or threat to the Church until he was old enough to figure it out for himself.

Before I do anything, though, I need to call Ken ASAP and set up some travel plans. This reminds me: I need to make sure I have my passport. I hadn't had to use it since I went to Mexico back when I was working on the Cappelano case. I could probably call and set up the travel plans myself, but I know Ken will do a better job of it than I will. Last time I made travel plans, I ended up paying twice the face value of a plane ticket because I didn't know who to call or how to do anything.

"Hey Ken, I know it's late, but I need you to do something for me."

"If you are asking about getting you a plane ticket to Poland, I'm already on it."

"You know me a little too well sometimes. I should probably be worried, but I'm just happy that I have someone to take care of me."

"Thanks for the vote of confidence; I just didn't want a repeat of what happened last time you tried to get your own travel plans together."

"That was pretty bad. I paid double for the plane ticket and didn't even have a place to stay when I got there, but then again, that's what I pay you for."

"Well, it's all taken care of. I've got a room for you down the hall from Christian and his cousin. Also, your flight leaves at six forty-five a.m. tomorrow/today. If I were you, I would just stay up all night because the flight is a long one."

"Just swing by tomorrow on your way out and pick everything up along with some information I'll have set up for you. Things like maps and a portable GPS unit."

"Thanks again for everything, Ken; I need to get to work on packing and calling Sheila to take care of the girls."

"All right, Neil, I'll talk to you later, then. I need to get going and get things together."

"Sounds good, Ken. I'll talk to you later."

Shortly off the phone with Ken and I finally found my suitcase, which is a good thing, since I have to leave for the airport in about four hours. I should get there with some time to spare, since I'm taking an international flight in a time of heightened security. I've got little time and a lot of things to get together; at least Sheila will be here shortly to help me do that. I could hear someone pulling up the drive and noticed it was Sheila.

"Hello? Neil, are you here?"

"Yeah, Sheila, I'm downstairs I'll be up in a minute. I'm just grabbing a suitcase."

"What are you grabbing your suitcase for?"

"I'm leaving to go to Poland in the morning; last-minute plans."

"I would say so. I just got off the phone with you moments ago, and you didn't mention anything to me about it. What time are you leaving?"

"I need to leave here about four or four thirty in the morning because my flight leaves at six forty-five."

"Well, then we better get to work and start packing for you. Why don't you give me an idea of what you want packed clothingwise and you can get to work on packing your work things?"

"Sounds like a plan to me. Just pack for similar weather that we have here and pack for about a week. Anything over that and I can just do some laundry."

"You're the boss; I'll get to work on it so we can maybe stop on the way out and grab a bite to eat or something."

It really is nice of Sheila to come over and help me out. She really is sweet with a big heart. I think that is half the reason I have so much trouble getting close to Maria. Or anyone else is allowing myself to be vulnerable with anyone other than her. I allowed myself to be vulnerable with Sheila, and although it has ended up manageable for both of us, I still went through a period in my life where I was extremely depressed.

It took me a long time to get over the heartache and questions I had within myself about why our marriage failed. Especially when we were civil after everything, it just didn't make sense to me that we couldn't make it work. Just ask Sheila, and she will tell you that there were many nights when I called her crying and asking her why we couldn't try to make it work. I don't have to tell you that I am a stubborn person in my own right.

"Thanks for everything. It shouldn't take me too long to get my things together; I'll be downstairs getting things done."

"Sounds good, Neil. If you hurry up and leave enough time, maybe I can give you a going-away present."

"As much as I would love that and trust me, I would, right now, I need to concentrate on this case right now and not lose focus. I'm sorry, cutes, but it's just that I can't take a chance of taking my mind off of anything."

"It's okay, I understand completely. I'm sorry for pressuring you into anything. I can only imagine what you're going through right now with this case."

"It's okay; I know you were only doing what we normally do. It's just that right now I know I haven't been focusing enough on this case. I've been allowing my employees to do all the work for me, and that is not something I am used to doing. I have never been someone that relied on other people to do his own work."

"Don't blame yourself for this; you've been going through a lot lately, and it's not your fault that you are taking advantage of what's at your disposal. You built this company from the ground up with Ken. Eventually you get tired of doing everything yourself."

"I guess that makes sense, but I've always been someone that likes to do everything myself when it comes to investigating something. It's not that I don't trust anyone, it's just what I'm used to. I've finally been able to let people help me, and now I'm half assigned to it. Just because I'm getting help doesn't mean I need to be lazy. I just wonder where we'd be with this case if I had given it my all from the beginning."

"You have an opportunity to make up for lost time, since you've been given a second chance in Poland having a tail on Andrew's mother and Cardinal Kelley."

"I'm really glad you came over tonight. I know we didn't get to have as much fun as we might have liked to, but you've helped to clear my head and refocus on everything."

She really is right in that I don't need to be so hard on myself. Although I didn't give my all and I got a little lax in my pursuit of Andrew's mother and Cardinal Kelley, I still gave an honest effort. Now that I am lucky enough to have this second chance in Poland, I am going to take full advantage and give my all into this case. In fact, I'm not going to have another drink or have sex until I finish this case. I don't care if it takes me weeks or months. I owe it to Glow, St. Mary's, and the Malinowski family.

"Well, Sheila, I'm going to go downstairs and get started so that I might have time to hang out with you before I have to head to the airport."

"I could always drive you to the airport if you would like."

"No, it's okay, I should probably drive myself, I've got to make a few phone calls anyway. I'd be on the phone the whole time, so it wouldn't even be worth it, but I do appreciate the offer. Let's get to work, and then we can relax a bit before I leave, or maybe we can just go and grab a bite to eat."

"That sounds good to me; I think you should get a good meal in you before you end up stuck on a plane for sixteen hours."

"Is the flight that long? Shit, I didn't even think of that. I'm going to have to bring something else on the plane to listen to other than my MP3 player. Its battery lasts only a few hours."

"Just bring your laptop with you; if you're flying first class, they will more than likely have an outlet for you to plug into. On these international flights, they have pretty much anything you can think of when you fly first class. They know a lot of businessmen fly internationally and need to get work done; they also know laptop batteries don't last forever."

"Wow, I didn't realize you were an expert on international flights. Oh, wait a minute, I forgot you used to date that airline pilot."

"Yeah, we dated on and off for a bit, I got to fly on a couple of international flights. But enough about my ex-boyfriends. Go downstairs; I'll see you in a bit when you're done."

Eventually I made my way downstairs to get my things together for work. I had an over-the-shoulder messenger bag to fill up with case files and other reading material for the flight. After twenty minutes I finally finished packing up the files and began getting my laptop and MP3 player together. It was almost two in the morning, and I'm running out of time to pack and hang out with Sheila. Speaking of her, I should probably head upstairs and see how she's doing, since I'm done down here with my work stuff. Luckily I already have Christian, his cousin Nicolette, and now Terrance. This will allow me to have some order when I get over there as well as all the surveillance equipment I may need.

"Hey babe, how are you doing up here? Are you having any trouble finding your way around the bedroom?"

"No, I finished packing everything up for you about fifteen minutes ago. I decided to curl up in your bed with the girls and get some rest."

"I see how it is, I'm downstairs packing up and getting things together while you're up here laying in my bed under the covers curled up with my dogs. It must be nice to be you right now?"

"I'm not complaining right now, I'm actually quite happy with where I am. How about we get going then and head out to Coney Island again and get something to eat?"

"Sounds good to me. Let's put the girls out and head out of here."

After the girls went out, we packed up my car and headed out to grab a bite to eat. Sheila followed me in her car, since we'd be eating at a restaurant right off the expressway. That way, I can just leave right after we finish eating and have plenty of time to spare. Being that it is the middle of the night, it looks like we are going to end up eating at Coney Island again, which isn't too bad, but I should probably stay away from the chili dogs. Although they are extremely good and tasty, having a stomachful of chili dogs while on an airplane for more than ten hours is not the best idea. Not only would it be uneventful for me but also for those around me. I'll probably just get a Greek salad with chicken added on; that's always a favorite of mine.

23

*I began my love affair with several small bottles of Jack Daniels
and a flight attendant named Annette.*

I don't know what you call a meal at three in the morning, but that's
what I just finished. Now that I have finished eating and made my
way to the freeway, I'm about twenty minutes from the airport, which
is a good thing because my flight leaves in a couple of hours and
we've all heard the stories about security now. The last flight I was
on took forever because I had surveillance equipment with me, and I
had to put up with hours of questioning. It wasn't until they finished
my background check and saw I used to be FBI that I got the okay to
get on the plane. Sometimes I wonder who decides the rules that we
follow at the airport because it doesn't make any sense to me. I can't
bring a pocketknife through the security checkpoint, but I can buy a
pocketknife on the other side of it. What the hell is that about?
Speaking of other annoying things, why do I have to pay for parking
at the airport?

Finally, at the airport, I decided to pay the extra money to get the car parked close to the airport because you never know what might happen when I return to Detroit. At least I will more than likely just write off the parking fee when I file my taxes, so that's a positive. As I made my way into the concourse, I noticed that the airport is quite slow at four in the morning. The nice thing about being here this early is that I won't have to put up with anyone standing in line; outside of the help, there really isn't anyone here. Another bonus is that the ticket counter clerk is quite a cutie.

"Hello. May I see your ID and ticket, please?"

"No problem . . . Sharon. How are you doing this morning?"

"Not too bad. I just started my shift a little while ago, so it's not too bad."

"Can you tell me how many passengers are going to be on the plane this morning? I'm just wondering if I need to get a few cocktails first. If it's a packed flight, I'll need some relaxing."

"I'm not supposed to say, but I wouldn't worry too much about the flight. The plane is barely half full, and there are only two other people so far in first class with you."

"That's a relief; I'm not a big fan of long flights, so having an empty plane will help."

"I can only imagine; I can barely handle a four-hour flight to Los Angeles. So why, may I ask, are you going to Poland at six in the morning?"

"I am on my way over there for work. That's why I have a one-way ticket. I'm not sure how long I'm going to be over there."

"What kind of work do you do, Mr. Baggio, if you don't mind me asking?"

"I'm a freelance investigator doing some work overseas. It's nothing too exciting, trust me."

"What type of investigator . . . like a private investigator?"

"You could say that I'm trying to locate someone's mother and father."

"Well, you are all set, Mr. Baggio. Have a safe flight and good luck with your job in Poland."

"Thanks for your help, and the lovely smile made my day; have a great day."

I am so happy right now that the flight isn't going to be packed. It's not as if I don't like other people; on a ten-hour flight, one can feel like a sardine in a can when the flight is full. Plus, I've noticed on long flights, the less crowded a flight is, the more likely people are to be friendly to others while in the air. I think it's because people are allowed their personal space when a flight is only half full; it allows them the choice to talk to others and not force it on them.

The walk from the service desk to the security checkpoint was a short one, and luckily so was my stay there. It's at times like these that I am extremely grateful I came to an agreement with the FBI after the "Veritas" case. I don't have to worry about getting the third degree from the security officers when I can show them an FBI badge. It is especially helpful when you are traveling internationally with a large amount of surveillance equipment.

"Sir, I need you to take off your shoes, jacket, and any metal objects and put them in a bin on the conveyor belt along with your luggage."

"That will be no problem, sir. I'm happy to oblige."

As I made my way through the metal detector, I noticed the look on the face of the TSA agent. She had a look of wonder, probably because she noticed all the equipment I had packed in my bag along with a few clips and guns. Luckily, for me, I have clearance to carry a weapon on airlines because of my setting with the FBI. The only catch is that I cannot carry on my person and that I can't have the gun loaded.

"Sir, may I ask you to step to the side and provide some identification?"

"No problem. I am already prepared, here is my license, my carrying permit, and my FBI badge. I understand if you want to make a few phone calls before you let me go anywhere."

"That won't be necessary; we have a list on our computers of those allowed to carry firearms on flights. We also noticed you've followed the proper guidelines for doing so, and we appreciate that. Just give us one moment to cross-reference your name in our system and you will be on your way, Agent Baggio."

"As I said before, no problem. I am here to cooperate with you guys. I understand what you have to do in your job."

"It looks like everything has checked out. Thanks for being patient and following the guidelines for carrying on a flight."

AVE MARIA

My flight was due to depart at six forty-five in the morning, and judging by the screen I'm looking at, it is on time. That means I have a good hour or so before the plane takes off. Maybe I'll go see if I can find something to read for some leisure. Since it's a long flight, I'll probably grab every magazine and newspaper I can find. I love my ESPN, and I love my sports; I'm just like the average guy when it comes to sports; I can never get enough. Hell, I even follow international soccer, as well as MLS. What can I say? When I'm not tracking someone down, I try to stay up on my sports; it's a nice outlet for me in which I can clear my mind without focusing it on something that might cloud my judgment.

Once through the security checkpoint, I made my way toward the gate while looking for someplace to grab a few magazines. Which shouldn't be too hard, since there is a magazine stand nearly every twenty feet in your average airport. If you have flown recently, meaning since the new security measures. I believe one would find that half if not more than half of the things they ban through the checkpoint can be purchased once past the checkpoint. Does that make any sense at all to anyone? I just don't get this country's policies sometimes. There wasn't anything major that happened to me from the time I passed the checkpoint and then on to the airline. As a matter of fact, I was barely paying attention to what was going on around me. I was too busy worrying about what was going to happen in Poland when I landed. Luckily for me, the flight would turn out to give me great insight into how I'm approaching this case.

AVE MARIA

From the moment I walked onto the plane, I was fixated on one of the flight attendants. There was something about her that grabbed my attention; it might have been because she looked like my mother. It was truly uncanny how much of a resemblance there is between her and my mother. Looking into her eyes brought me back to my childhood with memories of my mother's sweet honey-brown hair in the summer sunlight. I'm not sure if it was the lack of sleep, excess caffeine, and too many things on my mind. Either way, she reminded me of my mother. More than anything, chances are she was wearing the same perfume that my mother once wore, because studies show that the olfactory senses retrieve old memories more than any other senses. Come to think of it, the smell of Chanel No. 5 is in the air.

"May I help you with your bag, sir? I can put it upfront here and hand it to you on your way out. I can also take your jacket for you if you would like."

"I will take you up on that, but I need to keep my laptop bag with me for the long haul."

"If there is anything you need, sir, don't hesitate to ask. My name is Annette."

"Thanks, Annette. I just have one thing to ask you before I take my seat and you get back to the rest of the passengers. Are you wearing Chanel No. 5?"

"Yes I am. You have a very good sense of smell."

"In my job it pays to be extremely observant. Otherwise I wouldn't get hired."

"Are you some sort of investigator or something in that field?"

AVE MARIA

"I'm a partner in a private investigator and security business based out of Detroit."

"You guys must be doing well, since you are flying first class on an international flight. It's not like it is a cheap ticket."

"As I said, we do all right for ourselves, but we aren't international by any means. The case I'm currently on just happens to bring me to Poland."

"I really want to talk to you more, but I've got to get a few things to do, as you can imagine. I'll talk to you shortly."

After our short conversation, Annette went to the flight attendants' area to get things ready for the safety spiel that many of us are so common with. It took a good fifteen minutes for the plane to be boarded, which had fewer people on it than I expected. While Annette was getting ready for the safety announcement, I sent a few text/emails to Christian, Nicolette, and Terrance to let them know I was on a flight out there. By the time I had finished, they had made the announcement to turn off our cell phones and other electronic devices. After a short taxi on the runway, we began the short ten-hour flight from Detroit to Warsaw, when I began my love affair with several small bottles of Jack Daniels and a flight attendant named Annette. She was genuinely honest about and interested in what I do and my case; my guess is that long flights like this one get old after a while.

"How are you doing, Mr. Baggio? Can I get you anything to drink, seeing as it's a long flight?"

"I could really go for a Jack on the rocks right now."

I know I told myself I wouldn't drink until this case is over, but give me a break. This is a ten-hour flight; I've got to do something to pass the time. Annette, on the other hand, couldn't join me in the intoxicating fervor that is Jack on the rocks. She mentioned that ever since the day the two towers fell, flight attendants have become much more than servers in the sky. I can only imagine what it must have felt like to be working on a plane after that day, the fear one would have all day, every day. That's the whole point of terrorism, to strike fear into those who had no fear. Before that fateful day, Americans felt that we were safe from harm, at least to a point; once the towers fell, the view we had of our safety became tainted. It made it hard to fly or to do anything outside of one's everyday life; to that extent, the terrorists won on some level. My father told me that after that day, the best way to honor those who died then was to keep living life and not let fear control our lives.

"So, Mr. Baggio, why don't you fill me in a little more about what you do for a living? We've got a lot of time to kill, and you're the only person in first class that can carry a conversation."

"You know how to make a guy feel really special, don't you? As I told you, I'm a partner in a private investigating company as well as specializing in private security for high-class clientele."

"How did you get involved in that sort of work, to begin with?"

"As a kid, I always wanted to play cops and robbers; needless to say, I always wanted to be a cop. There was just about bringing criminals to justice that got my adrenaline pumping."

"I can relate a little bit; ever since I flew on a plane as a child I've always wanted to work in this field."

"I went to school and studied psychology as well as criminology; they always came easily to me. Shortly after graduation, I was offered a chance to study at the FBI academy. From there, it's a long story that this flight can't contain. Eventually I went into the private sector while keeping one foot in the door of the bureau as a consultant."

"Aren't you the adventurous type? Why don't you tell me a little bit about the case you're on? You don't have to give me any specifics; it's just that I've always been interested in things like that. I'm always reading books that deal with investigating murders and espionage."

"I guess it couldn't hurt; just one question before I start talking about this case."

"Shoot."

"Do you have any family that is in or involved with the Catholic Church?"

"Not that I know of. My family isn't very religious unless you consider going to Lions' games every Sunday for almost fifteen years."

Over the next couple of hours, Annette and I began talking about the case. Which was good because I was getting feedback and questions coming from someone extremely fresh and unaffected by this case. It allowed me to get a truly objective view of everything. You could tell she was well read as well as intelligent, which was odd to me at first because she never mentioned college. It seems as though she learned the majority of her knowledge the old-fashioned way, through reading and self-teaching. It has come to my attention that people who are self-motivated in their education seem to have better retention of the knowledge they have acquired over the years.

"So you're telling me that the basic premise of the case is that you have a dead boy at his high school. A mother that is being hidden and moved around by the Church. Then a letter addressed from the Archdiocese of Warsaw, Poland?"

"That's pretty much the basic idea of this case. To be honest, I'm at a complete loss because what little information we have on the kid who died is information that doesn't get us anywhere. We know who he is, we know who his girlfriend was, and we know who his mother is, but that is about it. We don't know if he knew who his father is or why there's a letter from the archdiocese in Poland. I figure the only thing I can come up with is that the Church is trying to hide the truth about the victim and his mother or that she is tied into the Church somehow."

"I see what you mean; you truly are in a bind in this case, aren't you? I take it, the reason you are flying to Poland is that you believe the mother is going to be there."

"You're a quick study, aren't you? We figure the only chance we have at cracking this case is to talk to the victim's mother and see what is going on. With our luck we'll find her, and she won't be of any help."

"It seems to me that you are taking this case personally. You are afraid of failing with this case, aren't you?"

"Some of it is that my ego doesn't allow me to accept failure in my life. There is also a tiny bit of information that ties me to this case in that the victim went to the same high school I graduated from. I am still very close to the headmaster and his students."

Talking about the case and how obsessed I've been with it really helped me to understand some of my weaknesses as an investigator as well as a human being. Talking with Annette helped me realize that I have problems communicating with others about what I am thinking without sounding condescending or belittling the person I am talking to. It is not my intention to do this by any means; it's just that sometimes I have trouble talking to other people outside of my head. Just ask my ex-wife, Sheila; she'll have no problem explaining my problems to you. Although now that I am aware of my problems, I can't excuse them, but I need to do something about them.

"You know, Mr. Baggio, I've been thinking about this case, and I know it sounds weird. What if the victim is the product of an affair with someone? Maybe of great importance in a political or religious sense?"

"I see what you're saying; that's one of the best ideas I've heard since I've been on this case. I know it's a little far-fetched, but chances are it's the key to this case. The challenge now is figuring out who the father is."

"Luckily for me, that's not my job to worry about. Instead, it's yours and that of your fellow employees."

I started this flight in a bad mood, and now I'm actually feeling quite decent about what lies ahead. As I glanced at my watch I noticed that we were almost six hours into the flight. I think it's time for me to try to get a little sleep, since chances are I'm going to get straight to work once we land in Warsaw.

AVE MARIA

24

The Polish didn't create coffee!

The flight was an interesting one and long, to say the least. With the time difference and the long flight, it is nearly seven in the morning on Monday morning. When I left, it was a quarter to seven in the morning on Sunday, and somehow a ten-hour flight makes it nearly seven in the morning on Monday morning. With the time change and crossing the International Date Line, it costs me a day; luckily, I'll get that day back when I fly back when this is all over. As for right now, I've got a few hours to kill before my ride shows up. I'm not in the mood to call Nicolette and Christian to tell them I messed up on the arrival time of the flight. I'll just get a bite to eat and walk around the airport until I find a place to lay my head.

After walking around, looking for a place to grab any form of nourishment, I realized that on international flights, jet lag is a bitch! I mean it's brutal; I'm going to be a zombie for at least a day. As I walked around, I realized the airport was much smaller than I was expecting. Then again, I don't know what I was expecting. It had about forty or so gates, and for a country of forty million, roughly four times that of New York State, I just assumed the airport would be bigger. For now, I have a stomach with some Polish snacks in it, water, and something else I'm afraid to know, but it filled me up. I just need to catch a quick nap and I'll be good to go.

Waking to the alarm on my cell phone, I noticed it was nearly eleven in the morning. I need to find Christian's cousin Nicolette, since she is supposed to pick me up from the airport, and once I get back to the hotel, I need to take a shower since I've been stuck in an airplane for more than half a day. I have to admit that my stay at the airport has been an enjoyable one over the past couple of hours. I've met some interesting people, and I even found time to catch a few more hours of sleep.

"Nice of you to join us in our bit of paradise here in Warsaw. How was your flight?" asked Nicolette.

"It wasn't too bad for a long flight. Luckily it wasn't too full, and I met a nice young lady on the flight as well as a friendly flight attendant."

"I would guess that a flight that long would allow you to meet a few people, especially since you are a friendly person."

"Yeah, I guess I can be quite friendly, especially when I am stuck on a plane. It's amazing how friendly one person can be when they are stuck in a confined place for a long period."

"Well, I've got a taxi outside waiting to take us to the hotel, where we'll get set and eventually meet up with Terrance and Christian. They are keeping tabs on Cardinal Kelley and Andrew's mother."

The two of us made our way from the hangar to a taxi out front of the concourse. I have to admit that Poland is not what I expected in the least; I guess I was expecting something from the Middle Ages. The airport is a little on the older side, but from the looks of things, I would guess that they are building a new airport soon. There are digital renderings of the proposed new airport all over the concourse. Either they are extremely excited about the project, or they want to convince everyone that it might be done. I couldn't get a good view of what was going on around the airport. It was a quick moment, then Nicolette and I were already in the taxi, making our way toward the archdiocese's headquarters.

"I meant to ask you, Nicolette, how far is the archdiocese from the place we are staying?"

"It's about a six-block walk from the archdiocese to the hotel that we are staying at. It isn't much more than a few minutes of a walk. We wanted to be close but not too close, where we would be obvious."

"That makes sense; why don't you have the driver take a route that passes the archdiocese if it doesn't already."

"We will drive by it on the way; it will be on our right in just a few minutes. The one nice thing about this city is that everything is in a centralized location. Their city planners really knew what they were doing when they rebuilt the city after World War Two."

"Well, that's good, because I want to get a good look at what I'm dealing with here."

I might even get out and talk to some of the people around the area. It's amazing how sometimes complete strangers can be very informative of another person's life that parallels their own without the other person noticing. Just imagine how much the local bartender knows about everything that is going on in the local scene. Who is dating whom, who knows what's going on, and usually where to find the best drugs? I'm looking for everything except the latter. We need to focus on information on the area, and a seasoned bartender is just the person to talk to in a situation like this. When you have no starting point in an unknown city, it is good practice to visit as many pubs as you can and talk to the bartenders. It's amazing how much information people will tell their bartender. It is a form of confession in some cultures; at least that's the way it is perceived.

As we passed the archdiocese's headquarters, it wasn't hard to see why the Church has been known as a political leader for so many centuries. The construction of the building is filled with historical context and strength. Just a glance at the building and one is taken back to the years of Church strength and complete control over its constituents. It really is an amazing sight to see the churches covered in biblical paintings, with vaulted ceilings creating an illusion that one is looking to the heavens. I could only imagine what it would be like to have been around when the churches were built; back when religion was the king of the lands, and the wrath of God was implemented by man. What a powerful tool to use when trying to contain or control a body of uneducated people.

"Nicolette, do you think you can have the driver stop at the closest coffee shop or bar in the area so I can get out and talk to some—"

"Wait a minute, Neil. Isn't Cardinal Kelley getting out of that car and heading into the archdiocesan building?"

"It sure does look like him. I don't see Ms. Malinowski, Andrew's mother, anywhere. I wonder where she is. Do we have one of our guys keeping a close eye on her and her whereabouts?"

"Yes, we do. Terrance and Christian are working together as we speak to keep an eye on her. We don't want to take any chances over here."

"I knew there was a reason I was happy with sending you and Christian over here. Why don't we stop up at the corner here; it looks as if there is a café there, where I can keep an eye on the archdiocese."

"What are you going to do there? It's not as if you can speak Polish or anything close to it. I'd be able to help you out, but judging by the tone in which you are talking, I'm guessing that you have something else planned for me and my services."

"Oh, how you know me so well in such a short time. I need you around the back to keep an eye out for Cardinal Kelley or anyone else that looks familiar leaving."

"I can do that, but if you need me or a few Polish phrases to get you by, you know I'm just a phone call away."

"Thank you very much, Nicolette, but I think I'll be all right. You forget that I can be very resourceful, not to mention that I have done my homework on the area surrounding the archdiocese."

"If you're going to head out there on your own, you will need some of the local money. I'll give you enough cash to cover you for the day."

AVE MARIA

As I stepped from the taxi and turned to the café, I noticed a student studying over a cup of coffee. It wasn't anything out of the ordinary, at least that I would understand it to be, being as I'm not from Poland. A small, noticeable logo on the student's hat caught my eye. He was wearing a sweatshirt with the emblem of the Warsaw School of Economics, and a Georgetown University hat. From the average view, it doesn't seem like anything important unless you realize that Georgetown University has an exchange program with the Warsaw School of Economics. It is one of the leading, if not *the* leading, universities on central European economics. This means that chances are the student is of American or Polish descent and able to speak both English and Polish.

I did not want to startle the student by stepping out of the taxi and directly approaching him; instead, I shall go inside and order a cup of coffee. This will allow me to make a slow play on the student in front of the café. Plus I could use a few minutes to go through my phone and check up on my emails and voice mails I've missed while flying to Warsaw. As I approached the counter, there was a young woman dressed in an apron asking me something in Polish. My guess is it was a simple hello, and how may I help you? She quickly learned that I didn't speak any Polish and followed suit with some familiar tones.

"I'm guessing English is more your suit?"

"What gave it away? Was it my blank stare to your first statement?"

"That gave it away, as well as the look of jet lag."

260

"For someone living in Poland, you speak pretty good English."

"Thank you; I'm studying English at the university so I can finish my studies at one of the economics universities in America. You'll find more than an average amount of young students in this area who can speak English and Polish as well as many other European languages. The Warsaw School of Economics draws attention from all over the world."

"That much I do know from my research on the area—"

"Before we go any further, what can I get for you today?"

"What is your house specialty, the drink of choice at this establishment?"

"All coffee is great in Poland. Don't you know that the Polish gave coffee to the world?"

"The Polish didn't create coffee!"

"That's not what I said. The Polish, after a war with the Turks in the late seventeenth century, brought coffee beans and brewed coffee to the rest of continental Europe. Before then, it was only found in England, Paris, and Marseilles."

"Damn, you learn something new every day, don't you? Then I will take an old-fashioned cup of black coffee; you choose the bean."

"Sounds good; if you're looking for someone to talk to while here today, the student out front is an American studying at the Warsaw School of Economics. His name is Trent O'Brien."

"Is he the one in the Georgetown hat and Cincinnati Bengals sweatshirt?"

"That's him out there; here's your coffee. I'll be out in a bit to see if you need anything."

"Thanks a lot. I never caught your name. What is it?"

"You can just call me Julita; I believe it is similar to Julia in your country."

"Thank you, Julita, I'll be outside talking to your friend Trent."

There really isn't anything quite like the feeling of walking up to a complete stranger, especially a man, and asking him if you can join him for a cup of coffee. Luckily for me, I've spent my life approaching strangers, so I've learned to get over the awkwardness of it all. My guess is that Trent finished his undergraduate work at Georgetown University, and he's here in Poland studying international economics, presumably that of central Europe. I had a little bit of help trying to guess the background of the student I'm about to approach; don't think for a moment that I'm a form of Sherlock. I'm just stubborn and persistent; those are what make me a good investigator, not having a brilliant memory.

"Trent . . . Trent O'Brien?"

"Yes. What can I do for you this afternoon?"

"I was talking to Julita inside, and she informed me that you were from the States and that you were studying here in Warsaw. I just arrived today and was looking for some good conversation. If you're busy studying, I won't bother you."

"It's okay, I could use a break. I'm just getting an early start on my finals coming up next month."

"You aren't kidding. That's a hell of a head start; I was a little bit of a late-night cram study student."

"If you don't mind me asking, what brings you to Warsaw: business or pleasure?"

"I guess it's business, but then again, my business is a pleasure for me. I'm an investigator whose case has taken me here to Warsaw. How about you? What brings you to Warsaw?"

"I'm studying at the Warsaw School of Economics, working on a PhD in central European economics. I did my undergraduate and master's work at Georgetown University, where I was presented the opportunity to study abroad here in Warsaw."

"That's interesting. I see that you're a Bengals fan?"

"I grew up in Ohio, in a town called Lima."

"It's a decent-size town right off of I-Seventy-Five, isn't it?"

"Nice job; it's very rare that anyone outside of Lima knows where the town is. My family has always been big Cleveland Browns fans, and I've always loved the Bengals."

Trent is the average person's idea of an Irish American: red hair, pale skin, and a boyish face. Next to the word "Irish" should be a picture of this kid. It truly is amazing to meet someone that looks like the idea you have in your head. It's like meeting a Sicilian that reminds you of every mobster you've ever seen, even if he's a priest or a teacher.

"I've noticed you've been keeping your eyes locked on the front doors of the Archdiocese of Warsaw. May I ask you why?"

"Let's just say that there is some information I need, and chances are the people in that building are my best chance for getting that information."

"Then I wish you good luck. This isn't your average Catholic, as it is in the States. This is Poland, a country that has survived because of its faith in the Church throughout history. The Church has more power in this country than many people can imagine."

"I must digress a bit. What made you come to Warsaw to study economics? Isn't it a school known for its central European economics studies?"

"That's what drew me here. I am a first-generation Irish American in my family. My parents were born, raised, and married in Ireland; I was born in Ohio shortly after their marriage in. I hope to someday go back to Ireland and get involved in politics and work to help the economic structure of the country that gave me life."

"I must admit, you sound like you have a plan and are very determined."

From the time I had seen Cardinal Kelley walk into the front doors of the archdiocese to now, the time has passed quite quickly. It was the middle of the afternoon when I arrived at the coffeehouse. Before I knew it, the sun was beginning to redden behind the Warsaw horizon. A good five hours had passed while talking to Trent about the school, economics, and the Polish socioeconomic infrastructure that he was studying and what it meant to the cultural society around us. He explained to me that the Church is into everything you can imagine, beyond politics, beyond social status. The Church holds equity in businesses through land contracts that it rents out to businesses. Land is the one commodity in this world that will never change throughout time. If you have it, you are in power, and if you need it, you are on the short end of the stick.

"Well, I guess this is the end of our conversation. I'm going to make my way to the hotel and get some things done before it gets too late. Here's one of my cards with my email and other numbers."

"Thanks again for everything, Neil; it was a pleasure talking with you. I will definitely keep in touch; if you need anything while in Poland, give me a call/text. I'll make sure to help you out in any way I can."

"Thanks again for the conversation and the coffee. Have a good night, and good luck with studying."

As I made my way from the café to the hotel, which was just a few blocks from the archdiocese, I noticed a figure out front hailing a cab. With the setting sun in my eyes, it made it hard to make out the figure at first. But once I heard his voice, even in Polish, I knew right away that it was Cardinal Kelley. He has a very distinct rasp to his voice; it is not commonly heard in a man of his stature. Standing at a mere 5-8 and weighing barely 170 pounds, you would expect his voice to be a little higher in pitch. Instead it is lower, as if he were standing over 6 feet and weighing nearly 300 pounds. I guess that the same can be said for some of the heavyweight boxers we see on TV that have high-pitched voices.

Before the cab could pull over to pick up the cardinal, I approached him to see if I could get close. I don't think he has any idea who I am, especially being in Warsaw right now. I'm going to see if I can get him to share his cab with me and allow a few moments of face-to-face time. Quickly moving with the sun as the advantage, I made ground on him. With nearly perfect precision, I approached him and said good day as the cab pulled up. I barraged him with a hearty handshake and an overly exuberant introduction. He quickly looks lost as I push the two of us into the cab, where he finds out what is really going on.

"Hey, would mind explaining to me what just happened and why you forced me into this cab?"

"You were getting in this cab with or without me; I just wanted to join you, that's all. That and I needed to ask you a few questions."

"You didn't have to jump all over me and shove me into a cab to do that. You could have just walked up and asked to talk."

"That wouldn't have gotten the result I wanted, which was to get your heart rate up and full attention to the situation. We have met once before, but it was under different circumstances, and you never saw my face."

"Are you that psycho from St. Pat's Church?"

"Yes, but I'm no psycho. I was pressed for time, and I was looking for information, and you didn't give it to me. That's why I'm here in Warsaw with you; I'm trying to get to the bottom of a young student's death. I'm hoping that you are going to be a little more helpful this time."

"For your information, I wasn't holding back anything the first time we met. I didn't have anything for you, but this time around is a little different."

Cardinal Kelley is turning out to be a completely different person than I had originally thought. Although a cliché, I did judge a book by its cover only to be surprised with a good story. He turned out to be more forthright with information this time around, and I felt like I should reward him for doing so.

"Seeing as I'm not the one who's ever been here and I'm guessing you can speak Polish. How about you tell the driver to take us to a nearby steakhouse or pub where I can make things up to you, as best I can."

"That sounds a lot better than hanging out in a confessional for an hour, thinking I'm dying of anthrax. I think steak and a nice drink will do the body good."

"If you know of just the place we can go to where we can talk and enjoy a decent meal, tell the driver."

"I know just the place. Sit back and relax; we're going for a drive."

25

It's going to take some work and creativity, but at least I'll have the resources I'll need to try and track down some answers.

The architecture of this city is modern, with reverence to the old ways. The Poles have done an amazing job of rebuilding a city once torn by the devastation that was World War Two. The cardinal had us take a drive past the Stadion Dziesięciolecia, which is Europe's biggest market and is still a tourist attraction. The city reflects a people that have gone through so many changes over the past hundred years. From a political viewpoint, Poland was at one point and, for quite some time, a Communist country. Shortly after World War Two, Poland turned to a Communist form of government and, in 1989, moved on to a liberal democracy. That's enough of a history lesson for you; I just wanted to indulge you in the same tour I was getting from Cardinal Kelley.

"Well, Neil, we are almost there. Just around the corner here, and we'll be at one of my favorite restaurants in Warsaw."

"I can't wait. After that long flight and several cups of coffee, I could use a good meal and a nice drink."

"I think this will suit you just right."

AVE MARIA

The restaurant was more modern than I would have imagined for driving that long. I was expecting something along the lines of a country market; instead I received a modern restaurant plush with large windows and a view that was just amazing. The restaurant overlooked the Wisla River, which runs through Warsaw. I believe Cardinal Kelley told me that or was it Trent? To be honest I'm not quite sure who it was, but I'm almost positive that it is the largest river in Poland. Either way, the view inside and outside was spectacular; if this is any lead into what the food will taste like, then this should be a great meal.

"Cardinal Kelley, from ambience and location themselves, you've outdone yourself; I can't wait to sit down and see what this country has to offer."

"We'll get the full course here, starting off with some Polish vodka. How do you take yours?"

"I'll take mine on the rocks with a lemon slice if that's all right with you. I like to enjoy the taste of the spirits."

"The locals will be glad to hear that you like to drink your vodka straight. Are you open to new cuisine, or would you like to eat something specific?"

"I'm up to trying the best the local restaurant has to offer."

As we sat down, Cardinal Kelley started talking to the server at some length. He later explained to me that he ordered our drinks and a full-course dinner, beginning with a beet soup, which was quite good. Next, we were served an appetizer of salmon with oil and vinegar; it was similar to a salad. But the best part of the whole meal was the entrée, a breaded pork cutlet followed by sauerkraut with sirloin and sausage. For dessert we enjoyed a fresh homemade piece of poppy seed cake. The best part of the whole night was sitting there talking to Cardinal Kelley about Andrew's mother and what he learned about her and her son while on the plane from the States.

"Like I was saying to you earlier, Neil, I wasn't trying to be short or withhold information from you on our first encounter. Instead, I had nothing to offer. That has changed since my flight overseas with Ms. Malinowski."

"So, what are you trying to tell me? Are you trying to tell me that you have more information now than you had before?"

"That is exactly what I am telling you about. The only problem is that I am still light on the facts. But I will tell you everything that I learned on that flight and on from those who overlook me."

"If that's the case, why don't you start at the beginning?"

"Can do."

The next couple of hours were spent talking about the case, what he learned from Ms. Malinowski on the flight. He informed me that once he was on the plane and built a sense of trust with her, the two of them began talking about her life and how she ended up in the situation she had arrived at. I'm just amazed at the turn this case has taken. Yesterday I thought Cardinal Kelley was part of the problem, and today I've learned he's trying to be part of the solution.

"Why don't we start with what you know about Ms. Malinowski's past, and we'll move forward from there?"

AVE MARIA

"Well, I found out she was born in a small town just north of Warsaw, and by age sixteen, she felt a calling to the Church. On her eighteenth birthday she arrived at a convent in Warsaw, where she would later meet Andrew's father."

"Are you trying to tell me she had a secret love affair with a priest?"

"I haven't gotten that far yet. Why don't you let me tell you what I know, and then you can just ask me questions from there?"

"All right, continue."

"It was then that I realized that Ms. Malinowski was involved at a young age. She isn't as old as she looks. Andrew was born when she was barely twenty years old. That means she is only in her forties. It's from all the years of holding her secret in. Also, all the hiding in the shadows that her age has presented itself."

"She's only forty? I would have easily pegged her for someone in their fifties. Wow, you aren't kidding, the time has not been kind to her; this is all the more reason to figure out what truly happened that night to her son."

"I am with you one hundred percent on this one. I will do anything I can to help; even if it may jeopardize my job, she deserves to know the truth. It isn't right what is going on with Andrew and his death."

"I can agree with you on that; the problem now is trying to figure out what really happened that night and why."

"From what little I was able to gain about Andrew's father, it seems as though he was either working at the convent or was a priest himself. She wasn't clear on which one he was. The problem now is who his father was, also why the Church would hide Andrew's birth for so many years."

"I guess that's where I come in. You've done everything you can for me and this case until now, but now I have to find a way to put everything together."

The conversation with Cardinal Kelley paid off major dividends for me. I was able to get enough information from him so I could build some sort of timeline to figure out when Andrew was born and who the father might be. Luckily for me, the Church has made a living out of keeping records. The Church and especially the Jesuit sector have held and created some of the greatest libraries in the world. Because of that, I should have a good chance of tracking down Andrew's father. It's going to take some work and creativity, but at least I'll have the resources I'll need to try and track down some answers.

"Well, Cardinal Kelley, I'm going to have to thank you not only for a great meal but also for your help on this matter at hand. You have given me a new breath of air to take this case head-on."

"I just want what's best for the Malinowski family; no one's death should ever be covered up regardless of the truth. I was trained and taught that truth, above all else, is what we must hold dear."

"I completely agree with you, Cardinal; I have made a living out of finding out the truth. That is why I've been going nuts over this case; nothing seems to be making sense. I think that is the hardest thing about this case to grasp; it is just hard to understand how something you are taught to revere all your life is the one thing that is keeping you from finding the truth."

"Imagine realizing the faith you have sacrificed your life to as being the bad guy in this, that's when you have to realize that it's the human condition that affects all of this. This isn't the Church's doing or the Catholic faith but instead that of man."

"I guess I see what you're saying: man is fallible, not God."

It really is true when you think about it that we sometimes judge our faith and that of our Church on the actions of man. It is not the Islamic religion that is killing people. Instead, man is using his religious beliefs to try and justify their actions. It is the same when we look at someone who says that it is God's will; sometimes it is just life and nothing more. We make choices in our lives that affect the outcome of our day; not everything is God's will. It has gotten to a point in our culture that we have found a way to take all blame off of ourselves and place it somewhere else. No one is fat anymore because they eat too much and lack work ethic; instead, they have emotional demons and not enough time to work out.

It's the same thing when people take another life. There is always some form of blame; the child wouldn't have killed his teacher had he not played violent video games. I played a lot of games as a kid, and I never emulated what I played. I understood the difference between right and wrong. It is just getting annoying hearing that people are always finding ways to get off free without punishment. I was always taught to fight to the death when you are wrongly accused but to admit wrongdoing when you are guilty. Some of it is the lack of repercussions our children have. We can't spank our children, teachers can't touch a student to show restraint, and we are losing all control of our children because we are afraid to offend anyone. In doing so, we are raising a generation that doesn't care about anyone but himself or herself.

"Well, I guess we should get a ride back. I've got a lot of work to do over the next couple of days."

"I'm actually staying across the street at a local inn. But I will have them call you a cab to your hotel. It shouldn't take long to get a cab out here at this time of the night."

"Thanks again for everything, Cardinal; I don't know where I would be right now in this case if we hadn't talked."

"It's all right. I will pray for you that you might find the truth beneath the lies. Be safe in your endeavors."

We parted ways as I made my way out to the taxi, where I would have plenty of time to think. The cab ride should take me two hours or so; I might even take a nap. That's probably the best thing to do. I'll worry about the case and getting everyone up to speed once I get back to the hotel.

26

Sit back and relax, there's a lot to go over.

I awoke to the cabdriver yelling at me to pay him something. I noticed the number on his meter and did my best to hand him the correct amount of cash for the ride. As would be expected, it cost quite a bit; any two-hour taxi ride is going to cost a few dollars. It's almost midnight; well, I've still got a good forty-five minutes until then, so I think it's about time I check in and head up to my room. Before I could even make it to the front desk, I was met at the door by Nicolette, and it didn't look like she was very happy with me.

"Where the hell have you been? I left you at the café around noon, and we hadn't seen or heard from you since."

"I didn't know I had to check in with you guys. Isn't that cute? You guys were worried about me."

"Oh, shut up, Neil, you are usually checking in with us every hour or so. It was just unlike you to fall off the radar like that. Especially when you are in a foreign country, where you don't speak the language, I figured you ended up lost or involved in something big.

Exactly what happened over the past couple hours that you were off the radar?"

"I ended up talking with a local college student who is from the States for a couple of hours. Then I shared a cab with Cardinal Kelley, where he decided to be of some major help. We went to dinner on the other side of Warsaw, and then I came back. As for what I learned, I don't feel like telling everyone separately, so we might as well head upstairs and get everyone together. We can just conference call in whoever is still following Andrew's mother. They could probably use a little bit of a distraction."

"I'll take you upstairs to show you where we are staying; we've got connecting rooms on the third floor. We've each got a bed and all the surveillance equipment one could need in a situation like this."

"We've even got some wiretaps and GPS units on the cars that the archdiocese uses. This way we can keep tabs on people even when we're outnumbered."

"I'm proud to see that you guys have everything under control out here."

"We are trying our best; we don't want to let our fearless leader down. You'll have to excuse me for a moment, though. I need to talk to Christian and have him get ahold of Terrance, who is keeping tabs on Ms. Malinowski right now. This way we can conference him at the meeting."

"I like the way you're thinking; it saves me having to tell everyone more than once what's going on."

It really is nice to see the growth of young investigators, especially Christian. He has grown leaps and bounds from the day he started at BCI. He has thought out plans, he's organized, and he always finds a way to get things done. You can't ask for much more from an investigator. As for Nicolette, she is coming along swiftly; it is amazing what a strong and heavily educated young woman can accomplish. I just wish more women knew what the world had for them; all they need to do is put forth the effort. After ten minutes, Christian and Nicolette had a conference call set up with Terrance so that I could work only once through the information I gained from Cardinal Kelley.

"Thanks, guys, for being here. Terrance, can you hear me clearly enough?"

"Yeah, everything is clear on my end. Let's get this going."

"Okay. I just got back from a long dinner with Cardinal Kelley that paid off some major dividends. It turns out that he isn't such a bad guy after all. He was just as much in the dark about the whole situation as we were. Luckily for us, he was able to get Andrew's mother on the plane for ten hours. After a while, she opened up about a lot of things that had us all in the dark."

"So what are you trying to tell us?"

"Sit back and relax, there's a lot to go over."

We spoke of what Cardinal Kelley and I had conversed about over dinner. Shortly thereafter, we spent the night planning where we would go from here with the case and how we would find Andrew's biological father. We could end the investigation right here knowing what we know, but that wouldn't solve the problem at hand. Why is this kid's death being covered up as if it is something more than it looks? I know I've said this, but the problem is that we can't figure out why anyone would want this kid's life hidden from the rest of the world. The thing driving me nuts is that now I know that Andrew's mother was a nun and his father in the priesthood. It doesn't seem to me that his parents' career choices are more than enough reasons to hide his life. I just hope we can come up with a good idea on how to track down Andrew's father. Once we get there, who knows where we will end up?

"I think I have an idea, but I'm not sure how it is going to work."

"Don't stop there, Nicolette. Share it with us."

"I agree with your cousin Christian. Spit it out, girl."

"What if we use a facial recognition program to track down his father? We can match his face against that of the Church's records."

"I like where you are going with this, Nicolette. The Church is known for being historians throughout our past. They record everything, including taking photos of themselves, as if to make a yearbook. I know who we have to call."

Before anyone could do anything, I grabbed the phone and started dialing Tony Johnson. It's almost three in the morning here, which means it's about six hours earlier back home. Tony should be hitting his stride right about now. His tech team and he are quite the night owl team, working very late and never around during the day, but they always get the job done. Even if they forget to shower occasionally, they are good at what they do.

AVE MARIA

"Hey Tony, it's Neil. I need to know if you can do us a favor."

"You know I'm always willing to help out in any way I can. What can I do for you?"

"I need to know if we can use a facial recognition program to compare Andrew's facial structure with that of men who were near his mother while she was in Warsaw."

"There are going to be two problems. One is going to be getting access to the photographs of those in school back then. The other problem will be getting them in clear enough quality that the program would work."

"What do you need us to do on our end?"

"I'm going to see if we can find and/or access some photos in the Church's database. But this could take a couple of days. I need you to track down some hard copies of those photographs. Also, we need to work on a timeline to narrow down the search."

"If we take Andrew's birth date and subtract ten months, that should give us a decent window to start looking at."

"Well, I'll get the tech team together and get started right away. We'll concentrate on gaining access to the Church's database. Let's hope that they have brought all of their records into the technological age and not kept doing things the classical way."

"The Church is always up on the latest ways to keep records; it wouldn't surprise me if they had every record ever written backed up on a database somewhere."

"That's true. The Church has always been a keeper of information. Plus they are always looking for better and safer ways to store that information."

"You get to work on your end, and we'll get started on our end first thing in the morning. Text or email me with any and all updates as they become available."

"Can do, Neil. I'll get started right away; good luck on your end. At least I don't have to leave the comfort of my office."

Finally, off the phone, I needed to get some rest soon. Tony wasn't kidding: tomorrow is going to be a lot of running around and sifting through books and, heaven forbid, microfiche. Before it gets any later—it's already four in the morning—I have to get some sleep. We'll need to get an early start tomorrow, which means that there won't be much sleep tonight. As long as I get two or three hours I'll be able to function without any problems. I just hope the other guys can keep up with me in the morning, although Terrance will probably need some rest since he's been tracking Andrew's mother for more than ten hours, and Christian is going to relieve him soon. For most of the day Nicolette and I will go through all the information we can get our hands on. More than likely it will help to have a feminine touch tomorrow.

"What did Tony have to say on his end? Does he think he'll have any luck?"

"He thinks he might be able to hack into the Church records; the only problem is that he doesn't know if the Church has put records that old on a computer backup. That is why we are going to track down what information we can at the library and any other resource we might be able to find."

"So we are going to do work that might not even be used? I'm going to have to get used to this kind of work."

"Look at it as covering your butt for the worst-case scenario. You'll learn that the more you do it, the better you will be at this job."

"Does this mean I might have a job waiting for me when this case is over?"

"We'll have to see when we are done; there are always opportunities for someone bright, intelligent, and multilingual."

"Thank you for the compliment, Neil. But it's getting late, and I'm guessing that you want to get a head start early tomorrow. I need to get some rest, which is something you might want to look into."

"I'll get to bed shortly; I just need to go over a few things before I lay down. I'll see you in the morning—say, about seven?"

"Sounds good. I'll see you then."

Before I could go to bed, I needed to check my emails and send one out to my little girl Carol Lynn back home in Detroit. I promised her that I would try and send her an email every morning so that she has something to read before she heads off to school. I know that I'm not always there for my daughter as much as I would like to, but I do try my best. I try to stay active in any way that I can, whether it is a phone call or an email to see how she is doing. I just want her to know that even when I can't be there to hold and hug her, I'm thinking about her and that I want to know how she is doing. I guess I could call;

there's a chance she might still be up, seeing as it's only ten o'clock at night back home in Detroit.

"Hey, Neil, what are you doing up so late? Isn't it nearly four in the morning there?"

"It sure is, babe, but I wanted to see if our little angel was still up by any chance."

"I just put her to bed, but I can see if she's still up if you would like me to."

"No, don't wake her up, she needs her sleep. She's a growing girl, plus she gets really cranky in the morning if she doesn't get enough sleep."

"Well then I guess you're just stuck with me. Is that going to be okay with you?"

"I guess I can manage; you truly are the beginning and end to my day. You are my best friend who drives me nuts. Thanks for always being there at the end of the day, Sheila."

"It's no problem, Neil. I know you are always stressed out, and you are a mess, but you are always there for your daughter and me at the end of the day."

"Although things didn't work out as we may have wanted, at the end of the day you are a good friend and the mother of my daughter, and to me that carries a lot of weight."

"You always knew how to sweet-talk the ladies, you know that. The thing about you, though, is that it was never fake, and that was the dangerous part about you. You were always speaking from the heart."

"I hate to cut our conversation short, but it is almost four in the morning here, and I have to be up and functioning at about seven, so I should probably get some sleep. I sent Carol Lynn an email. If you can print it off and put it in her room, I would greatly appreciate it."

"That's no problem, Neil. She really appreciates the time you take to call her and leave her emails. I know she keeps every email you send printed off in her school binder. Get some rest, honey, and I wish you the best with your case."

"Thanks, Sheila. I love you and Carol Lynn so much, I hope all is well, and I can't wait to be home and see you two again."

There is nothing left to say or think about that that can't wait a couple of hours. Currently my number one priority is figuring out a way to get some sleep.

27

The water was running and the steam was rising. My favorite part of the day has begun.

There seems to be a problem with my alarm; it is telling me to get out of bed, but I've been sleeping for just a few hours, and I'm not ready to get up. I just don't know what to expect today; I can only hope that Tony or I come up with something, because the longer time we spend, the less chance we have to figure out the truth. Before I had any time to debate with myself on getting out of bed, I was awoken by an angel.

"Wake your old ass up, we've got a lot to do today. Hop in the shower; I've already got the coffee brewing."

"Sir, yes, sir, I'm right on it. Damn Nicolette, you're nuts!"

"Neil, wake your butt up and get in that shower. And don't make me come after you in there. You've got fifteen minutes, and the clock is ticking."

This is going to be difficult; by now, you've learned that I love my showers and that they often run for more than twenty minutes. This is going to be hard for me to get out of here in less than fifteen minutes.

"I'm going to take my sweet time in there, and if you don't like it, you'll just have to come in after me."

"Neil, I wouldn't antagonize her; chances are she'd go in after you. She's not the shy type."

"I'll take that into accord, Christian. Shouldn't you be heading out to switch shifts with Terrance?"

"As a matter of fact, I'm just grabbing a few last things together to head on out there. We're switching at seven; is there anything I can keep an eye out for you?"

"Just the usual. Keep an eye out for everything because we still don't know who we are looking for."

"You got it, boss man; I mean Neil. I know you hate it; good luck out there with Nicolette."

"Thanks, Christian, I'll check in with you later and keep you up to date. As for right now, I need to jump in the shower because I'm running out of time."

I made my way into the bathroom and began to strip when I heard Nicolette yelling at me through the door. She was reminding me I didn't have too long in the shower. I would have to make it quick, which is not to my liking, but then again, it can't always be about me.

"Hey, old man, you are running out of time. If I were you, I'd have the water running already."

"Did you just call me an old man? I don't take kindly to idle threats."

"I'm not too worried about you, and the threat wasn't an idle one. Just hurry up; I'll be waiting for you shortly."

"Give me ten minutes and I'll be dressed and ready."

The water was running and the steam was rising. My favorite part of the day has begun. As the water ran down my back, the whole case took off as if I were watching a highlight reel of it. Andrew's body lying there placed ever so gently; some people forget that crime scenes aren't perfect and that there is always chaos. I could hear the conversations I had with Headmaster Glow and Cardinal Kelley. Things just don't seem to be what I originally thought.

"Hey, are you almost done there, old man? We're running out of time with this."

"I'm almost done here; just give a few more minutes—I'm thinking through something. Just ask Christian about my showers; he'll tell you."

"Hey Christian, what the hell is he talking about?"

"Oh, Neil's shower thing? Yeah, he says that he thinks better in the shower; he's been known to take twenty- or thirty-minute showers. It seems to be working for him, since he's always coming out of showers with good ideas. If you ever get a call to meet at the warehouse in the middle of the night, chances are Neil just got out of the shower." Damn straight!

"So you're telling me that I should let him take his time in the shower?" Yes, he is!

"I'm telling you to grab some coffee and relax because it could be awhile. Plus, the longer he takes, the more likely he'll come up with something. So chill out, Nicolette."

"I guess I should tell him to take his time then?"

"I wouldn't worry about it. Neil will take his time in there; just sit back and relax."

I could overhear Nicolette and Christian talking outside of the shower, which made me realize that these walls are extremely thin. Thin walls make for quiet nights; anyone can hear you on the other side. If you're the person on the other side it could be a long night. I can make out enough of what Christian is saying. It sounds like he is telling her to relax and let me take my time. He knows better than to rush my shower; I think my best is here. This reminds me: I need to focus on the case again, start with the basics, and work forward.

I know that Andrew is dead, and it is supposed to look like a suicide. I also know that his mother was and may still be a nun in the Catholic Church. The twist to this puzzle is that his father was close enough to Ms. Malinowski when she was in the convent. The question then becomes, was she pregnant when she entered the convent, or did she conceive Andrew after she began her service with the Church? Before we go searching for photos, we need to go looking for birth records, which will probably be nearly impossible. Still, we can work backward and look into Ms. Malinowski's birth records and try and get our bearings on this whole case. If we can put together a timeline with all of the information we have, then maybe we can narrow down our search criteria.

I really need to get out of this shower before I start to prune up, not to mention I've run out of things to think about. It's time to get a plan together and get moving. If I know Tony, he's already been working all night, and he'll have news either good or bad for me in the morning. This means I need to get going and fast so that I've got something to bring to the table; now that I'm out of the shower, we can get going.

"All right, Nicolette, I'm almost ready to go. How are you doing?"

"I've been patiently waiting for you to finish thinking in the shower. I've got the car waiting for us downstairs."

"Well, let me fill up my coffee thermos and let's get out of here."

"I've already got that done for you as well. With sugar and cream, just the way you like it."

"Since you've got everything covered for me, let's get going."

I couldn't help but think that I am missing something here. I wish I had someone to bounce some ideas off of, outside of those involved in the case. I need a fresh objective perspective; I need someone who looks at this from a different angle. What I need is someone that isn't involved in making good out of things that have gone wrong. The problem with talking to other investigators is we have preconceived notions as to what is going on. I need someone who can look at this from a different angle. I know I said that already, but this is driving me up the wall; I need to talk to Cappelano. I know what you are thinking, and no, I am not nuts. It's just that Cappelano can look at this from an educated perspective that is a little more twisted than mine is. I need to get ahold of him, and soon.

"Hey Nicolette, can you bring the car around? I'll meet you downstairs. I need to make a quick phone call."

"This better not be a way to stall me, Neil. We need to get this shit going—"

"Damn, girl, I just need to call Ken and talk to him about something, but I need a little privacy, so I'm going to give you a head start. That way I can walk alone and talk to Ken in privacy and not lose any more time than we have."

"Okay, I'll give you a five-minute head start. If you aren't down there five minutes after I am, then I'm going to the library on my own."

"Don't worry, I'll be there."

I let Nicolette get going. Then I grabbed the headset to my phone so I could walk, talk, and check email all at the same time. You learn to multitask like a son of a bitch in this business; it's rare that you get moments alone to work on one thing. As the phone rang, I couldn't help but question my own judgment to solicit advice from a man such as Cappelano. It is safe to say that I am running out of confidence and options.

"Hey Neil, what are you doing calling me at two in the morning? You know I don't operate on the same clock as you. This better is good, I mean *really* good."

"I need you to do me a huge favor. First thing in the morning, I need you to drive down to the prison and meet with Cappelano. I need to talk to him, and the only way we can do this is if he uses your cell."

"I'm not letting him get his hands on my cell phone. I'll get a prepaid phone and call you from his cell when we get in there. I take it you are going to make a few phone calls and set this up?"

"Yeah, I'll call my old college buddy Coby Shields. Chances are he's at work or going to be at work soon. Call me before you leave and I'll fill you in on how it is going to go down."

"All right, Neil, I'll head out there at six in the morning. That way I'll get out there before most of the inmates are up. It will give us a chance to get this done undetected, at least to a certain degree."

"Thanks a million, Ken; I really need to get a different perspective on this case, and fast."

"No problem; that's what I'm here for. I'll talk to you in four hours or so, okay?"

"Sounds good. I'll talk to you in a bit."

As soon as I got off the phone with Ken, I started scrolling through my phone book, looking for Coby's cell phone number and praying that he was going to be at work around six or seven in the morning. Coby and I went to college together; to be a little more specific, we were roommates for a year. It's quite funny how we met, but that's beside the point. Maybe later we can go over that, but for now I need to get ahold of him. We still keep in touch halfway decently for old college buddies.

"This is Coby Shields. Who may I ask is calling me so fucking late?"

"Your old roommate. Why are you so cranky? It's barely even two in the morning over there."

"We're not in college anymore, Neil. What the fuck is your problem? If I know you as well as I think I do, then you are calling to ask me a favor. And the first answer you are looking for is yes, I'm at work, and I'll be here until eight in the morning. What can I do for you?"

"I need you to let a friend of mine get in a private room with Cappelano so he can use a cell phone to call me. I need to ask him a few questions about a case I'm working on."

"If that's all you need, then no problem. What's your friend's name?"

"Ken Chamberlain is his name; you'll know who he is when he walks up. He should be there at about six or six thirty in the morning. Should I have him call you when he gets there?"

"Yeah, have him drop me a text, and I'll make sure and meet him at the gate. You are going to owe me one."

"No problem. Name it and you've got it."

"I'm going to need a letter of recommendation to get out of this prison and onto the street. How about you call some of your friends and see what you can do?"

"No problem. I'll get to work on it as soon as this case is over or in a week, whichever comes first."

"Sounds fair to me. Just give him my number and we'll be all set."

"Thanks again, Coby. I'll call you when I get back in the States. We'll get a drink."

"All right, by me, Neil. I've got to go, though."

That was easier than I intended, but then again, Coby and I go back pretty far. We've also been there for each other over the years, and he knows that I am good on my word. Now all I have to do is text Coby's number and the plan to Ken while running down to the car so that Nicolette doesn't leave me here. I guess I could wait and text Ken when I get to the car, but for now I need to haul ass downstairs. It's at this moment I am starting to remember I'm no longer in college, as Coby mentioned. The body doesn't move quite as well as it used to. It was quite funny to see the looks on the faces of those I passed on my way downstairs. People were probably trying to remember my face in case they get questioned about a man fleeing the building after committing a crime. It's not every day you see someone sprinting as hard as they can down eight flights of stairs and out the front door to a waiting car.

"I was just messing with you, Neil; you didn't need to sprint down here. I would have given you a few more minutes."

"I didn't want you to wait any more than you already have. It's the least I could do since you were so patient for me when I was showering."

"Shut it, Neil, you don't have to give me a hard time. Not to mention for someone who could barely get up this morning, you moved quite well. So where are we heading?"

"We are going to the archdiocese first; it's time to put on a good show for the Archdiocese of Warsaw."

"I don't if I like that look in your eyes' I heard about that stunt you pulled with Cardinal Kelley at St. Pat's Church. Are we going to do something that could get us kicked out of the country?"

"I'm not sure yet. Let's go get some breakfast at that coffeehouse where you dropped me off yesterday. I need a few moments to think and to call TJ."

"You've got a cup of coffee. Speaking of which, where did it go? I left it with you upstairs, didn't I?"

"Yes you did, but I lost it somewhere between the phone call I had with Ken and running down here. I really don't have any idea of where it is. Oh well, it was just a paper cup; we can always get another cup of coffee."

"I guess you're right, I know just the place. I'm not going to have to flirt or seduce any member of the Church, am I? I don't know if I can do that."

"I don't think you'll have to. We'll just see now, won't we?"

"I guess so, Neil. Sometimes I worry what I've gotten myself into, but then again, this is really fun."

I know we have to get into the archdiocese and see what we can come up with. We originally had some elaborate plan. Things have changed now that Cardinal Kelley is on board, helping us. I should call him and see if he can help us. I'll have Nicolette call the inn where he was staying. Let me text her real quickly, and yell through the door one last time.

"Nicolette, I'm texting you some info for Cardinal Kelley where he is staying. Call the inn, tell them you're working with Neil Baggio, and that you need to get a message to the cardinal. Let's see if we can get his help at the archdiocese. It's worth a shot; after yesterday, I think he'll help."

"Got it, Neil. Now get ready so we can be moving." Fair point.

28

If it isn't the American who ran off yesterday without saying good-bye.

We've been sitting at the coffeehouse for a little while now. I'm just waiting for a phone call from Ken and Cappelano so I can talk to him about this case. I need a fresh perspective, and there is no one I can think of with a more unique perspective than Cappelano. Luckily for me, this is a private case and not one for the bureau; they don't like it when you involve mass murders into the investigation. I don't see why it's a big deal; when you are trying to catch a psycho, why not ask one for advice?

Before I could order my second cup of coffee from the pretty Polish girl at the counter, I noticed my phone ringing insistently. This better is Cappelano; that's all I can say about that.

"Neil, it's Ken. You're going to have to make it quick. You've only got five minutes. I'm always here for you, but I think this is useless." Ken might have a point.

"Hello, Neil. What can I do for you? I hear you've gone and gotten yourself entangled with the Church, and you're trying to figure out a mystery. I'm intrigued, but I doubt I can help."

"Frank, I keep looking at this case, and nothing makes sense. If a young boy is the child of a girl from a convent, why ship her and the child to the States, have her work and raise him secretly? If you're going to disavow, separate completely? Then why go to lengths to throw people off the scent when he was tracking down his real father?"

"Neil, I'm giving Ken his phone back. You don't need me. You need a drink, maybe a long shower, and a good fuck. Or just talking to a strange bartender like you did in DC before you caught me. You always have it in there, just slow down."

What the fuck just happened? Did I go out of my way, risk a friendship, and call in a favor, only to get shot down? Fuck, I did not see that coming. He has a point, though: I have all the information, all the plays in my head. All I need to do is slow down, sift through them, and find a way to talk it out. Maybe I can go to that coffee shop again and find Trent, or reach out to Cardinal Kelley. He was a good listener.

"Ken, I'm sorry for wasting your time. You're always telling me he's useless. But I never listen, maybe I'll learn." Probably not.

"That's what I'm here for, to support you, even when the idea is dumb. That's what friends are for."

"Who's that laughing in the background? It sounds like more than one voice."

"It's Cappelano and your buddy Coby. They both liked my comment, I guess." Ken got a chuckle out of that.

"Well, I'll let you guys go. I have to figure this out, as usual. Thanks again, Ken."

I could see that Nicolette was getting really impatient with me. She had heard all these great things about the awesome Neil Baggio, only to find out he is just as lost as the rest of us. Searching in the dark for his socks, can't find shit, not even light, hoping for that lucky pull. I just need time to work through shit, I can do that anywhere. Let's see what she has planned.

"Nicolette!"

"Hmm? What? Oh, do you finally need me?" Fair enough.

"Yeah, I'm done with all my shit. How can I help you with what you had planned? Now that you have indulged me all morning."

"Well, I was able to get through to the cardinal as you asked me to this morning. While you were in dreamland dealing with Cappelano and your buddies back Stateside, the cardinal said to chill for an hour or so. He needed time to make some calls. Any ideas on what or where we can go?"

"Honestly, let's stay here. This coffeehouse is where I met Trent yesterday; I'm hoping to run into him again today. It's also right up the street from the archdiocese. Do you have a way into its headquarters while we wait for some recon?"

"Yes, I had an appointment there this morning with the human resources department; it was a job interview. I figured if I needed to get into any records, that's a great place to be."

"Smart thinking; I hope you get the job. You head on in, start the process. On your way over get a message to the cardinal to call me, since you'll be tied up."

"Got it. I might be in there a few hours. Hopefully you can keep yourself busy, or better yet, out of trouble." She's got a point there.

I watched Nicolette walk down the street, phone in hand, making her calls to track down and communicate with Cardinal Kelley as she approached the front door. She stopped for a few moments, paced around as she finished her call, looked down in my direction, then disappeared into the womb of the archdiocesan building. All I can do is wait for her, wait for Cardinal Kelley to get back to me. I think I'll go inside, grab a cup of coffee and a pastry, maybe ask the manager if they think Trent will be in today. She looks like the same girl that pointed him out to me yesterday.

"Hey, good morning, or almost afternoon, I should say. If it isn't the American. What can I get you today? Black coffee again, maybe something to go with it?" Great memory.

"Yes, I'll take a black coffee, different roast this time, and get me a pastry, something you'd recommend. Any chance that the Trent kid will be here again? It was a pleasure talking to him yesterday."

"He comes almost every day after class, so I wouldn't be surprised if he isn't here within the hour. We're not busy. Is there anything I can help you with, or any direction I can point you in?"

"No, I was just fascinated with some of what he was studying as it pertains to East European economics. I know it seems odd, but we had to cut short so I could catch up with an old friend."

"Is that where you went running off to yesterday? We saw you were hurrying down the street toward the archdiocese."

"Yeah, an old friend of mine from back in the States has been over here for a while. I didn't want to miss an opportunity to catch up with him. Thanks for the coffee and the scone. I'll take a seat outside and enjoy the view."

The view outside from the front of the café was picturesque; the scene fit what I was looking for. Fresh air, an old iron table and chairs mixed with moisture and mildew left from the morning dew. The shade from the tree above kept the sun from drying it up, keeping the chair ever so cool and refreshing for me. As I sat there, feeling the chill in my bones, it paused the world, gave me a moment to relax, to focus, and to sift through it all. What was Andrew going through? Why was his father ashamed of him? Could it simply be that Andrew's mother was a nun living in a convent?

There are so many random options on why someone could be ashamed of the situation and what the odds were that he wasn't the father, and Andrew just felt he was. If he wasn't, then why is the Church involved, and who is covering up the issue at hand and trying to hide the truth of Andrew's father?

A solid hour later, two pages of scribbled notes, graphs, circles, and what looks like a schizophrenic's mad writings, and I still haven't gotten any further in my thought process. How did Andrew and his mother end up in the States? Why would his father disown him? Why is the Church still playing such a big role in their family? If there wasn't a connection, then there would be no need to keep up this overwatch of Andrew and his mother. I'm not the kind of person who thinks Andrew is the Second Coming. This has more real-world, powerful daddy implications. I just don't know where or how yet.

"Hey, if it isn't the American who ran off yesterday without saying good-bye. Do you make a habit of sprinting out of cafés in Europe like you're in a James Bond movie?"

"If it isn't Trent, the economics major looking to make a difference in his hometown back in Ireland. As for sprinting out like a bad action movie, it depends on the day. Lately there have been a few."

"You'll have to forgive me. Unless you're as cute as Julita over there, I'm horrible with names. What was yours again?"

"Ah, there is a reason you come here daily, and it's not just for a caffeine fix. My name is Neil, and as for the girl, want me to do some recon for you? It's the least I can do?"

"I appreciate that, but I'm not sure it would matter; I struggle talking to girls either way. What brings you back to the café other than the coffee and Julita?"

"I was hoping to get some work done while a friend of mine is doing an interview up the street. And perhaps run into you so I could apologize for my abrupt behavior yesterday."

"Neil, no need. Though I appreciate the sentiment, especially from an American, not what your people are known for."

"I could see that. Side note on our friend Julita over there: she knows your name, knows your schedule, and lights up enough that when I talked about you, she had a positive tone. It may not be love or even infatuation, but it's a start."

For the next fifteen minutes we exchanged small talk, pleasantries about his struggles with women as well as the lack of cute girls in the economics department. I tried working in my case a bit, dropping little nuggets, a few questions here and there, getting a perspective here and there, and bouncing things off a blank canvas. Trent and I spoke about his degree, why he was into economics to help his local country. He had a really good answer.

"Trent, if you don't mind me asking, there are different ways or different majors you could specialize in if you're going to get involved in politics. What made you choose economics?"

"Well, Neil, to me, it's a matter of the impact I want to make; I want to do more than just local change. I want to impact my country on a grander scale. To think big, you must understand how the world interacts. My father wasn't educated, but he was smart enough to say always follow the money, that's where the power lies. Where people can lose money is where they can lose power."

"Smart man. If you don't mind me asking, as someone that grew up in Ireland—your father, that is—what was his trade? I'm assuming from the way you spoke of him."

"He was a carpenter; he framed houses and buildings, eventually did some contracting, but always had his hands to fall back on. He made plenty of sacrifices for my family and me. Reminding us that we need to work to make an impact on those around us, make a change, and not squander the sacrifices he made for us."

AVE MARIA

The more I talked to Trent, the more I was moved a little bit, the more I started to see the world through his eyes and started to look through this case fresh. I keep getting held up on Andrew and his connection to the Church. Not to mention his connection to the father, or how he plays in all of this. What if the connection lies with his mother? The burden is hers to carry; that is why so much has been done. She is the only person who has been there since the beginning I feel like this is a huge oversight by myself, my team, and even Cardinal Kelley. We were all so focused on Andrew, on the boy and his death, that we missed out on the mother; she was the quiet one, the one who needed consoling.

"Trent, I appreciate the conversation today; I would love to follow up some time. I'm not sure how long I'll be in Warsaw, I bought a one-way ticket, while I'm out here working. I'd love to continue this conversation. As for Julita, I think you should ask her out; I would do it today, before her shift is over. Ask her to go for a walk, just to get to know her. Sometimes the simplest gestures can be the best ones."

"Thanks, Neil, I appreciate the advice. I guess the old adage is always true. The answer is always No, if you don't ask the question." Exactly.

As we parted ways, most of the afternoon light had disappeared into the horizon, leaving a sky on fire. I just keep asking myself, what the next step needs to be, whom to call, and how to play it. I've been waiting for Cardinal Kelley all day, waiting for Nicolette all afternoon, and still nothing. Though I have some direction, I'm still missing out. I guess I can reach out to Ken back Stateside to see what he and TJ can pull up and maybe get a message to Glow about Ms. Malinowski to see what he has on her, if anything at all.

With the time difference, I'm not sure this is a wake someone up in the middle of the night kind of moment. I know I'm learning. If this were a hunt for a killer, it might be different. As I made my way around the square walking around, killing time, I decided to text Ken and TJ about my hunch with Andrew's mother. I'm starting to think back on what Andrew's birth date was. Why were we having so much trouble with his birth records? I bet you any money she was already pregnant when she got to the convent. My hunch is that she was the one being hidden. The child, Andrew, was just a bystander, a young kid dealing with a shit hand who couldn't deal with it.

Imagine being a teenager, as if that part of our lives weren't hard enough, now you add to it, being a foreigner in a country where you're not accepted. You don't fit in all the way, you know you stand out from the others, then add to it your mother's baggage and stress of not knowing your father, and the truth or story that she gave him. We really have to rely on the mother and perhaps anyone else we can find from her time, though short at the convent. As I was walking through the square and with these thoughts on my mind, I noticed my phone was ringing but didn't recognize the number. Let's hope it's helpful.

"Neil speaking. What can I do for you?"

"Neil, it's Cardinal Kelley. I was told that Nicolette might be tied up and to give you a call to see if I could be of help, or to give you some help. I did call the person interviewing her and gave a great recommendation, which should help get her hired and into the office."

"That's great, Cardinal, I appreciate it. But I think I have an idea or a new way to look at the case. Is there any way to get to Andrew's mother again, to talk to her for us? I have a feeling she's not going to want to talk to me, but I think she's the real reason all of this is going on, not Andrew."

"What do you mean? I thought this whole time you were looking into what caused Andrew's death."

"That hasn't changed. I'm just thinking that his mother played a bigger role in what happened than she is letting on. No one spoke to her in depth, which is our fault, but we all just looked at her as a grieving mother. It wasn't until recently that I started to piece things together. It makes more sense to ship her overseas and hide her until he is old enough to be on his own."

"I see what you're saying. She is staying out here at the same hotel with me as we try to find her a place to stay. I will see what I can do about getting her to open up. Why don't you come out here for breakfast tomorrow; we'll see if we can get her to warm up to you."

"Sounds good. I'll figure out the rest of my day and get out there. Shoot for nine a.m. tomorrow; it'll give me time to get there in the morning."

"That should be fine; we'll meet you in the lobby of the hotel tomorrow morning. I'll talk to you tomorrow. I'm supposed to meet up with her tonight, so I will press on her some more info, to see what I can learn about her past."

"The biggest thing I'm trying to figure out is detailed timeline info. Why did she end up at that convent? Why did she end up in the

States? And when did she get pregnant? The timing doesn't seem to add up the way it's been presented to us. I took it at face value, had no reason not to, but the more I think it through, the less likely it makes sense."

"Sounds good, Neil. Have a blessed night; may God go with you."

"Thanks, Cardinal. You too."

Well, I'm running out of shit to do. At this point I think I'm going to start my walk back to the hotel. I'm already halfway there. While talking to Cardinal Kelley, I had inadvertently started making my way toward the hotel, assuming that Nicolette was going to be working the rest of the day. Between her ability to sell herself and the cardinal's references, I'm assuming she should get the job quite easily. It's really turned out to be a great night. I have a decent idea of what to look for and people in the right places to get what we're looking for. I feel like we have a shot at finding something out. For the first time in this case I feel like we have some substance.

There's a small restaurant across the street from the hotel that has a great big window, with an outdoor seating area. Quite common, I've noticed in Warsaw. Then again, I feel like the European lifestyle gives way to outdoor seating and enjoying the weather. There's much more leisure, less worry about being done quickly getting to the next task. As for the restaurant, they had only ten or so tables inside and a few outside. But the restaurant smelled amazing. They had a brick oven in the back where they had been baking fresh bread all day, filling it with different things: soup, salads, and anything else you could imagine.

AVE MARIA

Dinner was going to be quiet and peaceful. I might not even drink just a coffee for a change.

29

This story has more holes, turns, and questions in it than we started with.

Dinner was simple, but what I needed, and with a coffee to go in hand, I was back in my room sifting through notes and details, trying to get organized for tomorrow. Waiting on Nicolette to reach out, I'm getting a little anxious trying to keep myself busy. I guess after a long day of sitting in the sun, talking and walking, I could take a shower. But I'll be honest: if Nicolette walks in I'm sure she's going to give me shit until the end of this trip—two showers in one day. Little does she know that I did four on one occasion.

I decided to call Sheila. With them being six hours behind, it would allow me to catch up with Carol Lynn and see how they were doing. It's been a while, and I miss them. I also want to see how the girls are doing with me out of town for so long. As the phone kept ringing, I was beginning to think Sheila wasn't going to pick up. I was starting to think there was no end in sight to this. I ended up leaving Sheila a text. I'm not a fan of voice mail; I feel it's almost rude when we can text. Why make someone pull out their phone and call their voice mail when you can simply give them the info in an easy-to-read format?

Well, I'm running out of options here; the last thing I want to do is fall back into some old habits that I feel have gotten me into trouble over the years. It's time to just figure out my next step; I'll probably end up falling asleep here chilling while waiting for Nicolette. As I'm about to fade into that space where your mind is pushing you into sleep but your heart is trying to keep you awake, I finally heard a knocking at the door.

"Neil, it's Christian. I just got back after my shift. I heard from Nicolette; she should be heading back soon. She said it went great, especially after Cardinal Kelley called in and gave her a reference."

"Why didn't she call me? I was waiting for her call all night."

"She did. She said your phone went to voice mail both times right away, figured you were tied up."

"Fair enough; I was on the phone a few times, we probably just got caught up. How long before she gets back to the hotel?"

"She should be here in a few minutes; she was already close to being here when she reached out."

"Did she give you any idea of how her day went, other than that she got the job?"

"No, Neil. She was pretty quick, sounded like she was hoofing it pretty quick. How'd your day end up? Get anything accomplished?"

"I think we're all looking at this a bit differently, a bit off. I think we need to put more emphasis on the mother. I don't think there's been enough attention put on her."

"Funny you say that. I started doing my own digging, started tailing her when she got here; it's why you haven't seen me around much when I'm not on post. I haven't been sightseeing, I've been up to where Cardinal Kelley is keeping tabs on her. Not sure why yet, but just a hunch, there is definitely something off about her." Christian looked dialed in.

"What do you mean? Give me a more detailed breakdown of your thoughts on her."

"Well, for example, when she and the cardinal go out, she is always preoccupied, always looking over her shoulder. You can tell she doesn't want to be back in Poland. There is a fear there, she is waiting for something to come, waiting for something to show up and grab her. She always has this look of fear. You can tell."

Christian is ex-military, he's a marine, and you never say ex-marine. Once a marine, always a marine. I only fucked that up one time, and he damn near ended me. I remember Ken tried explaining it to me and I didn't really get it, I honestly thought he was kidding, I wasn't trying to be a dick, I just didn't grow up around it. Even in the bureau, we didn't have a shit ton of marines, we had more eggheads than marines.

Christian was a scout in the marines, which is why he's ideal for missions like this; he can go days on end surveilling a target. He has natural instincts that he has improved over the years with experience in the field that come in handy and are showing true in this case. I can only hope he did more than simply review and report.

"Did you do any digging while you were out there, try to find any more info on her, maybe for starters the convent where she was before she made her way to the States?"

"Well, there is a problem with all of that. I don't think her story checks out, I also don't think her name checks out. That's where most of this got me confused; nothing added up. I was trying to get more confirmation before I came to you. Ken always said, be sure, don't just have a hunch unless it's dealing with a killer when you come to Neil." He's got a point.

"That being said, what do you have, lay it all out for me, start with the facts, then go into your gut feelings, or the items you have found but can get concrete evidence for."

Christian started explaining to me that he can't even find a history for Andrew's mother in Poland anywhere. He has struggled to find any information. This isn't uncommon to have lost records for families and children in Europe following World War Two. But as old as she is, and was, when she left to go to the United States according to her story, there should be something there.

He has a good gut feeling thinking that something is missing there. The question, though, is what we are missing. What part of the story are we not seeing? It's almost like not being able to see someone coming at you because something is blocking your view. It's not that they aren't there, it's simply that you can't see them. As Christian and I began trying to trace back Andrew's mother to where she might be from, what's missing, and where we can start, we heard a knock. It must be Nicolette.

"Hey guys, it's me, open up, I know Christian's in there because he texted me. Someone let me in the room, I have my hands full."

As Christian opened the door for her, I saw she had a crap ton of photo albums that looked like yearbooks as well as a crap ton of other documents. No wonder she got off the phone quickly with Christian; she was carrying ten plus pounds of books and paper a good couple of blocks from the archdiocese to the hotel.

"Holy shit, Nicolette, where did you get all that? Better yet, what is all that? Other than homework for the three of us?" I said with a chuckle.

"Yeah, cuz, I mean shit, we're going to have to get a few gallons of coffee to get through all of this." Christian has a good point there.

"Cardinal Kelley really went above and beyond for us. He not only spoke highly of me to help get me in. He also asked them to allow me to grab any information I needed in regard to yearbooks, old files, etc. for a research project I'm doing for him. This will give me access to all the old documents we need to sift through. The only problem now is, will we ever find what we are looking for?" Great point.

"Well, let's start with the first good idea. Christian, you go down to the lobby to see if they'll give us a pot of coffee and just bring one up every thirty minutes or so until we say stop. I think they'll take you more seriously if you go in person. Otherwise they might think it's a prank."

As Christian left to get us four bags of coffee, Nicolette and I started moving my room around, creating as much workable space as we could to start going through everything. We spent the next couple of minutes moving furniture around the room when we both had the same idea.

"Desks—we need desks from the other rooms here. We can take everything out but the bed and desks." We said it in unison.

As we made our way around the room moving furniture, Christian came up, hopped in, started helping, and like a good soldier didn't even ask what we were doing. He figured it's easier than asking what we were doing. As a marine, you learn when to ask and when to simply hop in and support your boss.

"All right, now we have working space. I can sleep in the corner, no problem. I should ask them if we can grab a twin bed for this room instead of this full; it would give us more room to work in."

"I think that might be going a bit too far, but then again, you are paying for three rooms long term, so they might say, when in Warsaw—"

"For now, let's get to work on this. What are all the different books? Did you just go back to the period that his mother and/or father would have been in? Maybe around a convent or church during that time frame based on what we know?"

"Yeah, it's a lot to cover, that's why there is so much to look at, but I figured it's better than leaving anything out."

"You thought well. Let's grid these out by time frame so we can work through them faster. We need to get bigger pictures of Andrew, his mother, and a younger picture of her if we have one. Or maybe we can make one; I'm sure TJ can get something done."

With the room set up like a 1970s newsroom, piles of paper all over, starting to pin it on the walls, pages paper-clipped and folded over, it was a beautiful mess. Christian had a tidy work space, methodically going through each page, sifting through, marking pages that might be important, then setting them aside. Nicolette, on the other side, had kind of a mess, her piles were a little disheveled, you could see she was getting a little worked up because Christian looked so organized.

"Have either of you found anything other than a bunch of ifs?"

"No, but I did find something that seems odd. I pulled up a picture that came up a few times over a three-year span. It looks like Andrew's mom. I might be seeing things, but I looked at the pic over three years, and it looks like Andrew at that age, and a young Ms. Malinowski."

"Let me take a look at that, Neil, come look at this."

"What do you mean, you think you found a . . . Oh, shit, yeah, that's a dead ringer for Andrew or his mother. And that name is definitely not Malinowski."

"No, that last name is Dombrowski, Anna Dombrowski. Wait a minute, I feel like I've read that name before, I know I've heard it somewhere." Nicolette was trying to pinpoint what I had on the tip of my tongue.

"You mean, as in the Dombrowski Field House, at the high school? That's where you heard it."

"No, that's not the only place I heard it. There were articles in one of the books that talked about a family named Dombrowski. They donated to one of the churches and their convent at about the time she would have been there, as well as the time the story was created." Nicolette was digging through some papers looking for an article.

"This story has more holes, turns, and questions in it than we started with, but at least we're looking in the right places now, or feel we're giving the right attention to the right place." So I felt.

"It just seems odd, it's not like you needed to excommunicate your daughter to another country just because she went and got knocked up, the math still doesn't add up. It also doesn't explain the constant paranoid look she has in her eyes since they arrived in Warsaw." Christian had that deep stare going on.

"Well, we have a ton to go on for tomorrow. I'll shoot Ken and TJ and email, have them start digging on this. Also, I'll press a bit on Cardinal Kelley and Ms. Malinowski in the morning at breakfast. For now, let's call it a night."

As Nicolette and Christian left my room with paper everywhere, I began organizing a little bit so I could gain access to my bed. I didn't even bother changing or getting ready for bed. I figured I'd simply set my alarm, get up early, and deal with it in the morning. Right now I'm tired, worn out, and need sleep. Surrounded by all this black-and-white paper has me feeling like a hamster in a cage trying to get sleep. All I'm missing is the big wheel and the water bottle.

30

That's what this case is doing to me, it's pushing my imagination and my wits to the end.

The morning started off as it usually does, me abruptly waking up to an alarm, but this time it wasn't to a cup of fresh coffee. The hotel life has been waking up to stale coffee, having it sit in a cup on one of the many desks. Found in my now makeshift command center, with a bed. Standing there in the same clothes I was in last night, hair all messy, with a cold cup of coffee in my hand. I looked to my phone for messages and noticed that I had a few missed phone calls from the office back home in Detroit. It's the main number, so I'm not sure who it is, they didn't leave a message, but they've learned not to with me. I'm sure they emailed me since that's what TJ usually does.

With them being six hours behind, though, I'm surprised that they did any work on what I sent, though TJ often works through the night. He gets a ton done for us during those hours. We call it wake to a TJ soufflé because it takes time, it's slow to rise, but it's almost always to perfection. As I expected, there was an email from TJ explaining to me that he found a similar trail to what Christian and Nicolette had surmised. It looks as if Anna Dombrowski is more than likely our Ms. Malinowski. We just need to find a connection, find a way to prove it. We can try to figure out what the hell happened. Part of me feels like we aren't going to get many answers from Andrew's mother, but it's worth a shot.

For now it's time to hop in the shower, get ready, and head to the hotel to meet up with Cardinal Kelley and Ms. Malinowski. Brunch at a hotel sounds good right about now. As I make my way into the small bathroom shower combo that is my old European hotel, I realize the small things we take for granted in the States. Even an average Motel 6 has a spacious bathroom compared to what you will find over there. It's not bad—just different, older, and smaller. We just like to build it bigger.

With the water hitting me, I feel my brain starting to feel a rhythm, falling into and out of thought, cycling through the ideas we covered the past couple of days. Circling through the conversations I had with Cardinal Kelley, Trent, and everyone else I have come in contact with and making a chart of ideas. To me a shower is a place of meditation; it's a calming place and always has been. There's just something about the water running over me that allows my restful mind to find peace, continuity, and symmetry.

If we're correct, why change your name, why hide your identity? If you're as scared as Christian feels you are, why allow yourself to be brought back to Poland? Do you miss it? Is there some form of unfinished business, or a bigger driving factor, guilt, at play? If she truly did change her name and run to the States to hide, then the motivation, the theory behind what happened to Andrew changes drastically, I also have to get with Glow and find out how much he knew and knows about Andrew and his mother.

"Hey, who's that knocking at the door?" I could hear a knock, but not who was there.

"It's Christian and Nicolette. We wanted to get into your room and grab a key from you before you headed out."

"Give me a minute. I just got out of the shower, I need to change, let me at least get some pants on."

Luckily, I try to stay in shape, working as much as I do, staying active. I'm not a fitness model by any means, but I can go to the beach confidently with my shirt off. I'm not rocking abs of steel, but maybe abs of kitchen countertop, functional and flat.

"Neil, what's taking so long? It's been almost five minutes. It doesn't take that long to throw on pants." Nicolette was a bit impatient.

"Fine. Here I come," I said, as I was pulling up my pants and buttoning them as I walked to the door.

"Finally, you took long enough. Do you think you're a supermodel getting ready in here or something?"

"Did Nicolette, with the consistent attitude this morning, wake up on the wrong side of the bed?"

"No, boss man, I just don't have all morning, I have to get moving before I head back to work. Remember, I picked up a job so you guys could figure this case out."

"That's right. But it's only six thirty. When are you due in? I have to leave here by seven so I can get there on time. It's a bit of a drive."

"I don't have to be there until nine, but I wanted to make sure I could get some work done with Christian this morning. Did you hear anything back from TJ? He's usually working all night."

"He emailed me a breakdown of similar items he found that coincide with our theory on Anna Dombrowski being Ms. Malinowski. The biggest thing he found was that she stopped having any footprint in her senior year in high school. It's like she just stopped existing."

"Like someone erased her, or the trail just stopped?" Christian was asking an important distinction.

"It looks like there was no intent to delete her from the record, but who she was did cease to exist from her senior year on. After the book and pictures were released, that's the final record. She doesn't even have grades posted for the final year, which says to me she was pulled from school early. TJ said he was waiting for some files he requested to try and find more information on Anna's parents, to see what connection there might be."

"I can check too in our archives at work, see if there is more information on her or her family. Now that I know what I'm looking for, it'll help me narrow my search. I'm going to bring back all the files that don't pertain to the Dombrowski family to the archdiocese, to ensure I don't keep taking things without returning them. The more I bring back, the better it looks." She has a point.

"Sounds good. I'm going to finish getting ready and head out of here. I have a car meeting me downstairs in a few minutes. I'll be out of your hair shortly."

"Okay, boss man, we'll keep digging. Can you forward me what TJ found so I can use it to cross-reference anything I might find?"

"No problem. Christian, I'll cc Nicolette on it just to keep us all on the same page."

After I finished getting ready, I spent a few minutes gathering my things, knocked out a quick email, packed up my laptop, threw it in my leather bag, and sprinted out the door. I've always loved this bag. I've had it for a long time, it's a messenger bag that sits just right and makes me feel like a professor out here, especially with the stubble I have going. Still, I figured it might make me look a little less professional for Andrew's mother. As I exited the hotel lobby, I saw a car waiting for me. Well, I *hope* it's for me.

"Mr. Baggio, I presume?"

"Thank you, yes, right on time. Thank you."

"Where are we headed today?"

"The Hotel Mansor. Are you familiar?"

"Yes, I am. It will be a bit of a drive. Are you aware?"

"Yes, it's fine, thank you."

"Then let us get on our way. If you need me to stop along the way just ask. It should take us about thirty minutes."

As I sat in the car, I dozed into and out of thought, trying to put together a picture of why or how this whole scenario played out. Even if you have a daughter that gets pregnant, you don't send her away.

You don't hide her from the world like that, make her change her name; so much doesn't make sense. I guess there is always the chance the family had money to donate to the Church. It is the oldest tradition, crime family supporting the local church. Maybe her family was tied up in something like that; maybe someone in the Church did them a solid to help get her out of a bad situation. I feel like I just described a bad version of a modern-day *Romeo and Juliet*. This case is pushing my imagination and my wits to the end.

"We'll be there shortly, Mr. Baggio; it was a pleasure driving you here. Do you have a plan on return?"

"I do not. If you have a card, I can call you directly."

"Just call our service; they will send the closest driver. Be safe, and have a great day out here. The weather is perfect."

"That it is. Safe driving today."

I walked into the lobby. It's gorgeous, modern, but it has that older feel to it. Meaning that though it looks new, they designed it with that open, large, and majestic feel that older hotels had, not the commercial, slap-up drywall jobs you see in the States. This hotel makes a statement, looks amazing, and makes you feel amazing. Cardinal Kelley is getting the treatment over here. This does cater to our idea that Andrew's mother is tied to something more than she's letting on.

"Good morning, Neil. I hope your ride over was easy and uneventful?"

"It was, Cardinal, thank you. Where is the guest of honor? I thought she would be joining us."

"She'll be down shortly; I've been learning she is always a good five to ten minutes late to everything. I now know where Andrew got it from—that kid was never on time to anything growing up."

"I didn't realize you had such a relationship with the family. You made it sound like Ms. Malinowski was new to you, new to getting to know you except on the flight over here."

"No, I said it took the flight to get her to open up to me. See, I was the one that brought them over to the States from Poland many years ago before Andrew was born when she was still pregnant with him. I played a big role in their lives until he was ten. Then the Church moved me around, and I lost contact with them for a while. It wasn't until a few years ago that I was able to rebuild a relationship with them. Andrew was open to it, but his mother was a bit bitter about the fact that I left them."

"I guess that is what you said; fair point. But it does come down to the details in life. I wish I had known you were more up front, with Ms. Dombrowski's history." Let's see what he does here.

"I beg your pardon. What did you say?"

"Sorry. I meant Ms. Malinowski. That's right, I forget, that's the name she goes by. Which is odd, since that name hasn't existed anywhere in Poland until recently. Also, Dombrowski seemed to fall off the planet in the middle of the semester from what we can find."

"Neil, I guess you have gotten some parts of the puzzle but not all of them. It's not quite as simple as you think."

"I don't think anything about this case and this lady is simple. That's part of the problem. I'm trying to get to the bottom of all this, and everybody is giving us only bits and pieces. If they give us anything at all."

"Have you thought there might be a reason it's so difficult and that she didn't want to be found for a reason?"

"That's great, Cardinal, but when it gets a kid killed, there it's time to start shedding some light on the subject, like for starters what your role is in this and why she is so scared. One of my guys did some tailing on his own and said it was pretty obvious that she was terrified something was coming after her."

I wasn't planning on giving the cardinal the business right now, but I didn't plan on having a one-on-one either. She still isn't down here. The cardinal and I are going back and forth in the lobby, almost making a scene. People are aware of who he is, so it makes me look like the aggressor, which I am, but with good reason. However, no one could care less when you're arguing with a man of the cloth, especially of higher rank and in a country such as Poland.

"Cardinal, we are getting nowhere, and fast. We simply keep arguing about vague points of reference, I'm assuming because neither one of us knows when Andrew's mother will be down here. Why don't we assume we are going to table this conversation now, pick up later when there is less chance of it ending poorly than either of us would like?"

"I would greatly appreciate that. Thank you for understanding the sensitivity of the situation. At this point I'm going to call up to her room. She should have been down here by now."

Just in time for the cardinal and me to find common ground and find a level head, he stepped away to call up to her room from one of the hotel desk phones. As the concierge kept trying her room, the cardinal had him try one more time, then began to walk back over to me.

"That's odd, she didn't answer in her room; maybe she's finally on her way down. If she's not, let's head up there and knock on her door."

We sat there for a solid ten minutes, much longer than either of us wanted to. It became a weird feeling bringing me back to high school when I was in trouble, and someone from the Church was keeping an eye on me for a period, which happened often. Come to think of it, this is bringing back some major déjà vu. I used to get in trouble a ton in high school, not for pranks or anything stupid. I was just always questioning authority, wouldn't listen, and I'm sensing a trend in my life right now.

"Cardinal, it's been ten minutes, we should probably go up and check on her; as I stated earlier, my guy said she looked terrified. You head up; I'll grab the manager to be safe."

"Do you really think that's necessary, Neil?"

"Yes, Cardinal, I do."

As the cardinal made it toward the elevators, I went to the front desk to inform them of the situation and the need for someone to aid us in a wellness check on a patron. They paged the manager, who swiftly appeared from the back. We decided to take the stairs, as it seemed quicker, and her room was merely on the second floor. As we were walking down the hallway, you could make out the cardinal raising his voice through the door, trying to get her attention, but to no avail; no one was answering. The level of panic in his voice was finally reaching what I had begun to fear downstairs.

"I'm assuming there is no answer here. Can you open the door for us, sir?"

"Ma'am, I'm the manager of the hotel. Your friends are very concerned for you. We are going to enter your room. I am opening the door in three, two, one."

"Cardinal, stay back, just to be safe." I pushed him and the manager back.

"I will not." I shoved again.

"She's not here, get out of the room immediately. Sir, call the police, judging by her room, the blood on the floor, and her phone being here, my guess is she was kidnapped at some point."

"Neil, there is no way. Let me see for myself."

"Cardinal, don't touch anything. Why don't we step outside, wait for the police, and you can begin to fill me in on who Ms. Dombrowski really is?"

"I guess it's time I do, isn't it?" He looked lost, distraught, and torn.

"It's the only shot you have at saving her."

31

Catholic archdiocesan office of Warsaw, this is Nicolette. How may I direct your call?

Why does he not get it? The secret is what got her in trouble in the first place. Come on, man, spit it out. We walked into the hallway, where we waited for the local police to show up. While standing there, in an eerie silence you could see the cardinal struggling to come to terms with everything; he was working through it all in his head. Was this his fault? Should he have brought her back?

"Cardinal, do you know who did this? Do you have any idea where or how this happened?"

"It's not that simple, Neil. Her background, the whole reason we left, and the reason we came back are much deeper than a simple Who did it?"

"Cardinal, if you're going to spend the whole time speaking in riddles, half thoughts, and keeping me in the dark, this is going to take a long time. I'm going to ask the same things the police are going to ask, but I'm not going to be able to listen in when you speak to them. We need to get this out of the way now; I have to get my team on this ASAP. We have already lost ground that we need to make up."

"I understand. I'm just trying to wrap my head around all of this, figure out where to start and get organized. I'm not sure how or what to do; this isn't the world I'm used to operating in."

"Why not start with, do you have a name we should be looking into, somewhere I can send my guys to start looking around? A starting point is often all we need; it's amazing what we can get done on our own from there."

"The name I have for you is Choike, the first name Jacob. His family has been bad news as long as history has recorded. His sister is the one to look out for, though. Her name is Marie; the two of them were causing issues when they were in high school when this all started."

Before we could get into too much detail, the police showed up and started doing their job. They took a few moments questioning the cardinal and me. They were quick to ascertain that I was going to be useless in this case, at least with giving them pertinent details. I also wasn't giving them anything helpful. As the cardinal was as helpful as he could be with them, I excused myself for a moment and made a few calls to Christian and the team.

"Hey, Neil, what's up? How'd the breakfast go?"

"We didn't get to breakfast; it looks like Andrew's mother was kidnapped, and injured in the process. We need to look into a brother and sister; they would be the same age as Ms. Malinowski, I mean Dombrowski—our instincts were right on the money. I haven't gotten any details, but we need to get that squared away ASAP. I did get some confirmation out of the cardinal that her name isn't Malinowski, but he didn't confirm it was Dombrowski, so that's still up in the air."

"On it, boss. What are you up to?"

"I'm going to hang around for a few, make sure the cardinal is in good hands, and have TJ do some deep diving on the names they gave us. Oh, before I forget, the brother and sister we are looking for are Jacob and Marie Choike.

"Got it. I'll get the information over to Nicolette too, so she can do some digging at the archdiocese, see what she can find."

"Thanks, Christian. I'll follow up with you in a few hours to see where you are, If anything comes up before then, let me know."

As I made my way back in, I was a bit perplexed because they had the cardinal in handcuffs. He was seated down the hall with his hands behind his back, which threw me for a loop. Why did they think he did it, and if they thought so, what did I miss? I guess the cardinal had the most contact with her and was the last to see her. My guess is they have a witness from down the hallway that saw or heard something. It looks like I'm going to have to ask someone what's going on. Judging by the look this guy is giving me, he might ask me something first.

"Neil Baggio, I presume, an associate of one Cardinal Kelley?"

"Associate, no; aware of who he is, here to meet him, yes; but we are not associated."

"If you are not associated, what are you doing here? Would you care to inform me?"

"Let's start over. Hi, I'm Neil Baggio. Who might you be?"

AVE MARIA

"I'm Captain Jan Duda. I'm here investigating this disappearance. With the amount of blood found at the scene, mixed with a witness and now blood found in Cardinal Kelley's room, we are going to keep him in custody."

"You don't think that a man of his age, stature, and cloth staged a kidnapping or murder of this woman in the middle of a hotel, do you?"

"No, not really, but the evidence points that way, so for now we will keep him in custody until otherwise found. Back to the original question, what are you doing here with him if you are not associates?"

"I am here, meaning in Poland. Trying to track down some information on a boy who killed himself back in the United States. His mother is now missing. I came here to talk to her; Cardinal Kelley was merely a contact helping me get in contact with her."

"You're here for law enforcement from the United States?"

"No, I'm merely looking into it for an old friend. He was concerned for the boy, for his mother, and I guess he was right, now that she is missing. I won't get in your way, I will let you do your job, I'm just here to ask some questions and find out information—that is it, not play a superhero."

"If you aren't lying to me, and play it that way, then we won't have an issue. Let's keep it that way. Now get out of here."

"Sounds good. Is there any way I can talk to the cardinal quickly before I leave? He was going to be my ride out of here."

"Don't test my patience. Just leave before I change my mind."

"Understood, Captain. Have a great day."

I guess I need to get a ride and head toward the hotel and figure out from there, but part of me wants to retrace all the steps that Cardinal Kelley and Andrew's mother took. I think it's time to just rent a car and make my way around Poland. Let me text Christian to find out what addresses they went to, and we can go from there.

It took me a good three hours to make my way around town and get a rental car, it's what you would expect in Warsaw on short notice. I ended up with a Volkswagen sedan, perfect for what I needed to get around, especially if I ended up having to shuttle around Christian and others. I was really hoping to get something a bit older, easier to hide in plain sight, but this will have to do with some AMEX points and an AAA discount. I was able to get a great rate on it. Not knowing how long this case is going to take, I need to watch every dollar I can.

I know I said catching Cappelano was good for business, which it has been, but I still like to keep an eye on my finances. Being smart is how you keep it; when you grow up poor, you get used to living light, surviving without the extra stuff. I think people can go one of two ways: they either want to buy everything because they never had it, or they just don't care still, and live a little better than they used to. I'm in the latter category; I just live a little nicer, but I don't go crazy.

Christian sent me the information from the stops that Cardinal Kelley and Andrew's mother made while he was tailing them. Most of them were consistent with someone trying to get resettled in a new place, or better yet, a new country. They went to a few different apartment complexes, looked like they put in a few job applications, even went to a few local municipalities. From the looks of it, she was trying to get back into the country. The question I have to get with Cardinal Kelley is which name she was using.

Maybe she felt pressured by someone to come back to Poland and she didn't want to be there. Was there an obligation that was bringing her back, something she was forced to do? Was she allowed to stay away with Andrew being alive, but now that he wasn't alive, she had to come back? That's the first good thought I've felt confident about this case since day one; it would make sense with the look in her eyes, as well as her disappearance. Someone wanted her here, needed her here. Now it's our job to find her and find the truth. Time to check in with Nicolette at the archdiocesan office.

"Catholic archdiocesan office of Warsaw, this is Nicolette. How may I direct your call?"

"Hey, Nicolette, any chance of getting you out of there early? I'm assuming by now Christian got ahold of you and you've been doing some digging of your own?"

"Slight problem, though. We may be running into a bigger problem. Remember how you said Cardinal Kelley kind of confirmed that her name isn't Malinowski but didn't confirm it was Dombrowski, in so many words? I know why he didn't do that; the problem is, we're back to square one on who the hell this lady is."

"Well, that was vague and a bit lacking in detail. I'm going to assume you're not in any position to talk in proper detail?"

"Exactly. I'll call as soon as I can from my cell."

She hung up quickly, then I was back to being in the dark, wondering what the hell was going on. It's like one horrible game of waiting for someone not to tell me the whole story. I'm sitting in the rental in a parking lot after a day of running around town, trying to figure out where Andrew's mother was, what she was doing, and what her next move is. From what I can gather, Cardinal Kelley was leading the way, and she was just along for the ride.

She was simply following him around, biding her time, not sure for what, why she even allowed herself to come back. Maybe she felt some form of duty, she knew it was coming, was tired of running and just wanted it over, wanted it to end. With her son being deceased, she simply wanted this other hell to be over. She wanted to confront it; she just didn't know how but figured if she were here, it would find her. About ten minutes into self-reflecting on the case, Nicolette finally called me back.

"Hey boss, sorry I had to step away and call you from my cell. I probably only have a few minutes, so I'll make it quick. From what I found, Anna Dombrowski died in high school, that's why she never finished. The names you gave Christian, the Choike siblings, they were responsible for it; from what I can tell it looks like they were the main suspects, but no case was ever brought against them."

"Good work Nicolette. That's a big break, a big turn and connection in the case. I can work with this. I'll get with Christian, we really need to track down these siblings, and fast. I'll get on TJ and see if he can find a digital footprint that can point us in the right direction."

"Thanks, Neil. I'll be out of here at about four today. See you back at the hotel."

"Talk to you later."

As I hung up, I was feeling confident we were getting somewhere. It was time to call TJ, get him digging, get the pit bull on the case, get his teeth sunk into the two Choike siblings, see what he can find out. He really is good once he gets rolling on something, it's hard to get him off it. As the phone rings, I let my mind wander for a moment, thinking of Carol Lynn and Sheila. I miss them, but it's hard to think of them this far across the world.

"Hey, TJ, how goes it in the bat cave?"

"Always rocking, boss man. What can I do for you: You know I relish these calls. What crazy tasks can I accomplish for you today?"

"We; those names I emailed you earlier to look into? Now it's more than some simple review. I need deep-dive, CIA-dossier-type depth. I want to know where they get coffee and their favorite chips from the grocery store."

"I got you, boss man. You want me to go crazy celebrity stalker on them. I'm on it. I have a base to work from 'cause I started to dive on them a bit when you sent me their names earlier, but this will get me to go deeper, harder."

"Please don't ever say that last part again, ever, I don't want to have Ken sit down with you and review HR rules."

"Shut the fuck up, Neil, quick busting my balls. You know what I meant; I got your back."

"Look at you, talking back to the boss man. Thanks, TJ. Hit me up, as usual."

AVE MARIA

From where I stand, the wild card is these two siblings, but not only them, their overall role in this case, where they come into play, what they did, how it affects Andrew and his mother. What are the chances Marie is Andrew's mom? No, that doesn't add up. If charges had been followed by a suit against them, I could see it, but not without it; it doesn't make sense. The math doesn't add up. Who is Andrew's mother and what is her tie to Poland? What has her so scared she is always looking over her shoulder?

32

As a father, I can only imagine the lengths I would go to protect my family.

Back at the hotel after a long day, I figured I'd try a long shot and call the police station to see if Cardinal Kelley had representation yet, but I have to come at them from the right angle, without triggering suspicion. Maybe if I call them, acting as a concerned media outlet, I can get some information from them.

"Warsaw Police station, Precinct 9. How may I direct your call?"

"I'm trying to get bail info on a friend of mine. His name is Cardinal Kelley."

"Let me look in the system. It looks like his lawyer made bail already, it says to direct all calls to Adam Horwitz. It looks like he was bailed out by an attorney. you'd have to contact them to get in touch with him, what did you say your name was again?"

Click.

That was quick, for someone not expecting to get in any trouble, he had a quick get-out-of-jail card. Then again, I'm assuming the Catholic Church came in and pulled rank. Just as the captain said earlier, he doubts he had anything to do with it, but the evidence pointed that way, for now, so he had to follow procedure, it's not his place to go against what is sitting in front of him.

Cardinal Kelley gets himself arrested, Andrew's mother gets herself kidnapped, I can't find either one of them, I'm in a country I barely know, my team that's supposed to be here around me is nowhere to be found. Nicolette is stuck at work because we made her get a job so we can gain access to old data, Christian is running around town, and Terrence is . . . where the *fuck* is Terrance? That's a good point, he hasn't checked in, which isn't surprising, he's kind of the rogue agent on the team, he'll disappear down the rabbit hole, be gone for days, then come up with information to turn a case.

Calling his phone is going directly to voice mail. That's annoying and somewhat stressing in this situation. Christian's doing the same thing. Maybe they're calling each other? I doubt it, but I feel like a stressed-out parent trying to look on the positive side; I'll call again in a few minutes. Nope, still nothing from either of them, I guess I can text them to hit me up ASAP when they surface for air. My last idea is to call Ken and check in, see if or TJ can ping their last known spots to see what's going on.

"Hey Neil, how is it in Warsaw? TJ filled me in a little bit. I have one of our people trying to get to Glow, see if they can get some follow-up info from him. We know he's a little shook, so we sent one of the girls over, a bit gentler touch." Ken's all over it.

"Thanks, bud, I'm having trouble right now getting ahold of anyone, you know how I get when I start calling and no one answers.

AVE MARIA

Nicolette is stuck at work, but Christian and Terrance's phones are off, going straight to voice mail. Can you have TJ and the crew look into when they turned off and where they were last, just in case?"

"No problem. Speaking of TJ, he has some info on Andrew's mother, he said it looks like the name Dombrowski isn't correct. Said it looks like Anna Dombrowski died in high school from an accident involving two other students, last name."

"Choike?!"

"Yeah. I see we're finally getting somewhere. When our findings start lining up, it means we're finally heading in the right direction. I'll get with TJ on tracking the guys down. Also, I'll have him email you the details of the accident ASAP. He was trying to verify a few more items."

"Thanks, Ken. As always, appreciate the hard work you and the team do."

At least for a change, we are getting somewhere, moving forward, and overlapping our findings. This crazy thing about working on a case in a foreign place with so many boundaries is that my usual distractions are limited. Not having my heavy bag to hit, my dogs to curl up with, or my exes to give me shit in person really change the routine. I've realized I'm not a fan of quiet unless I'm in a shower, getting lost in my thoughts.

As a father, I can only imagine the lengths I would go to protecting my family, I know the lengths I've already gone to trying to protect them from the Cappelano. When you're in fear for your family, you will do things you never thought possible and cross lines you never

335

dared before. As we get some semblance of a picture, even its bits and pieces, you start to see fear has driven this woman's life. To what extent she put that on her son, we don't know. We can't talk to him anymore; all we can do now is try and save her life, figure out what's going on, and solve this.

Back at the hotel sifting through emails, my notes, and starting to organize a plan of action. I kept coming across the same headline from a packet of snippets of information that TJ had emailed me about the death of Anna Dombrowski. It described a scene where the Choike siblings were driving down the road in the middle of the night. Apparently one of them had been drinking and driving, which led to an accident that killed Anna. The cops, though, didn't test either of the Choike siblings at the scene. All of the information about the drinking was considered hearsay. That, in turn, forced the police to rule the crash an accident.

TJ is trying to find more information on the crash, the statements from everyone involved; I need to see where we are with everything. I'm hoping to track down at least one of the siblings, that's where this case is going to open up, not only lead us to Andrew's mother but also the truth. I hope TJ can find a way to get his hands on that case file, at least the original officer on file; it will allow us to get some details.

"Knock, knock, anyone here?"

"You don't have to say it as you do it, Nicolette."

"I know, but it's a weird habit I have, I'll work on it."

"No, it's okay, I'm just giving you a hard time. How about we focus on what you found about the case, starting with the death of Anna Dombrowski?"

"Jumping right into it, as usual, I grabbed you a cup of coffee on my way in, figured you can always use a cup."

"Smart girl. You know how to get on the boss's good side."

"As for the case, it's pretty light in the details like TJs email stated, but what I found was a detail that might help us gain more information. The officer first to respond, who also did some of the follow-up, is still on the force. He has a higher title, Captain Duda."

"Awesome, he loves me already, that's a great start." Sarcasm was laid on thickly.

"Judging by your tone, I'm assuming not."

"Bingo. He wasn't a fan of mine, he was at the crime scene with Cardinal Kelley."

"I can see that you can come off as an aggressive American male, especially in these settings. You can be impatient, a little unyielding, and off-putting. We're used to it at work, especially since it gets amazing results, but that's what you've built up. You're in a country that doesn't know you, doesn't care, and just thinks you're Ass American."

"Well, tell me how you really feel. Can we focus on what else you found in the case file?"

"Well, that's the thing, the case file isn't even there, all I have is a few names of officers, date of the incident, it looks like someone deleted the file or removed it, I mean there is nothing there. I hope TJ has a better chance but I doubt it, looking into what I saw."

"Maybe we can get to the captain. We just need to try a different approach. Let's have you approach him tomorrow. I think you're going to have to call in sick to work, get over to the police station, and see if you can build some trust on this case."

"I can do that; I'll see what info I can find on the captain to make the approach a bit simpler. As Christian told me, never approach someone without knowing as much as you can know."

"Smart. Well, I guess we can call it a night from here. If we don't have anything else to go over, just waiting on info, talk to you tomorrow?"

"Sounds good, boss. I'll see what I can come up with for tomorrow. Have a good night, call if you need anything."

Nicolette and I have a game plan, but I still don't have a clue where Terrance and Christian are. Then again, as I glanced over my shoulder watching Nicolette leave, I noticed I had a few emails from Ken and TJ, I also had a missed call from Ken. Let me check the emails first for a change and see what's in there.

According to TJ, it looks like the only way to get our hands on the info we need is to get a hard copy. There is nothing backed up anywhere, and just like Nicolette, he found the person on file most likely to get us the information we need is one Captain Duda. Though we are still grasping at straws, when they line up, start to overlap, and confirm each other, it lets you know that you are on the right path.

Ken's email was in-depth, stating that it looks like Christian and Terrance were working together on something. He said that they crossed similar paths over the past week, which is not surprising, since they were tailing the same people and surveilling the same places. What they said did seem like they were working together—they turned off their phones off at different times but at similar locations. He thinks they met up to do something and are off the grid until they complete it. I'll just call Ken to follow up as his email said he'll be surprised that I actually read the email. I took Nicolette's comments to heart. I need to be more aware of how I interact with the team, especially in this circumstance.

"Hey Ken, I just got done reading your and TJ's emails about everything. What's up?"

"Wow, you actually read them first, before calling. Look who's getting better."

"Nicolette found similar info that TJ did; we have a plan to have her approach the captain tomorrow. He wasn't too keen on me earlier when we met, figured it would be a better approach. So you really think Terrance and Christian are just off the grid doing something? When do we know? What's the protocol for those two?"

See, for different agents, we have different rules. Some get a longer leash because of their backgrounds. It's not a favoritism thing, more of a skill and respect thing. Their backgrounds and experience say they can handle themselves. They also understand that we are operating outside the purview of our normal surroundings, which comes with higher risk and less coverage from the main office. But that's also what draws some of our best talent to us.

"Well, these two know what they're doing. They're pros with a history of scouting; they'll be fine for at least twenty-four to forty-eight hours. If we don't hear from them by tomorrow at four in the afternoon your time we can worry; by midnight we can start looking for them."

"We're really going to wait that long?"

"What if they are following a lead, undercover, playing a role to get the intel needed? You know they aren't going to risk themselves unless they felt it necessary."

"That's a good point. I'll focus on hitting up the captain tomorrow with Nicolette doing the soft approach, and we'll control what we can."

"Smart man. I'd call Sheila, I was talking to her earlier, she's worried about you."

"I'll call her as soon as I get off the phone with you. Have a good night, Ken."

"You too, Neil. We'll figure this out; at least we have something to go on."

He's got a point. For the first time in forever we have something to work with. Now I'm wondering what these two could be getting into. I shot an email to TJ asking him to dig up dirt on the Choike siblings, see what he can find, maybe we can get lucky and get some info on them since high school. Next up is to call Sheila and check in.

"Hey Sheila, how are you and our little girl doing tonight?"

"She's not so little anymore, you know that. But we're both good, just worried about you, as usual."

"I'm doing good, this case has been a fact-finding mission. It's not like I'm chasing a killer or a drug kingpin."

"You don't know that yet. For all you know, this case will take you down a wild turn."

"Fair point, Sheila. Let's focus on you gals. How's Carol Lynn doing? Is she up?"

"Hi Dad, I'm here, but I'm about to go to bed. Mom said you should go to bed too."

"She's right as usual, baby girl. I love you. Give your mom a big hug and kiss for me. I love both of you."

"Hey Neil, I'll call you right back. Let me put her down."

"Sounds good."

Just like that, I'm back off the phone sifting through emails, when I see TJ is already emailing me info back about the Choikes. It seems to be mainly the brother, though he said he can't find anything on Marie. The brother has a crazy rap sheet for drugs and has even been accused of a few murders. It looks like since high school, he's been busy growing from corner drug peddler to drug kingpin. Of course, Sheila's half-ass comment was quick ass foreshadowing to this moment.

"Hey Neil, sorry about that, but I had to put her down."

"It's okay, but I think I'm going to call it a night. I love you, Sheila. Talk to you tomorrow."

"Yeah, that's fine. Are you okay?"

"I'm fine, I just wanted to hear your voice. Now I need to crash."

Truth be told, she can tell when I'm scared or when I'm lying through my teeth or both. The last thing I wanted was her and Carol Lynn worrying about me all the way over here, where I have limited to no backup and all the stress it would bring. It looks like I'm going to spend the rest of the night going down the rabbit hole that is the Choike family.

33

Hey Nicolette, where are you going? The car's here, I'm here, so why are you going back inside?

Nothing quite like waking up in the middle of the night with a keyboard stuck to your face. I was able to get up and crash a few more hours and get some decent rest, but last night became an exercise in crazy. This Jacob character is nuts; he is all over the map with felonies and anything else he can get charged with or accused of. I'll give him this, he is one highly motivated individual, he is not a lazy criminal, he seems to be working his ass off. The question is, do we think he is the reason Andrew's dead and his mother's missing? If that's the case, what's the connection? Where do we go from here?

With a cold cup of coffee in hand, a consistent staple of my morning routine in Warsaw, I began reviewing my emails, the notes from the night before, and the thoughts I had. I started game-planning for the day, then hopped in the shower and began my routine While in there, I noticed my phone going off, messages coming in left and right. I wonder who it is. Only one way to find out, but I don't want to get out of this hot shower, it feels so good right now, but it's needed. I got out, dried off quickly, and threw on some jeans, standing there partially wet from a lazy drying attempt. I noticed that most of the messages were from Christian.

He said that he and Terrance got tied up with a local street gang, but they think it's tied to the case. They spoke of a lady they kidnapped from the Hotel Mansor the other night when they were getting acquainted. They're trying to figure out if they were simply hired for the job or if they are a group working for the person attempting to grab her. They'll reach out when or if they can. It's good to know that they are okay, not good in the situation there, but they can handle that pretty easily. It's not as if they're cops, so getting found doesn't carry the same effect.

From what everyone lacks in detail to be found, we are all working on the same puzzle and missing the same pieces. As we get different pieces, we will come together fast and be able to have an impact on the case greatly. It's a sign when you're about to make the turn, hit the final stretch. I'm going to shoot Ken an email to let him know about the guys, although with the time change he won't be up yet. Then it'll be time to get ready and head over to the precinct and massage the situation with Captain Duda; it's going to take some work. Let's see what Nicolette has found out about him.

As I began my morning routine, I realized I hadn't had a decent workout in days and really needed to get something in. I started to do push-ups, followed by some planks and sit-ups. When I was rudely interrupted by a knocking at the door, I'm sensing a pattern here as I heard a familiar voice along with the knocking.

"Knock, knock, it's me, Nicolette."

"As opposed to anyone else that says the words as they do it."

"Are you ready yet?"

As she opened the door, to her utter dismay she realized I was far from ready. The look on her face reminded me of being scolded by my mother as a child. Or an angry teacher when you failed to turn in your homework for the third consecutive week, pure disappointment.

"Well, it's not hard to see you're not going to be ready anytime soon. I'm going to turn around, go across the street, grab me a pastry, and two coffees for us. I'll be back in fifteen minutes. You better be ready to rock 'n' roll. None of this is personal shower time, not on my watch."

"Man, girl, you do realize I'm the boss man, right? You seem to be doing a lot of commanding for the newbie to the team."

"Leadership isn't about tenure, it's about performance. Now get a move on, Neil, we don't have all day."

"Yes, ma'am, I'll be ready in one hour and fifteen minutes," I said, giving her a hard time.

"What the—"

"Just messing. Get out of here, I'll see you in a few, I'll get ready quick."

"That's much better. See you shortly."

This trip is going to change the way I do a lot of things, at least while I'm over here. It's good to teach an old dog new tricks, even if

---

he gets a little whiny at times. No one likes being taken out of their routine, especially one that has made them successful, but life is about adapting, growing, and changing. After a quick shower, feeling a little out of sorts, I got ready, threw on a hat, threw on my favorite jeans, and some rocking blue Chuck Taylors I bought recently. All I need is my favorite shirt and I'll be ready to go.

I decided to try and race out of the room, down to the lobby, and toward the café to see if I could beat Nicolette back and catch her off guard. Maybe to flip the tide a bit in this power struggle. Sometimes the simplest things can change a power dynamic. I called ahead and also had the valet pull the car around. By the time I hit the lobby, I was getting into the car when she was making her way back from the café. She didn't even notice me downstairs, especially with my Detroit Tigers hat on low.

"Hey Nicolette, where are you going? The car's here, I'm here, so why are you going back inside?'

"When did you get downstairs? It's not like you to be quick. Did you skip a shower?"

"Good point, but I'm here now and time's wasting. Let's get a move on." She was still surprised.

"Okay, got it, Magnum." Nice Tom Selleck reference.

The trip from our hotel to the precinct would have been a short one had we not gotten lost. But the GPS mixed with our lack of understanding Polish and our distracted driving, from talking about the case, led to us miss a few turns. On the way over, we spoke more in detail about what she found out about the captain from researching him through social media, utilizing TJ's help, and doing his usual background dive. It looks like he was divorced a few years ago, not uncommon for us law enforcement types, and enjoys drinking; he posts lots of pictures of beer, she said.

"Since we're almost there I guess it's a good time to ask whether you even checked to see if he was going to be there."

"I had TJ pull their schedule yesterday; I thought it might be better than calling and giving away the element of surprise. He said he's on the morning rotation right now, so he's there eight to six daily, off occasionally, but not today."

"Sounds good. What did you find out about him? Anything you think you can use for leverage or in your approach?"

"His financials are good, but TJ said he feels they are too good; he makes too much with limited police pay normally. He rose through the ranks shortly after that case but has since stopped at captain for a few years."

"I wonder if he's just comfortable or if something stopped him from progressing."

"I guess we're about to find out; we just pulled up. You stay here. I'll head in and let you know how it goes."

"I'm not going to just sit here in the car and look like a creep. I see there's a coffee shop across the way, not surprising by a police station. I'll go hang over there. Hit me up when you have something."

"Got it, Neil. Wish me luck."

We parked the car, I tossed her the keys in case she had to leave, and I began walking across the street. As the station faded away in the background, I looked back and saw she was inside, doing her best to get his attention. She most recently went undercover with the Catholic archdiocesan office, and now she's on her way into a police station trying to stir up an old case that someone wants hidden, although "erased" is a better way of putting it.

While walking over, I searched how far the high school was from the station, out of curiosity, and noticed it's just a few blocks. That means that the case and all the people involved more than likely grew up around here; this is essentially the hub where it all took place. The coffee shop looked like a less branded version of a mainstream coffee shop.

Sitting inside at a table, coffee in hand, I pulled out my laptop. I started digging through emails, starting with the one showing Terrance and Christian's last known location before they went dark. Both were in this neighborhood, which makes me a little worried for Nicolette and what she's walking into; something just isn't adding up here. With someone working their way up the police ranks, stopping here as captain, staying in this neighborhood, where the accident happened, where the siblings are from. Too many coincidences for them to keep adding up like this. My phone began vibrating in my pocket. As I reached for it, I saw a car drive by the coffee shop with four guys in it; one looked like Christian.

"Neil here. What's up? Who is this?"

"That's no way to greet your friend from yesterday. I have your friend with me. She's sitting in an interrogation room."

"Captain Duda? Is that you? Why is she sitting in interrogation? What did she do?"

"It seems you and the people you associate with have trouble sticking your nose where they shouldn't. Now I'm going to have to make an example of one of you. This has got to stop now; I'm not going to let some cowboy American ruin what I've taken years to build."

"First of all, it's not like I can do anything, I'm just trying to find out what happened to a kid back in the States, that's all. Now his mother is missing, we are just trying to find her, get some answers, and then go home."

"Here's your answer: the mother is home, where she belongs. Don't worry, no one will harm her, she'll be treated like royalty here, returning to her rightful place." What the fuck does that mean?

"Captain, what do I need to do? What needs to be done to get her out of there and walk away from this?" Fat chance, but I need to get her out of there.

"As of right now, nothing, I'm going to keep interrogating her, see what she knows. I'll call you back. If you're lucky."

Click.

Just like that, it went from a slow, dull ass couple of days to full-speed oh, fuck mode. First thing I did was email TJ to turn on Christian and Terrance's phones remotely and text them with a message that says Nicolette was being held hostage, call me ASAP. Last year we put software on the phones so in case of an emergency we could turn the phones back on. Hopefully these two guys didn't pull their batteries. TJ will know in a few minutes anyway. I'll call Ken and figure out our next move, see if we have any friends out here, or close enough to get to Poland ASAP.

"Hey, did you get the info from TJ?"

"Yeah, I did. Neil, this captain got so spooked that he was interrogating her and called you out?"

"Yeah, Ken, it's safe to say he falls under one of those paranoid motherfuckers. My biggest concern right now is getting her out of there, getting her safe, and then going from there. He did say something strange as shit, though, about Andrew's mother."

"What's that?

"He said something along the lines of her being safe and sitting at her rightful place now that she's home."

"What the fuck does that mean?"

"Took the words right out of my mouth; no idea. The only thing I can think of at this point is she is tied to the Choikes, that much I'm almost certain, I just don't know how, nor do I know where to start since we don't know who she is."

"Speaking of which, we still can't track down the sister, she has had no footprint anywhere since high school. It's like Anna died and went missing at about the same time. Maybe she saw something, and the brother killed her? Maybe that's what Andrew's mother is tied to?"

"Did TJ have any luck with the guy's phones? I need to get them over to the coffee shop and pronto. We need to get a plan of action ASAP to get Nicolette out. Christian is going nuts, he's going to want to storm the police station, damn nearly go Steven Seagal on them or some shit."

"Yes, he got the phones on, but I don't know if they got the messages or what's going on. Just need to cross your fingers. I'll keep working on our end, I'll reach out to our network of military and security friends and see if we have anyone that can help if we need a fast exit or a wet team. At this point, nothing's off the table. you know our motto."

"All for one, fuck the rest. Don't fuck with our team."

"Not in so many words, but yeah, I see your focus. I'm going to get started. Let me know if you hear from the guys, keep me updated with what's going on. I'll keep the local news on just in case you can't, and you pull the usual Baggio stunts."

"Fair point. If you mix those two guys and me, chances are we are going to damage something or blow something up."

"Neil, please don't get arrested in Poland."

"I'll do my best. Peace."

Just like that, I was in creative mode. While I was waiting to see if the guys would get my bat signal, I started casing the block looking for ways to distract. Get half the police station out, get them wondering what's going on, get us a shot at getting in there. If I can get these two guys, I got a shot at getting her out of there. They are talented, resourceful, and scary as shit. I wouldn't want to be locked in a room with either of them, let alone both of them. That, along with motivation, that one of our own is locked there.

While I was waiting, I decided to do the smart thing and move my car to a block over, off the street, in case we needed to make a getaway and the car wasn't noticeable. It's the small things. While I was driving looking for a place to stash the car, I got a call from Christian Yes, let this be good news.

"Dude, give me good news. Where are you?"

"It's not bad news. I'm close to you, Terrance isn't far either, but getting to you might be hard. The guys we're with are a gang that works for the captain; they work freely in this neighborhood."

"Fucking A. Well, I need you two out of there, we need to get Nicolette out, I'm not letting this paranoid fuck continue to lean on her. How quick can you and Terrence get over to me?"

"We'll figure it out. Give us like ten minutes. I'll go grab him and we'll swing over."

The longest ten minutes of my life, I found a fire escape down the alley from where I had stashed the car, gave the address to Christian via text, and got to the roof. It gave us a great vantage point to see the station. From the looks of it, there aren't many officers working right now. Then again, it is the middle of the day, low crime, many are patrol officers just out and about, mainly office staff is my guess. The building isn't that big, which is a great help to us; that means there aren't many places they can stash her if we make a big fuss out here.

Twenty minutes of me running through a million scenarios in my head, and I heard some commotion down an alley. I made my way carefully to the other side of the roof, looked over, and saw my guys walking up the alley with Christian's car parked down the alley.

Which is good; he has that thing loaded with all the gear we might need. But the problem is I see a guy tailing them, coming up from behind them, keeping an eye on them. A quick text will help that: "tail, seven o'clock, red hat." In a quick move, Terrance flanked right, sprinted around, doubled back, and caught the guy from behind, a quick move to put the man to sleep, and the guys made their way to the roof.

"So when did a fact-finding mission become a full-on op, Neil?"

"When one of the main suspects turned out to be paranoid as shit and a prominent police captain in the area. I guess that explains why the file is missing. I doubt we'll ever find the information about it."

"No. I bet a guy like that keeps that shit at his house locked up for the security on people, to keep over them." Terrance has a great point.

"You guys don't happen to know where he lives? No, but TJ will soon, I already called him, had him start digging for us. Also, I have an idea on how we can get her out. Did he give you any clues on where he is keeping her?" Christian is trying to plan.

"He said he was going to interrogate her until he knows if she has too much info or not."

"Well, there are only two interrogation rooms in there. It's a small-ass station, which helps us a ton, and there's a back door, also helps us. We were in there yesterday for a meeting with the head honcho of the neighborhood." Terrance is full of details, as usual.

"Wait, you met Captain Duda and you guys were in there, walking around the station. Do you have any ideas about what you can do to get her out? If I find a way to get most of the officers in there out of the station?"

"Oh, here comes one of Neil's crazy-ass plans. I've always wanted to be a part of one of these. Terrance, you down to do some shit that might get us arrested, or on the run in Poland?"

"Shit, if we don't get caught, not to mention he's one dirty-ass cop, let's get our girl out, then we can take this dirty-ass cop down and find our missing mother."

"Sounds like fun. So what do you have in mind, Neil? We can get in, play it dumb for a minute, then you make the distraction. We'll do the rest, and double back to one of the cars. Let's split them up so we have two different options."

"All right, you guys head in, get the ball moving, and text me when you're five minutes out from needing a distraction."

"We're not going to know what you're going to do, are we?" Terrance looked concerned.

"It's better that way, trust me, plausible deniability, plus you'll be truly surprised that way, easier to sell it."

"All right, let's do this. We'll move the car, head in. and get this shit rolling. Let's go get our girl out. No one messes with our team and gets away with it. They don't call us American cowboys for nothing." Christian is all kinds of fired up.

As the guys drove around, doubled back, and made their way in, I found a decent-size truck for me to steal. I'm glad the guys used to teach me things like this back at the warehouse for such an occasion; it has come in handy time and again when out on ops. Now the key is how do I get Duda's attention and make sure he comes outside? I think I have the perfect idea—well, at least one that will work. I just need to wait for the signal from the guys. It's been about ten minutes; I'm sure they'll be ready any second now. Right on time, as usual, I see the text come through from Christian. It's a go.

As I called, I heard someone speaking in Polish. I could barely understand them, but I said, "this is Baggio, get DUDA!" They understood that. As I sat in the truck a good two hundred yards from the station, I waited for him to come to the phone. Once I heard him answer, I started revving the engine.

"What are you doing, Mr. Baggio? Revving an engine?"

"Why not look out the front window? You'll see I'm up the street in a truck."

Judging by the blacked-out Mercedes in the lot with a personalized plate labeled "KingPO," I'm going to guess that's his. This is going to be fun; I just hope I don't get shot in the process.

"What do you think you are going to accomplish with that piece of shit? Leave it to an American to think if he has a truck, he can take on a bunch of cops."

"I'm not going to take on cops, just going to smash your car. Maybe drive into the building and bring enough attention on this station that I get Nicolette in the proper custody, or better yet you out of this neighborhood."

"You know nothing of the power I have here, and you wouldn't dare risk it, one man coming to save his little girl. You crazy American cowboy, this is why we don't like you guys, except in the movies. Deal with it, she's mine, and there's nothing you can do about it."

"Fuck you, Captain."

Like that, I hung up the phone, started flooring the truck toward his car, and crashed into it. Metal parts flying everywhere. You could hear him screaming at me from inside. I peeled off. I started driving around the block, gaining speed, and texted Christian to stay away from the front of the station. As I geared up, getting the truck up to forty-five, taking each turn tight, the truck leaning, I found myself on the straightaway, now up to fifty-five, then sixty-five. I undid my seat belt. By now a few officers were outside, and I started honking and screaming, "Move!" As they made their way out of the path of the truck, I leaped from the truck into a patch of grass, leaving the truck with the cruise going seventy miles an hour heading directly at the front door of the station.

"You're fucking crazy, Neil. She's still inside. Good luck getting her out on foot. All you did was piss me off. We are going to hunt you down and kill you, you motherfucker!"

I could see Terrance and Christian slide out the back in full sprint, heading toward an ally where they stashed their car. From this vantage I could hear Duda screaming for his goons to start shooting me. That was my sign to exit stage right. I ran inside the building, already knowing I could make it through to the back alley, around the block, and to my car.

I just had to keep them off my ass long enough that they don't see my car. Most of them will be too busy dealing with a smashed-up cop car and a truck in their front door to get out to me. Their parking lot was all blocked off, and the only way to get out was to be blocked from the damaged car and truck. On foot, sprinting through the building, out the back to the alley, I still didn't see anyone, but I could hear them screaming at me as I ducked into the car. I peeled out. I'm sure they caught a glimpse of the car and would be able to track the plates from footage earlier when we showed up. I'm going to have to ditch the car somewhere. I need to call the guys, regroup, find somewhere to lay low.

"Christian, I saw you guys got out. Did you make it to the car?"

"Yeah, we're all here. You're one crazy son of a bitch, Neil. I love working with you. Are you okay?"

"Yeah, I'm a bit busted up, but I'll survive. How's Nicolette doing?"

"He roughed her up pretty good, but she said she'll be okay, just some bumps and bruises."

"Where are we meeting up? I'm going to have to ditch this car ASAP before we do."

"Since you already hot-wired one car, do you want to find a new car and meet us somewhere to pick you up, or rendezvous in thirty minutes back at the hotel, clean up, and head out?"

"Let's head back to the hotel, check out quickly, and find a seedy motel to check in under our aliases. I've got my crash kit with me. Do you guys?"

"I know Terrance and I do. not sure about Nicolette. I'll meet you back at the hotel; let's be quick. We'll have Nicolette find a place to crash in the meantime."

As we made our way back to the hotel, I called TJ and had him look up local home rentals off the grid. He found a few we could pay cash with, just outside Warsaw. This would allow us to regroup, stay clear of Duda, and find a way to track him down and Andrew's mother. As we pulled in, we barely parked, left the cars running, told the valet to leave them running hot. I tossed him some cash with my card and said if he sensed any trouble, call me and I'll double it.

"Hey guys, we have maybe five minutes to pack up and get out of here; let's make it quick. TJ already found us a place to meet up that's off the grid, just outside Warsaw. Since I'm sure my rental has GPS that the captain will track, let's have some fun, drive it around town, park it in a seedy neighborhood motel, then head out of town. Get it?"

"Works for us. Meet you back down here in five minutes, boss."

We all worked fast and clinically. Luckily, I had barely unpacked; most of my stuff was still in my bag. It made moving downstairs easy. I threw my stuff, except for my crash bag, into their car. As they came down, we all headed out and made our way to the rough part of town to look for a poor motel to drop the car. We finally found one but found an even better situation when I saw a kid looking bored and for something to do.

I went inside to rent two rooms with my credit card that we were never going to use while Christian and Nicolette talked with the local boy to give him the lowdown on driving our car around for some extra cash. If the car is moving, coming back to the motel, it'll keep up the looks to Captain Duda. Once all back in the car, we all had that feeling we actually pulled this shit off, headed out of town toward the bed and breakfast that TJ found us to rent off-grid with cash.

"So Neil, what's the next move? Since you went nutso on that police station and drove through it, it put a target on your back, and we're assuming at this point our faces are now involved. Though we dodged the few cameras there, they still know we had a role in this. You can bet they're coming for all of us." Terrance is always thinking about the next step.

"Yeah, Neil, that shit was insane I've heard stories about your crazy on-the-spot plans but never thought I'd be lucky enough to see one firsthand." Christian was still amped up.

"How about you, Nicolette? How are you doing? You still look a little roughed up?"

"Yeah, I'm hurting a bit, but I'll be okay. Just get me a drink and a bag of ice, a nap, and I'll be okay. I want to get this bastard just as much as the next person."

"How long a drive do we have until we get there, Terrance? I know it's a bit outside of town, and we just drove downtown."

"We should be there in five minutes, Neil. It's not as bad as you think. We're already on the highway; from here, GPS says only ten or so minutes."

"Well, once we get there, Nicolette will probably have to lead the way in case their English is lacking. For now, everyone get some rest, focus a bit, think through the next steps, what you saw, what you learned, and what we can review when we settle in."

The remainder of the trip was quiet, we just listened to the humming of the road, the wind ripping by with the windows down. We all needed that moment, to find some solace in a crazy day, trying to wrap our heads around the day, and what Captain Duda meant when he spoke of Andrew's mother. There are so many different things we have to review, but for now, we rest, find a center, and review internally.

34

Christian went soap opera, back from the dead theory.

The place TJ found was an old farmhouse on a functioning farm—barn and all—which will be perfect for parking the car off the street and out of the way. As the guys and I began unpacking, we realized that our rooms were in the barn. There was a makeshift apartment on the top story of the barn. Looks like we'll be living the country life for a bit. According to Nicolette, the toilet works out there, the faucet works, but they highly suggest we shower in the house, and drink only bottled water when we're in the barn; house water is fine.

"Did they really say the barn water is bad? Or just the house water is better?" I was stunned.

"They said the house water is treated and might taste more like we're used to. The water out there is well water, safe to drink, just different."

"I love well water, I'll be good." Terrance grew up in the sticks.

"I'll be fine. Sure beats some of the shit we drank in the desert." Christian is always making a good point.

"I'm not about to make an ass out of myself, I'm game. I guess that leaves Nicolette. What say you?"

"You bet your ass I'm taking the fancy bottled water and treated house water."

"Now that we have the water situation figured out, why don't we review the day, see what we can piece together, and game-plan for tomorrow. Someone wants to conference in TJ, let's see what he was able to dig up on Captain Duda while we were running around like idiots all afternoon." I was getting cranky.

"I'll call him; I haven't talked to him in a while. As for the day, other than the captain being your usual local lowlife crime boss. Not sure what to say. Christian can fill you in more." Terrance looked distracted.

"Yeah, he was into everything in the neighborhood. Guns, drugs, and an old-fashioned protection racket. I guess the classics never die."

"Anyone have any idea on Andrew's mother, who they think she might be? Especially after his comment to me on the phone earlier about her sitting in her rightful place, being treated properly." I was grasping, but I could feel it was coming.

"Everything seems possible at this point, but maybe Anna never died?" Christian went soap opera, back from the dead theory.

"No, I think she's related to Jacob somehow, that's how this all plays together. But who?"

Nicolette is still working something, she's just not quite there.

"I'm starting to think she's Marie. It has to be, it's the only thing that adds up."

"Neil has a point there, it would have to be Marie, but how does she play into this?"

"Christian, are you asking if she is a willing participant, or reluctant?"

"Exactly, Neil, we don't know what her role is, what she plays in it."

"Also, what is the significance of Andrew, why his life meant so much that she had to be exiled? Then without him, she is brought back home."

"I guess we start with digging up info on the Choike siblings, family feuds, and go from there. Maybe this goes back to something bigger, maybe Anna is from another crime family but we just aren't seeing it." Terrance is making a strong argument.

"Not a bad point there, Terrance. But for now let's get some rest, regroup in the morning. I say we see if we can break into Duda's place, look for any blackmail files. If he's there, it's not like he's going to be looking for us at his house, probably the safest place to be in the city, unless he's got it guarded."

"The rumor is that he leaves it wide open because no one is ballsy enough to break in and do it. Other than us, that is; then again, we're not from around here."

That line got a great chuckle, everyone looked at Terrance like he was crazy, but we knew he was serious. Breaking into the captain's house is probably the best thing to do; it'll generate the most leads, that's for sure. Not to mention it'll be fun to fuck with his place a bit, maybe even wait around to see his face when he realizes we broke in.

The nice thing about people such as Captain Duda is that they have built up such a strong ego, a social persona, they feel invincible in their neighborhoods. They feel they own them and can't be touched; often this is true, or damn close. When you introduce some American cowboys to the mix, that's when you get crazy ideas like breaking into the local kingpin's place.

As everyone started to get comfortable, I went downstairs into the barn with my laptop and headphones. Figured I would check emails and listen to some music. Believe it or not, this farmhouse had pretty good Wi-Fi. Much better than our hotel was; then again, it's not in the heart of the city and there aren't a hundred people trying to get on and push the signal to the limit. I could hear some footsteps, ever so softly, coming down, as they turned the corner. I could see it was Nicolette, probably struggling to rest from the beating she took earlier.

"Hey girl, what are you doing up? You need to get some rest."

"I know, I will, I just wanted to thank you, what you did, coming for me. I never thought someone would go to such lengths for me."

"When you're a part of our team, there isn't anything we wouldn't do. We might push you, we might ask a lot, but we always have your back."

"This is why guys never leave the company, Christian was trying to explain it to me, I just thought it was some ex-military macho BS. I didn't realize it's because you're one of the good guys."

"Don't take it that far, Nicolette. I have plenty of ex-girlfriends that will say otherwise."

"Fair enough, I just wanted to say thank you, count me in as a lifer too."

With that, she kissed me on the cheek, made her way back up the stairs, and turned the lights off. Just then I saw Christian look down to me and give me the bro nod of thanks; that's all we needed. He knows how much I appreciate him and Terrance. We're a big, crazy family; we make it work.

As I sifted through emails, I saw that TJ did track down Captain Duda's house; he also noticed there are a few different places that the captain has registered in his name—a storage facility, some wine storage place, and his house. I have a feeling the wine storage is where he has his shit hidden. I know his type; he's not going to keep it at his house, his storage is too obvious, but the wine storage has surveillance built in, and it's a great place to hide documents from prying eyes.

I saw an email from Sheila too, with some pics of her and Carol Lynn playing at the park. It made me feel great seeing them. Had Sheila known the shit I pulled today, or any of the days I do that shit, she would go nuts. When the guys let slip some of the craziness around her, she usually goes off on me, reminding me that I'm a father, a best friend, and an ex-husband with responsibilities. I know all of those things, but when one of our team members is in trouble, I get focused on that one task; it has to be completed, I can't break from it. I become like a dog ripping through a bone; it's all I can focus on.

I'm starting to get tired, but I don't want to wake them up. I think I'm going to lean back in this makeshift area I created on some bales of hay and just nap. Tomorrow we go after Duda hard. We wrap this case up and get out of here. I'm done with all this waiting around, we have strong leads and are starting to put it together. It's time to mess shit up and ruffle some feathers. I wouldn't mind finding this Jacob Choike fella. As I started to fade away dreaming of Sheila and Carol Lynn back home, taking care of my girls, oh, how I miss my dogs back home. I saw an email come through from TJ informing me, it looks like Anna Dombrowski's father and brother were both serving life sentences for a long rap sheet of charges; her family is the rival to the Choikes.

Fuck me—I'm caught up in a modern-day Polish *Romeo and Juliet*.

"Got to love waking up that way."

Waking up to the warm Polish sun as it rises over the horizon, hitting me ever so softly, would have been great. Not me; I woke up as I felt a large sandpaper tongue slather my face. Then I fell off my hay perch to hard ground, screaming a bit in the process, becoming the alarm for the rest of the team, or so I thought.

"Holy shit, look who slept down in the barn with the animals." Christian was laughing.

"Very funny, guys. After sifting through emails and work, I decided to give in and just sleep where I was. I guess I paid the price."

"I don't know, I think we all did. These mattresses are about as soft as that hay down there I bet, might have been a crapshoot." Terrance stood up stiffly, trying to stretch.

"Where's Nicolette? She still sleeping?"

"Nah, she's in the house, showering and talking to the house manager. She said breakfast will be ready shortly—the house manager, that is. I think Terrance has a crush on her."

"Dude, shut up. I mean, she's cute, but lay off me."

"Guys, get your shit together. Let's get organized, ready, and get moving. We have a ton to do, and we have to divide and conquer today. I'll go over everything at breakfast so I don't repeat myself."

As we made our way inside, Nicolette was done showering, enjoying some coffee, and talking to the manager. Terrance and Christian said they were going to do quick showers and make me last since I'm the one with the issue. I argued it wasn't an issue, just a preference, but they all ganged up on me. It took us guys a quick twenty minutes to cycle in and out of the shower, by the time I made it in there it was cold, but I made do. I figured it would wake me up anyway.

"All right, gang, let's sit at the table. Today we have three different spots to hit, but I'm pretty sure one is going to be useless, so we're going to start with two of them. According to TJ's email, Captain Duda has his house, a storage unit, and a locker at a wine storage facility. We're going to focus on the house and the wine place, leave storage for last if we don't find anything."

"Sounds good, Neil, but what are we looking for? That case file still?"

"It's less about that file, Christian; we are looking for Captain Duda's blackmail files, his leverage. That's what keeps him in power; without it, he loses it."

"Why do you think the wine facility is a place to look over the storage unit?"

"Well, Nicolette, it's got plenty of security built in, and if he goes in and out regularly to check on or add to it, no one will be the wiser."

After forty minutes of breakfast and game planning, we realized we were going to need another car; we couldn't split up with only one car. I'm not in the mood to steal another car. This shit is getting old, and as we were talking about the issue, the house manager told us she had some old motorcycles that were her dad's. They still ran great, they were in back, and we could use them. Terrance and Christian were all over that, which left Nicolette and me with the car. As I sent them to the house, I told them to be careful, as Nicolette and I went to the wine place.

"Guys, remember today is about getting intel, tracking down the Choike siblings, especially the brother, that will lead us to Andrew's mother and get some answers. That's odd; I'm getting a call from the cell we gave Glow. I'm going to step outside."

I made my way outside to where it was a bit quieter, took a deep breath, and answered the call. Why was he finally reaching out to me? It's been a while. I figured that at this point he was just staying away to be safe.

"Hey Glow, what's up?"

"No, Neil, it's Ken. We got a problem over here. We can't find Glow; no one can."

"What the fuck! Come on, man, you're telling me he just up and vanished? That doesn't make sense, especially with all the commotion over here in Poland. Does it look like a kidnapping?"

"I don't think so, it looks like he packed a bag and dipped, but we can't get ahold of him; his phone is off right now. I have TJ doing the usual dive on him; we should have something in the next hour or so. I'll keep you updated. From what we can tell, it looks like no one has seen him since last night."

"Okay, thanks, Ken. This case keeps getting worse."

As I made my way back inside, I realized we really had to ramp this shit up. Get this part of the case closed. We were about to get reckless a bit, turn some tables upside down, and make a mess, all in an effort to get the Choikes' attention so we can find out what we need to and move on.

"Okay, now to add to the mix, it looks like Glow has gone missing. From what Ken can figure, he dipped out. But no one knows where and probably sometime last night."

"Does Ken or anyone else out there think he's a suspect? Is that why he's running?" Terrance was just asking obvious questions.

"No, my guess is he's tired of sitting on his hands. It's summer, kids aren't there, and he is trying to solve this shit too."

"Do you think he's coming here then?" Nicolette was thinking the same as I was.

"That's the only thing that makes sense to me. Otherwise, why leave? There's no point. He knows where in the case we have agents all over. I think he knows something he's not telling, and he wants to confront Andrew's mother."

"That brings us back to the theory that she's the other half of the Choike equation."

"Exactly, Christian. Enough breakfast, enough chilling, let's get after it. We need to wrap this shit up and fast. Thundercat's HO!"

"What the fuck!" Christian looked confused.

"I forget, all you kids aren't as old as I am. Never mind, let's go."

We spent the next fifteen minutes gearing up, syncing up our game plans, and rolling out. Terrance and Christian took off, heading toward the captain's house. As Nicolette and I made our way toward the wine storage facility, we started preparing for how we would play it once we got there. Though Nicolette had plenty of bumps and bruises, she cleaned up like a champ. She had heels in the car in case she had to play the part; she really has come in handy out here. She's been rocking like a great agent, ready for any role needed. As we pulled in, only one car was parked in the lot, and only one person was working inside. It looked like a younger kid. Nicolette should be able to make this kid putty. We just needed to look up which unit is the captain's and find a way to get in.

TJ was working on most of this last night, he said he emailed me the info about the captain's stash, what his unit is, and possible lock combinations. He also emailed the team a spec of the captain's house, floor plan, and necessities. I was going to review everything before we went into the field today, but after the call about Glow, it threw me off my game. This case has me shooting from the hip, waiting all the time, and confused as shit. As we pulled up, Nicolette grabbed her heels out of the back.

"Nicolette, are those Louboutins? And did I buy those?"

"Well, you haven't yet, I was going to try and expense them, see what happened."

"Well, technically you are using them for the case right now. You'll have a good chance to get them approved."

"Hell, yeah. Well, let me go inside and make this kid my bitch. When I get in there, I'll get his keys so you can get into the captain's locker. As TJ said, there's a master key so the staff can add to and remove or ship bottles for their customers."

"We need something to go easy for once, go knock them dead."

Nicolette walked in, rocking tight black pants, a fitted shirt, and a little jacket, mixed with her heels And with her attitude she was sure to stun any man. The beauty of what she's wearing is to throw on some black tennis shoes or military boots and you're in good straits; she really knows how to walk that fine line. Christian has been coaching her up great, just as Ken said he would. She's walking in, seeing her amazingly petite body and fearless attitude. All I could do was think about how I ruined things with Maria.

I know what you're thinking. This is when I finally deal with it, when I go over; hell, when I bring it up to you. You know I don't like confronting my poor choices when it comes to women, that's why I always run back to Sheila, it's what I know, it's safe, we know where we stand, even if we know it's only going to work to an extent. I know it's not healthy, we both know it's not healthy, but we keep at it.

Maria, she really struck a chord with me, not just her beauty, but her ambition as well.

That plus Maria wanting me to really step back from Sheila and Carol Lynn. Not so much my daughter, but the way Sheila and I co-parent her. She said she couldn't compete, and I get it, but I kept trying to tell her, not to be self-conscious, that she had nothing to fear. I know that she felt she couldn't compete with the connection, with our history, but that's something she had to get over; I guess any woman that's with me will have to. I'm always going to be in this place because of the way Sheila and I have worked it out. It's like being forever single and married at the same time; its oddly lonely and comforting at the same time. At this point I've accepted that my life isn't normal, but I embrace and enjoy the chaos.

After thirty minutes of me getting lost in my shit, I noticed my phone ringing. It was Nicolette.

"Hey, I have the keys, and he's all tied up in the back. I improvised; let's see what we can find."

"Damn, girl, did he think you were super kinky and get his hopes up?"

"Yup, I know I can be harsh, but hey, he's got an amazing story for a long time to tell."

"I'm already on my way in."

As I made my way into the store, I got a text from Terrance and Christian saying they are coming up empty at the house. No one there, nothing to find. They are going to lay low and wait for us, head our way in case we need backup.

"You work quickly, don't you, girl?"

"I had some great teachers. Christian told me, don't wait around, especially when putting moves on a guy."

"He's right. Read the room, read the guy, make your move, no point in beating around the bush."

"You got the keys, TJ said its locker forty-seven, right over there."

"Really, locker forty-seven, station forty-seven. Dude, this guy has issues." She's got a point.

"Not surprising. I would be surprised if all that's in here is personalized bottles of his own wine that tastes like shit because he thinks he's going to make it."

"Well, let's see."

"Wait; not assuming he's smart enough to rig it, but let's open it from the sides, see if he at least has a camera or something. The last thing we want to do is tip our hand. Remember, he is paranoid as shit."

"Good point. Why don't you stand back and to the side so you can look in. I'll step aside and open."

"Good idea, Nicolette."

As she opened the door and turned the key, ever so slowly it's as if we could hear each other's heart beating quickly.

"Do you see anything from over there. I'm just happy it didn't explode."

"No, Nicolette, I don't see anything. But let me use my phone camera to be safe, just to keep my face out of it. Wait for a second, yeah, I see it back there, a small Wi-Fi camera looks like it's triggered to go off when the door opens. Hand me that towel over there; I'll toss it over the camera."

"Seriously? Just a dirty towel soaked in dried wine?" Nicolette looked disgusted.

"The simplest shit is the best."

"Fair enough. So is there anything in here we can use?"

"Lots of bottles of wine, as expected. But wait for a second, I think, yup, knock on the bottom here, with me, look to the sides here. It's a false bottom. I wonder how it opens, though, I don't see any loops or latches."

"Try simply pushing it down. maybe it's spring-loaded. From all the weight, might be worn out."

"Well done, girl."

As we delicately pulled out the documents from the false bottom, most of it was cash, some fake IDs and travel docs for himself if he had to run. With two different guns, which we made sure not to handle in case they had been used for murders. The thing is, there aren't any files here. Maybe he simply digitizes them, and stores them somewhere, keeps them to himself, to be safe.

"Is there a chance we're giving this guy too much credit?"

"What do you mean?"

"Maybe he's just a bully cop from the street who knew that the Choikes ran drugs for him and he covered their tracks, plain and simple."

"I did just say the simplest things are the best; I think you might be on to something. Let's have some fun at his expense; there have to be some drugs around here."

"Let's go talk to my new boyfriend; I bet he has some drugs on him or can get some quick."

"Good idea."

We walked into the office where she had him tied up, where we caught him struggling to force his way out. He had found a way to tip the chair over on its side, but he was no closer to getting out than he was before. She talked him down, told him we could care less about him, but asked if there happened to be some drugs in one of the lockers. He said one of the tenants keeps drugs in four different lockers there. They pay the owners plenty of cash for them to just them use it as a stash house. There was a lot of back and forth with her talking Polish to him and explaining to me what he was saying.

Eventually we found out that the lockers are under a fake name, no shit, but the phone number is real. They guy said he's been told that if cops ever show up, call that number. We emailed it to TJ, told him to back-trace it, and get as much info, maybe a location worst case. By this point we had texted Christian and Terrance; they were waiting for us outside. I decided to pay the kid five hundred dollars to walk away and call the local cops. Claiming the place was robbed, we opened up the lockers, knocked some things around, opened those lockers but didn't steal the drugs; this should be a pain in the ass for them.

As we walked outside, we would have to figure out who was going to sit on the store and see what the cops do if they called Captain Duda and who else might show up.

"Hey gang, we need to decide who is going to sit here, wait and see what's going down, and then who is going to chase down the cell phone number."

"Hey Neil, since we didn't get to do anything at the house but look around, can we go chase down a drug kingpin's cell phone? Sounds like fun." Terrance was amped.

"Yeah, you guys can, get with TJ, he'll get you the info. We'll sit on this place. There's plenty of retail spots around here, blending in should be easy enough for us."

35

Oh, fuck me, this just keeps getting better.

After a good hours plus, the cops had been there, called in backup, and had drug dogs all over. They had the place completely torn apart; we hadn't seen any commotion yet in regard to dirty cops, Captain Duda, or what might look like drug dealers looking in on their product.

"Hey Neil, look over there. I think we have some movement for a change."

"Oh shit. I think you're right, that guy is chilling over there, but kind of obvious. He's staring right at the building, making a call, and looks worried as shit. My guess is he's the guy who thought this place was a good stash house. I'll sit here, you get in the car, plan on tailing him if he leaves, let's see where he ends up."

"Got it, boss man. Where are you going to end up?"

"No idea. This situation is fluid; we'll figure it out as we go."

Nicolette disappeared, got in the car, and made sure she was in a position to keep an eye on our friend that looked a little suspect. One of my favorite parts of this job is coaching talented people, seeing them become great at what they do; it makes a difference. I can only do so much. If I have a growing team of amazing individuals, we can make a bigger impact.

Watching the scene being processed systematically was a bit mind-numbing, but it needed to be done. We had to see who was going to show up, especially if it was someone related to Captain Duda, but part of me feels like Duda would show up himself, especially after the show from yesterday, as well as us breaking into his locker today. The question is, how much control does he have, and does he have enough pull to make gun and drug charges disappear from his locker?

After an hour had passed, our squirmy friend got on the move, and Nicolette followed suit behind. Shortly after she exited stage right, I noticed a cop car with some newly earned fender damage, with "Precinct 47" on the side. Here we go; let the show begin. Let's see how he takes the news, see if he tries to pull rank. I noticed that the evidence team had already processed his locker, and from the looks of it, they have it all cataloged and packed up. That means if he's going to pull rank, they're going to have to change lots of paperwork.

I'm sitting across the street at a retail shop, keeping an eye on what's going on. It's off to the side at a ninety-degree angle, so I have a great view of what's going on.

I'll probably end up in a car shortly, maybe calling a cab in an effort to keep the staff from thinking I'm some weird guy creeping on them. I only wish I were closer, to hear what they were talking about, except it really wouldn't matter since I can barely say a phrase or two in Polish. Now that I know he's there, the data has been processed. I can have TJ or one of the other guys look into the case file tomorrow and see if Duda had a chance to pull it. Time to find a ride out of here; then again, according to the maps, I'm only a five-mile walk from the hotel. I might just get to walking.

As I made my way around the back, to ensure that no one would see me go a bit out of the way and steer clear of the scene, I noticed a few emails from TJ. I decided to call him for the rundown. I'll make sure to follow up with the other guys after I get off with him, see if they were able to track down our cell phone.

"Hey TJ, what do you got for me? From what I just saw, Captain Duda just showed up, probably going to cause a bit of a stir, but I didn't want to hang around and risk getting noticed."

"Well, I have some good news. Terrance and Christian were able to track down that cell phone. It turns out it's the same person Nicolette is tailing as we speak, so Terrance decided to widen his perimeter, and Christian is on his way over to you to pick you up. Just hang tight."

"Thanks, TJ. Any other good news, any chance on getting a recent pic of Jacob Choike sent to the team and me so we can be on the lookout for him?"

"Yeah, I emailed one to you guys a bit ago, figured it might come in handy as you tailed that other guy. Also, I found Glow—well, sort of."

"What the hell does that mean?"

"He's on a plane, looks like he bought a ticket to Warsaw. He lands in an hour."

"Oh, fuck me, this just keeps getting better. I guess Christian and I can go see why he felt the need to come to Poland."

"Ken said to give him a shout, he did some interviews around campus, got a pretty good feel for what he thinks happened."

"Okay, sounds good. Thanks, TJ."

The only thing I can think of is that Glow knows something, or better yet, is just pissed. Us OLSM boys take care of our own. Glow is an alumnus, not just the headmaster, and is the heartbeat of the school. This is going to eat at him, especially if he finds out the mother had anything to do with Andrew's stress. I really wasn't in the mood for another call, so I simply texted Ken, asking him if my hunch was correct, and he confirmed. I think he appreciated the brevity. I know I did because shortly after, Christian pulled up on his ride.

The bikes, both of them, were a pearl color, looked like Polish off-white, with chrome all over. They were a little bit older, not quite classic. I think the manager told us, 2000s, BMW R1200C was the model. The quickest way to describe them is if you took James Dean's personality and put it in a European motorcycle in the 2000s you'd have this bike.

"Hey, boss man, I hear we are going to the airport to meet Glow, see what he thinks he's doing out here, other than picking a fight we're already picking."

"Christian, most principals would take it personally when one of their students takes their own life. You have to understand Glow, and our school is a different kind of community that you're tied to forever. He'll look at what I'm doing for this case."

"Good point. They really get you boys trained up good, don't they?"

"It's not that. They pushed us, almost broke us like mules, but I'll tell you college was a cakewalk compared to high school. They aren't kidding when they say it's a traditional college preparatory."

"I didn't mean to get you all fired up. I can see and have learned your school means a lot to you and others like you. That's why we have your back. Let's head to the airport and make sure we get there before he lands."

Having to hug another man tightly on a motorcycle is a test of how comfortable you are with your masculinity. You laugh, but there is no way to embrace a man tightly while going sixty or seventy miles an hour without it getting a little awkward. It's just par for the course. As we pulled in, I looked down at my watch, then my phone to check the flight info that TJ had sent us and then directed Christian to head out.

"Hey, I'll be good. Let me handle this solo. I'll just grab a cab from here."

"You sure, Neil? I can hang, it's no big deal."

"I know, Christian, but I want to get Glow one on one, see where his head is, break it down."

"You plan on getting in a cab with him, talking to him on a ride to his hotel, I'm assuming?"

"There ya go, that's the idea."

As Christian pulled away, I walked in, then walked over to baggage claim to check his flight status with the info on my phone. It says it should be deplaning about now, which means I have about five to ten minus max until he makes his way through here. I'll just chill over here until he makes his way through the terminal. Might catch him off guard, but I'm sure he'll be happy to see me. If he isn't, that will be a telling sign. After sifting through emails and unsubscribing from a few spam emails from the usual department stores, I noticed Glow walk by me.

"Hey Glow, fancy meeting you here."

"I figured you would meet me here; I knew I wouldn't have to call. Who noticed first?"

"You mean, how did we figure it out? We tried getting in touch with you, so I could talk to you and saw you had dipped out, didn't look forced, so we did some digging, found out you bought a ticket to Poland."

"That's right. You're good at this job, which is why I called you. Want to share a cab? I'm assuming you want to talk about why I'm here."

"Yeah, why are you here, Glow? Even if you're here for Andrew to get closure, he's passed on, this isn't going to change anything.

"I need to see for myself, I need to hear from her, look her in the eye and ask her what the *fuck* she is thinking."

"Do you know something you're not telling me? Maybe that her name isn't Malinowski, it's actually Choike, and her brother is a crime boss, son of a legendary crime boss in Poland?"

"I could tell you that, but you already apparently know it for yourself. Let's get a cab; I'll tell you more on the ride."

We got into a cab. He gave the cabbie directions, detailed where he wanted to go. That's when I realized he didn't have anything but a backpack with him, he didn't have a suitcase, didn't have a carry-on, just a backpack.

"Packing light for the trip. Going back soon?"

"You could say that my flight leaves tomorrow morning. I'm staying at the hotel by the airport, going right back. I just flew out to talk to her, then I'm going home."

"Why didn't you give me all this info about who she really is when you called me out that night?"

"Well, that would be from the fact that she just called me and dropped all that shit on my plate yesterday, offered to fly me out here, to tell me in person the truth and apologize. I'm fucking livid, so I took her up on the offer. No one puts my kids in harm's way."

"Want to share with me where we are heading so I can give my team a heads up? I won't have the storm in, just be close in case we need them."

"Sure, it's a restaurant called the bent spoon, in Polish obviously, but the sign is pretty clear."

I shot the team a text, let them know what was going down. Terrance and Nicolette were finished tailing our friend, who led them back to a warehouse, but nothing came of it. They were just sitting on it; Christian was just waiting for his next assignment, so the three of them made it there to the area where the restaurant was to be our backup if we needed it.

"Okay, it looks like my guys should be in the area in ten minutes, give or take. Did Marie Choike give you any idea what the hell all this is about?"

"On the call yesterday, she said Andrew started to figure out who they really were when he started trying to find who his dad was. He realized his father was scared of his mother and her family, which didn't make sense. He eventually got some information out of her about him."

"That's what this is about. Andrew was struggling with being the heir to a crime syndicate and not a poor immigrant in the States? Just the complete one eighty of it?"

"Andrew was a really good kid, extreme salt of the earth. I think finding out that he came from a family with such a dark secret was very hard for him to comprehend. According to his mother, she told him she was disappointed in him that he didn't show a bad streak."

"What the fuck, are you serious? Who says that to their kid? I guess the daughter of a legendary crime boss in Poland."

"I guess so. We're pulling in according to the driver. You are coming in?"

"You bet your ass. I got your back, Glow. Let's end this shit, find out what the fuck is going on out here."

As we walked in, I noticed that Captain Duda's cruiser from earlier was parked out front. I grabbed my phone and texted Christian, *GET YOUR RIFLE, COVER US—DUDA WAIT FOR MY SIGNAL!*

The only problem is we don't really have a signal, but I'm sure I can come up with something. I just hope Christian can get set up quickly enough and that Duda doesn't shoot me in the head two seconds in the doorway.

36

Duda and I began our high-school cockfight like two roosters.

As we entered the restaurant, it looked like an old diner. (When I say "old" I mean more than a hundred years old. The tavern, from the turn of the twentieth century, had been slightly updated—just enough to cover the health code. There was more wood in there, than a moose ski lodge, but it did have a kind of ambience to it. What it lacked in overall cleanliness and basic restaurant decor, it made up for in small size and a great big window for Christian to see into, or so I hope.

"Fucking Baggio, I should shoot you right now. Come to think of it, I just might."

"Good to see you make friends everywhere, Neil." Glow wasn't amused.

"Calm down, Duda. Mr. Glowacki here was personally invited by Ms. Choike herself. She is expecting him."

"How do you know she's here, or who she even is?"

"Enough, Duda. Shut the fuck up, and be a better host to our guests." Enter Ms. Choike.

"Hello, Ms. Malin . . . I mean Ms. Choike. Thank you for the invite; sorry it took so long."

"I hope the flight was very comfortable?"

"Yes, you didn't need to fly me first class, but I'll take it."

"Nice to see you again, Neil. I hear you had a little fun yesterday at the precinct giving the captain a hard time."

"Yes, sorry for causing such a stir, Ms. Choike, but I wanted to ensure the safety of my team member, and the captain here was a bit chippy yesterday."

"Neil, I swear to God, I'm going to shoot you and risk my boss killing. If you mouth off one more time, you will show me respect. By any chance, were you the one who fucked with my wine locker?"

"What are you talking about? Wine . . . what?"

As Duda and I began our high-school cockfight like two roosters fighting over a hen, Glow and Ms. Choike walked to the kitchen to talk. While they were back there, I noticed her whole demeanor change from a sweet old lady to a dark princess with a secret. It was like watching a supervillain change in a movie. While I was arguing with Duda, she was getting in Glow's face, he was giving it right back, but I'm not sure that was the best move. I was trying to keep an eye on Glow and Duda, but I kept getting a light shined in my eye, almost a reflection of sorts, when it dawned on me that it was Christian letting me know he's in position.

"You know exactly what I'm talking about, Neil."

"Duda, what the fuck is your problem?"

I moved around him, putting me in a better position to see Glow. I had Duda lined up with his goons behind him where Christian and my team could peg them off, and I could see Glow. Which is good because Ms. Choike was getting heated; it looked like she was a moment away from pulling a gun or a knife on him. I could barely make out what they were arguing over while Duda was yelling at me.

"That boy had an amazing future; you took it from him?"

"Shut up. You're his mother, you took it from him, forcing your family shit on him."

"You and your school filled him with that service shit, that care for your brother shit, you took my boy. I should take your life for his, a life for a life."

Like that she pulled a gun on Glow, Duda followed suit on me, and we were in a bad situation, but I had one ace up my sleeve. I just hope Christian knows to shoot the old lady. I mouthed Glow, three times to the window, almost confusing Duda.

"What the fuck are you looking at? What are you saying? Are you praying? No one is coming for you. You're going to die here tonight, Neil, there's no one with a truck coming to save you."

"You're right, come closer, get up close, put the gun to my head."

Now Christian can't shoot at Duda; he'd hit me. This way, he has to shoot Choike, which made me think for a moment we still haven't seen the brother, haven't even heard a word, just that mug shot from TJ that's about a year old. Well, if I go down, this is one hell of a way to go out. Guns blazing in Poland with your high-school principal.

"Tell ya what, Duda, I bet you're too weak to shoot me this close, afraid of the mess."

"Fuck you, Neil. Fuck you, bro. Back the fuck up!"

"Shoot me back, you dumb piece of shit."

I lifted my finger, flipping them all off, then quickly turned it to an imaginary gun, and that's when I heard the crack of Christian's rifle. I turned, punched Duda, busted his nose, and did my best Ray Finkle impersonation score for the dolphins, right between the poles. As he hit the ground, grabbing his crotch, nose bleeding, I saw Terrance and Nicolette come barreling in, shooting, and disarming the three other guys in there.

"Shit, please tell me he didn't kill her. I want to talk to her."

"No, Neil, your guy is a hell of a shot; her hand is pretty fucked up, though. Tell him thanks for me."

"You can tell him yourself; I'm sure he's already on his way."

"You set all this plan up off a few text messages on our way over here?"

"No, we just winged the whole thing, dead serious, luckily no one died, especially you."

"I didn't need to know that part, but thank you. So back to this lovely lady." Glow sat down.

"I'm not going to talk to any of you. Get me a fucking ambulance."

"Nah, I'm thinking we're going to leave here in a minute, but can you tell me something first? Then I'll call you a ride to the hospital. Where is your brother, and why are you the rightful heir?"

"My brother died a few months back; I was going to leave Andrew back in the States after graduation and come home to run the family business. We kept up appearances that he was still alive. Now call me that ride."

"Nicolette, can you get her a ride to the hospital?"

"Two more questions. When did Andrew find out the truth about his family? Is that what pushed him over the edge?"

"The reason he killed himself is that he was weak like his father. When I told him that, he killed himself. His father was from a rival family when he found out I was pregnant. He freaked out and killed himself; that's why I ran to the States, for my safety. From his family, they blamed me for his death, just like you blame me for my sons."

"You don't see the trend here," Glow chimed in.

"Yeah, lady, really, what the fuck, maybe you're just a piece of shit."

"Terrance, not necessary." Even if true.

"Glow, we got clarity, you good. Want to go grab dinner and a beer before you head home?"

"Wait, he's heading out tonight?" Nicolette was confused.

"No, he leaves first thing in the morning. But he needs to crash with us tonight. Let's be gracious and get the fuck out of here." I was tired and happy to be done with this shit.

"Her ride will be here shortly. Let's get out of here." Nicolette had a good point.

"Hey Nico, who did you call for old lady cranky pants?"

"I called her a cab. You just asked me to get her a ride."

"Hell, yeah. Well played, Nico."

"What's up with the Nico nickname all of a sudden?"

"It means you're part of the team, kiddo. Welcome aboard." Christian was on point as usual.

As we walked out of the diner into the Polish sunset, I was reminded how much of a pain in the ass this case has been for almost nothing. There was no killer to be found, no one is going to get arrested because they carry too much power, and we have to go back to our lives in Detroit. But I can tell you—

"What the *fuck* was that?!" Terrance screamed.

"That was the restaurant blowing up!"

We all turned around and saw the restaurant go up in flames. My guess is that the bullet from Christian's rifle ended up hitting a gas line in the kitchen, not unlikely, eventually leading to the issue. But what would cause the spark? Maybe Duda's dumb ass was lighting up a cigarette. That would be poetic justice if he killed himself by accident, by a cigarette. Let's hope no one else was hurt.

"All we can do is say a prayer." Glow was right.

For more updates sign up at

www.BHPubs.com

The Neil Baggio Universe

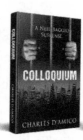

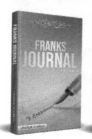